Tender Prey

by

R.C. Morris

"Tender Prey," by R.C. Morris. ISBN 1-58939-812-2 (softcover); 1-58939-813-0 (hardcover).

Library of Congress information on file with publisher.

Manufactured in the United States of America.

For my wife, Brenda

For all her enthusiasm, love, support, and encouragement,
and for inspiring me to live my dreams

PROLOGUE

New Years Eve, 1984

When the frosty gray mist rolls in off the waters of cold Puget Sound, the old house is spooky enough. Its tall narrow face, gingerbread trim, gabled windows and dark balconies only add to its sinister force, reminiscent of an old Alfred Hitchcock film. Yet for one small mind, it's more, a virtual den of horrors as evening darkness descends and shadows fill every nook and cranny. Particularly frightening is the poorly illuminated third floor bedroom with its single window. Fat furry creatures, their eyes wide and shiny, align the shelves. Cute and cuddly during the light of day, they quickly become smirking, evil little critters in the twilight dimness, awaiting their chance to pounce on the small trembling form on the little white metal bed.

Through the glimmer of light from a partially open door, the lovable, funny clown with big red shoes, such a joy only a few hours earlier, seems diabolical, capable of evil deeds and untold mayhem. Even the soft, fat teddy bear transforms to become bloated and malicious.

Occasionally a wind gust will brush some bare Madrona branches against a windowpane or the shingled roof, making it very easy for a young mind to imagine demonic fingernails tapping, seeking to be let inside. A dull light two levels below faintly glows through the small door crack. It should bring a small measure of comfort to the frightened child. Instead, it only adds to the hellish atmosphere casting its shadows, evoking distant memories of a Halloween horror house the family had visited once in a far away place called California. Etched into memory from this single visit is a vision of a flickering gate leading to hell, a shadowy figure beckoning just inside its darkened passageway.

A shrill, intermittent scream slices through the night air, inciting the tiny hands to clutch at the bedcover. Wild laughter outbursts emanate from the bowels of the creepy old house, amplifying the grotesque effects of the dark room ten-fold. The displaced gaiety of clinking wine glasses and the surging and waning disco music periodically float upward, creating macabre sensations — akin to finding a perfectly formed rose in the midst of a bloody accident scene. From afar, a lonely barking dog wale punctuates the eerie night.

Under the soft yellow happy-face blanket, a small form huddles in a fetal position — as if this will afford some protection. It won't. At least it hasn't before. The sounds subtly change as the boisterous party below finally begins to break up. They would be coming soon. They *always* came after a party. As the thin arms hug at cramped knees and the weary, tired eyes squeeze tightly shut in a valiant but vane effort to hold back time, the small figure tries to will itself invisible. A soft sob escapes as the all too familiar sounds reach the bedroom door. *There!* The first tiny squeak—the seventh step of the old stairway! Those alert little ears know there will be yet another on the fourteenth — this one, louder. This dreaded knowledge gained from other episodes of lying awake late into the night, listening — listening for each memorized squeak to announce their coming. *There!* The loud fourteenth step. The squeaky door opens wide, a tall shadow filling the doorway. Pausing briefly, the male crosses to the bed, casting his shadow over the bright yellow bedspread. Frozen and terrified, eyes tight, the frightened child holds its breath, pretending sleep.

"Daddy and Mommy are giving our friends a ride home," the deep gentle voice sooths, as huge hands snugly gather the happy-face blanket around the small trembling body. "They drank a little too much and aren't feeling very well, so we don't want them to drive. We won't be gone long, so stay awake and wait for us sleepy head. Mommy and I will be back to tuck you in and play some of our games before we all go to sleep."

The tall shadow moves away, exits, and the room falls silent once more. As the door closes, a click echoes off the old plaster walls, plunging the room into total darkness.

OK. There, it's the *loud* squeak again — and finally, the *last* one, signaling retreat of the immediate threat. As the silence settles, the child shudders, and with a deep sobbing breath raises a comforting thumb, then quietly begins to cry.

———————

New Year's Day, 1985

Doctor Ben Popham observed the small child waiting patiently in his oversized leather chair; stoically quiet, with none of the fidgeting or squirming typical of kids that age. As he meandered about his large book-lined study, the wide, liquid eyes obediently follow him. Lonely and distant, they possess a lingering quality of... it was difficult to identify. Sadness maybe? At seventy-four, Doctor Popham had been practicing medicine for more than fifty years, frequently being called upon to break sad or unpleasant news to friends and surviving family members. He'd found the old saying, 'Practice makes perfect,' certainly didn't apply in these cases. He'd never done it well, nor found it to be easy. Having been this family's physician for about ten of those fifty years, he'd treated them all for common ailments, even attending to the birth of this disturbing child.

This won't be easy, he thought as he faced away, staring through the sizeable picture window overlooking some bare maple trees that lined a large circular drive. He'd always enjoyed the view from his home office, especially during the fall when the leaves exploded with color. Now the sky and limbs were depressing, matching his mood. Having put off the inevitable for as long as possible, he sighed deeply, reluctant to turn. Carefully choosing his words, he cleared his throat.

"Corky, do you remember when God took your kitten so it could go live with him?"

"God didn't kill Cupcake. A dirty white van did." the child muttered defiantly.

He was right. This wouldn't be easy. The old doctor continued to face the window, intent on not looking at the child's sad eyes during the next part of his message. "Yes, yes. I know, I know. But you remember what your mother told you about it not being the driver's fault? That it was just God's way of taking Cupcake to Kitty Heaven so he could be with God." Thick silence greeted his remarks so he plunged blindly ahead.

Best to just get this over with, he thought again, as he hastened on.

"When something dies, Corky, it doesn't just go away and that's the end of it. It's not really gone at all because it lives on in heaven, forever." He paused, but greeted with silence, continued, carefully selecting his next words. "Last night, God took your parents, like he did Cupcake. They're going to live in Heaven with him from now on. As they drove friends home from their party last night, they skidded on black ice and failed to negotiate that curve by the small bridge near the main road. Their car plunged into the water and never came up. Honey, all four of them drowned."

The child emitted a small muffled sound. Hot tears sprang to the old doctor's eyes. He stared straight ahead, daring not to turn until his task was completed.

"Does that mean they won't ever be coming back again?" The tiny voice sounded so very distant, frightened.

Popham steeled himself for the final part, that which would come when he finally faced the child and attempted to offer whatever comfort he could manage. "Yes, I'm afraid it does, Corky. They're with God now," he replied, rapidly blinking his stinging eyes. The old man removed a handkerchief from his jacket pocket and dabbed at his watery eyes, his voice cracking, "I'm terribly sorry, Corky. So very sorry."

Those small sniffling sounds had grown stronger. He knew the time had finally come for him to face the child's sorrow. Sighing deeply, Doctor Popham stiffened his resolve, reluctantly turning to face those large, hauntingly sad eyes. Corky had not moved, but the eyes were no longer distant. Startled, chilled to the bone, Popham discovered he'd been badly mistaken about the noises he'd thought were sniffles. A dark realization washed over him as the child struggled to hold some emotion inside—it wasn't grief and tears! The hair on the back of the old doctor's neck stiffened as shivers shot through him. These weren't the sounds of a child's grief. It was *laughter*!

Corky was happy!

April 14, 2005

The Seattle rain deluge was heavy, even for this early in the spring. Beginning as intermittent showers just before noon, the steel gray sky had finally split wide open and by late afternoon the weather had turned into a real "*rat drowner*", as locals often called it. By evening, rain still continued to pour steadily, then off and on, well past midnight. Slackening momentarily, the clock tower in Pioneer Square could clearly be seen for the first time in several hours; 2:21 a.m. Glistening puddles dotted the cobblestone plaza while torrents of dirty water threatened to inundate swollen gutters.

Only one vehicle could be detected in a nearby alley, a late 1980's battered white van with tinted blackout windows. Parked in the shadows, it might never have been noticed had it not been for the flashing neon lights of a nearby espresso shop. To a casual observer the van could've seemed deserted; just another vehicle left overnight from the day's bustling activities. A closer more careful scrutiny, however, would reveal thin vapors whiffing skyward as the raindrops splattered upon its warm hood.

The driver's side door finally swung wide. A black clad figure emerged, briefly glancing at the dark sky, seemingly impervious to the chilling rain. Yanking the van's side door to the rear, the figure entered the dark interior, then reappeared, hoisting a heavy elongated plastic wrapped object. Stooped by the weight of this heavy burden, the figure walked briskly to the center of the alley, slowly knelt, then gently placed the bundle onto the wet pavement.

Quickly reentering the van, the figure retrieved another parcel, round but much smaller, placing it beside the first. The figure carefully unwrapped each, working over the objects lovingly for several minutes, then straightened briefly as if to admire the finished work. Apparently satisfied, the plastic sheets were hastily collected and tossed into the rear of the van.

Without warning, a heavy squall hit, then quickly began to dissipate as the van crept slowly toward the street entrance, as though reluctant to leave. Midway to the exit, the powerful engine finally revved and labored as it gained speed.

A young black woman, clad only in a brief camisole, a short leather skirt and spiked heels, tried to hold her umbrella low to protect her carefully braided hair from the wet wind. She stepped into the alley entrance just as the van lurched in front of her—traveling any faster it might have easily hit her. Startled, she jumped backward.

"Motherfu...!"

She gestured angrily, belligerently glaring at the black tinted windows, then continued her stride toward the red Mustang parked near a dim gaslight half a block away. The van paused briefly, accelerated, then swung out of sight around the next corner.

Chapter 1

J *ust another shitty day in Paradise.*
   That's what Frank Murphy thought as he hurried to a job that he'd grown to hate lately. He'd been awake since dawn, had watched its first promising blush give way to the impending gloom he felt more and more to be an actual part of him. Black ominous clouds hung through some blue sky patches as though pinned to a backdrop, until finally, they'd catch a stiff breeze and rush to obliterate the morning sun again.
   Ghosts die with the dawn.
   He'd read the phrase somewhere as a teen, and it'd stuck with him. Or maybe it hadn't been *ghosts*, at all. Maybe it had been *bad spirits* that were supposed to die with the dawn. Only his bad spirits hadn't died. Not this morning anyway. They'd lingered on the edge of his consciousness and were stubbornly hammering against the mental firewall he'd so carefully built into his psychic to contain them. At least during his waking hours. With dogged determination, he forced himself to think of other things. There would be plenty of time to revisit the dreams when the sun went down.
   The last time he remembered checking the clock on his nightstand, it'd been 2:05 a.m. He'd barely slept four hours. Sluggish from lack of sleep and drained by depression, sleeping pills and raw whiskey, he'd been jerked wide-awake, only to lie and listen as waves lashed against the side of his forty-foot, live-aboard trawler. Around 6:30 a.m., he'd finally forced himself to move from beneath his warm down comforter and face the day, telling himself that the sun would eventually pop through the dark clouds to offer him a new start.

1

But like his mood, the day had remained dark, the sun stubbornly refusing to show its face for even an instant. When the rain finally hit, it'd first rolled across Elliot Bay as a foggy mist, then pummeled in thick sheets. For nearly a week angry waves had been cascading against the boat's deck and bursts of wind hammered at it, violently rocking the wood and fiberglass craft he'd called home. Huddled beneath his warm cover, he'd justified his tardiness by telling himself it would clear up soon. Then he'd get ready and go to work — to the job he once loved, then simply tolerated — and now hated.

Finally dressing and hurrying up the dock, the sun flirted, first peeking from behind the swift black clouds for only an instant, tantalizing with its brilliant but fickle nature. To those unacquainted with the Northwest's intricate weather patterns, it's easy to mistake a day's summer appearance for what it actually will be. On days like this one, it's easy to spot the tourists. They're the ones dressed in shorts and shirtsleeves, sporting cameras — the blue-lipped folks with goose bumps. Puget Sound residents seem to understand the weather's unpredictability, the whimsical way it can transform a simple sunny outing into a miserable soggy mess. They are the ones with the umbrellas clutched beneath their arm, or carrying a rain jacket, just in case. Murphy had neither. His mind just wasn't on the weather at the moment.

Pigeons scattered as he walked across the cobbled square, to immediately return once he'd passed, settling a few feet away from where they'd originally started. A young mother in a hurry yanked on a little blond girl's arm, remanding her in a harsh breathless voice.

Tina! Don't start with me this morning. No! Of course not!

The sight of the little girl's bouncing ponytail felt as if a stake had punctured his heart. *Stay focused, Sport. Stay focused.* Yes, he had to stay focused. Just the same, his heart ached and his step faltered as he attempted to force last night's *bad spirits* away and focus on his present task — the bad spirits that were supposed to have fled with the dawn— the difficult task of just making it through another day.

Take one step after the other, Sport. One day after the...

As always, he managed this morning by finding black humor regarding his situation, life in general — and about his life in particular.

2

Detective Sergeant Frank Murphy hurried up the station steps hoping he wouldn't encounter anyone he knew. *Damn, almost an hour late again! The second time this week. Shit!* As he reached the top, two uniformed patrolmen whom he knew only by sight exited the door and nodded noncommittally. *So far, so good.* Murphy quick-stepped to the men's room, hurriedly emptying his bladder, pausing in front of the sink to wash his hands. The rumpled man in the mirror could've used a shave. He'd shaved in a rush and he could tell the effort had been sort of hit and miss. By late afternoon, the five o'clock shadow of his coarse black beard would reappear as if he never had made the effort. Not wanting to waste precious time, he hadn't combed his shaggy dark hair, preferring to hastily run his fingers through it. His wrinkled white cotton shirt, with an equally wrinkled silk tie he'd knotted loosely, looked as though he'd slept in them. In short, he conceded, he looked like death standing on the corner eating onions.

If you think it's bad out there, Sport, ya oughta be in here with me, Murphy thought, as he stared back at his red-eyed reflection in the dirty mirror.

It'd been another bad night despite the whisky and sleeping pills. He figured one or the other would probably kill him someday —maybe then he'd get some real rest. With an unexplainable sense of impending doom, he'd fallen asleep on the couch around ten o'clock, dozing fitfully until awakened at 2:00 a.m. with the old nightmare about Tina. Afterward, he'd gulped three sleeping pills, two more than the instructions called for, and crawled into bed. While the recurring nightmares hadn't returned, he didn't awaken again until the Bremerton ferry blew its distinctive whistle for the 6:00 a.m. return trip.

He'd lain in bed for a long time, exhausted, drenched in sour sweat, waiting for the thunderous rain to slack off and the fickle-fucking-frivolous sun to pop out to give him his bright new start in life. When it hadn't, he'd finally acquiesced, hurriedly showered, thrown on the same suit discarded the previous night and rushed to his car, only to become hopelessly snarled in Seattle's morning commute.

Pushing Tina's image into the back of his mind, Murphy studied his shaking hands briefly, then stared deeply back into his own eyes, annoyed he couldn't seem to connect with this man in the mirror. He was a cop. His father had been a cop, and two of his uncles had been cops. But he was different from other family members who'd chosen the profession. They'd loved being police officers. Not Frank. Oh, maybe once, but no more. He'd chosen this line of work because he'd seen the dark side of human nature and hoped to change the way things were — at least that's how he'd felt at first. Discovering he could change nothing, the job had now simply become a habit. At age forty-three, he stayed because he didn't know what else to do.

Behind his eyeballs were the beginnings of what was sure to be the mother of all hangovers. Tasting a dry bitterness in the back of his throat, he suddenly retched over the sink and suffered through several dry heaves. His nausea temporarily relieved, he scooped a handful of water into his mouth, swished it thoroughly and spit. It didn't help much. He repeated the process. It still didn't help. Cupping the tepid water, he splashed his face and reached for a paper towel from the stack on a small shelf over the sink. Suddenly, his head pounded like a jackhammer. Frank stared at the red-rimmed eyes of this stranger, searched his coat pocket and retrieved a Cert, popping it into his mouth.

That's as good as it's going to get, Sport, he thought ruefully. *Better not breathe on anybody for a while.*

Covertly checking and looking both ways, he left the washroom, pleased he'd been lucky enough to catch the elevator door just as it closed. He and Drake had timed the damned thing one day when they'd missed it, and it'd taken a full six minutes to make the return trip. His good luck with the elevator suddenly offered him a glimmer of optimism. Things were beginning to look up. He knew the fire exit stairwell only took a minute and a half to negotiate, and he'd used them before, but only in an emergency. He knew, without a doubt, that he'd die on one of the first landings if he chanced it this morning, probably not to be found until the next fire drill.

At the fourth floor he exited, inhaled deeply and entered a large double door labeled HOMICIDE. His partner, John Henry Drake, was at his desk. Glancing around quickly, he noted everyone was already at his or her desk. The beautiful BJ, casually elegant in tailored black wool slacks and matching leather sport jacket, was on the phone. Rumpled Charley Booth was also on the phone, but by contrast, easily looked as though the cat had

4

dragged him home. BJ's voice was cultured and refined—Booth's, vulgar and profane. *Two-Gun* Colburn and Joe Yates held their heads close in a corner of the large squad room, probably stabbing one of their fellow officers in the back. Detective Alvin Lee, their Asian-American investigator, questioned a Hispanic male with tattoos on both hands proclaiming *mi vida loca*. The young man was adamant about not being able to speak English, despite having lived in the United States for more than six years. It was clear Alvin wasn't buying any of it. He was the primary suspect in a grisly ice-pick murder of an elderly woman. Lee's sidekick, Dick Fletcher, leafed through Seattle's Yellow Pages for pawnshop addresses where they hoped to locate some of the dead woman's stolen property. Red-haired, freckle-faced Fletcher, the newest member of their group, had been assigned to homicide only a few months earlier and was still learning the ropes.

None glanced up as Murphy approached the work area he and Drake had shared for the past seven years. Drake's massive body filled his over-sized chair, his large buttocks oozing over the edges, tilting it slightly to one side where his broad butt had long since destroyed the springs. The large man always seemed on the verge of toppling onto the tile floor. Drake had been offered a new chair numerous times, but always indignantly declined, stating it'd taken him fifteen years to properly break in the one he had. Glancing up through lazy, half-closed eyes as Murphy approached, Drake whistled softly, his glistening black face breaking into a broad grin.

"Morning Murph. Man, you look like shit."

"F.O.," Murphy growled back. He was still experiencing the sour taste of his hangover, and a thin wet sheen covered his face. He loosened his tie more as he approached his own chair. He'd been determined to ignore any rude remarks his partner might come up with this morning, being in no mood for Drake's caustic brand of humor. Drake's description of his disheveled appearance was a bull's-eye, as usual, and the only reason Murphy relented was because he'd suddenly remembered he was out of smokes.

"Morning, Bear," he finally said, using Drake's nickname.

"I've been trying to get in touch with you all morning, Frank, but you seem to have changed your address," Drake said accusingly.

Murphy looked embarrassed as he dropped his head and fumbled with a stack of papers. "Yeah? Well, I've been living on the boat lately. I probably should've told you earlier, but Elnore and I have been having some marital problems and we just thought it might be better if we each had some space for a while."

Drake raised his brows suspiciously, suspecting more to it when Murphy didn't meet his eyes. Murphy had purchased the old tub five years ago from the previous owner's widow. The once proud forty-foot trawler had been a masterpiece in its hey-day but had fallen on hard times, was seriously neglected and accumulating mildew and grime.

Murphy had come upon it quite by accident during one of his investigations near the Cozy Cove Marina. He'd noticed the dilapidated old boat pitifully covered by a dirty blue tarp. A small hand-printed sign simply read, 4-SALE, with a telephone number. He knew he probably didn't have the financial resources to purchase it, but nonetheless jotted down the number, then promptly had forgotten about it. He'd discovered the slip of paper again while cleaning out his jacket pockets and called on impulse.

It seemed the owner just wanted to get rid of the headache of having it around, and quoted Frank a ridiculously low figure he couldn't pass up. Two days later he became the proud owner, registering it as *Crime Pays*. With Olaf's help at the marina, he began a labor of love to restore the fine old vessel to its former grandeur. These days it looked better than most its age; it was Frank Murphy's pride and joy.

Smirking, John Henry Drake, "*Bear*" to everyone, leaned back in his damaged chair until it appeared it'd topple. His hands folded in his wide lap, he critically studied his partner's disheveled appearance. Drake's broad black face suddenly displayed impossibly white teeth.

"Captain Brooks has been out here twice this morning, asking for you. Said he wants to see *both* of us in his office the minute you arrived."

Murphy perched on the corner of Drake's desk, searching through his rumpled jacket pockets for a cigarette. Seeing his discomfort, Drake picked up an opened pack lying in front of him and pitched them to his partner. "Here, take these. I quit last night." Grinning broadly he unwrapped a stick of gum and poked it into his wide mouth.

Murphy knew this would be at least the third time in a month his partner had given up smoking, but gratefully accepted the offered cigarettes. Removing one, he stuck it between his lips and immediately fumbled for a match.

Drake tossed Murphy his lighter. "Keep that, too. I've quit for good this time. I promised Mable."

"What do you think we ought to do?" Murphy mumbled, lighting up.

They'd worked together for a long time and Drake knew exactly what his partner meant. The prospects of facing Captain Brooks this early in the morning somehow made him feel worse than his hangover did.

"As I see it, we got one of two choices," Drake replied. "One, we can suck it up, walk in and face the music like men. Or two, we can go on down to the locker room, stand in the shower so we don't mess the area up too badly and just shoot ourselves."

"Number two doesn't sound too bad," Murphy muttered solemnly.

Suddenly, the office bustle was shocked into complete silence.

"*Murphy!*"

He grabbed his aching head between both hands and grimaced, his eyes on the floor.

"Murphy! You and Drake get your incompetent asses into my office. I mean *now!*" Captain Brooks glared at the two men from his doorway for an instant more, then whirled and marched back inside, slamming the door—loudly.

Drake's appreciation of black humor neatly paralleled that of Murphy's. They did a pretty good imitation of a slow, exaggerated gallow walk toward the captain's office, like condemned men, while co-workers gazed silently with pained expressions of mock sympathy. It was evident this good-natured drama was just one of several the two partners had enacted many times. A few seasoned bystanders handled their roles with a practiced flair, shaking bowed heads in mock sorrow while emitting soft ticking sounds with their tongues.

Drake always got to ask the drama question first, and it was always uniquely common. "Where do you think we went wrong, Murph? Was it the blond with the microfilm and the suitcase full of money?"

"Nah. It must've been the brunette with the killer jugs. I think she slipped me a micky when I frisked her." Murphy adlibbed his role with practiced ease. Despite lingering depression and a raging headache, he forced himself to go along with the ritual even though it was substantially harder to do this morning.

In the background, two pencils beat a slow drum-roll on an ashtray as someone hummed taps, slightly off-key. The choreographed scene was a time honored office tradition, done in good-natured fun. That's to say *most* was good-natured. Frank caught a snicker and jerked around in time to see *Two-Gun* Colburn and Joe Yates' nasty smirks. *Yeah, laugh, you horse's ass. You'll get yours.* He suddenly felt terribly sorry for himself and on the verge of puking again to boot. *God, I don't need this shit right now.*

"Guess it's too late to just run for the shower room and eat our pistols, huh," Drake said in a loud stage whisper, smiling radiantly.

This time, Murphy felt far too sick to respond.

Drake opened their boss's door and moved aside for Murphy to enter first, drawing a cold stare from his sick partner. Captain Brooks continued shuffling papers as the two men entered, making no mystery that he was making them wait. The next five minutes Murphy stared impatiently at Brook's prominent bald spot as he worked. He'd threatened to plant a big wet kiss right in the middle of it someday, but mostly just to hear Drake go ballistic. He felt an overpowering urge to walk over and do it. Pondering the repercussions, he wondered if he'd lost his job over it, would it matter? Not much, he concluded. Fighting the impulse, he shifted his weight and felt the room begin to sway as bile tried to enter his throat.

What the hell is Brooks trying to prove?

He marched to a large chair and sank heavily into it, trying not to think about puking. Drake rolled his eyes, then uninvited, quietly squeezed his broad butt into a smaller straight-backed chair with padded arms. Brooks, absorbed in his work, totally disregarded them.

Ignoring the no-smoking signs, Murphy belligerently lit one of Drake's strong unfiltered smokes, puffed deeply and blew in Brooks direction. Drake rolled his eyes, which usually meant, "quit farting around." Murphy opted to ignore him as Brooks began to sniff loudly and repeatedly, finally raising his eyes coldly at

Murphy.

"Put that out!" he said evenly, trying to contain himself. "You know better than to smoke in here! What the hell's wrong with you, Murphy?"

Murphy pinched off the end and carefully stuck it back into the pack. Drake squirmed more, trying to distance himself from his obnoxious partner by innocently admiring the plaques on Brook's office walls. Among them were numerous photos of a much younger Brooks posing with celebrities Richard Nixon and former Governor Dixie Lee Ray.

Brooks stared a hole through Drake and then Murphy, and finally spoke. "Well, Frank, you certainly look nice today, like you spent the night in the detox tank. Since you don't come into the office much any more, I suppose it's safe to presume you and Drake have already solved the Asian gang case." Brooks smiled sweetly, forming a temple with his fingers.

The two partners glanced at each other; both hoping the other would go out on a limb by opening his mouth first.

"Well? *Talk to me*!" Brooks slammed his hand hard on his wooden desk. The low hum in the outer office abruptly ceased.

Drake squirmed uncomfortably and cleared his throat. "We got a couple of leads we're working on, Captain."

"Well, that's what I like to hear! Leads are *good*. Leads are what solve cases, right? Leads like *what*?" Brooks persisted, glaring at the two homicide detectives. "Talk to me!"

Brooks was a small, mean man, hard as nails both inside and out. Behind his back the others called him *Tas*, short for Tasmanian Devil. He'd been Captain of Seattle's Homicide Division long before Drake or Murphy had been hired, and there were very few things he hadn't seen or heard during his tenure with the department. He'd pulled his time on the streets, received numerous awards, and despite being black, had been promoted ahead of his contemporaries prior to such things as EEO or minority quotas. He was proud of that fact and had been known to take it personally if threatened with anything that might *blemish* his record. Things like his current situation.

Drake shifted uncomfortably again and glanced to his partner for help. Finding none, he bravely plunged ahead. "Oh, you know, the usual small things."

"You got *shit*! That's what you've got, Drake! The Mayor, Chief-fucking-Williams and half the media in this frigging state are breathing down my neck to nail those guys, and you two — *you two* sit here jerking me around!"

He fumed at the two fidgeting men a moment longer while sucking on an antacid. Finally gaining control of his breathing, he shot Murphy a frosty, studied look.

Brooks had been watching Frank Murphy for several years. Like others who'd made it through the ranks to a position of authority, Brooks knew a successful career often depended exclusively on political contacts made during days on the streets. Cops frequently asked each other, "Who's your Daddy?"

Successful careers didn't always hinge on solving cases or catching criminals and Brooks knew this. Such victories were few and far between — sniper attacks in a war already lost. Fighting crime appealed to him mostly as a result of a strong Christian upbringing idealized from his youth, remaining with him after thirty years. That was what kept him going. He doggedly believed, despite evidence to the contrary, that a man had to fight evil every day of his life. A practical man, he was careful to keep his ideology hidden from others, particularly his superiors. Early in his career, Brooks had discovered the department was not a place to demonstrate such convictions. The departmental slogan was that crime in Seattle was like the rain; it couldn't be stopped. Those who tried too hard were considered fools. The inference was clear. Fools didn't get promoted.

Those targeted for the fast track were rated on their ability to get noticed by the right people — and the image they presented. Brooks had once thought Murphy held those qualities and had secretively become his "Daddy," slowly helping to craft an image for him. Murphy was tough, resourceful, and decisive, all the traits Brooks admired in a young cop, although he thought he needed to tone down his fiery temper and polish some rough edges. Brooks perceived Murphy's limited ambition and enthusiasm as strengths, and carefully set about refining the young officer's image. Although scarred and weary from his own former battles, he still believed in the old adage, "one man can make a difference."

Lately, Murphy had become one of Brooks' greatest disappointments. During his earlier years on the force, he'd impressed everyone with an uncanny ability to zero in on the heart of problematic cases. He easily discarded irrelevant details, little things that seemed out of character or behavior and didn't align with expected patterns. It was precisely these unique traits and Brook's constant mentoring that Murphy had been promoted first to detective grade, then to sergeant, well ahead of his peers.

His early assignments had been only the most difficult and perplexing cases; those that others clearly wanted but probably couldn't have handled anyway. This was a source of resentment among some of the more ambitious officers. Recently, his first major bust had come back to haunt him, about the same time as his carefree happy life began to unravel.

The case had involved a prominent attorney and his wife, seemingly gunned down randomly after attending a fund-raising dinner for a popular politician of Italian descent. The newspapers had been quick to recycle allegations of Mafia ties, corruption and pay-offs. The messy crime scene photos sold a lot of newspapers, reminiscent of the bloody east coast Mafioso gang wars. As others sought links, Frank had taken an unlikely approach that the attorney's wife and not the lawyer may have been the killer's target.

He discovered she'd had a romantic liaison with a younger man she'd met at the museum where she volunteered two days a week. Uncharacteristically, she'd covertly met him at a small motel near the city limits where they'd spent the day. Suffering remorse, she'd decided to break it off with the single encounter but the man wouldn't accept it. Unsuccessfully attempting to entice her further, he relentlessly stalked her, deciding if he couldn't have her then no one else would. He'd purchased an automatic twelve-gauge shotgun from a local pawnshop the day before the murders, and emptied it into the couple's car as they returned home — killing them both.

The couple's telephone records had tipped Frank off. During his investigation, he'd come across dozens of calls to the residence, each less than a minute in duration. Tracing them, he'd discovered they had all been made from the killer's apartment. It wasn't long until he'd located the motel where they'd initially met. When shown handwriting samples of his signature on the motel's register, and presented with facts of a newly purchased shotgun found in his garage toolbox, the killer grudgingly confessed. Frank Murphy had his first major homicide bust.

Thereafter, he'd been given most of the high visibility cases. His work on the Green River killer task force stood out among his peers. Yes, Frank Murphy had accomplished great things for the department—until his personal tragedy put an end to his life, as he'd known it.

Brooks was still speaking softly.

"Frank you used to be one hell of a cop. I know you've been through a rough time, losing Tina and all, but it's time to either put it behind you or hand in your badge."

At the mention of Tina's name, Drake saw the color drain from his friend's face. His hands grasped the chair arms so tightly his knuckles turned white. Recognizing these very real danger signs, Drake quickly jumped to his feet, towering over Brook's desk.

"Captain, we've been working this case hard. Frank has a pretty good theory about it."

"Well, let's just hear Frank's *pretty good theory*," Brooks sneered sarcastically. His lip curled nastily, just enough to expose the edge of his gold-rimmed front tooth.

Growing up in low-income housing in West Seattle, Drake had spent hours watching cop and gangster movies. But unlike most of his friends, he'd always identified with the police officers, a fact he'd kept carefully hidden from his rowdy friends. The movies he'd liked the best were the ones with hard-boiled detectives who could sneer. Of all the actors he'd seen sneer, Brooks' classic sneer topped them all.

I hate it when he does that! Drake thought. *No matter what you say next, you're gonna get skewered. Bend over and grab your ankles, girls— here it comes again!*

In desperation, he shot a frazzled glance at Murphy, hoping his partner would pick this particular moment to jump right in. It didn't surprise him to find Murphy absorbed in the wall plaques.

Trapped but undeterred, Drake breathed deeply and continued. "All the businesses hit so far have been Korean establishments."

Brooks tapped his fingers impatiently, already aware of this information. Drake hurriedly went on.

"Several victims—the few still alive—said the men who robbed them spoke Korean. Now, me and Murph both spent a few years in

Asia, and while most Americans can't tell one Oriental from another, we know there are definite cultural differences."

Brooks continued to glare, not making it any easier on the big detective.

"Most Asians have a strong sense of family and the values of *old country* culture. We've noticed some of the young Vietnamese and Cambodian gang members don't show the least respect for anybody, or anything, including their elders. They've got guns, and they'll use them. The trigger-happy little bastards just *love* to shoot people, and it doesn't really matter if it's one of their own.   The Korean gangs, on the other hand, still have *some* sense of family for the most part, but usually only within their *own* communities. So Frank thinks that since it's been primarily Korean stores being hit and the gang speaks Korean, they might not be from the Seattle area at all. We figure they rob here, precisely because they *don't* know any of the families they're hurting."

He finished and smiled.

Brooks peered at Drake through the triangle he'd made with his fingers. "So?"

Feeling on firmer footing, Drake was only too happy to continue. "Me and Frank believe these guys are from out of town. Vancouver, B.C., San Francisco—someplace like that. If we put out an all points for Asians cruising with out-of-state tags, we might get a lucky hit. We'd run it to find out who the car's registered owner is, and bingo, maybe we get a lead. What do you think?"

Brooks rubbed his bald spot, a mannerism he frequently used when seriously contemplating a situation. Drake took this to be a good sign, smiling encouragement at Murphy. He was wrong. Brooks abruptly straightened in his chair, glaring at the two of them.

"I'm glad to see somebody around here is using their head to try to nail these guys. Yes, it is a *theory*. As theories go, however, it completely *stinks*. In fact, it's the *stupidest* idea I've ever heard in twenty-five years of police work. But . . .it is a theory."

Brooks leaped from his chair and pointed toward the street. "You two ass-holes get out there on the street and start interviewing people! You hit every owner, witness and resident in the area. You talk to every shopkeeper, window-peeper and floor-sweeper in the city if you have to, and if you come up with nadda?

13

You start over again—and again—and fucking again, until you come up with *something*! I've got Councilman James, Chief Williams, and the Mayor up my ass all day from sunup to sundown while you two jerk-offs run around playing with yourselves!"

Brooks squinted through his glasses, glaring as if resisting the urge to pull his service weapon and solve at least two of his problems.

"Now get out of here and try to act like cops for a change," he finally growled, popping another antacid while brushing them off with an indifferent wave of his hand.

Drake rolled his eyes toward Frank and headed for the door.

"You have a fine morning, Captain," Murphy tossed pleasantly over his shoulder.

Drake grimaced as if he'd been poked in the kidneys as Brooks jerked his head up to glare some more. Smiling apologetically in an attempt to distance himself from Murphy's actions and show his abject displeasure at his partner's behavior, Drake grabbed Frank's arm in a vice-like grip, pulling him roughly towards the door, apologetically smiling over his shoulder.

"Wait a minute!" Brooks shouted, stopping the two men dead in their tracks.

Brooks held out a folder.

"Here. On your way out take a look at this. A hooker was waxed in Pioneer Square last night. The call came in about twenty minutes ago. Don't waste a lot of time on it. Just put in an appearance to let the news media know we're still interested in the occasional murder of a hooker. Then get back on that Asian gang thing."

Drake respectfully took the folder and quietly closed the door behind them. Brooks never even looked up.

Chapter 2

People watching the evening CNN weather report incorrectly presume it rains all the time in the Great Northwest. They're correct only about seventy-five percent of the time. The rest of the year, the days are spectacular. After a winter of continuous gray malaise and cold drizzles—while the rest of the country has been frozen, pelted with sleet, dug from snow banks, and lost battles with sandbagged levies—Seattle actually has a spring like everywhere else. When the Korean Dogwoods bloom, the pink and white popcorn balls burst forth from the magnificent flowering cherry and plum trees that align city streets. Pikes Place Market becomes a beehive of activity as tourists and locals press against its seams for the fresh seafood catch and farmers' vegetables. But mostly, they come for the waterfront ambiance and breath-taking views.

Frank Murphy had traveled the world during his military years, but was convinced nothing could compare with Seattle in the springtime. This wasn't on his mind at the moment though, as he slumped in his seat, taking in the sights as Drake worked his way through morning traffic. Instead, he contemplated the events that had led him to this point in his life.

He and Drake had been working the Asian gang case for about four months. If the crimes had only been robberies, they wouldn't have received it at all. But these were different. Four men, each armed with a shotgun, had been robbing small Korean businesses about twice a month and shooting all eyewitnesses. So far, the gang had hit six establishments, killing eight and wounding five. The newspapers were having a field day with it, and on the eve of

Seattle's elections, the candidates were, as Drake put it, "Happier than a pig in shit."

Robert James, according to the polls, Seattle's next mayor, was the most vocal among the department's critics. He was the one man Murphy hated more than anyone. Councilman James was sleeping with his wife, Elnore. Ex-wife, actually. Well, *estranged wife*. Of any men who might've been the cause of his marriage's demise, the knowledge that Robert James been the one caught *back-dooring* him had been the most distasteful pill he'd ever swallowed. He and Robert James had been bitter enemies long before this latest run-in, but their bad blood had nothing to do with the councilman's current relationship with Elnore.

His disdain for James was rooted in what he'd discovered during an earlier investigation, the case of the attorney and his wife murdered by her jealous lover. While checking the couple's telephone records, he'd discovered James had also made numerous calls to the attorney's young wife, and furthermore, had been meeting her for secret liasions.

Routinely following up on the calls, he'd attempted to question James about the meetings. James had become unreasonable, then furious with him. Shortly after his confrontation with the new city councilman, Murphy had received a surprise call from Chief Williams ordering him to cease and desist.

Stubbornly Murphy did neither, and soon it'd been open warfare between he and Robert James. He'd learned that the couple had been gunned down by the woman's other lover, but Murphy had secretly hoped right up to the end that James had somehow been involved. When the evidence proved he hadn't, Murphy never made public his knowledge about James and the victim. However, Murphy suspected that simply having this knowledge still worried the politically ambitious James, and he was concerned disclosure would thwart his run for higher public office. At the very least, Murphy *sincerely* hoped it would. In any event, ever since that investigation James went out of his way to create problems for Murphy and others within his department.

Two weeks earlier, Frank had discovered Elnore's adulterous affair with James and suspected him of purposely setting out to seduce her as revenge for their past differences. The burden of her sleeping with James had been the final straw and he and Elnore had finally split for good. This revelation, on the heels of Tina's violent death, the *real* reason for Frank Murphy's tardiness and drinking binges, had sealed his ruination.

Tina. Little seven-year-old Tina…she would never grow any older. God, how he missed her.

When Elnore had given birth to their only daughter, he'd been thirty-six, and Frank's entire world virtually changed overnight. After a life of kicking around, hanging out, drinking beer, and drifting wherever the urge took him, he suddenly couldn't wait to get home every night. His little girl simply became the center of his universe. They developed a special bond, one that he relished in his new role as father. At first, Elnore seemed jealous and a little resentful of their relationship, but eventually relieved when she'd been able to come and go without restriction.

Then six months ago, Tina had been snatched from the school ground; her mutilated body fished from Puget Sound a week later. Distraught, Murphy couldn't bear to ask if she'd been sexually assaulted. Only upon recently reviewing her file he'd learned it. Afterwards, Frank Murphy's life just unraveled. Tears could still flood his eyes at any reminders of her, and terrible nightmares continued to haunt him. After her death, he'd managed to sleepwalk through department duties, barely able to function. Then when Elnore had started sleeping with Councilman James, he couldn't seem to care much about anything.

He'd met Elnore in her third year of law at Gonzaga University. It'd been an extremely hot, scorching summer, even for Eastern Washington, and Murphy was feeling a bit sorry he'd accepted the university's invitation to address its student body. He'd been asked to lecture an advanced evidentiary class of law students on advanced police procedures. He'd been in his fourth year with the Seattle P.D., had just passed his detective examination, and was considered an up and comer. Elnore had been taking summer classes so she could graduate early and accept an appointment offered by King County as a junior deputy prosecutor. She'd sat in the front row during his lectures, and Frank had found her to be the most provocative creature he'd ever seen. The attraction had been mutual. Within a few days their relationship had progressed to a whirlwind courtship, passionate couplings, tearful farewells and discussing future plans, all compressed into a short three-month relationship.

Neither wanted to bear the uncertainty of a relationship only consummated on weekends, so despite strong objections by Elnore's wealthy parents, they'd been married by a Justice of the Peace in the small town of Moses Lake. Even as newlyweds, money had never been a problem. Frank's salary wasn't large, but it was adequate, and Elnore's law-school tuition and expenses were being paid from a trust fund her wealthy grandfather had left for that purpose. After Elnore's graduation, she'd immediately accepted the position her prominent family had arranged with the King County Prosecuting Attorney's Office. She'd been a deputy prosecutor for more than three years.

After Tina's untimely death they'd drifted apart, going separate ways, barely speaking about anything that really mattered. Maybe they'd simply been slipping from each other for a long time, but it had taken a tragedy like their daughter's murder to bring it to a head. Murphy had given it some thought but could never seem to reach any conclusion. Tina's conception had not been planned. Throughout her pregnancy Elnore had fretted about the loss of her figure, and suffered constantly from severe morning sickness and depression. As far as Murphy was concerned, he'd been simply elated, believing a child could draw them closer. He rationalized what went wrong was simply two people with separate careers, living together yet circling in their own little orbit. A baby might turn them into a *real family* and bring them together again.

Instead, having a child completely fractured their already fragile relationship. Tina's birth had the effect of polarizing them, already slipping away from each other. Elnore resented the additional burden her pregnancy placed on her, just as she was making a name for herself with the prosecutor's office. Within weeks of giving birth, she returned to her job, essentially turning over all of the baby's needs to her husband.

Murphy couldn't have been happier to inherit the sole responsibility of caring for his darling baby girl. It'd been love at first sight between the two. Dirty diapers, spitting up and middle of the night feedings, all evoked immeasurable pleasure. Drake, who'd raised two children of his own, remarked more than once that he thought his partner was ready for the *white zip-up-the-front jacket*.

When Tina began to walk, she learned to reach up and place her hands on the front windowsill, watching for his return each night. Spying her father's familiar car pulling into their driveway, she'd squeal, clap her little hands and toddle quickly to the door, waiting for him. Frank would growl like a big old bear, swinging her onto his shoulders and hoisting her to his neck, laughing and squirming, then stomp around the house ignoring Elnore. Each night, it'd been the same routine, never getting old. Whenever he worked late, he'd often find her with her blanket on the window seat where she'd fallen asleep while waiting for him. Those nights, he'd gently carry her to bed and lovingly tuck her in.

On October 21st, a day forever etched into his mind, Murphy had arrived, as usual, to pick Tina up after school. He'd been running late, so initially he wasn't worried that she hadn't been waiting near the gate as normal. If he was running behind a few minutes he'd often instructed her to go back inside, stand by the door and he'd come in to get her. That fateful day, she hadn't been at either place. Murphy remembered his overwhelming sense of panic when he fully realized she was gone, and it still haunted him.

As a cop, he'd watched other parents literally fall apart when one of their children turned up missing, but like most parents, thought it could never happen to him. He'd become so shaken he could barely explain what had happened to Drake over the phone. Within minutes, a dozen police officers swarmed the neighborhood, but to no avail. She'd simply vanished. Three days later she'd been found by oyster hunters during low tide near a jetty on Bainbridge Island, floating among driftwood and debris.

Heavily sedated, he'd barely survived those first days. When lucid, they'd finally told him of the body's discovery. The saltwater decomposition had made positive identification difficult, and Elnore, nearly hysterical, flatly refused to go to the morgue to identify their daughter. Murphy became completely unglued as he identified Tina's remains, and couldn't bear to hear any of the details. When learning of them later, he'd needed to be sedated again. Although the department had given him thirty days bereavement leave, he'd returned to his job after only a week.

Following Tina's death, Murphy found returning to the lonely, silent house each night extremely difficult. It wasn't that he didn't want to be with Elnore; it was just that he couldn't bear the thought that his nightly ritual with his baby girl would never again happen. Although Elnore had somehow worked through her own grief by remaining busy, she'd never seemed to completely understand what he'd been going through. Murphy began to work longer hours, arriving home later and later, often reeking of alcohol.

Several months had passed when he came upon an article about another missing girl, and decided to finally look at his daughter's file. Aware the departmental brass would frown upon his investigating his own daughter's case, he'd talked Drake into removing the file, secretly slipping it to him inside another folder.

Drake had admonished him soundly as he handed over the file, "You get me fired, Murph, and I'm gonna live with you until I'm a hundred and sixty. You can support us both, and my whole damned family!"

For nearly a month he'd emerged himself in the file, finally realizing he hadn't drank a drop during the entire time. *I can catch this* sick *creep*, he thought. *I know I can!*

Not long afterward, the department had selected five officers to attend the Law Enforcement Commission's convention in Washington, D.C. Frank T. Murphy and John Henry Drake had shown up on the list of officers chosen. Throughout the trip, Frank maintained his abstinence from alcohol and pondered the turn of events his life had taken, to include his faltering relationship with Elnore. He became determined to salvage his marriage, an important part of his life that had been missing since Tina's death. Although attendees were scheduled to depart on Saturday, Murphy moved his departure up and left a day earlier.

After buying a bouquet of flowers on his way home from SeaTac Airport, Murphy had arrived home at ten-thirty that evening to find a strange car parked in his driveway. He'd let himself in through the kitchen entrance and silently moved through the house, pausing at the oak stairway. In the foyer, sounds floated down from the bedroom he'd shared with Elnore for the past ten years. He recognized the familiar throes of his wife's passion, her throaty moans and husky urgings, as familiar to him as his own breathing. Stunned, he'd remained until he heard

Elnore's low cry of fulfillment, then sadly turned and walked out of her life.

Elnore found the flowers and card on the kitchen table the following morning. That was the last time Murphy had been in the two-story house where he'd thought he'd spend the rest of his life.

Chapter 3

Bertha May Thatcher struggled with the heavy vacuum-sweeper as she pulled it up the remaining flight of terrazzo steps to the vacant condo. It was an old but elegant Magnolia Bluffs landmark, built in an era before most folks thought they needed an elevator to help them climb a trifling three flights of stairs. Usually she would've agreed, but today the sweeper seemed extraordinarily heavy and clumsy. The previous owners had occupied the second-story unit for the past thirty-five years, but when the old woman had been diagnosed with Alzheimer's, her husband sold it and placed his wife in a nursing home.

Bertha was the complex manager and normally wouldn't be doing this, but her worthless handyman had called in sick for the second time in a month and the new owners were scheduled to review their unit this afternoon. So here she was, again cleaning up after that worthless skunk. She swore it'd be the *last* time. When he came in on Monday she'd have his check waiting. Bertha May banged the heavy contraption against her arthritic ankle for the third time and muttered an obscenity that would've shocked most of her elderly tenants. Guilt ridden, she glanced up and down the stairwell to see if anyone had overheard her profane words. Satisfied her reputation remained intact she muscled the heavy sweeper to the top level, tossing its awkward coil of hose on top of it.

Regaining her breath, Bertha May fumbled with her key ring to unlock the door, just as Margaret Bodine left her unit a few doors down and limped down the hallway toward her. Hurry as she might, she was unable to find the correct key to enter before the older woman approached.

"Good morning *Bertha May*. I might as well inform you right now that I've taken it upon myself to call the Home Owners' Association and report your lack of promptness in dealing with tenant complaints. Nothing personal, but you *are* the manager, even if you do have your own condo. You have yet to fix that terrible dripping faucet in my bathroom. Lord only knows how many times I've told you about it."

Ms. Bodine hooked her cane over her flabby left forearm. Bertha May knew that meant she would be sticking around for a few moments, which also meant she'd be on the receiving end of Bodine's terrible wagging finger. She was right about that, for the old woman shook her long bony finger directly in Bertha May's drawn face.

"Another thing I'm going to tell them, too. I just know the Johnstons have a child living with them. That's a clear violation of the rules. I know because I hear that kid running across the floor over my head, day-and-night... night-and-day. Between the dripping and the running I'm just about to lose my marbles. I'm sorry if it causes you any trouble, Bertha May, but *someone* had to report it, and you've got no one to blame but yourself."

Bertha May watched the old woman's bent back disappear out of sight, her cane and the handrail being carefully used to negotiate the stairs. *Yeah, I'll just bet you're sorry, you old... biddy.* For the past ten years, she'd been secretly hoping the old gal would die, but like the persistent moss on the north side of the building, she just kept returning every spring. Sighing deeply, Bertha May finally located the right key, inserted it, and went inside.

The elderly retired couple who'd lived here before had painted the wall lime-green, a shade reminding Bertha May of snow cones. The paint's pale tint made the red stuff appear almost purple. That's why initially she didn't fully comprehend exactly what she was looking at. She went all the way in, gawking, trying to comprehend the large purple splotches on the walls. It was only after she'd seen what had caused them that she gasped, backing away blindly, in horror. Gagging on sour bile that threatened to rise in her throat, she tripped over the sweeper twice in her haste to get out of the door, banging her bad ankle again. This time, she never noticed.

The Pioneer Square section of Seattle is history rich and money poor, suddenly popular with tourists... *a good place to build ballparks, but I wouldn't want to live there...* Along with its numerous arts and crafts, antique stores and coffee-houses, it boasts of some of the best eating establishments in the world. Gaslights, totem poles and the Seattle Underground all combine to make it a warm, cozy, traditional day out for the family. For locals and visitors alike, it's a real *feel-good* kind of place where famous sports figures mingle with common folks and where '50's beatniks, '60's hippies, and eternal bohemians still co-exist. Unfortunately, the cheap flophouses and deserted alleys also make it popular among drug addicts, panhandlers, the homeless, and hookers. Such as the one they were now rushing to see.

Pioneer Square is the oldest part of the city. The original buildings that Doc Maynard and Seattle's other *floundering* fathers had built, remain standing along haphazardly arranged streets that still cause heartburn to this day to even the most knowledgeable drivers. And if city dwellers find it frustrating, for outsiders, the traffic patterns are nothing less than a nightmare.

One might not realize it just by looking, but the streets today are a vast improvement from what the city's fathers initially intended. The original stores and shops, built in the mid-1880's, were constructed with little regard or consideration for traffic flow — or for that matter, Puget Sound's drastically fluctuating water tables. Consequently, the streets had been built fifteen to twenty feet above the shop entrances with ladders for brave shoppers leading down to the stores. Many a drunk staggering home late at night met his maker when stepping off a curb while crossing to the other side, unexpectedly plunging twenty-feet to his death.

The businesses and stores tourists know today have been built above those old shops, actually the second story of the original old buildings. The lower level, which sprawls for miles beneath what is visible to modern day shoppers, had been the original city. Now Seattle's Underground, it is locked at night and available only during scheduled tours.

Half-sick and still on the verge of heaving his guts out, Frank Murphy slumped in the passenger seat of the unmarked patrol car as Drake expertly wheeled them through the heavy morning traffic

24

toward the murder scene in Pioneer Square. Shops and businesses were in full swing as they sped past well-dressed men with briefcases and long-legged professional women, all clutching umbrellas. Suddenly the traffic lurched to a standstill, and Murphy knew they'd arrived in Pioneer Square. Against a red light, a silver-haired old woman, her overcoat tattered and soiled, pushed a shopping cart brimming with her lifetime of possessions. Drake courteously paused for her to cross and as she labored past their unmarked unit, she shot him the bird, toothlessly grinning.

"And God bless you, too, old Mother," Drake muttered.

Across the street, a shopkeeper argued with a wino about panhandling in the doorway of his shop. The wino, shouldering a small tattered backpack and his sign proclaiming him to be an out-of-work and disabled Vietnam vet, staggered away shaking his fist and mouthing profanities. As a soft drizzle started falling, Drake turned on the windshield wipers, smearing it with bug guts.

"*Shit!*"

It was Drake's favorite word of choice when all others failed to adequately describe how he felt about some rotten situation. Unwrapping another stick of gum, he stuck it into his mouth. "You still feeling like you're ready to toss your cookies, partner?"

Murphy stared sullenly out the opposite window without answering. Unfazed, Drake kept right on needling him, confident that if their roles were reversed and he was the one with the horrendous hangover, Murphy would do the same to him.

"You want to just sit there like you got a turd crossways and wallow in self-pity, or do you want to tell me about it?"

They'd been partners for more than ten years, ever since John Henry had persuaded him to join the police force. He and Murphy had served together in Desert Storm as members of the Marine's First Force Recon. It'd been the first time Murphy had gotten to know a black man very well, and he'd certainly never thought he'd have one as his best friend. He hadn't grown up in a prejudiced home, but as young people often are, his peers had bombarded him with small doses of bigotry. The war had changed him. It'd been different there. In Iraq, there was no black nor white — just the man on your right and the man on your left whom you trusted and depended upon to survive.

John Henry had saved Frank's life scarcely a week after he'd joined the unit, and they became inseparable once discovering they both claimed Puget Sound as their home. They'd always arranged it so they'd go on patrols and ambushes together. Once, they took R&R together in Spain, and made plans for when they returned to *The Real World.*

John Henry returned to the states first, giving Murphy his address and instructing him to call the minute he returned. Murphy remained with the military for an additional year, and when discharged, had decided he'd go back to school to get his degree. After arriving in Seattle and being accepted at the University of Washington, he'd contacted his old Desert Storm buddy. Drake, an officer with Seattle P.D. by then, convinced him to join the department after his graduation. That'd been nearly ten years ago. They'd had no secrets from one another during all that time, no matter how tender the subject.

Still, Murphy decided to ignore Drake's sudden interest in the regularity of his bowels, and continued to stare silently out the passenger side window.

"Well. *Are* you?" Drake persisted.

Resigned to the fact that Drake didn't intend to back off, Murphy sighed deeply and started talking. He told Drake about his coming home a day early after the conference, only to find Elnore in the sack with another man. He related how he'd illegally run the license plates through the department's computer and discovered the car belonged to Robert James. Councilman — soon to be Mayor Robert James. He concluded about his living on the forty-foot boat he'd been restoring, and Elnore lived... who knows?

"That just about sums it up, partner," Murphy finished lamely.

"*Shit*," Drake offered again. "You should've shot the fucker. You want me to?"

He didn't have time to answer. Just ahead, in the next block, several police cars blocked traffic, their emergency lights flashing through the rain, which was now falling steadily. Drake pulled in beside one of the patrol units and they exited, ducking under the yellow crime scene tape.

"I don't see Hemphill's team." Murphy noted the obvious, meaning that the scene hadn't yet been processed.

A uniformed officer with a lot of service stripes down his sleeve was standing in a nearby phone booth speaking quietly into the phone. It was a booth open to the wind from the waist down, installed so it could no longer function as a bedroom or latrine by Pioneer Square's legions of junkies. Reinforced flexible cables bound the receivers to the boxes. Nonetheless, this one looked as though someone had taken an ax to it. Murphy was mildly surprised it even worked. He watched the sergeant hang up, suddenly longing for someone he could call and tell he'd probably be working late — someone who'd care.

The young officer hurried forward, raising his hand to halt them. John Henry towered over him, glowering as he shoved his shield into the guy's startled face. "Drake and Murphy, homicide. Is she in the alley?"

The young uniform nodded his head and swallowed hard. "Yeah. It's pretty bad, sir."

"They all are, son," Drake reassured him, shoving a third stick of gum into his wide mouth.

Murphy headed off in the indicated direction while his partner lumbered behind, like a big black bear. He was glad it was raining. Somehow the rain seemed to wash away, or at least cover up, most of the crud and urine odor that accumulated in these back alleyways. Twenty feet inside the entrance another uniformed officer waited impatiently. Twenty-feet further, a small lump had been covered with a raincoat by some caring soul. A chill shot up Murphy's spine at the hint of some unwanted memory. He hesitated slightly, leaving Drake to deal with the officer as he moved forward cautiously, then stopped, staring motionless at the covered remains.

Suddenly disoriented and seeking some sort of reassurance, he turned back toward the two men. Fighting off a spell of vertigo, he saw Drake squinting at the nametag on the officer's breast pocket. Through the ringing in his ears, Drake was saying softly, "Officer Gates, you can wait outside by the street. We got it now."

"I'm supposed to remain with the body until the forensic team arrives," Gates replied with uncertainty.

"Who told you to do that, Officer?" Drake stared disgustedly at the raincoat-draped object.

"My sergeant. Watch Sergeant O'Donnell."

"Well, go find *Sergeant* O'Donnell and you two have a nice latte' or something out of the rain. Tell him Drake told you to do it. Got that?"

The young officer hesitated, swallowed hard and nodded, grateful to be dismissed from having to guard the grisly remains.

Recovering somewhat from his panic attack, Murphy turned back to the object of his dread. He knelt beside the body, lifted the edge of the yellow raincoat to peer at the young victim's face and recoiling — nearly tumbling over backwards.

"Oh, for Christ's sake, Bear! The head's missing!"

He stared numbly at the bloody stump of the victim's severed neck, and fought down the gorge threatening to overcome him. *What in the name of God happened here?* Forcing himself to remain focused and professional, his eyes trailed downward, seeking answers. The pounding of his heart seemed to be drowning out every other sound around him — except for the rain, which had suddenly increased its frantic tempo. His mouth felt full of cotton as he continued his inspection of the pale, lifeless body.

She was a slender girl, almost skinny. Her thin ribs protruded, casting ripples beneath the pallid skin. Murphy finally seemed to place his finger on what was causing most of his discomfort. She looked like a small child! Hastily, Murphy pushed that thought from his mind, concentrating on the chore at hand. Someone had taken the time to carefully wash all the blood splatters off the torso before positioning her here. *Why?* Was that important? Her small breasts were bruised with black and blue marks, and one nipple appeared to have been partially severed. The raincoat covered the remaining torso from the waist down.

Through his concentration, he felt Drake as he kneeled beside him, his saddle-sized hands tenderly peeling the raincoat from the girl's body. She appeared to be a teenager; thin, vulnerable and completely nude. Her sparse blond pubic hairs were slightly matted—made thinner by the rain. This time, *both* men recoiled. The missing head was positioned facing her crotch.

"Ah, Shit!" Drake groaned in alarm.

Murphy's vision blurred as he finally lost his focus and the severed head suddenly became Tina. Quickly squeezing his eyes tightly to clear them, he waited for a moment and when he opened them again, the thin stranger's face was back, eyes dim and staring, filled with some kind of unmentionable horror. With shaky hands, he rubbed his five o'clock shadow as he continued his visual search of the girl's body.

An odd pattern of ripped flesh protruded from the raw, ugly stub that had once been the girl's neck. Still fighting down sour gorge, questions swirled in Murphy's mind. What kind of weapon could have caused it? What kind of monster could've done this awful thing? Who was she? Who were her parents? He observed the wound for several moments, but the answers continued to elude him. Drake's voice quickly jarred him back to the present.

"What do you make of it, Murph?"

Murphy wiped his eyes with cold wet hands. "Damned if I know," he said. "What kind of person does this, Bear? It makes no sense."

Drake picked up on the stress in his partner's tone, and correctly suspected it had something to do with Tina's death. "Just another of your run-of-the-mill, everyday psycho, Murph. You have to let it go."

"Yeah, just another psycho. Who can tell these days? The whole world's fucked up."

Still crouched beside the body, Murphy continued studying the headless body, his trained expert eyes roving slowly, inch by inch, as a collector might view a specimen. He suddenly tensed, alerting Drake that he'd noticed something else.

"What is it, Murph?"

Following Murphy's gaze, Drake noted the girl's right index finger missing; it'd been cleanly sliced off near the knuckle. Straightening upright, reading each other's minds, they scoured the alley, but couldn't find it.

Voices were approaching and Murphy turned to watch a short fat man scurry toward them. It was Paul Hemphill, the department's forensic expert who usually headed up the crime scene processing team.

"Stand back! *Stand back!* Quit tramping all the evidence into the ground and give me something to work with!" he shouted angrily.

Hemphill was heavyset with a large red nose, and his bloodshot eyes magnified through thick, wire-rimmed glasses. His close-cropped hair, or what remained of it, was somewhere between a washed-out brown and gray. An ugly cold sore at the corner of his mouth had burst and his tongue couldn't stop probing it. Rumors circulating around the department were that he was a confirmed homosexual—a rumor neither Murphy nor Drake gave much thought to.

Murphy caught Drake's grin as the two men stepped aside to give Hemphill his space. Both men agreed he was a crotchety old fart, but as forensic specialists go, Paul Hemphill was still as good as they come. The ME examined the body carefully for a long time before stopping to look back, signaling his team — two young assistants waiting to take their crime scene photos and scrub the area for evidence. Hemphill retreated to the street with Drake and Murphy in close pursuit.

"What do you make of it, Paul?" Murphy asked. The trembling in his hands had ceased, but his face remained pale and drawn.

"She died," Hemphill answered shortly. "Some asshole cut off her head and she died. Any more brilliant questions?" Even in the rain, his face beaded with sweat.

Instantly, fire shot from Murphy's eyes, his face clouding up. Drake, reading the danger signals, quickly stepped forward. "You got anything else to give us, Paul? We've got a special interest in this one."

"Yeah? Okay. The amount of rigor mortia and livor mortis suggests she's been dead about twenty-four hours. It's cool, so it tends to last longer under these conditions, but that's still a ballpark figure. She wasn't killed here. Someone dumped her after they knocked her off. Probably some John who didn't care for her skinny legs. I'd say she was raped—probably sodomized, too. I won't know for sure until after the autopsy."

"Right! Some dissatisfied John did it," Murphy put in sourly. "Oh, and by the way, he just happened to have a little extra time, so he stripped her, hauled her down here to the Square, and repositioned her body like that. For God's sake, get real, Hemphill."

"What about the finger?" Drake asked quickly.

"Which one?" Obviously stung by Murphy's sarcasm, Hemphill appeared to be pouting.

"*God dammit*, Hemp! *Work* with me on this!" Drake drew himself up to his full height and glared down at the pudgy Paul Hemphill. Early on, Drake had earned the nickname, Bear, due to his amicable disposition and easy-going manner. But some of the other officers had seen him really lose it on a couple of occasions, and word spread quickly it wasn't wise to piss off the Bear.

"Okay, okay. It's just been a long day," Hemphill stated, squinting through his rain-splattered glasses. The water on his thick lens made him appear like a frog peering through a block of ice. "It's only ten o'clock and I've already got another call waiting in Magnolia Bluffs. After that, *maybe* I'll get a chance to eat breakfast." Scratching his thin beard, he went on.

"The finger's hard to figure. Could've been pulled off in a car door... you know, someone got in a hurry to get her out of the car and closed on it. Or, it could've been torture... hard to say at this juncture. The nipple appears to have been bitten off. If so, there may be teeth marks. I'll know more after Sally does his autopsy and I write my report."

Drake still towered over the small man, unbending, although his tone had lost some of its edge. "When do you suppose we could get a copy of your report, Paul?"

"Try late tomorrow afternoon. That is, if we don't have any more bodies pop up tonight." Hemphill climbed into the passenger's side of a waiting police car and it quickly roared away.

Murphy came along side of Drake. "Likeable puke."

Drake automatically reached for his partner's lit cigarette and Murphy slapped his hand away. The big man scowled and poked another stick of gum into his mouth. Murphy estimated he was probably chewing roughly six sticks, and wondered how many more he could stuff in.

"Cut him a break, Murph. Think about how it must be doing his job."

"Yeah. Not like the glamorous one we enjoy, right?"

Climbing into their unmarked patrol car, Drake started it up and the warm air from the heater vents felt good.

"Ah!" Drake muttered. "Spring in Seattle. Ain't nothing like it."

He pulled into the solid line of traffic without looking, ignoring the horns of other drivers. They rode in silence for several miles, Drake periodically cussing the smeared bugs on his windshield and the other drivers as he picked his way through the crowded wet streets. Murphy slumped in the passenger's seat as

31

before, brooding silently. From the corner of his eye, Drake watched him unconsciously touch his jacket pocket where he always carried a worn laminated picture of pony-tailed Tina riding her Big Wheel.

Murphy *was* brooding, and he was troubled. The murdered teenage hooker had reminded him of Tina. His hands began to tremble again and he wanted a drink. "Who do you think she was, Bear?"

Drake hesitated, then said, "Oh... *her*. Just some young hooker, Frank. Probably came to the big city with dreams of becoming a model and got ground up in the machinery. Happens all the time."

"That should be some comfort to her parents," Murphy said dryly.

Drake shot him a concerned glance, maintaining his silence.

"Let's run by the station and pull Tina's file," Murphy said suddenly, sitting upright. He had a dark look that Drake instantly recognized. It usually meant trouble for *both* of them.

Drake emphatically shook his big head. "No, no, and no! Let's drive over to Rainier Valley and interview some of those *victims* like Brooks told us to before we lose our jobs!"

Murphy hesitated as though he was going to argue, then visibly deflated back into his seat. They rode without talking for a while, Drake casting worried sideward glances at his suffering partner. Murphy's pained expression finally got the best of him and Drake acquiesced.

"*Then* we'll go look at Tina's file."

Murphy slouched and scowled. "You know as well as I do it's a frigging waste of time trying to get *those* people to talk to us. They had no reason to trust the police or anyone else in authority where they came from, and they're not going to start trusting us! It's too deeply embedded in their culture, and we're not going to be the ones to change them."

"You're probably right, Murph. But we gotta try."

Drake took a one-way street and doglegged two blocks off Rainier Avenue, the four-lane thoroughfare that runs from one end of Rainier Valley to the other. They were headed to a business park in a seedy section of Seattle, dotted with small minority businesses, run-down homes and dilapidated housing projects for the poor. Gang graffiti was boldly scrawled on every wall. It was an area responsible for a major share of the drug deals, murders, robberies and rape statistics published in the city's annual crime report. Despite continual efforts to clean it up by various citizen groups, that section of the city remained one of the worst crime areas in King County.

By the time they arrived it appeared Mother Nature had finally made up her mind about the weather, and a hard, driving rain had set in. They'd come to interview the owner of a small Korean restaurant in a horseshoe-shaped shopping center containing half a dozen mom and pop businesses. The lettering and advertisements on all the businesses were written in both English and Korean. The Seoul Garden Restaurant had been the latest establishment hit by the so-called "Asian Shotgun Gang."

What could be so lovely as a day in May?" Drake grinned, holding out his palms, eyes skyward.

"It's April, and this is nothing but a frigging waste of time," Murphy grumbled as they hurried through the downpour to the front door of the small business. Crowding into the narrow foyer, a diminutive old woman, followed by a young man, rushed to greet them. Exotic smells filled the air, making Murphy feel a little light-headed.

"Welcome! Welcome, Sirs! You come this way please," the old woman said, bowing and gesturing with her hands. She seated them at a corner table as the young man rushed off to retrieve a menu and a pitcher of ice water.

Murphy noticed he and Drake were the only customers and wondered how these businesses ever survived. The dining area was decorated in red and gold art of the old country, most likely carted in when the family initially immigrated. A grossly fat teak Buddha stood erect in one corner, his arms outstretched toward the heavens. Exquisite glass and stone Jade trees dotted the small room. Despite his earlier misgivings, Murphy was surprised to find he liked the ambiance, and since he'd skipped breakfast, the smells emanating from the kitchen were driving him absolutely bonkers.

Both detectives flipped open small black cases displaying their gold badges to the old woman. Her face changed instantly. Stunned and afraid, she shrank back. Murphy risked a smirk, hoping Drake would remember his prediction concerning the cooperation they could expect from the Korean community.

"I'm Sergeant Murphy and this is Detective Drake, Seattle P. D. We're investigating the recent robbery and murder that occurred here, ma'am."

The old woman simply stared at the two men, her face white and drawn. "No understand. No speak English." As though to prove her point, she bustled off in the direction of the kitchen, waving her arms about and speaking loudly in her native tongue to someone in the back.

"Like I said, a frigging waste of time," Murphy stated self-righteously, smirking again, just in case Drake missed it the first time.

The young man who'd seated them earlier hurried over and began speaking in excellent English. "May I be of service to you, gentlemen?"

Drake started it off this time. "We need to ask some questions about the robbery. Is there some place we can talk?"

"Only here, or the kitchen, sir. Allow me to introduce myself, gentlemen. I am Kim Nam Ho. Everybody calls me Jimmy Ho. Our family owns this place. My mother understands English well enough, but you must understand she is from the old country and is a little distrustful of the authorities." Jimmy Ho smiled. He had a nice smile. "I will be more than happy to answer all of your questions."

Murphy jumped back in at this point. "Were you here the night the place was robbed, Jimmy?"

"No. I attend Seattle University in the evenings and work here during the day. On the day we were robbed, only Yong Mi, the young girl who was murdered and my mother were here. My mother was working in the kitchen when she heard the screams and the gunshot. She hid in the freezer until they were gone. She didn't see any of their faces but repeatedly heard the names, *Kisop* and *Pak*, called out by one of them. The leader seemed angry and told them to quit using names. She said from the sound of their voices they were all young men, late teens, maybe early twenties — somewhere around there."

"Did she happen to see the car they arrived in?" Drake asked without any hope.

Jimmy Ho hesitated. "No, but next door is a tailor shop. My mother's friend works there. She saw the car but I don't know if she'll talk to you. I'm sorry sir, but old people have long memories concerning their handling by the police. I've explained that to you."

Murphy leaned forward. "Do you suppose you could talk to your mother's friend for us? Maybe she will provide you with the information we need."

Jimmy looked doubtful, but nodded his head. "I will try," he said. "What do you want me to ask her?"

Murphy jotted a few notes and Jimmy slid them into his coat pocket. Before departing, Jimmy convinced them to try some specialties from the extensive menu. Never one to skip a meal, Drake eagerly selected several items, and with some initial misgivings, Murphy selected two dishes. Smiling graciously, the young man took their orders and hurried toward the kitchen. Within minutes the old woman reappeared balancing several steaming dishes and a large bowl of rice. Despite Murphy's mother-of-all-hang-overs, the food smelled enticing.

"Hey man, this is good!" Drake mumbled around a large mouthful of fried rice. Murphy nodded, eyes downcast but continuing to eat. As they finished off the last of the hot green tea, Jimmy Ho returned, sliding into the booth beside them. Jimmy passed information about the automobile and killers to the officers, non-stop for the next fifteen minutes, pausing only for a series of questions for clarification.

As they departed to return to the station with several pages of notes warming their pockets, Drake asked smugly, "Don't you ever get tired of being wrong?"

"I didn't say it *was* a total waste of time," Murphy said. "I said it *might* be."

"You said," Drake recanted, "and I quote, 'it's a *frigging* waste of time to talk to *any* of these people.' End of quote." He grinned with self-satisfaction and poked another stick of gum into his large mouth.

"Well, no matter. We were just lucky to get what we did."

"What we got, my good man, is two suspects, a pretty good description of the car, and the fact it had out-of-state license plates. Not a bad mornings work. Now, if you'd be so kind as to call it in to have it put out to the field, we may get a break and save our jobs."

It was clear Drake wasn't going to let him just slip off the hook without the obligatory wriggling, so Murphy settled in for a long assault on his dubious record of *right guesses*, as opposed to his partner's *two in a row*. Even though he wasn't in the mood for it. Finding Murphy's foul mood the perfect time to push his advantage, Drake wanted to brag about the score because they usually stayed about even. But as luck had it, Drake was slightly ahead on points.

Self-righteous asshole, Murphy thought, glancing resentfully at his big partner. Drake smirked with self-righteousness, obviously ready to needle his partner some more.

A sensuous breathy voice caressed the radio and suddenly warmed the interior of their patrol unit by several degrees, interrupting their exchange. It had the affect of instantly taking their minds off their immediate contest. The deep voice, oozing pure sex appeal and sparking their imaginations, belonged to a young lady all the cops called *Hooters* —Samantha White—a buxom twenty-five year old beauty, the department's dispatcher. She had a husky, wet voice that made men's arm hairs stand at attention, and according to Drake, everything else. She was secretly referred to as *Hooters*, but to date, no one had been incredibly stupid enough to say it to her face until just recently. About a month earlier, the desk sergeant inadvertently asked a young rookie officer to tell Hooters to call one of the field units with information about an on-going case. The green, inexperienced young man did just that—opening his remarks with, "Morning, *Hooters* ma'am…"

That one small slip of the tongue had the affect of a terrorist attack on the entire Seattle Police Department. Sexual harassment complaints multiplied overnight followed by mandatory attendance at workplace diversity and sexual harassment classes. A multitude of touchy-feely documents immediately began plastering bulletin boards. Murphy and Drake were cautious to never refer to Samantha that way—even in the privacy of their patrol car. Nonetheless, her deep throaty mutterings still sent both men straight to hell.

"Something's getting awfully rigid in here," Drake mumbled toward the window. It was his opinion that a sexy woman was the one topic that remained every man's right to think about, talk about, and look at without having to justify it. That was as far as it went with him though. As long as Murphy had known him, the big man had never cheated on Mable — not once.

"Really."

"I shit you not. Harder than Superman's kneecap!"

Murphy rolled his eyes toward his partner and answered Samantha's call, bolting upright in his seat as they received the message! It was another victim just like the last—the one Paul Hemphill had remarked about earlier in the morning, found near Magnolia Bluffs. The M.O.'s were identical; young girl, body nude, head positioned between the victim's legs. Drake turned on the lights and siren and gave the big cruiser the gas.

Hemphill was just wrapping things up and preparing to leave as they arrived. He walked outside the condo with the lime-green walls, leaned against the stair rail and stoically watched Murphy and Drake huff their way up the last of three flights of stairs.

"No need to hurry," he shouted down to them. "She ain't going nowhere."

Murphy made it first and gasped for breath as Hemphill went on. "Almost identical to the other one in Pioneer Square, Frank," he said. "Only this one appears to have been killed here."

"Any ID on her, yet?" Murphy could hear Drake panting below them as he dragged himself up the final flight of stairs. He sounded like the two-ton water buffalo that had chased them from a flooded Southeast Asian rice paddy one hot day during a training exercise. Hemphill was suddenly all business. "We're working on it. Looks like you'll get this one too since it's probably the same sicko that killed the hooker."

Hemphill started back down, edging past Drake who'd finally given up and was now seated on a step about half way up the last flight. Drake, opting for an easier way out of his predicament than completing the climb, apologetically smiled at Murphy and followed the forensic specialist down the steps.

"*Great*! Thanks pal!" Murphy didn't sound as if he meant it.

He walked to the apartment door and peered inside. The area was drenched in blood; further evidence the crime had been committed on the premises. He spotted a medic placing the remains in a body bag to transport to the morgue and quickly moved toward him. Squatting beside the bundle, he gently unzipped it, exposing the contents.

Like the last victim, she appeared to be about fifteen or sixteen, fair-haired, slender, and probably very pretty — before some monster cut off her head. A trace of sticky substance dotted the corners of her mouth, indicating, like the other victim, a heavy cloth masking tape had been used to keep her quiet. He carefully observed that both hands had been incased in clear plastic baggys for later testing to detect any skin under the victim's nails. If so, he couldn't see it. He checked the young girl's breasts and found them intact. Satisfied he couldn't get anymore from the crime scene, he traversed the stairs again, sighting Drake and Hemphill, who'd found shelter under an overhang. Several news vans now aligned the street.

"No missing finger and the nipple wasn't bitten off," Hemphill stated, stealing Murphy's thunder.

"Same guy?" he asked.

"No doubt in my mind. Though it's unusual for one of these guys to knock off two in one day like this. Really unusual for him to do it here, where he might be interrupted." Paul Hemphill looked tired even though it was still early in the day. "Looks like he whacked this one around midnight, give or take thirty minutes." He smiled smugly as Murphy visibly flinched at his crude choice of words, then they made a mad dash for their waiting cars.

A dozen reporters huddled under a large oak near the street trying to stay dry. A husky youth holding a monstrous camera, *Channel 5 News*, filmed a pretty woman speaking into a microphone. *Molly Atwood, the barracuda*, Murphy thought, as he ducked between cars to avoid her spotting him. He was too late—hearing his name called repeatedly.

Reluctantly turning, he slowed as the attractive woman ran toward him. He was conscious most of the males present stared at her trim legs flashing beneath her short skirt. Molly had that affect on men.

"Frank, are you going to head up the investigation on this serial killer case?" she said as she approached. The youth struggled with the tripod-mounted camera, trying to keep her within its lens.

Murphy sighed deeply. "Molly, who said it *is* a serial killer?" Murphy sourly retorted, quickly turning away.

"Oh, *come on*, Frank! Two young girls killed in one day. Both decapitated and raped. What would *you* call it?" Molly Atwood stated indignantly.

Murphy eyed her as if she were something he'd just scraped off the bottom of his shoe. "I'm not calling it anything. You seem to have much more information than I do, Molly. Maybe you should head up the investigation." He quickly closed the car door in her face. Drake took his hint and pulled into traffic.

Molly stood motionless, her hands resting on her shapely hips, glaring after them. She muttered a four-lettered word and stalked back toward the news van. She knew Frank Murphy very well. Ten years ago, after she'd been given her first big break as a reporter for the Daily Report, she'd even slept with him—three times, to be exact. That was before he'd discovered she'd leaked information gained during their encounters to further her career.

The scene had been ugly and Frank hadn't willingly spoken to her since. Atwood knew about the death of Frank's daughter, and she'd also heard the rumors concerning Elnore Murphy and Robert James—and Frank's escalating drinking problems. Molly shoved the knowledge to the back of her mind, reserving it for later.

Murphy and Drake pulled into the underground garage, just in time to see Captain Brooks speed away in his personal car. *It might turn into a pleasant day after all*, Murphy thought, as he watched his boss disappear up the ramp.

Homicide was its usual chaotic self when they entered; a dozen phones ringing off the hook, BJ arguing with a well-dressed older woman over her right to question the woman's twenty-two year old son, and Booth's radio blaring an old Rolling Stone ballad. Detective Lee yelled across his desk at a huge black man with neatly parted dreadlocks that out-weighed him by at least a hundred pounds. Lee suddenly jumped from his seat and glared at the man as if ready to take him apart, his head barely level with the man's chest. The large man didn't appear too concerned. A slick defense attorney attempted to converse with Fletcher over all the commotion, then growing frustrated, finally slammed the lid to his briefcase and stormed out.

"Don't ya just love your job?" Drake said. Amazingly, his tone implied he actually did.

Charley Booth, who'd been assisting in their investigation, saw them enter and quickly moved to intercept them. "Good job getting that info on the perp's car, guys! We ran it and already have several possibles. The best lead is a car with Vancouver, B.C. tags."

Murphy pulled a crumpled pack of Camels from his jacket, shook a bent one free and stuck it between his lips. As he searched for his lighter, Drake unconsciously reached for the Camels. Murphy, grinning maliciously, snatched the pack away and stuffed them back into his own jacket.

Booth smiled at the exchange and went on. "The registration is under the name of Kisop Shinn. The spelling on that may not be exactly right, but it's close. It's a 1989 Olds sedan, light green four-door. An almost identical match to the description given by the old lady at the tailor-shop." Booth's excitement was contagious to the others.

"When we find it, if there's primer on the right front fender, we've got 'em!"

Booth's features were exactly like the old Sunday morning TV cartoon character, *Deputy Dog*. Deep hanging jowls and sad eyes made him appear slow-witted and ponderous, yet he was one of the finest investigators in the department. Long ago, he'd accepted the fact that he'd never be promoted beyond sergeant—if lucky enough to advance to even that grade.

Though well dressed, his clothes always appeared rumpled. It gave him a friendly and forgiving appearance and strongly influenced his success as one of the finest hostage negotiators and interrogators in the department. He was the kind of guy who could wear a five-hundred-dollar suit and still look rumpled. On the plus side, Charley had a great sense of humor and everyone in the department liked him. He was the first to admit his lack of Hollywood good looks made his advancement unlikely. Disarming as he appeared, he could also be tough, as Murphy had discovered the first time he'd seen the rumpled little man in action. He'd been stunned at Booth's ferocity in going after an escaped felon.

"Put everything you have out to the field units, Charley. The more eyes we get on it, the sooner we'll find these ass-holes," Drake said.

"It's already been done, Bear," Charley replied. "I'll bet you a Big Mac the son-of-a-bitch is still in Seattle. Want to bet?"

"I think I'll pass. Watching my fat grams, ya know." Drake answered, rubbing his large belly.

"Which means Mable's got him on another diet," Murphy said dryly. Drake shot him a dirty look.

While they waited, Murphy and Drake scoured Tina's file, cover to cover, then ran computer checks on all the deaths of young girls within the state for the past two years. Then they repeated the process, going back five years. It was a long list. Murphy drafted a message to transmit interstate to other law enforcement agencies throughout the country. From his experience, he knew it'd take some time to receive any responses.

He and Drake updated their report for Brooks on both the gang case and the deaths of the two decapitated girls, requesting that certain information be withheld from the media about the latter, at least for the moment. They especially wanted to keep secret the aspects of how the severed head had been positioned and other specifics that'd only be known by the killer. These small details would help to identify the person responsible from all the nuts sure to crawl out of the woodwork and confess once it hit the papers. The report was waiting when Brooks returned, red-faced and unhappy.

With much less trepidation than they'd felt at the earlier meeting, they entered without knocking. Brooks glanced up at their entrance and nodded them toward two chairs. This appeared to be a good sign. Drake happily hurried to take possession of the large overstuffed one, leaving the functional straight-backed chair for his slimmer partner. He smiled smugly, sinking into the soft leather.

"Good job on the information about the car," Brooks started off. "Stay with it until we nail those bastards." He uncomfortably sifted through several sheets of paper on his desk, failing to meet either man's eyes. "I'm going to put you both on it full time until you get them."

Murphy caught Drake's eyes while mulling over Brook's last remark. His face registered alarm as the realization slowly began to set in about the inference.

"In the meantime, you'll be turning your other case over to Yates and Coleman," Brooks said matter-of-factly.

Murphy jumped to his feet. "What the fuck is going on here, Brooks? What're you trying to pull, anyway? That's *our* case! You

41

know it's only a matter of time before this gang thing is nailed down. The other case has been ours from the beginning and by god, we're going to keep it!"

"Sit down. *Sit down!*" Brooks shouted over Murphy's objections. Murphy glared back, his face flushed as if he were ready to lunge over the desk at any second. "Just sit down and shut-up for a minute!" Brooks shouted again, this time louder. The outside office noise level ceased abruptly.

"*Bullshit!*" Murphy remained standing, his face crimson with rage.

Both men stood toe-to-toe, glaring into each other's face, completely unyielding. Drake shouldered between them, trying to usher his partner away before he landed in deeper trouble. He strong-armed Murphy to his seat, noticing the fire still shooting from his partner's eyes. Drake effortlessly held him in the chair by placing his ham-like hands on his friend's shoulders.

"Let me handle this, Murph. Okay? *Okay?*" he said soothingly.

Silent and stone-faced, Murphy finally nodded, continuing to glare at his boss.

Drake glared at Brooks with cold hostility. "What's going on here, Captain? This isn't *your* policy. The team that starts a case finishes it. You've always run things that way."

Brooks knew Murphy's hot-headedness was one thing, but watching the controlled fury just behind this big man's dark face prompted him to handle it with unusual finesse.

"Sit down Bear," Brooks said softly.

Drake remained standing, staring obstinately back at him.

"Please."

Like the huge animal that was his namesake, Drake finally lumbered to the chair and sat down.

Brooks took a deep sigh of relief, and said, "That second young girl they found in Magnolia Bluffs wasn't just *another hooker* like the first. Her name was Bobbie Holcomb. Her mother is the Honorable Ethel Holcomb, the state senator from Pasco. I spoke to Paul Hemphill earlier, and he thinks we've got a serial killer on our hands."

"Whew," Drake whistled softly, shooting Murphy a sharp look to keep quiet. "Be that as it may, Captain, we can handle it. The

Asian gang situation is all but wrapped up and we can go full bore on the other one now."

Brooks shook out a cigarette, gazed at it for an instant, then stuck it behind his ear before he rose and walked to the window. He stood with his hands clasped behind his back for a moment before he spoke. "I just returned from the Mayor's office, Bear. Chief Williams, Robert James and Helen Walcott were also there. James doesn't want you and Murphy on the case, period. Particularly *you*, Frank. The others don't care much one way or the other as long as we get results—quickly. That said, the Chief will probably follow James lead, seeing as how he's likely to win the election.

Brooks whirled to face them. "Chief Williams instructed me to form a special full-time task force to solve this before it gets out of hand. He doesn't want another Green River killer fiasco going on for ten years. He expects a full-court press using all the resources at our disposal before this guy can strike again. He knows Colburn, and Two Gun is his preference to head up the task-force."

The captain breathed deeply and looked back dejectedly. "That's just the way it is. I'm sorry, Murph. I really am."

Murphy rose without answering and left, leaving the door ajar. Brooks and Drake watched him as his back disappeared from sight. Drake's unrelenting eyes leveled on Brooks once more. "You and I have been friends for nearly twenty years, Tom. There was a time when you wouldn't have stood for something like this. You realize this'll likely finish Frank as a cop."

Drake advanced to the open door and grasped the knob, then slowly turned back to face Brooks. "If I find you didn't do all you could to stop this, Tom, you and me are quits." He quietly closed the door as he left.

Brooks's shoulders slumped as he stared vacantly at his desk.

———

Magnolia Bluffs, isolated from the hustling masses of downtown Seattle by the Ballard Bridge, boasts of some of the finest view property in Puget Sound. Tastefully decorated homes, manicured lawns, gardens and gated residences overlook the gentle waves and white sailboat masts at the Elliott Bay Marina. Slow-moving cargo ships continually traverse wide shipping lanes between the clay bluffs and Bainbridge Island, as high-speed motorboats and sleek sailboats dodge nimbly between them. While few can afford to live this lifestyle, many Seattleites cruise through the area on sunny days, fantasizing while enjoying the spectacular view.

With building amusement, Corky stood among the silent crowd watching the commotion near the upscale condos where the girl's body had been discovered. An ambulance and several police cars with their flashing lights and blaring sirens added immensely to the thrill. Blending in with the other spectators huddled tightly in the drizzle, Corky contemptuously studied their faces. Pale expressions drawn haggard by fear and shock, they shivered as they clutched their pathetic little umbrellas against the cold rain.

What would they do if they knew the person who did it was standing right beside them? But they won't know, because I'm smarter than all the Keystone Cops in the world! Fucking smucks.

Corky knew about rejection . . . and the consequences of that rejection. Consequences like what they'd found upstairs in the vacant condo with the shitty green walls.

Like that gorgeous little thing huddled next to the old woman, right over there. My, oh my. So innocent. So...fresh.

Unaware they were being watched, both females stood close, shivering under a large umbrella, as though it might somehow protect them. It wouldn't. *Yum, yum,...fifteen, maybe sixteen, long blond hair, very pretty—just the kind that thinks her shit doesn't stink. Probably lives right around here, too.*

That'll be something to think about. Corky smiled.

Chapter 4

Elnore observed Frank and his big partner walking briskly across the street, returning from lunch at the nearby McDonalds most of the downtown cops frequented. She knew that's where he and Bear usually went and therefore, had been avoiding it lately. She'd been tempted to cross and intercept them, but at the last moment had decided against it, opting to skip what would be a sure altercation with her ex-husband. Just the sight of him with his tousled dark hair made her heart ache, but she knew that in her current frame of mind she'd be no match for his sharp tongue.

She'd just left Carl Allen's office, the King County Prosecutor, and her head was still spinning from their conversation. She'd gone to present an ultimatum; she was fed up with the *good old boy* judicial system network. When she'd entered, Allen had been seated as usual, reclining in his big overstuffed leather chair, his fingers intertwined behind his head. The spacious wall of glass behind him was one of Puget Sound's most beautiful views, coveted by many of the city's most powerful people. At one time even the mayor had made a power grab to take possession of the prosecutor's office, but somehow Allen had always managed to hold on to it. Outside, tugs pulled at the huge container ships bringing their goods into port while some sail boats with colorful spinnakers nimbly dodged among their wakes. Five square blocks of chaotic gridlocked city traffic completed the scene.

Carl Allen was a small, distinguished man in his mid-fifties. His gray hair was thinning rapidly, and there was a bald spot about the size of a large cup on the very top. The few remaining strands of hair had been combed over the top; he was vainly aware of his impending baldness. His wide nose was slightly off center and made him appear more interesting than ugly. His deep penetrating gray eyes missed nothing, and Allen could be alternatively warm and totally unforgiving in the same sentence. As usual, he'd been blunt and to the point. Elnore's mind flashed back to their conversation...

"When we spoke on the phone, Elnore, you seemed to have something particular on your mind. Why don't you tell me what it is?" His tone was smooth, but the coldness in his eyes belied his remarks.

She didn't intend to be bullied. "Carl, I didn't sign on here to handle the leftovers," she replied sharply. "Oh, at first I realized I'd get a good share of them. Those I did — and I think you'll agree — I handled very well."

He failed to acknowledge her tart remark, so she'd hurried on. "I came to work for you and to build a reputation. There are cases I feel strongly that we should pursue, but because they would be very difficult to prosecute we usually end up settling for a plea bargain on a lesser charge. Others are frequently dismissed, simply because they appear so hopeless no one in the department is willing to take them on. To be honest, sir, I think that's wrong."

"You're ill-informed, Elnore. We're operating short-handed," Allen retorted bluntly.

His patronizing tone irked her, so she blurted out, "That doesn't seem to stop the good old boys from getting the plum cases though, does it, sir?"

At that, Allen leaned forward, placing his fingers together in a temple, pondering her remarks. "Ah, now I see what this is all about."

Elnore hadn't tried to hide her irateness, firing back angrily. "I just think everyone deserves proper representation under the law, victims deserve retribution, and each of us deserve a chance to handle the impact cases that come along."

Despite her antagonism, Elnore had known she was on firm ground. She was an excellent lawyer and knew her worth to the department. She'd worked the trenches for the past three years, becoming one of the prosecutor's most experienced officers. She'd taken some small, but not insignificant cases that otherwise might never have been prosecuted, and to many of her colleague's surprise and envy, had won them all. Recently, the news media had begun to follow her court battles. Now the time had arrived and she wanted her due — bigger, complex cases — and more visibility.

A week earlier, the senior partner of Becker, Becker, and Price, one Seattle's most successful law firms, had approached her. They'd offered more than just a job. They'd offered her a carrot—a possible junior partnership sometime down the road. Although emboldened and intrigued by their offer, she hesitated. Elnore had loftier ambitions. She wanted to be the county prosecutor someday, then perhaps Attorney General—or governor. After all, Dixie had become Governor. Why *not* her?

As it'd turned out, she'd been on firmer ground than she'd imagined. Only two days earlier, Claude Becker had cornered Prosecutor Allen at the Rainier Club and mentioned the offer he'd made to his prized employee. Overburdened, Allen couldn't fathom how he'd get along if his most productive deputy left. To aggravate the situation even more, Councilman James had also been pressuring him to give Elnore higher profile cases. Allen knew James had been slipping the meat to his deputy prosecutor and correctly surmised that James' sudden interest in her career were the wages of their sin. On the other hand, James seemed a sure bet to be the next mayor, so it certainly couldn't hurt any to cement some future ties with City Hall.

With this in mind, Prosecutor Allen said, "I think I may have a case like the one you've got in mind, Elnore. It should prove to be interesting." He smiled thinly.

———————

Murphy and Drake placed their protective vests in their lockers, preparing to leave for the day. Most of the shift had already changed and they were alone in the basement. It was the time of day Murphy most dreaded. *Home*, he thought contemptuously. He'd probably just head over to O'Mally's instead and down a few. Maybe several. When numb, he'd somehow find his way back to the boat, pop a handful of pills and pass out. Murphy had been around long enough to know he couldn't fight the system. Well he could, but the prospects of winning weren't all that good. He knew from first hand experience. He'd spent most of his life fighting the big boys and here he was, still a bottom-feeder. In the end, they always find a way to grind you down.

Lower than whale shit, Sport — and that's on the bottom of the ocean.

"Why don't you come on over and watch the game? The Lakers are in town and it's going to be televised for a change. My treat." Bear said. "Mable likes the Sonics too, so we'll order out for pizza and drink that case of beer I've got socked away in the garage refer. The season's about over and they need this game to stay in the running. What'd ya' say Murph?"

"Thanks for the offer, Bear, but I've got a hot little number waiting at O'Mally's. She'd be so disappointed if I stood her up that she'd probably pick up one of those county-slobs who wouldn't be nearly good enough for her."

He felt his partner was just trying to keep him from feeling depressed and spending all night alone in O'Mally's. He was grateful, but tonight he didn't feel like he'd be good company for anyone. He could tell Drake knew he was lying about the hot number, but his big partner let it drop.

"Well, if she stands you up or you want to drop by later, just come on over. Don't matter how late it is," Drake said. "Hell, you can sleep on the couch."

From the stairs, boisterous laughter and loud voices abruptly interrupted their conversation. They turned to see Colburn and Yates entering. Recognizing Murphy and Drake, the two men's demeanor instantly changed as they headed toward their lockers. There'd been bad blood between Murphy and Colburn ever since they'd been students at the police academy. Murphy believed the philosophy that every so often you just happen upon another human being you just naturally hate, and generally, the feeling is mutual. Most sensible-minded people are able to work through it, never letting it interfere with their daily lives. That hadn't been the case between he and Colburn.

"Hey, heard you guys did a fine piece of police work on that Asian gang case." Yates winked conspiratorially at Colburn.

Murphy and Drake pointedly ignored them.

"Yeah," retorted Colburn. "If you ever get it wrapped up, you might be able to do some leg-work for me on *my* new case. Got a serial killer to catch. It's the kind of case that can make you or break you. Not everyone can handle 'em."

Colburn, just over six-foot one-inch, wore his black oily hair slicked back, several inches too long. His wide necktie, barely reaching the mid-point between his thick neck and belt-line, was splattered with large purple petunias resting short over the beginnings of a potbelly. He'd been the topic of many discussions between Murphy and Drake, and they'd conceded he seemed more like a used car salesman than a plainclothes detective. Begrudgingly, they did have to admit that what they'd heard about his work indicated he was a competent investigator.

"Fuck off." Murphy said without looking up. He was instantly angry with himself for responding to their digs, but in his black mood he wasn't about to be pushed very far.

"I just thought it'd be nice to have someone with connections working with us on this one. Hey Joe?" Colburn winked to Yates as he spun the combination lock on his locker. "Did you know Frank has connections over at City Hall, Yates? By way of the Prosecutors Office."

Drake saw his partner stiffen, but before he had time to react, Colburn made a serious mistake. "Yeah, his wife has an *in* at City Hall, too. Someone important, I hear."

A younger Frank Murphy had fought Golden Gloves for three years. Some said he'd been good enough to turn pro. It showed as he smoothly came off the bench and put Colburn on the floor with a solid left to the jaw. Dazed, Colburn didn't move as Drake instantly grabbed Murphy's arms in a vise-like grip, hustling his struggling partner up the stairs toward the parking lot.

"Jesus, Murph! Are you fucking *crazy*? Do you *want* to get kicked off the force?" They both knew if Colburn turned him in, it'd mean suspension at the least, and likely his badge.

"It doesn't make any difference to me anymore, Bear," Murphy answered honestly after Bear released him. "Not one damned bit."

He slid under the wheel and drove away, leaving Drake staring after him, his face etched with worry.

Located near the Ballard Locks is a favorite cop hangout called O'Mally's. The owner is an ex-cop named Sean O'Mally, who'd been Frank Murphy's first street partner as a rookie. Murphy had learned a lot from the old cop. Entering through the rear-parking door, he saw the place was busy as usual. Maggie O'Mally saw him instantly and shouted across the bar, "Hey, Murph! Where ya been keeping your raggedy ass? Come on over! Have a seat. The first one's on me."

She favored him with a warm affectionate grin reserved for special customers and friends. Maggie—Ma to the regulars—was married to Sean, now medically retired and still one of Frank's oldest friends. Recently Sean had suffered a stroke, leaving him partially paralyzed with difficulty speaking clearly. He generally came to their bar only on Friday and Saturday nights, watching quietly as his pudgy wife of thirty years attended bar. Frank hadn't been in to see them for almost a month, although he had been in the previous night on Ma's night off.

"I'll take a bourbon with a beer chaser," Murphy said, straddling the nearest barstool.

Handcuffs, batons, and cop photographs wallpapered the walls, some dating to the first of the century. Many of the photos were of a much younger, leaner Sean O'Mally, grinning broadly among the ranks of other uniformed police officers in variously dated uniforms. The most recent was Sean in a Seattle Public Safety uniform, wedged between Frank and Bear. All three smiled happily. It'd been taken just a week before his crippling stroke.

"Going to get serious tonight, huh? Drinking that shit will kill you." Ma's tone was one of undisguised disapproval as she drew a glass of suds from the tap. When he didn't answer, she went on. "How's the job going, Murph?"

Murphy gave her his best disarming grin. "Great. Brooks took me off the only case I've had an ounce of interest in more than a year — I decked Two Gun earlier tonight—and I'll probably get kicked off the force first thing tomorrow morning. Couldn't be better. Yourself?"

He swallowed a deep pull of the ale and wiped off the foam moustache.

"You socked Colburn? Tsk, tsk, tsk," Ma mouthed. Then leaning closer, she whispered, "I hope you knocked him on his slick ass." Nodding her head in total approval, she moved to take the order of another couple just sitting down. Frank winked at her and was still smiling when he caught the eye of a tall redhead he'd seen the previous evening. She sat six stools down, the same place she'd occupied before. She'd caught his eye and stared back last night, too. Frank downed his shot, gathered his mug and slid uninvited onto the vacant stool beside her.

As she turned, he gazed into the deepest green eyes he'd ever seen. *Irish*, he thought. *A real knockout, too!* She took his breath away.

After just the right amount of pause, she smiled a slow dazzling one that displayed incredibly perfect white teeth.

"Julie. It's Julie Harris."

The voice matched her looks — sensual, deep, and entirely sexy. "Aren't you going to ask what a nice girl like me is doing in a place like this?" Everything about her said money — grossly understated. She wasn't what you'd expect to find in a cop joint like O'Mally's.

"I already know what you're doing in a place like this," he commented. Julie Harris's eyebrow lifted provocatively. *God, what a sexy creature*, he thought again. "You're here because you thought I might be back tonight."

An amused smile toyed at the corners of her lips. "You don't think too much of yourself, do you?"

"I just believe in cutting through all the crap right up front. When two adults meet and like what they see, they shouldn't have to play games."

Light danced off her shiny copper waves as she tilted her head back and laughed — rich and husky, like her voice. "You always come on this romantic?"

"Not always. Sometimes I'm pretty blunt."

Murphy realized his approach was chancy, but instinctively he continued. Scoring had been the last thing on his mind when he'd come in tonight. In fact, these days, women in general had about as much appeal as did sticking a sharp stick in his eye. But that had been before he'd seen Julie With The Fabulous Eyes. After encountering this green-eyed walking orgasm, he found he was having second thoughts.

"I'll bet you don't get lucky too often with that approach." She closely observed his reaction.

Those eyes! He could drown in them. "No, but when I do, we both know what we're there for," he stated frankly.

Julie sipped her nearly empty drink and set it down, and he motioned for Ma to bring a fresh one.

"I may be the kind of woman who needs to be wined and dined first. Some are worth it, you know." Julie slowly crossed her long legs, an expanse of smooth tan thigh teasing beneath the short cream-colored skirt.

The motion wasn't lost on him. Aware of a surge below his belt-line, he thought, *This has got to be love, Sport. Love at first sight!* He swallowed hard and with difficulty, finally found his voice.

"Are you?"

"What? Worth it?"

"No. I already know you're worth it. I mean, the kind who needs to be wined and dined first."

"No."

Her answer caught him by surprise. "Then maybe I will. How 'bout dinner? I know an excellent Italian place near the Space Needle. Want to take a chance?"

"How do I know you're not a rapist or murderer like Ted Bundy?" She raised one eyebrow, tentatively cautious before committing.

"Cause I'm a cop!"

"How do I know you're not a rapist or murderer like Ted Bundy?" she repeated.

Murphy threw back his head and laughed loudly. It'd been a long time since he'd laughed. It felt good.

"Touché, touché."

She rose and placed her warm hand on his arm. "Just to be safe, I'll pick the restaurant."

As she guided him toward the door, he was conscious of the envious stares he was getting from all the other off-duty cops. He seriously hoped none would shout any crude advice as he left. This time he was lucky. Ma saw them leaving and smiled.

Julie opted for the Edgewater Tower, a popular waterfront eatery on the top floor of a new twelve-story luxury hotel in the north end. The staff seemed to know her well and gave her preferential treatment. A pretty hostess led them to a coveted corner table surrounded by a wall of glass where they could gaze at the spectacular view. Across Elliott Bay, city lights danced on the water, while a ribbon of soft moonlight reflected thousands of bobbing boats tied at their moorage. The food was simply the best he'd had in months.

From the outset, Murphy had pretty much intended to treat her the same as any other bimbo he'd run into since he and Elnore had split. In other words, tolerate 'em, get 'em into the sack, bust a nut and get the hell out of Dodge. But as the evening wore on he began to observe her more attentively, watching her grace and beauty as she transformed even the most minor act into one of charm and elegance. She was clearly among the most breathtaking and intriguing women he'd ever met. The realization scared the hell out of him. He felt out of control, like being sucked beneath quicksand. It was a feeling he didn't want at the moment.

"Why me?" he said, downing the last of his wine. Her sexy eyebrow arched again, her lilting smile turning his insides to oatmeal. "I mean, I'm not one to look a gift-horse in the mouth, but ya really gotta wonder. When a woman like you lets herself get picked up by someone like me... she's either slumming, or I've just won the lottery and don't know it yet."

"You were a lot more sure of yourself in O'Mally's." She sipped her wine, her eyes lingering on his face with a hint of amusement.

Something about that irked him. "Maybe I've had time to think about it!" he retorted more harshly than intended and was instantly sorry.

"Oh, come *on* Frank! You're a good-looking guy with a flat stomach. You can't be so naive to have gone through half your life without knowing the impression you make on babes. Quit sounding so innocent." Her moist red lips slowly curved into a crescent, taking the sting out of her words.

Murphy reached for the wine bottle and poured the remainder into their glasses. She seemed to be giving serious thought to his question.

"I think there was a certain look in your eyes that drew me to you. Like you've been beaten up very badly and don't know exactly what to do about it." The corners of her shapely lips turned slightly downward. "Although... I have to admit your caveman approach is wearing thin."

"I'm a victim of my environment," he said.

"Want to talk about it?"

"No."

Her deep green eyes lingered on him, unwavering. "Okay." Silence lay heavily between them for a moment, and then she said, "Do you want to fuck me then?"

Startled, his eyes jerked back to hers, his hand nearly spilling his glass of wine. Over the hammering of his heart, he said, "It surprises me you'd even use that word."

"Typically, I *don't*. I just wanted to fit into your crowd. Did I shock you?"

He paused, then relaxed and grinned. "Uh huh. You really did."

"Good."

Murphy silently pondered, then said thoughtfully, "Look, Julie, can we do this over? I mean, I've been treating you like a piece of meat all night and you've just been ignoring it and making me the envy of every hairy-legged guy in the place. Then...wham, you let me have it in a way that makes me realize what a jerk I've been. So...can we start over?"

She chewed on a pouty bottom lip, making him wish he were the one doing it. She smiled, extending her hand.

"Hi. I'm Julie Harris."

With all the sincerity he could muster, Murphy's eyes met hers. "I'm honored to meet you, Julie Harris. Frank Murphy, cop and part time jerk. My friends call me Murph. I hope we'll be friends. Maybe if I order another bottle of wine, we can start getting better acquainted."

They remained at their table through most of the expensive wine, listening to the piano player, softly talking and staring into each other's eyes. Preparing to leave, Julie excused herself to the ladies room, while Murphy motioned for the check.

"It's been taken care of, sir," the well-mannered waiter politely informed him. Julie waited for him near the door.

"I don't usually let the girl pay for the meal. It tends to threaten guys my age with a loss of masculinity."

She laughed huskily in the throaty manner he liked so well. "Please don't think of it that way, Frank. My family's been coming here for years. Dad and the owner are good friends, and my family maintains an open account. It's just become a habit for me to eat and leave, and honestly, I didn't even think about it."

"Good. Next time we'll go to my favorite place and I'll feed you ballpark franks," he stated. "One must protect the old family jewels. It's a guy thing, ya understand."

She laughed again and used her automatic remote to unlock the door. Murphy climbed into the passenger side of her Jaguar and settled back into luxurious leather. *I could get used to this.*

Julie drove directly to her place. This time there was no pretense. Neither spoke as she pulled into the reserved underground garage, the door automatically closing behind them. She led him into the garage elevator, pressed a single button, and when the door opened they were viewing her spacious foyer and sunken living room. He was impressed but somehow managed not to let it show. It was an expensive high-rise condo that most folks only see on TV. The living room was approximately the same size of the entire ground level of the house he'd purchased for Elnore. One wall was completely clear, facing an array of city lights.

Julie motioned toward a small but well-stocked bar in one corner of the tastefully decorated, champagne color room. "Pour us a drink, Frank. White wine for me, please. I've got to get out of these tight panty-hose and heels before they kill me."

She hastily moved toward a partially open double door, through which he caught sight of a round king-sized bed covered in quilted blue satin with matching pillows. *The playroom,* he thought, and felt a familiar stirring. *Behave yourself, Sport.*

He took his time pouring the drinks, left her wine glass on the bar and carried his toward the large sky-wall, staring out at the city lights and harbor far below. He could barely hear the muffled city sounds—the hustle and bustle of horns honking, the muted shouts of throngs of passing people. Immersed in the panorama, he didn't hear her as she approached from behind.

"Nice, isn't it? I've lived here more than a year and I never get used to it."

Murphy didn't turn right away, but could feel her heat nearby. He swallowed, weakly attempted to compose himself, then finally just thought to hell with it, and turned. Her hair, no longer pinned back, cascaded in shimmering waves. She'd changed into a white silk robe elegantly clinging, accentuating her soft body curves. It complimented her emerald eyes.

He licked his dry lips and whispered, "Yes, very nice."

Taking the glass from his hand, Julie placed it on a small marble table nearby, her disturbing little smile playing at the corners of her pouty mouth. She moved closer, raising her lips to be kissed. Blood pounded inside his head and heat rushed to his loins as her fiery tongue slipped into his mouth. As if of their own free will, his hands found and cupped her warm firm breasts inside the robe. She frantically tugged at his belt, then the zipper, her soft palms enveloping his hardness. He groaned into her open mouth. Murphy realized they had somehow ended on the plush carpet, pulling at clothing, touching, kissing, and gasping with intensely growing pleasure.

Burying his face in the musky hollow of her neck, the blood roared in his ears as her demanding hands sought to guide him to Paradise. She smelled of jasmine, sunshine — woman. He thrust blindly into her soft warmth. Her wet lips pressed against his ear, her moans growing more intense…she cried out sharply.

"Oh, God." she moaned softly, kissing him back, climbing him. "Oh, *God!*"

Her back arched, she rubbed against his length, savoring his body. As her pleasure peaked overwhelming her, her eyes became glassy as she thrust frantically, grabbing onto his hips to maintain depth. Shuddering and quaking against him, her breath exploded in panting bursts against the side of his neck. Then, he was there, too.

Caught up as if flowing in lava-hot river, he was oblivious to the rest of the world moving far below them. All that mattered was the pounding in his ears, the soft mewing of this beautiful creature beneath him and the awesome heat of her passion. It was a long time before he thought of anything else.

He was the first one at the office the next morning and it felt good for a change. Dumping a half-pot of day-old coffee into the commode, he whistled as he rinsed the pot in the sink and made a fresh batch. Then he washed all the dirty cups he could find on the desks and filing cabinets. He'd already begun to review Tina's file when Drake entered, followed within seconds by Booth, who nodded in their direction then proceeded straight into the men's room.

"You go home at all last night?" Drake chided. "Or did you just sleep here?"

"Berry funny. Berry, berry funny." Murphy didn't even glance up. Instead, he moved to the copier and began feeding in Tina's file, ignoring the horrified expression on his friend's face.

Drake hurried over, nervously glancing around the office. "Are you *crazy*?" he whispered urgently. "You can't copy official files like that! If anyone sees you, you're gonna be history, Murph!"

"Big deal. I figure once Colburn and Yates get their greasy mitts on it, I'll never see it again," he grinned. "Besides, if I do get fired, I'll need something to keep me busy."

"You *are* crazy!" Drake hissed, wide-eyed. "Totally bonkers— certifiably — iron shackles and chains—walk-into-a-white-jacket-that-zips-up-the-back, crazy as hell!" He watched, his mouth gaping as Murphy slipped the warm copies into his Samsonite and locked it.

Chapter 5

Jamie Burgess caught Murphy and Drake whispering over the copier as she slipped off a shimmering silver windbreaker and draped it over the back of her chair. It was made from a new kind of material that always looks wet even when it's dry outside, but this time it *was* wet, her light mocha skin still glistening from an earlier rain shower. Jamie, nicknamed "BJ" for the reverse order in which her name appeared on departmental rosters, was a tall, immensely attractive officer who'd been promoted to detective two years earlier. Murphy and Drake had both worked with her on several cases and found her to be quick-witted, physically fit and totally fearless. They'd quickly formed a three-way friendship built on mutual trust and admiration.

One evening after she and her two friends had consumed too many beers at O'Mally's, she'd confessed she'd studied to be a model and worked at the profession for nearly three years. Murphy could believe it, for she was always stylish and tastefully dressed, clearly fashion magazine material. BJ had given up any ideas of a modeling career twelve years earlier when she learned she was pregnant with her daughter, Amanda. She'd never named the father, and to the amazement of all that knew her, she'd managed to remain single.

Police officers ran in the Burgess family. Her father, with the department for more than two decades, had been killed in the line of duty while chasing a man suspected of robbing the First Interstate Bank. An older brother served as a supervisor with the Bellevue Police Department, but BJ's world was Amanda, and she made no excuses about it, although her job ran a close second.

Jamie knew the other cops in homicide considered her to be a good cop, and she was proud of what she'd achieved.

Bear and Frank had gone out of their way to make her feel at home when she'd first arrived, and she knew they truly liked her. They were always quick to point out her competence to others, but despite her attractiveness, neither had heard of her dating, either within or outside the department. The three of them had formed a closely-knit group, and her only source of socialization seemed to be their weekly pizza and beer sessions at O'Mally's — until a few months ago, when she'd suddenly quit going with them.

There was a reason—an awkward, uncomfortable feeling that would've been too difficult to explain to them. She and Frank Murphy nearly had a *thing.* They'd been attracted to each other from the very start, each trying to simply ignore it. It'd happened one night at O'Mally's when Bear's daughter, Jo Jo, had been ill and Bear needed to go straight home after work, leaving her and Murphy alone at O'Mally's to carry on their Wednesday night tradition.

She'd wanted to dance to a slow jukebox favorite, and after making a couple of crude jokes about two cops dancing together, he'd finally relented. As for BJ, she'd been surprised at the ease and familiarity at which they'd fit together as they glided across the dance floor. During the dance something had happened and when the music ended her feelings for Frank Murphy were changed forevermore. BJ never knew exactly what the *it* had been, but returning to the table, she felt tongue-tied, her heart pounded a mile a minute — and she'd soiled her panties just like some damned adolescent schoolgirl.

She'd noticed that Frank hadn't been totally able to hide the fact that he'd been affected, too. He couldn't have hid it even if he'd tried. She'd *felt* him! Never had she experienced such a yearning, as intense a desire for any man, as she felt for Frank. Suddenly the pizza had tasted like cardboard and the beer had no taste at all. In an embarrassed silence, they'd both searched for something to say. Murphy had tried to avoid eye and knee contact and tried not to stare at her heaving bosom while self-consciously swilling beer. Hating her trembling hands and ragged breathing, BJ had desperately wanted to reach out and touch him. All it would've taken was for one or the other to make a move.

In the end, they'd both valued their friendship more than a quick roll in the hay. Frank had been married, and all he ever talked about was his baby daughter, Tina. BJ couldn't see herself cast in the role of a home breaker. Besides, she was secretly terrified of getting involved with another man. She'd stopped going for pizza and beer with Drake and Murphy shortly thereafter, but whenever Frank passed her in the hallway, or when unavoidable circumstances placed them alone for a few moments, her heart still raced and her pulse quickened at his nearness. Then she'd find herself fighting the urge to flirt, leading him back into her life.

BJ felt Murphy's eyes on her, looked up and gave him a comely smile. He quickly looked away.

God, he looks so good! Stop it you stupid, foolish girl!

Moving closer, she could inhale his spicy male scent, with just a hint of musk. She moved toward the copier to assist him in gathering up the papers that he'd been reproducing, holding them out to him. His fingers lightly brushed against her arm and he jerked away, but not before his fingertips had burned her skin. Like an adrenaline rush, she wanted to brush the wayward lock of dark hair from his forehead — hold him — kiss him. Instead, she pushed all such thoughts from her mind and calmly said, "The Judge called right after you left last night, Frank. He said he wanted to see you *right away*, but you didn't answer when I called."

"Well, yes... um, stayed on my boat last night," he lied, not fully understanding why he didn't want BJ to know about Julie. "I'll leave a cell number if he should call again." His cheeks flushed at the obvious lie.

"He won't. He wanted me to tell you to get over there the minute you came in today. He's probably waiting," she said, grinning openly.

"Oh *shit*." Frank groaned as he grabbed his jacket, sprinting for the door. "Cover for me, will you, Bear?"

"Don't I always?" Drake said warily. "Don't I always?"

Murphy drove his own car to the Judge's house on Mercer Island, an affluent neighborhood on the shores of Lake Washington. The new Interstate-90 floating bridge was a vast improvement over the old one, so he made good time. During the commute he had a chance to reflect upon the Judge and the last time he'd seen him, perhaps six months previously. A sudden pang of guilt ate at him.

Damn, I should've called him on his birthday. Damn!

Judge Thurman Q. Woods had once served on the 9th U.S. Circuit Court of Appeals, then as a Washington State Superior Court Judge. He'd retired almost twenty years previously. At ninety-two, he was still on a first name basis with most state and federal judges, and many senior legislators.

Early in law school he'd discovered he had powerful language skills and his orations were usually eloquent and always effective. He'd authored numerous legal articles on the floundering justice system, deviant social behavior and trends in juvenile delinquency. As the demand for him to speak became so heavy, he found himself turning down many speaking engagements and curtailed his participation in seminars and public forums.

He'd often been invited to serve on political advisory committees by both parties, cutting across all philosophical and political boundaries. News columnists, editorials, and television commentaries often referred to his work and many universities and colleges used his books exclusively. He'd already been a highly successful attorney noted for strong liberal views when asked to serve in the Department of Justice. Later, he'd been appointed to the President's Special Commission on Crime and Violence.

Judge Woods had been an unofficial counsel, mentor, and legal consultant for virtually every judge who'd served on the state or federal Supreme Courts during the past fifty years. Considered by many to be one of the finest legal minds of the century, he was also one of the first black judges in Washington State.

Judge Thurman Q. Woods had been a life-long friend of the Murphy family, especially to Frank's grandfather, *old* Frank L. Murphy. *Young* Frank T. Murphy was named after them both, the 'T' for Thurman. *Frank T.* sped toward the Judge's home, anxious about the reason he'd been summoned. As he zigzagged through neighborhoods of immaculate lawns and stately three story homes, he was once again impressed by the immense wealth consolidated on Lake Washington.

Uh oh, he thought.

The iron ornate gate stood wide-open—a bad omen—since it was nearly always locked to keep obnoxious reporters at a distance. Those hoping to enter usually had to explain who they were and their business to the cool voice in the speaker-box in order to gain entrance to the Judge's estate.

As he drove under the portico on the circular drive, Murphy remembered how gigantic the estate had first seemed when his father brought him here as a child. Now, he realized the estate was smaller than others were, but still very impressive. Coming upon the old mansion, he was engulfed by a sudden and unexplained melancholia. He left the car in the circular drive and approached the doorbell, but before his hand could touch it, a rather pompous, bow-tied gentleman appeared, summoning him curtly.

"Please follow me, sir. The Judge is *waiting.*"

The old residence had been built more than a hundred years earlier, when choice heavy-grained timbers, fine trim and elaborate carvings were affordable. Pompous *Bowtie* led him into the large study overlooking the garden. He remembered it well. As a child, he'd climbed all over the bookshelves and leather furnishings. Filled with nostalgia, he longed for those carefree days.

"Is it as you remember?" The soft, firm voice came from behind him.

He turned to find Judge Woods leaning on a sturdy walking cane, gazing at him. The slight of build, bent individual bore little resemblance to the powerful judiciary Murphy recalled from the old man's glory days on the bench. Not that the Judge had ever been a particularly large man—he'd just seemed larger than life to a much younger Murphy due to his presence and demeanor.

"Yes sir, it is," Murphy answered.

They shook hands briefly and the Judge waved him toward a comfortable leather chair. As Murphy took his seat, Thelma Budd, Judge Wood's housekeeper of thirty years, magically appeared, setting cups in front of them. She poured steaming coffee into his cup first, then tea for the Judge, leaving without a word. Murphy knew Thelma could neither hear nor speak. It'd always been a mystery how she seemed to know within seconds when someone had arrived, and always had fresh drinks ready.

"How's the wife, Frank T?"

Judge Woods had never called Elnore by her name, always, "The wife." At first it'd angered Murphy as insensitive, but gradually he realized it wasn't because he disliked her. It was simply the way he thought of her.

"Um… she's fine Judge. Just fine."

"Uh huh, right," Judge Woods mumbled, waving his hand in the short jerky motions for which he was known. "And the job? How's the job going these days?"

Figuring the Judge was making small talk before getting down to the real reason he'd been summoned, Murphy said, "Great! It's keeping me really busy, Judge. By the way, sorry I didn't call on your birthday. Just too busy at work, you know." *If things get any better*, he thought, sourly, *I don't think I'll be able to fucking stand it!*

The Judge mumbled softly and to Murphy it sounded like '*hoarse words*'. He leaned slightly forward, saying, "Beg your pardon, sir?"

The old man jerked his head, his eyes penetrating as he said with clarity, "*Horse turds!*"

Murphy recoiled, flabbergasted.

"All of it…a bunch of horse turds, Frank T. Your job — Elnore — everything! All, *horse turds!*" He tentatively sipped his steaming tea and set it down. "You want to tell me what's really going on that's all of a sudden got you trying to drink up the state's whisky reserve?"

Murphy stammered, tempted to lie, then breathed deeply and collapsed back into his chair. He'd never lied to the Judge — couldn't in fact.

The Judge struggled to his feet and limped to an expansive wall of bookshelves. "When you were a boy, I used to make you read one of these, every month. I'd some vague notion that you might learn something from them. Guess I was wrong," he said in his usual blunt manner.

Wheeling around quickly for a man his age, he sternly peered at Murphy with the same feared expression he'd shown to a thousand others who'd cowered before him just before his awesome sentences were pronounced. That's how Murphy felt, as if he was about to be sentenced.

"Of all my nephews and nieces, Frank T., you've caused me the most anxiety. I've always told you if you had a problem to come see me. I promised your granddaddy, Frank L., I'd look after you. Now you're going to give me a chance to honor my word to him." The use of middle initials was his way of differentiating between all the *Franks* in the Murphy family.

Judge Woods returned to his desk, eased into the leather chair, and placed his hands together forming a steeple.

"I saw you at Tina's funeral. All pasty and white-faced, you looked as if you'd died, too, Frank T. Well, maybe you did in a way, but *dammit* boy, life goes on, and the living have no choice but to go on, as well. They've *got* to go on. I know. I've been where you are, boy."

"It was Drake, wasn't it, sir? He called you."

"Frank T., *Frank T.* Nothing happens in this town that I don't know about. No, it was *not* Drake, nor for that matter, anyone *else* in the department. But word usually gets around, sooner or later," the Judge answered. "I know all about Elnore, and I know all about Councilman Robert James wanting you off this new case. James is a maggot — a maggot that's about reached the limit that some will put up with. We're keeping a close eye on him, but forget James for the moment. It's you I want to talk about. I figure you want the case because it's very much like Tina's. Probably feeling some terribly misplaced sense of guilt, too. Am I right?"

Murphy nodded mutely.

"Well, do you still want it?" the Judge demanded.

"Yes sir. I still want it," Murphy answered, this time barely whispering. "I want it so bad, I get a pain in my gut every time I think about it. If I can just catch this guy, even if he's not the one who killed Tina, I think it'd help the way I feel. A closure of sorts."

Judge Woods pondered Frank's remarks, resting his elbows on his large oak desk, peering at him through his locked fingers. He nodded, his mind made up.

"All right, Frank T. I'll make a few calls — but there's a price tag. No more hitting the sauce, and start acting like a cop again."

"Anything else?" Frank asked dryly.

"Yes, as a matter of fact, there is," the Judge said. "Do you remember my niece, Lisa Kinard? You may have seen her a few times briefly after you and Elnore married. She was about fourteen at the time. Hilda and I had become very good friends with Lisa's grandparents when we all attended U.W. When their son, Tom, married Nancy, it felt as if someone in our family was getting married. They both also attended U.W. and in the family tradition, Tom became a fine surgeon, and Nancy, a popular and respected clinical psychologist. Both remained very prominent in Seattle's social circle and their tragic deaths attracted a lot of interest, fueled by the press. Lisa was only ten when she lost her parents in a terrible accident, and she took it extremely hard. Her grades plummeted, she had difficulty making friends and disciplinary problems dogged her throughout high school — maybe drugs."

The Judge filled Murphy's coffee cup, then warmed up his own tea, dropping in two sugar cubes while stirring. He sipped appreciatively, nodding, apparently to his liking.

"She bounced from relative to relative. One day Hilda asked if Lisa might stay with us for a while. It seemed like a dandy idea at the time, and it was. When Tom and Nancy were alive, Lisa, and our granddaughter Jennifer were the best of friends. So when my daughter died of cancer, Jennifer came to live with Hilda and me. We loved that child so much. It was like having our baby daughter back. After Lisa came, the two girls became inseparable.

She was with us two wonderful years, right up to Jennifer's tragic death. I guess it was just too much adversity to expect one so young to handle, and I don't suppose Hilda and I were of much help. We had our own difficulties in accepting our granddaughter's death. I think it finally killed my dear wife, bless her soul."

The Judge stared blankly at the far wall, recalling a memory from the past.

"During the last ten years of my Hilda's life, we never spoke of our granddaughter in this house. I watched, dreading the day, as Hilda became progressively frail through those final years. I think, in the end, she just gave up. Anyway, after Jennifer's death, Lisa asked to be sent to school back east. She'd lost so much during her short life."

The Judge moved toward a grouping of photographs on the fireplace mantle, pointing at a grinning, blond teenager and the Judge's deceased granddaughter, both holding tennis rackets.

"That's Lisa and my granddaughter just before her death. Hilda and I always figured the strain might finish Lisa, too, but she's sturdy stock, just like her folks. Lisa has kept in touch, eventually graduating from Rutgers University. Recently, she moved back to Seattle. She was just a baby the last time you saw her, but now she's all grown up — a truly beautiful girl."

Murphy wondered where all this banter was going, but felt so grateful at the judge's decision to help him get what he wanted more than anything else, that he could only listen, despite his growing impatience to return to the office and get started.

"She'd always wanted to be an Olympic gymnast and for years practiced hard. About four years ago during practice, she fell and injured her arm. Oh, it wasn't serious enough to keep her from a normal life, but she'll never go to the Olympics. Just another big disappointment in a long series of them, but she kept bouncing back. Since then, she's expressed a desire to become a policewoman, a cop... don't ask me why. She first landed a job as a probation officer with the Department of Corrections, and then as a presentence officer. Lisa finally got her chance last year when she graduated from the Police Academy — at the top of her class."

The judge gazed thoughtfully at the girls' photo for a moment longer, then said, "Of all the kids I've helped through the years, I suppose I'm the most proud of Lisa and what she's accomplished, despite all her pain and loss."

He paused until his words had soaked in.

"She's part of my price tag in helping get your case back. Lisa's always been ambitious with a great desire to succeed. She says she expects to become Seattle's Chief of Police some day. Don't laugh, she'll probably do it!"

Judge Woods returned to his original seat and carefully lowered himself, relying heavily on his sturdy cane.

"Anyway, I want you to place her on the task force. If you catch this guy, it could give her the break she needs to make detective."

"Does she have any experience? Other than writing traffic tickets, I mean?" Murphy said with a straight face.

"She's worked two stints, each several months in the Sex Crimes Unit. My feedback is that she did a good job. What do you say? Do we have a deal?"

"If you get me on that task force, Judge, you can have anything you want," he stated. "If you wanted, I'd hire Thelma Budd."

An hour later he left, walking on air.

Chapter 6

Back at the station, Murphy found things in an uproar.

"*Murph*!" Drake screamed as he entered, "Where the hell have you been? We've been calling your cell phone for the past hour."

"I had it turned off," Murphy admitted sheepishly. "What gives?"

Drake tossed him a vest. "We got the *Shotgun* gang in a house on Capital Hill. Booth talked to the landlord and he confirmed who lives there. Said the Olds with the primer painted fender is in the garage. We've *got* the assholes, Frank! We were just waiting for you to get back so we could make our run." Drake grinned, ready to bust. "I'll brief you on the plan as we ride. If you don't like it, we can change it before we move in."

Murphy knew the area well. When he and Drake were in uniforms, they'd worked the neighborhood for three long years. It was in one the roughest housing complexes in the city, and more than one police officer had been shot at while there answering calls.

Ten years ago, only three blocks from the address they were headed, a drunken husband had shot Sergeant Joe Banis to death after they'd responded to a routine domestic disturbance. The man had immediately dropped his shotgun and placed his hands on top of his head. Murphy could still remember how desperately he'd wanted to kill the bastard anyway. As friends of the deceased, he and Drake had been given the task of reporting the old sergeant's death to his wife and ailing son. It left a bad taste in his mouth, even after all these years. The killer was released after serving less than two years in Shelton.

The SWAT team waited impatiently, and it was apparent they'd been in place for some time. Lou Bateman, the team leader, chewed relentlessly on a cigar butt, pacing back and forth in the falling mist.

"Well shit, fellows, it's really decent of you to show up. I hope we're not taking you away from anything *really* important?"

Lou, who'd been the driving force behind the SWAT team's inception in Seattle, was widely known as a national expert in special operations. He didn't pull any punches when he had something to say. The fact that he was within a few months of retirement didn't make him any easier to get along with.

"*Yeah, yeah, yeah,*" Drake said. "Some people got *real* responsibilities, you know. They can't just up and walk out every time the phone rings. Charley Booth brief you on the situation, Lou?"

"We know *our* jobs. Just be sure you got the paperwork straight and the right house this time. Nothing stirs up the newspapers and good citizens like a SWAT Team wiping out an innocent family." Bateman turned and walked away, gnawing on his unlit cigar.

"Pleasant sort." Murphy said, watching his back disappear around the SWAT van.

"A real sweetheart," Drake agreed.

"You know, I really hate working with these elite units. They always act like they've got a cob up their ass— they think they're the Marines or something. Next time, maybe we'll just do it alone."

"Yeah, but they sure got some neat toys," Drake said, as he climbed back into the car. Bateman gave him the high sign and sped forward toward the targeted house. Even though they'd been following directly behind the SWAT van, the team was already entering the house by the time Drake pulled up in front.

"How do them guys do that?" he grumbled, as he heaved his bulk out of the car and lumbered toward the front door.

Murphy passed him halfway up the walk and cautiously peered through the open doorway. The SWAT team already had three individuals sprawled on the floor, their hands cuffed behind their backs. Another lay spread-eagled on a bedroom floor in the rear of the house. None matched the description of Kisop Shinn, the owner of the damaged Olds.

"Car in the garage?" Drake asked Bateman, who nodded and continued his search of the cuffed man's pockets. Nearby on a chair laid a wallet, switchblade knife, and an automatic 9mm handgun with several loaded magazines. One of the SWAT team members scurried past carrying three twelve-gauge shot guns and a GLOC automatic. A search of the house and garage revealed several more handguns, ammunition, another shotgun with a pistol grip and six thousand dollars in small bills.

Murphy left Booth behind to tidy things up at the arrest site, and he and Drake returned to the task force office. Several newspaper reporters were already waiting on the front steps when they arrived

"How do those parasites find out everything so fast?"

"Sergeant Murphy! Frank Murphy! Can I ask you a few questions?" It was Molly the *Barracuda*.

Murphy didn't look up as he hurried up the steps. "Don't have time. Got to write my report."

Drake paused long enough to hurl a suggestion at the reporters. "See Captain Brooks. He'll be glad to make a statement." He grinned at Frank as they squeezed through the entrance together. Inside they opted for the stairs and found an excited group waiting in the office. Exchanging gleeful high-fives with Jamie Burgess and Fletcher, Murphy noticed Colburn and Yates looking on with very dour expressions.

"Way to go, fellows!" B.J. told them with obvious sincerity, laughing happily. "How do you do it, Frank? Every case you touch turns to gold. What's this, your lucky number seven this year?"

Murphy's face flushed. He was unaccountably pleased to receive her compliment. Yates whispered something to Colburn, who smirked and softly snickered. Frank favored the two with an overly warm smile, lingering just a moment longer than he had to on the small bluish mark on Colburn's jaw. He fought to control his steady expression and silently prayed for the Judge's successful intervention on his behalf.

He and Drake spent nearly two hours putting together their report, while Murphy, in a hushed tone, described the details of his meeting with Judge Woods. Drake grinned brightly and leaned forward so only Murphy could hear his comment. "I'd give my left nut to be a fly on the wall and see Colburn's face when Brooks tells him he's out on his ass. Better yet, when he finds out *you're* the one that'll replace him."

"Well, don't count your chickens yet, Bear," he replied. "I've got a lot of faith in the Judge, but I think I'll hold off celebrating until Brooks personally tells me it's a done deal."

Scarcely thirty minutes had passed when Brooks stuck his head out of his office door and shouted, "Murphy! Drake! Get in here. *Now!*"

Colburn and Yates snickered loudly from the corner without looking up.

This time, it was apparent Brooks wasn't going to invite them to sit before he started in on them. Drake and Murphy remained standing, smiling innocently, waiting for their boss to gain his composure long enough to begin. "You two ass-holes are going to be the ruin of me yet," he started off, sounding exasperated and totally defeated. "I got a measly fourteen lousy months until retirement and it seems you two have made it your personal goal to see my bleeding ulcers turn into stomach cancer — if I don't get fired and lose my pension before then. I don't know how you did it, Murphy, and I don't want to know, but you'll end up getting your ass in a crack before it's over," Brooks said dejectedly.

"Shit Captain, we thought you'd be pleased we nailed that Shotgun Gang," he replied innocently.

Brooks slammed his hand explosively on the desktop. It sounded like a rifle shot. "*God dammit*, Murphy! That's not what I'm talking about and you *know* it!"

As usual, the outer office buzz abruptly ceased. Brooks swallowed twice, deeply inhaled repeatedly, reached for his roll of antacids and popped two into his mouth. Trying hard to collect himself, Captain Brooks said calmly, "Sit down."

Both men instantly plopped into chairs, smart enough not to say anything.

"All right… I don't know how you got the Chief to change his mind, nor do I want to know," Brooks said again. "He called me about thirty minutes ago and told me you and Drake were back on the serial killer case." He stared directly at Murphy. "I told the others to get all their belongings out of that small storage room next to the underground parking area. You'll be using it as your task force headquarters."

"Nice view."

Everyone knew there wasn't a window in the place. Irritated, Brooks glared at him. "I didn't choose it because of its aesthetics, Murphy. I chose it because it has its own entrance, enough phone lines, a toilet and is of sufficient size. It can also be easily secured.

And that's the name of the game until you catch this guy. *Security.* Nothing gets leaked to the press unless I personally okay it. No grandstanding or hot-dogging. It's going to be a *team* effort if I have to publicly flog everybody in the frigging department twice a day!"

He continued his direct stare at Murphy as he said this. It irritated Murphy that his own partner was also watching him so pointedly, and there was no mistaking the fact that Drake personally agreed with this part of Brook's speech.

The Captain spoke again.

"…select your team by close of business today. Two caveats, Frank. One, the task force reports directly to Lieutenant Borden, and two, Yates stays on the task force. Both directives come straight from Chief Williams."

Murphy was stunned! Color shot to his face and his jaws clamped. He jerked toward Drake and saw by his partner's incredulous expression that he'd received the news with the same reaction. "Butthead" Borden, as he was known among the staff, was Chief William's personal spy.

Dirty little ass-kissing stooge, Murphy thought, feeling his blood pressure begin to pound in his head. Chief Williams took every opportunity to shove Borden into the spotlight, grooming his little snitch to be his eventual replacement.

"Chief, Borden's got his nose so far up the chief's ass that if Williams turned a corner too fast, he'd probably break the little fucker's nose!" Murphy felt very close to saying something else extremely stupid but valiantly fought the impulse.

Everyone in the department was well aware Chief Williams was Borden's "*daddy.*" He went out of his way to ensure Borden's superiors perceived him as tough, but reasonable; decisive, yet conservative; ambitious but not a cutthroat. Unwittingly, Borden continually sabotaged his chief's efforts by writing idiotic memos and voluminous garbage e-mail, outlining incredibly stupid proposals on everything from departmental reorganizations to new sports uniform designs. His idea for the sweatshirt with a pig wearing a cop's hat had brought the house down.

Borden hadn't pulled a single day of field duty since his graduation — without distinction — from the police academy. An anal-retentive paper-pusher, he insisted every "i" be dotted and every "t" crossed. The few times he ever left his office was when there might be media coverage, and he never missed a photo opportunity or a chance to get his name into the newspapers.

Old, everything by the book, Butthead, Murphy thought. *Jesus, sometimes life can be so cruel.*

Drake noted his partner's crimson face, his white-knuckled hands gripping the chair arms and quickly intervened before Murphy could explode. "Why not you, Tom? You're our superior."

Brooks's top lip curled distastefully. "Because Robert James has expressed a particular interest in this case, and Chief Williams wants to impress upon the future mayor of Seattle just how responsive the department is. James was livid that you'd been brought back at all, Frank, but someone with real horsepower scared the shit out of Williams. He's adamant now about your staying with it, despite James bitching. In any event, James gave up on his demands that you be replaced, but you could tell he wasn't a happy camper." Brooks suddenly stood and vacantly stared through the window, facing away from them.

"Plus, there's likely to be more than the usual amount of media coverage. These cases have a way of peaking the interest of those who wouldn't normally touch it with a ten-foot pole."

Murphy and Drake exchanged puzzled looks. This was the first time in all the years they'd worked for Captain Brooks that he'd remotely criticized his superiors. Drake silently whistled and rolled his eyes. His expression reminded Murphy of a black comic in some of the old time movies he'd seen as a kid. The only line he could remember was, "Feets, don't let me down."

Brooks turned to face them. "You can bet your ass none of them will hesitate to hang either of you out to dry at the first sign of trouble. You'll have no friends on this one, Murph. Road blocks and outright interference wouldn't surprise me." He sighed deeply. "I'll help all I can, but be forewarned." Tired, he returned to his chair, dismissing both with a wave of his hand.

As they started for the door, Brooks glanced up. "Oh, by the way, you guys did a hell of a job getting that shotgun gang. Great work, just like some of your earlier cases, Frank. On your way out, tell Colburn to come in." By the time they exited, he was emerged in the stack of papers on his desk.

Murphy sauntered past Colburn's desk, paused, put on his best pained expression and said politely, "Captain Brooks asked me to send you right in, Phil. Guess he wants to discuss your new assignment."

Colburn's chest puffed up as he smirked. Murphy struggled to keep a straight face and avoid laughing outright. Barely maintaining his doleful expression, he slowly made his way back toward the work area he and Drake shared. From the corner of his eye he caught the motion of his big partner's shoulders, shaking so hard his desk rattled as he silently fought for control. Within five minutes, Colburn stormed from Brooks' office, pausing only long enough to fire off a scorching look in Murphy's direction then slammed the door so hard the windows chattered. Murphy favored Yates with a friendly smile across the room and arched an eyebrow in his direction.

"Must've had something to do with his new assignment,"

Murphy immediately selected BJ and Charley Booth for the task force. Detectives Lee and Fletcher both volunteered and Murphy promised to use them anytime the situation allowed.

Stripping to tee shirts, the taskforce members began the process of transforming the old basement storage room into an acceptable work area. Charley, with an innate ability to scrounge, quickly traded the salvage reject desks and beat-up file cabinets for a few reasonably functional pieces of furniture. Within no time, he'd located desk lamps, city, county and state maps, chalkboards and other items they'd need to organize their operation. BJ set about getting the phones operational and hooked up, and managed to get a computer terminal installed, too.

Late in the day, Anita Garza, one of the department's newest administrative assistants appeared, stating she would be available for taskforce supply and admin support. That evening, Murphy and Drake remained long after the others departed and discussed strategy for getting the operation off the ground.

As Drake finally prepared to leave, he said, "Don't stay and work all night, Murph. You won't do us any good if you conk-out from exhaustion the first week."

"I'll be right behind you, Bear," Murphy assured him. "Give Mable and the rest of the family a big kiss from me."

Despite his promise, it was well after midnight when he finally left, but he believed he had a solid plan to submit to the rest of the team the following morning. It felt good to be doing something constructive once more.

The dark slender man slumped in the front seat of the dirty white van, watching as the flashing legs of young schoolgirls passed on the sidewalk just outside his window. *Oh yes, that one*, he thought, his pulse quickening. *The little blond one with the bouncy ponytail.* His eyes darted hungrily to yet another, the blonde's olive-skinned companion. *Better yet, the exotic black cunt in that short skirt and ankle bracelet. Oh, she's just right!* He felt himself stiffen beneath his clothing and his imagination soared. Leaning his head against the headrest, he closed his eyes and imagined having the two girls in the back of his cluttered van.

His cycle was coming much faster now. That's what his counselor had called it—his *cycle*. Until now, it'd only reached this intensity about once a month. This time however, it'd been only three days since he'd last fed it, and already the hunger was nearly overpowering. He knew from prior experience that it'd soon be unmanageable. But he couldn't act now. *Not yet!* He needed to wait for the voice to tell him what to do.

The *voice*, that's how he thought of the mysterious messages he received. The mysterious all-knowing *voice* would tell him when it was the right time to act. The voice had always seemed to know just how long he could hold out, but would it know if his cycle had sped up? Unconsciously, he began stroking himself through his clothing. Breathing rapidly, he groaned softly, a seeping wetness saturating his pants. His eyes closed, he remained still for a long time, leaning against the headrest, breathing deeply as he regained his composure. Wearily, he forced his trembling hands to shift the van into gear and pulled into the rush hour traffic, his mind still on the little black girl. He hoped the *voice* would hurry. The hunger had abated for the moment, but knew he would start feeling it again before the night was through. The porn magazines and videos he kept in his room in case of emergency could only do so much to slow the insidious thoughts eating at his mind when his cycle hit.

As Amanda Burgess passed by the parked van, she thought she detected some movement behind the black-tinted windows. *I hate those windows*, she thought, shivering uncontrollably. *They remind me of those sci-fi movies...* ooooh, *hungry monsters stare at two girls from behind, ready to pounce. I wonder if there's a monster in there?* She shivered again. Briefly, she remembered something about a law being passed against the windows. She'd ask her mother. She was a cop. She'd know.

Her friend Kathy swished her blond ponytail impatiently as she waited for Amanda to respond to her question. "*...Amanda!* Did you hear *anything* I just said?"

Amanda turned her attention back to her friend, and immediately forgot about the dirty white van.

Chapter 7

Elnore lay beside the snoring man and wondered if she should get up and make the drive back to her house in Everett. It was already nearly midnight, but by the time she got home and into bed, it'd be at least 1:00 a.m. and besides, she hated to go back to that big dark house alone. It wasn't that she was particularly frightened, it was just that... well, it was so damned empty.

It hadn't always been that way. Not when Tina was alive... and Frank was still there. Elnore felt the tears suddenly burn her eyes. *Shit. Guess I've really messed things up royally this time. But I've made my bed and I guess I'll just have to sleep in it now,* she thought, snickering in disgust at the trite saying.

Maybe if she'd tried a little harder, things would be different. She could see how Frank suffered over Tina's death and knew how close the two of them had been. *Dammit, how could he be so selfish about it all?* She'd suffered too and she'd done her suffering alone without the comfort of her husband. That is, until Robert James had shown up.

She'd been at an all time low when she met him during the Annual Law and Order meeting with the City Council. He was smooth, good-looking and confident, all the qualities in a man that appealed to Elnore. Still, she'd always felt he'd sensed how vulnerable she was and secretively resented the way he'd taken advantage of that vulnerability.

She quickly learned Robert was a tireless, inventive lover, and once hooked, she had to have more. With Robert, she'd done things she never would have dreamed of. The longer she was with him, the less inhibitions she felt— and the more he demanded. She remembered the day he'd insisted she perform oral sex on him as they traveled up Interstate 5 crowded with holiday travelers. She'd eventually complied and was confused to discover how much the act had excited her. Another time in Victoria, he'd approached her from behind as she stood on the small balcony of the old inn where they'd stayed for three days. In broad daylight, he'd clandestinely lifted her skirt and entered her, as unwary strollers passed just below. She'd been aroused to an unbelievable level.

After that, he knew he had a hold on her and became even more daring and uninhibited with his suggestions. No, suggestion wasn't the right word. Demands. She willingly acquiesced to his dominant demands. Growing ever bolder, last night he'd suggested a ménage trois, actually bringing another person into their lovemaking sessions. Frightened by unwelcome feelings, she'd nervously asked if he meant a man, or another female. She reflected back on his raised eyebrow and cold smile as he replied, "Whichever you prefer, my dear."

Satiated and exhausted, the mere thought of what they had done repulsed her, even though a shiver of anticipation shot through her as twisted images from the previous evening flashed across her tired mind.

At first, it'd been deliciously evil to slip away with Robert twice a week for afternoon sex, especially since she'd known about the animosity between her husband and him. She'd heard Frank rant about Robert James, what a "back-stabbing *prick*" he was. Once she'd met the suave attorney though, she'd instantly found him alluring. She supposed the taboo made it seem even more daring, and just knowing the way Frank felt about him somehow made their liaisons all the more dangerous — and *exciting*.

As time passed, they'd become more bold and brazen as opportunities frequently presented themselves. That's why — she recalled bitterly — they'd been at her house fucking their eyes out the night Frank returned home early from New York. Maybe if they'd been more careful...better yet, if she'd never started sleeping with Robert James, she and Frank might've worked things out. Tears stung her eyes as she thought about Frank again. She ached inside from missing him. These days when Robert made love to her, she'd pretend she was in her own bed, and she was with

Frank—thrusting and groaning above her. Nothing inventive, nothing unexpected, just a welcome familiarity.

She'd tried unsuccessfully to talk to him numerous times, but he never returned even one of her phone calls. On the two occasions she'd inadvertently run into him in the courthouse, he'd stared right through her, completely ignoring her.

Shit, Elnore thought miserably, as tears burned her eyes again.

Robert James snored loudly on the pillow beside her, then exhaled deeply and evenly.

Even if Frank was willing to take her back, Elnore knew all James had to do was to call and suggest some sick session and she'd drop everything. Oh, maybe not right away, but eventually she'd go. Eventually, she'd have to. She wouldn't be able to help herself. Whatever Robert had, she desperately needed. She was hooked!

Elnore slid off her side of the king-sized bed and reached for her panties lying in a crumpled heap beside the bed.

Everyone but Anita Garza had arrived early, excited about being assigned to a special task force that was to investigate the recent murders of two young girls. Murphy had arrived first and already had coffee going when the others walked in. Jamie Burgess and Drake arrived together, and Charley Booth came in just moments later.

"Now, that's more like it! Dedication, devotion to duty, ambition..." Drake started in when he saw Murphy already there.

"Give it a break!" Murphy groaned pitifully.

BJ and Drake gave him a big *Brooklyn cheer* by squeezing their lips together with thumb and forefinger, then blowing the air out harshly through closed lips. Charley, who'd entered a little behind them and had no idea what was happening in the encounter, nonetheless joined in on the crude gesture.

"Fuck you all, very much. I want to remind you that I *am* in charge around here, and as your superior I will require a little more respect from now on."

That drew another Brooklyn cheer from the group.

"Now, if you're finished with your insults and sophomoric

humor, grab a cup of mud and have a seat," Murphy chided. "We have work to do. I worked up a plan last night before I left to use as a starting point."

As he outlined his previous night's work, the door opened quietly and Joe Yates sheepishly stuck his head in. Everyone's head turned toward the newcomer until he awkwardly began shifting his feet.

"Come in and take a seat, Joe," Murphy said softly. "We're just getting started."

Yates settled on a chair at the far side of the room, noticeably as far as he could get from the others. He seemed terribly ill at ease, and more than a little bit embarrassed.

"First off, the door between us and the stairs leading to the rest of the building will remain locked at all times. We will use only the entrance you entered this morning. Furthermore, everything about this case is confidential and *will not* be repeated outside this room. I mean to *anybody*! If Captain Brooks or anyone else needs to be briefed, I'll do it. That goes double for the media. That's the one hard and fast rule that I insist upon. Break it, whoever you are, and you're out. Period. Any questions about that before we get started?"

There were none, and after pausing, he went on.

"Okay. BJ, when Anita reports in, have her get into the database for a profile of every case in the U.S. within the past two years that is similar to these latest killings. Anything with decapitated young girls... sexually assaulted... all the rest. Joe, you and Charley, start talking to hookers working the Pioneer Square area. See if you can get an I.D. on the girl who was found in the alley, and anything else you can find out."

He thought for a minute. "Bear is my second in command. Anything he tells you, just consider it as coming from me. He and I will go over to the Medical Examiner's office and see how Sally is coming along with the autopsy. BJ, take a run out to the condo complex in Magnolia Bluffs where they found the second body. Interview everyone who works in or around the building, neighbors too. See who owns the condo where the body was discovered, who found it — all the usual stuff. See Jim Keith. He was handling the initial investigation.

Everyone keeps copious notes. We'll meet here every morning

at 0800 from now on to compare notes and war game our daily strategy. I'll be around most evenings too, in case you've got something on your mind. Think out of the box on this thing. Nothing is too far out."

He looked around the room, meeting each person's eyes.

"Some within the Department are already referring to this killer as the *Headhunter*. I don't want to see that name show up in the press, okay?"

As the meeting broke up, everyone left, except for Drake. "What do you think?" he said.

Sensing he was asking about Yates, Murphy frowned. "We'll give him a chance. If he runs to his *Daddy* with anything, we'll change the locks on the door and forget to give him a key."

———————

Murphy and Drake arrived at the Medical Examiner's office thirty minutes after it was scheduled to open and encountered Shelly Durham, Sal's assistant, coming from the autopsy room.

"The ME's in there, Frank." She smiled sweetly for his benefit. "I think he's working on *your property* now. Go on in, if you can stand it." She winked conspiratorially, swaying her firm buttocks under the sheer white uniform as she hurried briskly up the hallway and around the corner. Drake stared after her, loudly smacking his broad lips.

"Oh, grow up, Bear," Murphy responded. "I've already told you, I don't have anything going with her. It's all in your mind."

"Just the same, she makes my dick hard."

"I would've bet you were going to say something like that."

"A *boner*-a-fied fact. Harder than Chinese arithmetic."

Murphy didn't bother to answer his partner, hoping he'd drop the subject. He knew Drake was just trying to keep things light, because what awaited them behind the swinging double doors leading into the lab would be gruesome. At the door to the autopsy room he hesitated, breathed deeply and grimaced, his face dour.

"Of all the things I like about my job, this is not one of them." He headed toward the double doors behind which their *property* awaited.

"I know what you mean, partner. I know what you mean,"

Drake said, reluctantly following him inside.

Antonio "Sally" Salvatore was just beginning to work on one of the murdered girls as they entered—the unidentified hooker. Pretending not to see them, he adjusted the microphone attached to the front of his green surgical gown, pulled on a pair of rubber latex gloves, pushed his acrylic visor down then picked up a clipboard and began to dictate.

"This is Case Number 95-32-3750, unidentified, Jane Doe. The body is that of a well-developed, under-nourished, approximately sixteen-year-old white female with blond hair and blue eyes. The body is 62 inches long and weighs 105 pounds."

He laid the clipboard aside and stood beside the body, briefly scanning the x-rays, photographs and general data obtained earlier. Completing his brief external examination of the body, he adjusted the bright overhead light to his best advantage.

"Rigor mortis is present in the extremities, but showing signs of dissipating," the ME continued. "Skin is of normal texture; there is a single seven centimeter scar on the lower center abdomen from unknown causes, a colored butterfly tattoo inside of the right thigh, and a one centimeter mole on the upper right buttock."

He picked up a plastic ruler, holding it against the stub that was once a slender white throat. "A jagged rip, or tear, starts just under the right jaw bone and extends to the left ear — made by an extremely sharp instrument — most likely a serrated knife. The same type instrument severed the spine. Reference photo and note, 1-A for follow-up information. The wound appears to have been the cause of death due to trauma and blood loss.

There is a two-centimeter ulceration consistent with anthropophagi over the right breast nipple, and what appears to be other bite marks and bruises on the mammary gland itself. Photographs, exact measurements, and teeth mark casts are found at reference 1-B."

Murphy sensed Drake shifting about behind him, and knew he was growing restless.

"Vaginal, anal and throat swabs taken and deposited at reference 2-B for further study. Due to substantial bruising and tissue damage, it's the Medical Examiner's opinion that the victim was sexually penetrated in each of these areas. A white substance, appearing to be semen, was collected and captured on the swabs.

81

Ligature bruises were found on both wrists and both ankles, indicating Jane Doe had been securely bound. There are no defensive wounds on either hands or arms. Nail scrapings taken from each finger and toe are contained at reference 2-C."

Sally picked up a sharp instrument, grinning to himself, and although he had yet to acknowledge their presence, Murphy was sure it was only for their benefit—an attempt to convince them he'd reached the part of the procedure he enjoyed most. Having been through all this before with the baby-faced ME, both detectives knew he did it just to shock observers and to relieve the boredom and stress associated with his job. Still, it had the desired affect.

Murphy forced himself to watch as the ME made a standard thoracic-abdomen "Y" incision, first across the chest, slicing through the skin above the girl's small breasts; then continuing from the lower tip of the sternum down the length of the abdomen to the pubis. He looked away momentarily as Salvatore sawed through the rib cage and cartilage with a crunchy sound, exposing the heart and lungs. Frank struggled to remain expressionless, but his stomach churned and he swallowed hard several times.

He forced his attention back to the operation just as the pericardial sac was opened and a blood sample taken to determine the victim's type. He looked away again as the heart, lungs, and other organs were removed. He knew they would be preserved for later examination. The insufferable Sally suddenly spoke to the two officers, pretending he'd noticed them for the first time.

"Frank... Bear, good to see you guys," he said pleasantly. "There's some coffee and donuts in that box by the phone. The jelly rolls are particularly fresh this morning." He arched his eyebrows twice in a bad Groucho Marx imitation.

Murphy glanced at Drake, his black face washed-out and strained. He felt just as rotten, but was determined not to let Salvatore get his goat. He pretended to stick his finger down his throat and feigned a gag, as if to acknowledge this was Sally's sick way of yanking their chain when they came in to watch him work. Drake swallowed painfully and looked at the ceiling.

"Gentlemen, this young lady is the Pioneer Square hooker. I did the senator's daughter earlier." He didn't look up from his task, grimacing as he poked around inside the cadaver. "Looks like she had a hamburger a few hours before she was killed. With onions."

He wrinkled his nose. "I hate onions!"

From the corner of his eye, Murphy saw that Drake had become even paler, almost green, and he was swallowing much harder as he studied the ceiling moldings.

"Hemphill agrees she wasn't murdered where she was found. She died yesterday afternoon, someplace else. The body was first molded into the position the killer wanted her to be in when found, then rigor mortis set in and she was simply placed in the alley where she was discovered."

Sally paused and looked intently into the bloody cavity. "Fries, too," he said. "That stuff can really ruin a person's colon." He glanced at Drake, apparently disappointed the big man wasn't already heaving onto the septic tile floor. He went on. "Might be able to get some teeth marks from the breast bite and match them up when you get a suspect. I made casts. I'll have DNA run on the semen, too. Just in case."

Murphy's mouth felt full of cotton, but he managed a little saliva and wet his lips. Just to have something else to think about, he said, "What killed her, Sally?"

When he answered, Sal's tone was soft, more kindly.

"She was alive when he started to cut off her head, Frank. Marks from around the back of the neck and small cotton particles found in the mouth indicate she was gagged so she couldn't make any noise. In her struggles, she broke off two teeth at the gum-line as the sick bastard slowly sawed off her head."

Drake suddenly had enough, covering his mouth and hurrying from the room. Murphy stared sympathetically after his buddy.

"I found the same thing on the Holcomb girl. Both bodies almost identical, Frank, but unlike the hooker, there was no semen present in the Holcomb girl. I'll send over copies of my autopsy reports later this afternoon."

"You saying the Holcomb girl wasn't raped?"

"No, she was raped all right. Sodomized too," Sal responded, his eyes still glued to his task. "Only... there was no semen. Maybe he used a condom... didn't complete to ejaculation... or used some foreign object like a dildo... hell, I don't know. She was pretty torn up internally." Sal finally looked up from his work, staring at Murphy for a moment. "Except for the absence of semen in the other case, I'd say they were both done by the same person."

Sal continued in a low monotone voice. "The Holcomb girl died around midnight. 'Jane Doe' was killed the previous day. Probably kept someplace cool, perhaps in a locker... a basement... something like that... until she was placed in the alley in Pioneer Square."

He watched the procedures until Salvatore picked up the small circular saw and approached the girl's skull, appearing just a bit too gleeful from Murphy's standpoint. Imagination overcoming him at last, sour gorge rushed into his throat. Spinning on his heel, he gave up and sprinted for the door, trying to keep from tossing his cookies. He tried to ignore the buzzing behind him. Drake was already seated on the steps outside and he saw his ashen face as he hurried down the brightly-lighted hallway toward him.

"Sally's as sick as the bastard who killed those girls," Drake said with rancor as they left the building.

"It's just his way of getting his rocks off," Murphy replied dryly, still shaken at what he'd observed. "I guess if I had to cut up people all day as a living, I'd look for an escape, too.

Chapter 8

Lisa Kinard was *excited*! Smiling, she hurried through the underground staff parking lot toward the task force headquarters. She'd chosen her best-fitting uniform, shined her brass and primped before the mirror for an hour, making sure she looked just right for today's meeting with Sergeant Frank Murphy. After all her hard work, she was finally being given a chance at the kind of case she'd always dreamed about.

So what if the position hadn't been awarded as recognition for her abilities? If she'd waited she might never have been given an assignment like this. Sometimes opportunities just knocked once and you had to be ready! The Judge had offered it, and she'd accepted. That was that! It was now up to her to show everyone his trust hadn't been misplaced. She knew she could pull it off.

At a very early age Lisa Kinard had discovered a smile and a pretty face could get you a long way in life. But that wasn't her style. She wanted to get to the top, but she preferred doing it the old-fashioned way, hard work and *smarts*. School had always been easy for Lisa; straight A's throughout high school and college, an honor student, the Dean's List — always at the top of her class. She knew she was smarter and more qualified than most of the men she met, but her youth and attractiveness had been an encumbrance rather than an asset.

Lisa brushed away a minor irritating thought. *Always some jerk trying to get into my pants.* But now she had her chance, she'd show them what she could do. *Lisa baby, you're on your way!*

It was almost noon when Murphy and Drake returned to the task force office in the basement of the Public Safety Building. An attractive blond female officer in her mid-twenties was seated on a bench outside the door. Murphy immediately recognized her as the Judge's "niece." Through the years, he'd never known anyone who thought it strange that Judge Woods would refer to all the young people he'd helped, regardless of race, as his "nieces and nephews."

"Sergeant Murphy?" she said standing, formally extending her hand. "I'm Lisa Kinard. I've been assigned to work on your task force. That is, if you approve, sir."

Despite earlier reservations, the girl's infectious grin warmed his heart. He returned her smile as he shook her hand, then unlocked the door and held it open. "Let's make a deal. I'll just be Frank and you can either be 'Lisa, or Officer Kinard.'"

The grin grew broader. "Lisa, then."

"Okay, come on in. The Judge said you'd be around to see me. You'll be sharing that desk in the corner with Detective Jamie Burgess — known as BJ around here — and Joe Yates. We have a scheduled briefing every morning at 0800 until we get too busy to have one, and I hope that'll be soon."

Murphy tossed a package of cigarettes onto one of the two remaining desks and took a chair behind it. "You have any previous experience in homicide investigations?"

"No sir," Lisa replied honestly. "I did a few months with the sex crimes unit though." When Murphy didn't answer right away, she blurted, "I'm a quick study and I *want* to learn."

He suddenly recalled the Judge's story about this girl's tragic life and searched her face for any hint of it. His only impression was she was very intelligent and overly enthusiastic. He remembered he'd felt the same way once, but lost it somewhere along the way. Instantly, he warmed toward her.

"Uh huh. Well, just stay close to Joe Yates, Bear or BJ for a while and you'll be into it before you know it." He pushed a folder toward her. "The locations of where the bodies were found, along with the names of the two victims we know about are in this folder. Get some colored pins and string from Anita. I want to see the exact location, name and a picture of each of them on the large wall map behind you. After you're finished, give Sally — he's the ME — a call at the morgue about every two hours to see if his reports are ready. Keep calling, no matter how pissed he gets, until he tells you to come over and pick them up. Do the same with Hemphill in Forensics."

He watched with satisfaction as Lisa scribbled notes in a small black book, which then disappeared into her back pocket.

"I'll have more instructions for you in the morning after our meeting," he stated as he walked to the door. Drake waited outside in the parking area, fumbling through a thin folder. He looked up as Murphy approached.

"This is Anita's research on the VICAP and HITS systems, Murph. We're also running the DNA sample through the Washington State Patrol Lab. If we don't get a hit there, we'll try the national database. If our guy has a previous felony, we may be able to wrap this up before the news media turns it into a complete circus. There've been four other girls murdered during the past three years who match at least part of our guy's M.O."

The Violent Crime Apprehension Program (VICAP) had been set up during the Green River Killer investigation as a nation-wide method for tracking serial murders. The Behavioral Sciences Unit of the FBI Academy was housed at Quantico, Virginia. Murphy knew it would give his task force instant access to a nationwide centralized information and analysis system that collected, sorted, and compared all aspects of a current investigation with similar multiple murder patterns, regardless of the number of police agencies involved.

While Murphy was glad to have these resources available for the task force's use, he remained apprehensive about using them because of the FBI's propensity to jump in and take over at the slightest pretense. He looked over his partner's wide shoulder, as Drake continued.

"Not all of them were in Seattle — scattered mostly around the Puget Sound area. There's one that looks promising. It happened in Portland a while back. Anita is working on a national scan now. She said she'd work as late as needed to finish it. Hemphill is trying to lift potential prints from one of the victims, but the rain probably made that impossible. I spoke with Brooks and he authorized overtime for everyone."

"See if you can round up the investigative reports on those potential cases and give them to Lisa to post, okay?" Murphy said.

"Have her mark them appropriately so no one confuses them with the two new ones. I've got to see Brooks again about getting rid of Yates. I don't trust him not to be a stooge. The last thing I need right now is a spy in our camp." He walked off toward the basement elevator, grumbling to himself.

"Now remember, just remain *cool*, Murph," Drake yelled after him anxiously, worried his partner's short fuse would land him into hot water again. "You want me to go with you?" He continued to stare at Murphy's retreating figure until it rounded the corner and disappeared inside.

Murphy returned fifteen minutes later, silent and glum. Apparently, his meeting with Brooks hadn't gone well. Moping into the office, he strode directly to the coffeepot and poured some of the thick concoction into his stained cup. Observing his cloudy mood with mild apprehension, neither Drake nor Lisa dared ask how his meeting went. They decided to just let him brood in solitude for a while.

Murphy took a sip and grimaced, staring into his cup like he'd discovered something unpleasant in the bottom. "Leave out those new folders. I want to go through them before I leave tonight."

Laughter interrupted them as Charley Booth and Joe Yates chose that particular moment to enter. Booth hustled to the coffeepot, picked it up and studied the less than a cup of liquid remaining in the blackened bottom. Purposefully disregarding the hand-made sign taped nearby on the wall — IF YOU TAKE THE LAST OF THE COFFEE MAKE A NEW POT — he poured exactly two-thirds of the raunchy stuff into a dirty cup and returned the pot to the burner. Yates disgustedly eyed what was left, decided against it and returned to his desk.

"Find out anything?" Murphy wanted to know.

"Yes, and no," Charley said, smacking his lips over his coffee as he gazed smugly at Yates. "Most of the ladies working the Square didn't want to be seen talking to us. A few offered us some free poon or a blow-job—which we turned down, of course— but most were scared shitless, worried they might be next."

He took another sip of the vile stuff before he continued. "All together, we talked to about twenty hookers. That may be only about half of the ones who work that area, but as I said, this thing has them spooked."

Booth retrieved a battered black book from his jacket pocket and flipped it open. A rubber band marked a page.

"Two of the regulars, 'Salina,' and another one named..." Booth paused, searching for the name, then continued, "...*Brown Sugar*, both said they had seen a white van in the alley where the body was found. That's it. No license plate number, nothing about the make, model, etc. Salina did say it was a big one, like a Ford Econoline. You know, one of those V8, American-made gas-guzzlers... late eighties, maybe early nineties. She claimed it almost ran over her as she was heading home. The time frame sounds about right, too. Both girls have been working the Square for about two years. They said if the dead girl had worked there, they'd have known her." He finished then flipped his notebook closed and waited.

Murphy thought for a moment. "Anyone say anything about seeing a white van around the Magnolia Bluffs crime scene?" He caught the blank looks around the room and sighed. "Well it's a shot in the dark. Charley, you and Joe go to the Bluffs tomorrow and ask around. Maybe if you mention a white van it will jog someone's memory."

The group spent the next thirty minutes planning their next day's activities, then departed. Murphy settled down alone with the new files Drake had brought in.

After about an hour of heavy reading, his mind wandered and he suddenly thought about the woman he'd met in O'Mally's two nights earlier. Julie — red hair, green eyes, long tanned legs. *Long, long legs.* Remembering the events of that night, he found himself suddenly responding and felt a growing tightness. He shifted uncomfortably in his chair to ease his discomfort, trying to concentrate on the paper in front of him. It did little good. They'd made love three times before he'd departed at 8:00 a.m. It was by no means a record for him, but the intensity of their couplings had stunned him.

Another thing that had amazed him was how easy it'd been to talk to her. He'd easily disclosed to her the details about his break-up with Elnore, Tina's death, the nightmares and how his heavy drinking had nearly led to his being fired. With some pride, he'd related his recent appointment to head-up the new task force, glad to finally share it with someone who seemed to care. As the pent-up emotions spilled out, he'd gained insight and feelings he'd been totally unaware of. Afterward, he'd felt completely free, unburdened of excess baggage that'd been weighing on him the past six months.

What had astonished him most about his situation was that he usually didn't trust most women enough to confide in them. The few times he had, he'd been burned badly — Molly Atwood and Elnore, stinging examples. Julie just seemed different than all the other women he'd met—elegance, style or beauty; he couldn't quite put his finger on it.

It'd been nearly three a.m. when they'd finally drifted off to sleep, her face nestled against his shoulder. He'd been awakened by soft kisses on his eyelids and mouth at six, followed by more lovemaking, this time gentler, slower. Then, he'd hurriedly showered, snatching a quick kiss at the door with promises to call later. That'd been two nights before, and he still hadn't called.

As if it had a mind of its own, his hand slowly snaked toward the phone. Pausing, his hand resting on it, he felt undecided about whether to make the call or not. He readily admitted he was more than just a bit scared, too. *Why not, Sport? It's just a roll in the hay. It don't mean nothing. After all, there she is... obviously a lady with money, upper crust, and here you are...yeah...here you are. Well, let's not get into that.*

Too many words could easily describe his predicament these days — an under-paid drunk, strung-out living on the edge, psycho-cop cock-hound. There were probably others better left unmentioned, he admitted guiltily. He felt his face flame, suddenly ashamed by the self-flagellation and his sudden unexplained propensity to wallow in self-pity.

Okay, okay! Shape up, dammit! So take whatever she has to offer, for as long as she offers it, then tip your hat and say, adios, ciao, sayonara... and hit the bricks. Not-a-problem,Sport.

That'd suit him just fine. One thing he didn't need right now was more complications in his life. Especially *women* complications. Hell, maybe she just wanted a little fun out of life, too. He could handle that. Yeah, he could handle it just fine.

The problem was he was beginning to feel as though he couldn't handle it. He'd struggled every conscious moment to keep her memory from invading his thoughts. *Shit, I don't need this right now...and I sure as hell don't have to call*, he thought, as his alien hand picked up the phone, dialing Julie's number. Okay, he'd just let it ring a couple of times, then hang up if she answered. Her answering service would probably be on anyway, and he wasn't about to talk into one of those damned things.

"Hello."

It came after the first ring. Murphy sat stunned, unnerved.

"Frank?"

"Yeah. It's me...how you doing?"

She paused, breathing into the phone. "I was afraid you wouldn't call."

Murphy felt a surge below his belt and took a deep, steadying breath. "You busy?"

"No! You want to come over?" she said hastily.

God did he *ever*! If she told him not to, he'd probably get arrested for kicking down her door and ravaging her on the living room floor. "I don't know if I have time tonight," he answered. "I'm kind of tied up right now. Maybe we can get together later in the week."

"Oh." She sounded disappointed.

Shit. This wasn't going the way he wanted at all. Frank breathed deeply. All he had to do was say he'd be right over. *Easy as pie*!

"I'll give you a call," he said instead, and hung up.

He picked up a file and threw it savagely across the room. *Way to go, Sport*! *God dammit*! He needed a drink. That would perk him up. *No.* He knew what he needed. Picking up the phone, he dialed again and Julie's husky voice answered on the other end.

Murphy spoke into the mouthpiece. "I'll be there in fifteen minutes."

"Yes," she whispered.

―――――――

Robert James reclined in the tufted leather chair behind his large mahogany executive desk, gazing through the wall-sized window at the boat activity in the harbor. Reluctantly, he forced his attention back to his day-planner and reminders of an ambitious agenda; an early meeting with his campaign chairman — lunch with Councilman Haines—a ground breaking dedication at two—

Phantom of the Opera and dinner with the Mayor at seven. Not *too* bad. It'd be even more hectic after he won the election.

A soft knock forced him to look up as the short wide frame of Betty Higgs entered, carrying a stack of papers. Although she had a pretty enough face, he'd purposely hired Betty for her secretarial skills rather than any physical attributes. Adapt at reading the weaknesses of others, he knew his own weaknesses as well, and thought it best not to tempt himself around the office. Besides, there were always plenty of other women who shared his unique tastes.

An intelligent man, he'd often analyzed his motives as they related to women, determining that he wasn't a sex addict, although it'd always played an important role in any of his relationships with the opposite sex. The fact was, he loved the domination aspects of his sexual *involvements*. In fact, being in total control was *essential* to his enjoyment. It'd always amazed him how certain beautiful women would willingly subject themselves to degradation and humiliation for their own sexual fulfillment. They actually seemed to thrive on his style of controlled pain letting.

James watched Betty's plump butt slip through the door, as it softly closed behind her. She wasn't much to look at, but the thought had crossed his mind that he could have her squirming too, if he really wanted to. Elnore flashed into his consciousness.

He'd sensed Elnore leave his bed the previous night, and smiled as he recalled her meekness as she'd sneaked about the dark bedroom gathering her scattered clothing, trying not to disturb him. She'd developed more quickly than *any* of the others. Elnore had thirsted for his every demand, like a duck takes to water, as if she actually *needed* his humiliation. It'd been easy for him to spot her vulnerability, intuitively see the guilt she carried the first time he'd met her at the DA's office. He'd known just which buttons to push right from the beginning, and she'd quickly accepted some of his most deviant ideas. At this point, all he had to do was to suggest something and she would start to tremble in fear, and anticipation. Yes, he liked to dominate. That's what it was all about!

Robert James liked being in control. He understood *power;* the illusive sensual qualities of domination that he relished. A career in politics had been a natural evolution for a man of his tastes. It'd certainly hadn't been the money that'd drawn him to this particular vocation, although money had been an intricate part of his power, too. It'd been his lustful appetites that'd gotten him into trouble once before, but he knew the pit-falls and had become much smarter. Since arriving in Seattle he'd been very careful, not wanting to slip up like he had back east while still in college. He could think of only one local incident where he could be remotely embarrassed, but he intended to rectify that soon.

Frank Murphy! Goddamn you to Hell!

He'd scarcely been able to contain his rage when Williams informed him Murphy was back on the new serial killer case. No one had to tell him this was going to be high profile, and he sure as hell wasn't going to share it with the likes of Frank Murphy. It was that Nigger judge again. James was certain Judge Woods had been somehow involved, because Woods had interfered once before with his attempts to discredit Murphy. Well he'd bide his time. The old fool was still too powerful to buck overtly, but he was…what? Ninety-three? He couldn't live forever.

Remembering the day Murphy *interrogated* him like a common criminal made Robert James's heart race. *What gives some nobody like Murphy the right to interrogate me?* He'd offered the detective a peace offering, a hint of future rewards when he became Mayor. Murphy had just sneered at him and thrown it back into his face. No one did that to Robert James and got away with it! That's how these things started. First, a small affront, if left unanswered, could grow into something like that embarrassing episode he'd had in college. No, he'd nip it in the bud this time. Frank Murphy was history.

The phone purred softly and he lifted the receiver.

He listened to the familiar voice on the other end. Then he spoke. "No, not tonight. I have other plans. What did you find out?"

Again, he listened intently.

"Good. Keep it up and maybe I'll reward you…I *said* not tonight! Remember your place!" He smiled thinly as he replaced the phone in its cradle. Yes, they *were* easy to find.

The others had arrived by the time Frank came to the office the next morning. He removed his portable shaver from a drawer and began to work on the worst of his growth. "Okay, who's first?" he said as he ran the dull blades over his stubble.

Drake spoke up first. "You see the Daily Report this morning, Murph? Our little friend, the Barracuda, has been at it again." He held up the front page. The headlines screamed:

HEADHUNTER STRIKES TWICE!
Serial Killer Rapes and Mutilates Two Seattle Girls!

There was a lot more, but Murphy had a pretty good idea about the rest of the story.

"She even mentioned your name, Murph," Drake pointed out helpfully. He seemed to be enjoying Murphy's discomfort.

"I'll bet." Murphy growled, as though glad to get this part of the meeting behind him.

BJ, aware of his previous fling with the reporter, and mildly amused by his predicament, cleared her throat politely. "I canvassed door-to-door through the entire neighborhood. Two men stated they'd seen a stranger several times preceding the murder. White male, stocky build, stringy dark hair, olive skin — rough dress; old fatigue jacket and dirty jeans — a person who'd stand out in a neighborhood like Magnolia Bluffs. Both descriptions could've been written by the same person."

As she spoke, BJ removed a small stack of papers from her briefcase. "I took Jan Parker by late yesterday. That's why I missed the meeting last night. Jan drew two composites based on the descriptions. Both are almost identical."

BJ smiled, obviously pleased. "If you don't have any objections, I'd like to return and show it around the neighborhood today." She handed out copies to the others.

"Good job, BJ", Frank praised her efforts while the others loudly applauded.

BJ curtsied politely. Anyone else and the motion might have seemed contrived, but with BJ it was just cute. Her effort was wasted on Frank, however, for he hadn't even glanced up.

Instead he said, "Joe, you and Charley go with her. It's the strongest lead we have right now, so let's push on it hard and see what develops."

Murphy addressed the newest member of their team. "Lisa, you mentioned you've worked the sex crimes scene a couple of times.

"Yes sir," she answered. "I'm attending evening psychology classes at U.W. with one of the guys who works in Vice."

"Either 'Frank' or just plain 'Murphy' will do fine, Lisa. There are no sirs around here."

"Yes... Frank. What do you want me to do?" She smiled sweetly.

"Take one of the composites, just on the chance he's one of theirs. Also give them a copy of Hemphill's profile. You never know when you'll accidentally hit pay dirt. Remember, criminal investigation is forty percent technique and sixty percent luck."

Murphy turned his attention to Drake. "Bear, the Captain stopped me on my way in this morning. We may have a lead on the last member of that Asian shotgun gang — that Kisop, guy. Brooks has someone doing the legwork for us. You want to finish that job if we get a chance?"

"Damned right!" Drake answered promptly. "That trash needs to be taken off the streets." Once immersed in a case, Drake never liked to give up on it.

"Okay, hang loose and we'll see what develops." Murphy said, distastefully eyeing a growing stack of computer printouts strewn across a table in the far corner. "That's our manifest of lists. There's more than four thousand released mental patients, fifty thousand domestic-built white van owners, two hundred who admit to knowing one of the two victims, nine hundred van owner names of those who live in the immediate area where the two bodies were found, and zero suspects."

Drake, who hated paperwork even more than his partner, rolled his large eyes and remained silent.

"By this time next month, we'll probably have 300,000 more names to add," Murphy continued. "So, if you folks don't want to spend the rest of your lives pouring through that stack as it grows each day, I'd suggest you hit the bricks and come up with some leads!" He watched as all their eyes got bigger, then smiled politely. "Any questions?"

There were none.

———

Murphy and Drake broke for lunch at McDonalds. Drake, hungrily eyeing Murphy's juicy Big Mac and fries, finally ordered a salad and diet Coke. They slid into a corner booth where they could quietly talk.

Drake paused, frowning at his salad while Frank zealously tore into his dripping burger.

"Does that have cheese on it?"

His mouth full, Murphy simply nodded as he continued to chew.

Drake sniffed twice. "God, that smells *great!* I *love* the burgers with all the cheese and stuff—the fries, too." He still hadn't touched his food. He sniffed loudly again, enraptured.

Murphy gently laid his burger back on his plate, clearly annoyed. "You are not getting any of my food, Bear! You do this every time Mable puts you on one of her diets. You insist on ordering that *rabbit food,* and then annoy the hell out of me while I eat mine, hoping I suppose, that I'll share it with you. Well, it's *not* going to happen this time. If you want a burger, go order one. If you want two, order two. Hell, I don't care if you order a dozen of them, but this one's mine. *Mine!*"

Ignoring Drake's envious eyes, he deliberately bit into the oozing bun and closed his eyes as he chewed, savoring it.

"I can't do that. I promised Mable." Drake sounded pitiful.

"What's the big deal, whether you order one or simply eat mine?"

Drake squirmed and poked at his salad. "Mable always asks me what I *'ordered'* for lunch. Not what I *'ate'* for lunch. What I *ordered.*" The big man's eyes lowered.

"Why you dishonest *asshole!* That's just a technicality and you *know* it, Bear! If I were her I'd make you take a polygraph every night."

"Don't give her any ideas," Drake said sullenly.

He poked a fork of the green stuff into his wide mouth, grimacing as he chewed, and pouted. At last, Frank snorted in disgust and shoved the fries in his direction. Bear grinned broadly and reached in.

———

Returning after lunch, BJ, Lisa, Yates and Booth all awaited in the squad room, grinning as if they'd swallowed the collective canary.

"Okay, I give up. What's the big secret?" Murphy said impatiently.

"Got 'em," BJ said exuberantly. "We ID'd the man in the composite."

Shocked it'd come so quickly, but very pleased, Murphy and Drake took their seats.

"Faster than a speeding bullet, more powerful than a locomotive, able to leap tall buildings in a..." Drake started. BJ gave him the finger and he shut up.

"Who is he?" Murphy said after he'd restored order.

BJ pulled out her always-present notebook and flipped it open. "Albert Burbakowski, a twenty-six-year-old lawn maintenance worker employed by Green Acres Lawn Service. Lives on Queen Anne Hill, on Stover Street. I drove by on my way in. It's just a ratty little apartment complex that ought to be razed. Your typical neighborhood drug den."

Murphy nodded for her to continue.

"He's been working in that part of the city for about a month. A check with his company shows he had three jobs lined up within the Magnolia Bluffs area the day the Holcomb girl was murdered. Should we pick him up?"

Frank remained pensive, then said, "In good time. But first, run a criminal history check with WASIC and the FBI. I want to know everything there is to know about this guy. Where he goes at night, where he eats, *what* he eats, everything. Lisa, start the paperwork for a search warrant, DNA tests, and a mouth plaster. I want to be ready to roll as soon as we pick him up."

He paused and stared intently at the group, first one, then another. "I shouldn't have to say this, but I'm going to anyway. This information does *not* leave this room. Not even to Brooks... until I give the okay."

"Charley, you and Joe stake out his residence. Call in when you spot him. Be careful that he doesn't *make* you. If he is the killer, he's no dummy—and we already know he's dangerous. We'll shoot for a meeting back here at 1800. If anyone can't make it, call in."

The door burst open unexpectedly, filling the room with the strong odor of cheap cigar smoke. Behind the smoke came Lt. *Butthead* Borden, followed by the Barracuda and reporters from two other Seattle newspapers.

"This is the *Headhunter* Task Force I immediately set up after the first murder." Borden strutted, waving his hand in a circular motion. "I believe most of you know Detective Sergeant Frank Murphy. I've appointed him officer-in-charge, and these are other task force members." Borden paused in his prancing long enough to start to remove the drape hiding the large operational wallboard.

Murphy was aware that each of Borden's three sentences had begun with 'I'." Infuriated, he lunged, grasped a corner of the cover and held on tightly. "That information is only available on a need to know basis, *sirrr*. If you'd like a briefing on it after our media friends depart, I'll be happy to do so, *sirrr*..." His slurring of the term *sir* conveyed subtleties of disrespect, completely lost on Borden.

Assuming an air of importance, Borden sucked an exaggerated draw on his cigar and plopped his butt on top of a vacant desk. "How about *you* telling us all about it then, Frank?" he smiled widely.

Murphy paused, raised one eyebrow and prompted, "All about...?"

There was another pregnant silence as the others began to stir uncomfortably.

"Uh... you know... this *Headhunter* thing," Borden stammered, uncertain now.

Another long pause.

"I'm sorry Lieutenant, but I'm afraid I'm not familiar with that term. Is that a new case?" Murphy said innocently.

Borden was becoming noticeably agitated, his thin neck pulsing, his long pointy nose flaring a deep red. "This goddamn headhunter serial killer thing, Murphy! What's going on with it?"

"*Sirrr*...," drawn out again. "I feel incredibly stupid, but I'm afraid I haven't heard any of our cases officially referred to by that term. Do you happen to have the victims' names?"

BJ sniggered softly behind them.

Borden had trouble swallowing. "The Holcomb case, Murphy," he hissed between his teeth. "The goddamn Holcomb case," he finally choked out in a harsh whisper.

"Oh… yes sir. We're looking into that one. Yep, we're looking into that one for sure." He nodded his head earnestly, eager to cooperate. "We may even have a lead." Looking at the newspaper personnel gathered, he said in a conniving tone, "You can print that."

It was evident that Murphy didn't intend to go any further, and Borden's red face indicated he wasn't going to force the issue. But, sensing Frank wasn't overtly bucking him, and growing increasingly unsure of himself by the minute, Borden quickly jumped to his feet, turning to address the reporters.

"Well, we just got the task force set up and there's not much to report right now anyway. Let's go back to my office and I'll bring you all up to date on some other things that are happening."

He shot Murphy a furious glare as he led the entourage out the door. Molly Atwood tried to catch his eye as she was ushered out, but Murphy ignored her.

When they were beyond earshot, he exploded. "*God dammit*! I want that door locked all the *goddamned* time! *All* the time! Who the hell was the dip-shit that came in last?"

Searching the subdued faces around the room, he paused as Drake grinned widely, raising his big right index finger, pointing directly back at him. Murphy's ears burned crimson and he dropped his eyes, blankly staring unseeingly at a file folder on his desk.

"Okay." Murphy grinned sheepishly and mumbled, "We won't make a big thing about it this time. Just be conscious of it from now on." He heaved out of his chair and began to pace. "But you see why you can't tell that asshole Borden anything about the operation, don't you? Okay, we've wasted enough time on this. Let's get it done, folks."

———————

Drake invited Murphy over for dinner after work and he'd readily accepted. Julie would be visiting some friends in Portland for two days so it was just as well. Murphy needed his rest anyway after last night. He'd been surprised how comfortable he felt with her after such a short time. She was drop-dead gorgeous, they enjoyed the same things, and she was a good listener. Having someone to confide in had been great therapy for him. Often, after making love, they'd just lie awake, talking for hours. Murphy smiled. Yeah, he was getting used to having Julie around.

Mable Drake met them both at the door and planted a big wet kiss on Bear's mouth. Murphy got an identical one.

"Frankie! Frankie!" she shouted. "It's been months since you dropped by."

It'd only been two weeks, but he maintained a respectful silence. Jo Jo, at sixteen, the Drake's youngest daughter, swooped down the stairway and wrapped her arms around him.

"Jo Jo, if you aren't the prettiest thing I've ever seen!" He watched intently as Jo Jo signed with her hands. He looked at Mable, questioningly.

"Same old subject she always brings up, Frankie. She just asked if you'd wait for her until she's finished with high school, then you two can run off and get married," Mable laughed loudly. Jo Jo had been mute since birth.

Walking arm-in-arm toward their comfortable living room bursting with family photos, Mable admonished, "John Henry, will you get Frankie a beer 'fore your friend dies of thirst!"

"Yeah, John Henry. Your friend is thirsty," Murphy said, smirking.

Drake lumbered down the hall, returning moments later with a couple of frosty mugs and two cold beers. Frank sank into the middle of an incredibly soft sofa, while Jo Jo plopped down beside him, worshipfully engaging him with her large brown eyes. He poured his own beer, basking in their warm friendship, happy to be with them. Since his parent's death over ten years earlier, they were the closest things to a family that he had.

Murphy didn't linger after dinner as he normally would've done, nor did he consume most of Drake's beer supply either, as he usually did — a fact not lost on Mable. After receiving hugs all around, he hastily said his goodbyes and headed toward the marina, anxious to finish a small sanding project he'd begun earlier in the week.

From the dock ramp, he saw Mama and Olaf working on Mama's old sailboat, and knew his good intentions were thwarted when Mama Elsa spied him, waving frantically for him to join them. The *Passion* was a dilapidated forty-five foot schooner, owned by Mama's late husband, Jorge. Originally christened *North Star* almost a hundred years earlier, Jorge had renamed it *Elsa's Passion*, but after his death, Mama had ordered Olaf to shorten it to just *Passion*.

"I don't vant someteen vat ugly vit my name on it!" she'd proclaimed adamantly.

Frank and Olaf had made it their personal project to refurbish the proud old vessel to its former glory.

Murphy stepped carefully around a square black hulk in the middle of the pier, Olaf's fat bulldog, *Ape Shit*. Stripping to his waist, he hung his shirt and jacket on a nearby post. Working on any boat quickly became contagious for Frank. Once started, it was hard for him to stop until the task was finished. He and the big handyman worked steadily with little talk as the hours flew by, Mama supplying a continuous flow of cold beer and snacks.

Unnoticed, the sun dipped below the horizon and the light sensor halogen lamps began illuminating the marina. Olaf stretched as he began to put away his tools and lowered himself onto a dock box near Murphy.

"Someday, I want to sail around the world in one of these," he said solemnly, catching Murphy by surprise. Given Olaf's propensity toward hard work, he'd never have suspected the big man had such aspirations. Olaf appeared a little embarrassed at his admission.

"Maybe you'd like to come with me, Frank. I've been saving my money, and Mama would let this old tub go for a song. She knows how I feel about the *Passion*. Anyway, think about it, Frank. We could have us a time."

Mama hadn't rejoined them, so they remained for another hour, talking about boats, the sea and far away places. At last, Frank rose and strode toward his own boat.

Sail the world. What a grand idea!

———

Amanda and her best friend, Kathy, were just two blocks from home when BJ pulled along side of them. The dark sky appeared about to open up at any minute and soak the area again.

"Hi kidos! Want to ride before you drown?"

"Thanks for the offer, Miss Burgess, but I only live in the next block. It'll be out of your way," Kathy declined.

BJ watched Amanda slip out of her treasured blue London Fog raincoat and hand off the matching umbrella to her best friend.

"Here, Kathy, take these so you don't get drenched. We'll get them later."

Giving her friend a quick hug, Amanda climbed into the passenger seat beside her mother, basking in the heater's warmth.

"Thanks, Mom! See ya tomorrow, Kathy! Call me later!" she shouted as her mother pulled away from the curb.

A dirty white van with its smoked-glass windows rolled forward in the block behind them, slowly keeping pace.

Chapter 9

Warden Cummings strode through a final security gate before entering the Intensive Management Unit (IMU), housing Walla Walla's most dangerous prisoners. Forsaking the open van that usually carried personnel across the courtyard, he walked slowly and deliberately. He wasn't in any hurry to see the inmate who'd sent him the message he carried in his coat pocket. In fact, Cummings dreaded it immensely each time he was forced to meet with *John Lee West* — the evil man with a pleasant name.

The warden, in the correctional system for twenty-two years, was keenly aware of the prison hierarchy and of the contempt inmate populations held for sex offenders and those serving time for crimes against women or children. Nowhere was this more apparent than at Walla Walla State Prison.

At the top of the dung heap were the respected macho crimes of robbery, assault and murder. Then came those who had committed lesser crimes, forgery, embezzlement and dealing illegal drugs. The most despised inmates were the child molesters, rapists and wife beaters. West fell into this last group. His notoriety and the length of his spree made him a prime candidate for strict seclusion.

Cummings had segregated John Lee West soon after the infamous prisoner arrived, for his own protection from the other inmates. He wouldn't have lasted a week among the prison population before someone sunk a shank between his shoulders. Probably after they'd made him "pull the train," a term that meant providing sexual gratification for the entire cellblock.

The heavy outer door crashed open and he stepped inside. Recognized immediately by the supervisor of the Watch, he was waved through by uniformed personnel sitting inside the two protected booths within a round room reception area.

Cummings followed a towering black officer toward one of the eight pods within the IMU. In the pod marked *D*, each cell door was constructed with a small upper panel enclosed in heavy unbreakable Plexiglas and a lower panel, a "wicket." A latched metal cover, locked from the outside, secured each wicket. Anytime a prisoner was removed from his cell, he'd back to the wicket, place his hands through it, and be cuffed from behind. Once handcuffed, leg shackles were applied before he was allowed to leave the cell.

As the warden peered inside, West was busy at a small computer, furnished at the insistence of an influential civil liberties organization after his initial isolation placement. When he could no longer visit the computers in the library, he'd complained he'd been deprived of his civil right to seek legal information for the filing of writs and appeals. Although Cummings had protested vigorously, his famous prisoner had finally won out. The warden had been ordered to provide a small television, writing desk, and any authorized reading material West requested, including current newspapers.

Salvaging a small victory, he'd ordered the usual security measures on these items, the same as those provided to the general prison population; anti-tamper seals to prevent entry inside the equipment, and restricted access and uses. He'd argued, unsuccessfully, that previous inmates, none nearly as brilliant as John Lee West, had been able to construct weapons and bombs, and just from the electronic parts.

Cummings noted an early edition of the Seattle Post laying on West's small writing desk bolted to the far wall. *All the comforts of home,* the warden thought bitterly.

Cummings knew West was keenly aware of his presence, although he gave no indication of this, as the prisoner continued pecking at his keyboard. Attempting to hide his irritation, the warden spoke through the small holes in the glass.

"All right, I'm here, West. What do you want?"

John Lee West glanced up from his computer monitor as if surprised, although Cummings knew he must've heard them coming. West's boyish, pleasant face lit up with an infectious grin as he pushed aside a wayward lock of hair from his eyes.

"Why, Warden Cummings! This is certainly an honor, sir. It's nice of you to entertain my message... so soon."

"Cut the crap, West. Tell me what's on your mind so I can get out of here."

"Certainly, Warden. I know you're a busy man and I don't want to hold you up any longer than I have to."

Cummings observed West as he spoke and for the hundredth time, found himself wanting to doubt the awful stories about this wholesome looking young man. Inwardly, he scolded himself and concentrated on the business at hand.

"Captain Thompson said you had something to give me?" the Warden said.

John Lee West immediately retrieved an envelope from his desk. "Lately I've had trouble getting my mail through the institution's post office, sir. Don't know what the problem could be—do you?" He grinned engagingly. "This is terribly important to me, so I wanted to give it to you personally. That way, I know for sure it'll get to the person intended."

"That's all?" Cummings was eager to be gone.

John Lee grinned. "That's it, sir."

Moving forward, West placed the envelope on the small ledge below the wicket and immediately backed up five steps. The large officer standing nearby opened the metal flap, removed the envelope and handed it to Warden Cummings.

"Have a pleasant day, Warden," West said, as he returned to his computer.

Cummings walked away without answering. Outside, for the first time, he glanced at the name on the envelope,

Detective Frank Murphy
Seattle Police Department

What the hell does Johnnie Lee West want with Frank Murphy? Cummings felt an ominous foreboding.

As she guided her Honda Civic into the last vacant parking space, Lisa spotted Officer Tim White waiting outside the classroom door. She was aware he was sexually attracted to her, but didn't particularly find it mutual. She had to admit, however, that he was a good source of information and she had several questions she wanted to ask tonight about one of his clients from the new Sex Crimes Unit.

Lisa smiled warmly, waved at him, and sprinted across the street just as the rain began to sprinkle.

Later, her two-hour class concluded, she felt good about her studies, but turned down White's offer for a nightcap. If she were lucky she'd be in bed by ten. She was very pleased by all the useful information she'd acquired from her admirer, Tim White.

It was well past midnight and Corky had been catatonically staring vacantly at the ceiling for hours. Visions and words filtered through as they had every evening since that memorable day by the river. They'd both been fifteen; it'd been the *first* time — and *first* love.

Jennifer. Sweet Jenny.

Corky had loved Jennifer even in grade school and upon reaching puberty often dreamed about how she'd look, completely naked, her legs spread wide, smiling invitingly. But of course that would've never happened with Jennifer, Miss-Goody-Two-Shoes, cheerleader and valedictorian, little Miss-Rich-Bitch.

You're my best life-long friend in the whole world, Corky remembered her saying as she reclined on the lush grass, her eyes closed.

She'd looked so sexy that day — maybe too sexy. That'd been the only reason it'd happened, anyway. Why did she have to look *so damned* sexy? Half asleep, Corky could almost smell the river air dampness and the cool prickly grass as the details of that day returned for the hundredth time.

The others had been far across the park, near the picnic area — so far away they couldn't be heard playing volleyball. It'd been so quiet and peaceful by the pond. Corky hadn't meant for anything to happen. It had… just happened.

Abruptly Corky's hand had slid up the girl's slender bare leg. Jenny's eyes snapped open wildly as she'd gasped, her mouth ready to register alarm. But Corky didn't let her. With superior strength, Corky had held her down, placed a hand over her mouth to muffle her protests and quickly slipped a finger beneath her pure white panties.

Reliving it, Corky's heart hammered wildly, the breaths quickening, becoming shallow, hands flashing faster and faster as the welcome explosion neared. Through the years the daydream had been the source of many exciting masturbation sessions.

Years before, when it was actually happening, it'd seemed as if Corky had been only a bystander to the event, watching it unfold from nearby. The handle of Jenny's hairbrush had replaced a rough, probing finger as the helpless girl whimpered and struggled, her eyes pleading with her attacker.

Corky had violently climaxed. Afterward Jenny had just layed on the grass, sobbing as if her heart had been broken.

Ah, sweet Jenny. Sweet, sexy Jenny. Well, I couldn't have let you live after that! You would've only run right back and told everyone. Besides, we could've never been friends as before and you would've never let me come near you again, anyway.

It'd been easy, actually, almost too easy. Corky had dragged her into the water and sat on her chest until she'd drowned, then pushed her body out into the swift current. Corky had nearly climaxed again at feeling Jenny's tiny hands feebly beating, trying to push the heavy weight off her chest. The event had been over way too soon, and then Jenny was gone forever.

It'd also been quite easy convincing the others that despite all efforts to save her, the water had just been too swift to save Jenny — that it'd nearly drowned them both. Corky, in fact, had become somewhat of a hero over the episode.

Corky, Corky, Corky! What a corker you are!

Chapter 10

Robert James drove toward the large gray stone and stucco house he'd purchased soon after coming to Seattle. As usual, he drove slowly, appreciating the neighborhood ambiance; high-bank view homes overlooking Lake Washington, affluent carefully maintained homes with their owners BMW's, Mercedes sedans, and sporty foreign coupes in the driveways. He'd come a long way in the few short years since arriving in the Northwest, and he'd planned to go a lot further, too. If the polls didn't lie, it was almost a certainty he'd win the mayoral election in four months.

After that, who knows? Maybe the governor's mansion in Olympia— or perhaps becoming the new Washington State senator. They both had a nice ring.

Elnore's face flashed across his mind again—as it had been doing all day. Instantly, he felt the familiar uncomfortable stiffening in his crotch. He knew keeping her around was dangerous—but essential.

She was the key to how he'd eventually take care of Frank Murphy. But he'd have to be careful with her. Passionate beyond belief, she was also unpredictable and extremely headstrong.

Now he had her where he could get her to do *anything* he wanted, but he still needed to maintain secrecy. He didn't want another episode like the one that had disgraced him in college. It'd been a good thing his parents had still been alive and were able to hush it up with money and influence.

Could've put a real cramp in my lofty political ambitions. He smiled.

Robert James had two smiles. His *political* smile was reserved for constituents and old ladies from whom he hoped to wring a few more critical votes. It was warm, charming, beguiling. The smile that fewer people got to see was much different. It curved slightly at the corners of his thin lips, cruel and malevolent; the one used when demanding Elnore or the others to perform an obscene, degrading act, pushing the limits of their tolerance — and watching them struggle with their self-respect, before meekly complying.

It was the unguarded, honest smile that burst forth whenever he thought about ambition — power. It was the one he used now.

Yeah, Elnore would be fine as long as he remained in total control. He was convinced that a little innovative sex play was all right. He'd just have to keep it under wraps. As he thought about Elnore again, the familiar tightening caused him to shift his weight once more. He had a plan for her tomorrow night, but first, some unfinished business to take care of.

It was pitch-black, and Kathy didn't know where she was. She finally became conscious enough to comprehend she wasn't home in her own bed. *Can't see — or move — talk. Help!* The last thing she'd remembered was waving goodbye to her best friend, Amanda. There'd been a dirty delivery van, and the strong smell of medicine.

What's in my mouth?

Panic stricken, she tried to scream and swallow at the same time, only to find the attempts gagged her severely. Forcing herself to remain calm, she attempted to figure out why she couldn't see or move.

As some sensations gradually returned to her limbs, Kathy realized she'd been lashed to a hard, rough, wooden surface. *That's why I can't move! Okay, I'm not paralyzed! Cold, so cold!*

Although the room was dark, she barely detected some small patches of light through cracks in the window covering.

An old blanket? Where am I? Who brought me here? Mother will be worried sick!

She suddenly froze! Scratchy noises, like tiny running feet, seemed to be coming from the floor beneath her. *Rats! Oh, please God, don't let it be rats!*

Of all things she feared most, it was *rats* — even more than spiders. Much much more than spiders. She squeezed her eyes tightly and prayed harder than she had ever before. An hour dragged by before she heard footsteps overhead, seemingly approaching. Kathy opened her eyes, just as a blinding light caused her to wince, then quickly closed them again.

"So, my sweet. You're awake now." The voice was soft, not unpleasant. Almost... *friendly.*

She cracked her eyes a little more, turning her head toward the voice, and squinted directly at... *Mister Rogers! It's Mister Rogers, from TV!*

As he came nearer, Kathy could see him much better and then quickly realized it wasn't him after all. A much younger man than the TV personality, he nonetheless wore the same distinctive haircut and famous cardigan sweater of the kiddies show entertainer she'd watched many times.

Looks a lot like Mister Rogers, though.

She wanted to speak, to ask if she could go home now, but that *thing* in her mouth wouldn't let her. All she could do was move her eyes.

Mister Rogers stood next to her, gazing down almost tenderly. He traced a latex covered finger up her calf, along her thigh, finally resting by cupping her small cold breast. *I'm naked!* Kathy whimpered in terror, and squeezed her eyes tightly, praying to disappear.

"Now, now, sweetheart," the man said softly. "Don't be frightened. We'll have a long time for you to get used to it."

Tears slid down her cheeks as she recoiled and whimpered again. The stranger who looked a lot like Mister Rogers gently touched her lips and Kathy, wrenching her head to avoid his hand, tasted the latex glove's after affects. They were like those she'd seen doctors wear.

He pinched her breast nipple hard and her eyes flew open, gagging as she tried in vain to scream her terror. That's when she first noticed the thick leather wrist bracelet attached to a metal ring, anchoring her arm to the heavy table. The sight drove her to a sudden awareness that her feet must be affixed in the same manner, for something also held them fast. She tried to sob, but the rubber-tasting object kept the muffled sounds from coming.

"So my pretty, let's begin. Not the *right* one, but you'll do," came the soft voice again. "Yes, you'll do just fine."

Kathy wondered how she'd ever thought this sick syrupy voice ever sounded friendly. The heavy table barely budged as *Mister Rogers* climbed onto it with her. She could tell he'd removed his clothing, at least from the waist up. She recoiled in terror as he lowered his head and licked at her tiny breast.

Seemingly pleased with her resistance, *Mister Rogers* groaned softly and licked on down her stomach as she strained and jerked against her bindings. Her struggles did no good; his wet mouth suddenly covered her, devouring her.

It seemed to go on forever. Kathy felt nauseous and fought down the urge to vomit. Her instincts told her that if she did, the gag in her mouth would cause her to drown. Terrified, her stomach churned as she strained against her bindings; then at last, relief that he was finished.

Through her tightly clinched eyes, she felt his weight and sensed a shadow position itself over her, momentarily blocking the bright light. Shaken, gasping for breath, Kathy squinted just long enough to see her tormenter's gaze fixate on her — akin to worship. Then he thrust forward, an excruciating tearing sensation ripping through her.

Kathy passed out—mercifully unaware of what he did next.

———————

The phone had been ringing incessantly when BJ, stepping from the shower, grabbed a large terry-cloth towel. Dripping water across the carpet, she rushed to pick it up.

"*Hello!*"

"Jamie Burgess? I'm Betty Farmer, Kathy's mother... Amanda's friend. My daughter didn't come home after school and I was hoping she's with Amanda."

BJ recognized the controlled panic in the woman's voice, and tried to calm her by remaining composed. "No. I'm sorry, Mrs. Farmer. I picked up Amanda about two blocks from your house tonight. Kathy said she was headed straight home." BJ heard the woman's soft moan on the other end.

"I hate to impose upon you, Jamie. But I know you're a policewoman and... well, I wondered if you could do some checking for me to see if... you know... she's shown up... anywhere?"

As a mother, BJ could understand her panic and rushed to reassure her. "Don't worry, Mrs. Farmer. Just give me about five minutes to rinse this soap off my hair and I'll call around a little. Try not to worry. I'm sure she's all right. I'll get back to you within the next thirty minutes. Okay?"

"Thanks, Jamie. I can't tell you how much I appreciate this," she said, followed by an inaudible click on the other end.

That poor woman! I know how I'd feel if anything ever happened to Amanda. Well, it's probably nothing to worry about, but it won't hurt to make a few calls, just to be on the safe side.

Chapter 11

It was late as Albert watched the gritty peroxide blond go down on the guy resembling the mouthy pro-basketball player, the one named, *Akeem* — *Abdul* — Mohammed — *something-or-other*. The skinny black man was clearly six-eight, his head shaved and large gold earrings in each pierced ear. He was the proud owner of a cock that had to be at least twelve inches in length and the thickness of a woman's wrist. It was a new film, but this was the third time he'd watched it today, each time with the same results — nothing.

Albert looked at his flaccid penis and sighed deeply. *Oh, to have a cock like old Akeem there*, he thought.

It was pouring again outside and he glanced up at the plasterboard ceiling and watched it drool. What a dump! His tenement had already been in desperate need of repairs when he'd moved in three years ago, and that damned Jew of a landlord hadn't done a thing since. *Drip, drip, drip*. As he watched, the drool shifted to a full-fledged leak.

Lifting his head, Albert could hear rats scratching behind the walls, squealing as they scampered to get away from the encroaching dampness — the same dampness that always brought out the strong odor of urine in the hallway each time it rained. Though he knew he'd never complain to the landlord. If he did, the old woman might actually fix the leak, then raise his rent — or worse yet, kick him out. She didn't like him anyway and was just looking for an excuse to run him off. *What a dump.*

The blond with black roots forced another millimeter of the stiff black meat down her throat as Albert pulled frantically at his own limp appendage. Once, just once, he'd like to see what it felt like to have a woman.

He'd come close when he was a teenager, he remembered, his face burning with shame. The girl had been younger than Albert, but certainly knew what she was doing. She'd taken his embarrassingly tiny penis into her mouth and worked at it with practiced skill, trying to get it up. Realizing it was useless and giving up, she'd really been *pissed!* So pissed that she'd told her parents that Albert had tried to rape her. The cops showed up at his house soon afterward and carted him off to jail — where he'd remained for the next six months. He was now a "Registered Sex Offender," according to the King County Sheriff's Department records. It was a secret he hoped those at his church would never find out.

It amazed and depressingly frustrated him that every other man seemed to have no trouble getting it up, but that he'd never been able to — not once!

Like Uncle Jason.

Albert had been five when his Uncle Jason started grooming him for sex. He remembered how Jason had given him candy to sit on his lap. Later, he'd been instructed to place his small hand inside his uncle's fly and rub his crotch. For bigger rewards, he'd done it with his mouth. He remembered how hard Uncle Jason had gotten — how he'd been sick afterward, and how Jason had always laughed when it'd happened.

Albert had hated it every time his uncle touched him, and had always felt as if he'd done something terribly bad. At age ten, when they'd told him his uncle had suddenly died of a heart attack, he was secretly glad. For years he'd prayed the old man's death had been painful and he'd burn in hell; now... he just didn't care anymore.

When he watched these movies or looked at the dirty pictures in his magazines, he still felt guilty, like he was being bad again. But he just had to get it to work. *Had to!* The blond was kneeling now, the black man thrusting into her from behind as she moaned disinterestedly. Still nothing was happening for Albert.

It happened so fast that it's suddenness terrified him. At first he thought it might be the big earthquake that Nostradamus guy had predicted would happen. It was only when he'd been spread-eagled on the floor with hands cuffed behind his back, that he

114

realized the noise had been his door splintering—and he knew the tan trousers with broad stripes belonged to the cops.

———————

Upon leaving Olaf at the old sail boat, Murphy tiredly made his way toward *Crime Pays* to spend what was left of the night. Through the building's small window shaped like a boat's portal, he could see Mama Elsa still at work in the marina office and decided he'd stop in. As usual, the door was unlocked.

"Mama, you've got to be more careful about locking your door. There're a lot of bad people in this world." He'd chided her repeatedly about it since he'd first rented his slip at her marina, but to no avail.

"Oh, posh, Frank! I don't vorry about things like vhat. You know I've got Olaf and his ugly mutt running around out there," she replied with her usual bright smile.

Mama had a deceptively ageless agility some people envy, despite being nearly seventy pounds over weight. He guessed her age to be about sixty-eight. He didn't let her ready smile deceive him, for he knew she'd immigrated from some Iron Curtain country, and figured she could be a pretty tough cookie should the occasion ever arrive.

Grunting, she eased her chubby frame from the too-small chair and automatically poured them a cup of the aromatic coffee she kept brewing. There were a couple of things about Mama you could always expect—a good cup of coffee when you stopped by, and the always-present box of assorted jellyroll donuts. He reluctantly selected one and nibbled on it. Coffee and jellyroll donuts, Mama's only remaining passions.

Mama watched the handsomely dark detective nibble his donut with a special tenderness. She liked Frank. He reminded her of her third husband — the best of the lot. *Quiet, too,* as she'd mentioned to Olaf. *Just like Jorge.* Because he *was* quiet and tended to brood, it'd taken Mama longer than usual to find out everything noteworthy that'd ever happened to him. Mama Elsa was nosey, and admitted it freely; she considered it to be her greatest vice. The more secretive or withdrawn a person, the more challenged Mama became to discover their hidden secrets.

Of course, she'd never tell anyone what she'd discovered; after all, she *wasn't* a gossip! The fun was in the finding out. The *finding out* in Frank Murphy's situation had made Mama's heart ache.

She'd told Olaf once that if she'd ever had a son, she would've wanted him to be just like Frank — but that he needed to get out of his terrible job as a cop and do what he enjoyed best — namely, fixing boats. She'd observed the young policeman at work on her old sailboat, and on his own boat *Crime Pays*, admiring his meticulous, detailed care. He'd even impressed the perfectionist, Olaf. She watched him finish off the last of his donut.

I'll just have to work on him a little more.

Mama also freely admitted she was a meddler.

Murphy downed the last of his coffee, and stood to leave. "Lock... that... door!" he reminded pointedly as he left.

Listening for the dead bolt to slip into place, he wearily headed toward Pier A where the *Crime Pays* swayed gently in her moorage. Although he loved the old boat, there was something sad about walking down the long floating walkway each night. He never did it without a flashing image in his mind of a little girl's face peeking out from an illuminated picture window. It happened again and just as quickly, he suppressed it, but the heavy weight of sadness washed over him just the same.

This night he was tired to the point of exhaustion, so he skipped his usual three sleeping pills, instead pouring himself a half glass of water, followed by a double straight shot of Old Crow. Drake had told him the combination could kill him. Well, he could only hope. Unlike most nights, his back had barely touched the bed and he was asleep. As usual though, it was a fitful sleep, punctuated by graphic images and flashbacks.

———————

Frank was happy! His heart simply *pounded* with happiness as he climbed out of his Suburban and walked toward the schoolyard entrance. Tina squealed and ran toward him as she waved goodbye to some of her little friends, giggling happily. There was an aura about her, glowing brightly, warming her surroundings. She looked *angelic*! Frank was overcome with his love for her.

As she passed a dirty white van, a long arm snaked out, wrapping its bony hand in her flowing mane, causing her to cry out. Horrified, Frank tried to run to her — but his feet were mired; they wouldn't move. He screamed silently. *Please let me go to her, this time! Please God…!*

Looking down, amazed to find his feet stuck ankle deep into molasses sludge, he continued to struggle forward — in slow motion. The shadowy figure seated in the van held his kicking daughter off the ground with one hand, producing a long gleaming knife in the other.

Again, Frank screamed silently. *No! Please dear God! No!*

Crying and kicking, Tina screamed to him. *Help me, Daddy! Please, help me…!*

Frozen, he watched in horror. *No. No! Oh, Jesus, no!* He groaned pitifully and sunk helplessly to his knees, watching as the person in the truck slowly turned toward him and grinned. He knew the killer, but somehow couldn't recognize him.

Frank screamed out and lunged forward, knocking the brass lamp off its ledge onto the floor. Tina, a sinister grinning Robert James and the street suddenly evaporated. He bolted upright in his bed, staring wild-eyed around the boat's master suite. His sheets were soaked, and he felt nauseous. The nightmares were back!

Oh Jesus! It'd seemed so real this time.

His legs trembling, he climbed the three steps to the head and relieved himself. It'd been the third nightmare in a week — only this one was the worst. *Shit!* His clammy hands shook out two of the pills Doctor Larsen had prescribed several months previously, swallowed them without water and lie down on the couch, tucking his legs beneath his robe. As he dropped off, he cursed an unmerciful God who'd let such a monster take the little girl he loved.

An obnoxious ringing assaulted his ears… it seemed like he'd just fallen asleep. Groggy, he slapped the alarm clock off the bedside end table, only to discover he was on the couch and it'd been his telephone, instead. Groaning, he picked it up from the floor, vaguely trying to decide whether to toss it overboard or answer it.

"This better be important," he mumbled into the receiver.

"Murph? Jeeze, what's going on there? It sounded like a fight."
It was Charley Booth.

"I dropped the phone — all right? What's up?"

"Better get dressed, Murph. There's been another one. I'll call
Bear and have him meet us there." Booth gave him an address in a
residential district on Capital Hill and hung up.

A three-quarter-moon still reflected brightly off Elliot Bay as
he rubbed his eyes and tried to wake up. Murphy glanced at his
watch. He was surprised to discover it was only four-thirty a.m. To
the west, a solid wall of dark clouds raced across the water towards
him, threatening to destroy the tranquil setting. He knew that in
just a few more minutes, these streaking clouds would completely
hide the bright moon.

Feeling as if he'd never slept at all, he brushed his teeth and
slipped on jeans and a sweatshirt. By that time, a soft rain had
begun to pelt the water and deck outside. Grabbing his holstered
pistol and raincoat from a hook near the door, he slipped them on,
hurriedly walking along the floating pier toward the parking lot.

The stiff ocean breeze and rain made everything smell clean,
and despite the early hour he was glad to be out of his small
prison.

Booth's directions had been good; the place wasn't hard to
find. A major residential street, it was now packed by police cars
with flashing red and blue lights. Booth and Drake were already
waiting outside when he arrived. Both were in shirtsleeves and
drenched, like drowned rats.

"It's another young girl, Murph" Drake said, handing him a
steaming white paper cup with its distinctive green logo. The
coffee was scalding hot and burned his tongue. "We're trying to get
an ID on her now, but like always, he didn't leave much to go on."

"Same as the others?" Murphy was reluctant to say the words.

"Yep," Booth said. "Hemphill arrived right after we did and
he's processing the scene now. If it's like all the rest though, there
won't be any prints, or much else." His tone was fatalistic. "We'll
know more when he finishes. I called BJ but she was already in
route to the station to check on any missing person calls that
might've come in last night. I don't know how she found out about
it so fast. She seemed pretty uptight about something. Thought
you'd like to know."

Murphy nodded and lit up a smoke. Drake nonchalantly reached for the cigarettes he held in his hand, but Murphy jerked the pack away, holding them just out of his reach for an instant. Then he returned them to his inside pocket, grinning with malice.

"Some friend!" Drake pouted, sticking a piece of gum into his large mouth. "Anybody ever tell you you've got a mean streak, Murph?"

Murphy's grin grew wider. "Smoking is bad for your health. Especially if Mable finds out."

Two coffees later the squat form of the forensics specialist headed toward them.

"No secrets here," Hemphill said, reaching for Murphy's coffee. "When you gonna catch this pervert?"

They ignored his dig, and Drake said, "She like the others?"

"Like I said — no secrets. Raped her, sodomized her, sawed her head off, and then rode off into the sunset, yodeling. Just another happy fucking ending."

Hemphill drained the last of Murphy's coffee and crushed the container. "She was transported here after she was dead. Then he unloaded the body, carried her up three flights of stairs, entered an unoccupied condo and arranged her in his favorite position. After that, the son of a bitch left — just walked out and drove away — all without ever being seen.

Who the fuck *is* this guy that he can just come and go whenever he wants, anytime he wants, and nobody ever sees him? Hou-*fucking*-dini?"

He threw the crushed cup onto the sidewalk disgustedly, turned, and climbed inside a waiting sedan. "I'll call you when my report is complete. Oh yeah, there's a tire track on the grass back there. It may be his, or it may be someone else's. If it belongs to the killer, the bastard might've made his first mistake."

They watched him as he disappeared into the rainy morning darkness.

"Shit." Murphy didn't have to look to know it was Drake.

"I'll double that," he said.

They remained for another thirty minutes before heading for the squad room. Commute traffic was just starting to thicken so Drake took to the side streets to make better time. Each nurtured their own thoughts along the way, and the silence was welcome to them both. Murphy reconstructed the nightmare he'd had a few hours before, while Drake relished the thought of slipping his big hands around the neck of this unknown monster that slaughtered little girls for his perverted pleasure.

Murphy slammed into the task force room ahead of the others and was the first to see BJ. Her head was bent forward and her face drawn as she stared at the tile on the floor. Drake, Booth and Yates all stopped abruptly, stacking up behind him. He hesitated, taking in her unmoving form, realizing from her posture that something was very wrong.

Worried, he spoke softly. "Talk to me, BJ."

She looked up, suddenly aware of him for the first time. "Kathy Farmer," she said.

Murphy looked puzzled, clearly not understanding her meaning.

"Kathy is Amanda's best friend. She didn't show up after school last night." Her voice trailed to almost a whisper. "Her mother thought she might have stayed at our house because of the rain storm. But she didn't."

Murphy saw the tears on her cheeks, the terrible anguish in her eyes.

"She and Amanda were walking home from school and I stopped to give them a ride. We were only a block or two from her house, so Kathy didn't get in the car.

She never made it home. That's Kathy in the morgue." More large tears spilled over as she choked out the words. "If I had just insisted that she ride, she'd still be alive."

Murphy laid his hand on her shoulder. She was clearly in pain. He knelt by her side, staring into her eyes.

It… is… not… your… fault, BJ. Get that through your head *right now. It's not your fault!*"

A sudden alarm displaced the anguish and as it registered in her eyes, she jumped to her feet. "My *God*! Amanda! She's at home *alone!*" BJ grabbed her raincoat and bolted for the door.

"Go with her, Charley! Stay with her as long as you're needed," he said. Booth nodded and raced into the rain after the distraught woman.

"Jesus," Drake said, as he dropped into a vacant chair. "That's getting too close to home."

"Way too close. I've got a funny feeling about this. I want to pick up that maintenance man we've got the composite on. Maybe if we sweat him, we'll get something. I don't want the papers to get wind of it until we've got him under lock and key. Until then, he's only a person of interest. Hell, we still don't have anything to link him with any of the killings yet, other than the fact he was in the area the day one happened."

"Yeah, him and about four thousand other people," Drake said dryly.

"It's raining pretty hard today so he probably won't be out mowing any lawns this morning," Murphy stated. "Plan to hit his apartment at 1000 hours. Just the three of us. No media, no Lieutenant Butthead, no SWAT—just you two and me. Real quiet like."

"Got ya, boss," Drake said. Yates nodded his agreement.

Within minutes they poured intently over the arrest plan, reviewing everything they knew about the suspect, Albert Burbakowski.

As it neared nine o'clock, Murphy picked up his rain jacket and waited while the others gathered up their gear. Locking the door behind them, they exited the side entrance and rounded the corner toward the front of the station. They heard the commotion before they even saw it. About twenty people were milling about in the rain on the front steps of the station. Most were reporters, a few were cops, and the others were from City Hall.

Murphy froze, as did Drake and Yates, and they watched as Borden led a dazed Albert Burbakowski in cuffs up the granite steps. They had no difficulty recognizing him. He looked nearly identical to the composite drawings. Camera flashes popped through the gray morning mist as Borden smiled, acknowledging each and every one of the reporters.

"That the killer, Lieutenant Borden?" someone shouted.

"Looks like it!" Borden shouted back. "We've found news clippings of all the murders, porno films, dirty pictures and magazine — the whole nine yards."

"Shit," Drake muttered his favorite word from behind.

Borden paused at the top step and smiled even broader. "I'll have a statement for you as soon as we get this guy booked. Let's do it inside, out of the rain, okay?"

The reporters cheered as they raced up the steps, crowding into the door behind Borden and his prisoner. Molly Atwood turned her head and smiled prettily at Murphy's group standing in the rain, just as she vanished out of sight into the dark doorway.

"*Shit!*" Drank used his favorite word again — louder.

Murphy turned and stared directly at Joe Yates, the fury in his reddening face clearly visible. Yates' features suddenly registered the realization of what Murphy was thinking, and backing up, holding his palms outward, blurted, "Now wait a minute, Frank! You're dead wrong this time! I didn't do it, I swear!"

Murphy balled up his fists and stepped toward Yates, who retreated, alarmed. Drake slid between them quickly, shielding Yates behind his bulk. "He ain't worth it, Murph. Let it go."

"I'm telling you guys it wasn't me! I had nothing to do with letting Borden know about Burbakowski," Yates insisted. "Look, I ain't afraid to go toe-to-toe with you if I have to, Frank, but *I didn't do it!*"

Disgusted, Yates finally threw up his hands in defeat, wheeled around, and marched toward the parking lot.

"You should've let me clobber the son-of-a-bitch, Bear!" Murphy reprimanded Drake, the fury on his face still evident.

"Yeah? Well, you were lucky the last time," his partner told him. "Smashing Yates's face in might've felt good right now, but you'd be off the task force this time and you know it."

"Yeah, yeah, yeah..."

The two partners walked toward the parking area.

"Murph, I've probably seen a thousand arrests come into this building for booking since I've been here. Ya know what? That's the only one I can remember that wasn't brought through the underground entrance. This was a real Butthead special."

———

For a reason she couldn't identify, BJ was terrified for her daughter's safety. She drove like a person possessed for fifteen white-knuckled minutes before she brought the car to a sudden brake-locked halt in front of the small split-level home she shared with Amanda. A thousand horrible images had flashed through her mind every mile of the way. The screech was loud enough that seventy-six-year-old Fred Phillips, her next-door neighbor, stopped stuffing his trash bags into his garbage can and frowned in her direction. Booth's face was drawn and pale as he kept to her pace.

"*Crazy broad.*"

BJ jumped from the vehicle, her car door left swinging from its hinges, and raced for the front door, followed closely by an ashen-faced Charley Booth. Both had their guns drawn in a two- handed grip — BJ covering the left side of the house — Booth covering the right. Literally exploding into the living room, they found themselves staring into the wide, startled eyes of Amanda and a young boy, hunkering over a heap of textbooks and note pads.

"Ah geez, Moms," Amanda's voice quivered. "I know I said I'd call if I was going to be late for school, but I didn't know you felt that strongly about it."

BJ pulled Amanda to her feet and held her tightly against her own trembling body. Amanda stared wide-eyed into her mother's watery gaze.

"Jimmy, you need to go on to school now," BJ said calmly, composing herself. "Amanda's staying home today."

"Yes, Miss Burgess." The scared boy stuttered, hurriedly gathering his scattered books and beating a hasty retreat out the door—glancing apprehensively over his shoulder.

"I guess you know you've just spoiled the best chance I'll ever have at marriage," Amanda quipped, still quite shaken. Observing her mother's face more carefully, she said softly, "What is it, Moms? What's happened?"

"Come sit, Sweetheart. I've got some bad news."

The killer hadn't moved in hours, rarely blinking at a candle flame flickering in the middle of the bare wooden table.

He was *pissed*! Not only did he get the wrong girl, but also he'd had to kill her too soon when she'd almost gotten away from him. The *voice* wouldn't be pleased. He knew he'd be punished for his mistake. The thought crossed his mind that he wouldn't be allowed to have any more girls. *No! I'll just have to make it up, somehow*!

It'd been an honest mistake — he could explain it. How was he supposed to know the little black girl would give the blue raincoat and umbrella to her friend?

I'll just go back and grab the little black cunt. That's the one the voice instructed me to get. I'll do just as I've been told.

He could wait... until he had the right girl.

Chapter 12

Drake and Murphy drove to the shabby apartment building Albert Burbakowski called home. The address corresponded to a four-story tenement in a row of rundown dwellings on a narrow side street, where the sun seldom shined. Drake drove past it twice, while Murphy searched for a number. On their second pass, he decided it had to be the building on the right.

Drake pulled into a bus stop area on the street, placing the police plate in the windshield. Garbage bags were stacked along the sidewalk. One had busted open between two abandoned cars. A skinny cat clawed at its contents through a rip.

Four young black males, their blue bandanas visible from beneath reversed baseball caps, loitered around a doorway halfway down the block. They were listening to painfully loud Rap music, flashing gang signs at passing cars. The group ceased their activities, giving the two strangers a hard stare as they entered the apartment building.

Murphy glanced around nervously, and with some resentment, noticed Drake's stride, his walk suggesting just a bit of the same arrogance — as though he'd like nothing better than to be accosted, or at least interfered with a little. He was at home here. He'd grown up in an area much like this one.

Forty or fifty years before, this had been one of the better neighborhoods in Queen Anne Hill. Now it was a war zone. These old masonry buildings had started out as stately townhouses with large stone steps and heavy imposing wooden doors. Now he and Drake passed steps that had been broken off, like bad teeth, the doors stained with graffiti. Along a wall of shattered plaster, a row

125

of mailboxes hung loosely from a two-by-eight. Several discolored smudges indicated where others had once been attached before being ripped from their mounts. Only a couple bore names. Most remaining had been jimmied open at one time or another, probably to steal welfare checks.

On the first landing, they encountered several tattooed able-bodied men. Big heavily muscled men. Ex-cons who, with nothing but time on their hands, had all buffed up in the prison gym — poked at, the needle and raw ink art etched into their laborious skin designs. Men without jobs — men living on their women's welfare checks — or what they could just take — men who knew the system was corrupt and believed that legitimized whatever they had to do to survive. The kind of men Murphy and Drake dealt with on a daily basis.

And they were packing. At least the ones who had their shirts hanging outside their pants. He and Drake studied the men's belt lines, the drape of their shirttails. Of the four, three were clearly carrying firearms. The other probably had a prison made shiv in the small of his back.

The laughing and joking ceased abruptly as they recognized the officers for who they were. Not by their faces, but by their type. *Cops.* Just as Murphy and Drake had done, men like these could also read the clothing and demeanor of approaching strangers.

He watched as the group took them in, reading them, and could see it reflected in their eyes. That and — hate. He could almost hear what they were thinking; a black man and a white man together, their jackets with bulges in the wrong places, the way he and Drake stared back, without fear — that meant they were armed. These strangers with bulges — on their turf, unafraid and staring back… *Cops.*

They passed two dark-skinned women gossiping across the hallway through their open doors. As they approached the women fell silent and stared at them as they walked by, only to resume their whispers after the two men were well past.

Murphy, who could almost sense what Drake was going to say before he even spoke, wondered if he'd ever understand these people. He knew Drake felt the same way. Murphy had the same kind of connection with Mable and the girls as he did with Drake. But not here. These streets were another planet.

126

A faded cardboard arrow pointed the way to the manager's apartment — on the manager's door a small sign, hand written in Magic Marker, stated *I'LL BE BACK!* Empty beer cans and trash littered an empty hallway containing the entrance to six other apartments. Strong cooking odors filled the corridor. From one apartment, a heavy bass dun pounded relentlessly as loud Rap shook the ground. Ignoring the sign, Drake banged on the door. It did not open. He banged again.

"What d'ya what?" It was a woman's voice.

"Police! Open up!"

The door opened a crack and Drake displayed his shield. The acne-faced white woman looked young, probably not yet twenty. Several small children peeked out from behind her skirt, their skin tones varying shades of brown and olive; the oldest no more than six.

"Burbakowski. Which apartment?"

"4-G. Fourth floor, rear," the young woman said. "He ain't there though. You guys took him away. He owes back rent."

"Sue him."

Carefully avoiding piles of trash and garbage bags, they made their way up two more flights of dingy stairway, locating the mustard colored and mildewed green apartment on the street-side of the building. The hallway reeked with a multiplicity of odors, the strongest — urine. Nodding to the uniformed policeman on guard at the door, Murphy removed the yellow ribbon crime tape across the doorway and went inside.

A foul stench assaulted their nostrils, nearly knocking them back, but Murphy and Drake forced themselves to search through the rubble and clutter. The apartment was actually only two small rooms, with a small bath and no shower or closet. The only bedroom, a nine-by-eight hole, had one small window, probably opened earlier by a searcher to relieve the stench. It allowed space for little more than a single bed and a cigarette burned orange crate nightstand. On the crate a small metal lamp stood with no shade and only a dirty light bulb. It was the room's only source of light.

The remaining room was larger; a small refrigerator, rusty sink, a hot plate in one corner, and several unpainted wood shelves utilized as cabinets. Dirty dishes stuck together in the sink, resting in a dismal gray water substance floating with colorful disgusting stuff. It'd obviously been like that for days — maybe weeks. Everything was uniformly filthy. Their shoe soles stuck to the linoleum tile with each tentative step.

"Wheee! This place would stink a dog off a gut wagon," Drake blurted, looking a little green. "How can people live like this?"

Murphy didn't answer, looking thoughtfully at the squalor. Drake tried for a response again. "Looks like they've pretty well picked it over, Murph."

"Yeah. What a dump." Murphy gazed around, puzzled.

"What's eating you?"

"Well, Borden and his crew took all the nasty stuff, right?" Murphy said, as he waived his hand in a circle and surveyed the room. "That makes it easier to see what's left."

"For instance?"

Murphy walked to a low, round coffee table in front of the tattered and stained plaid couch. It was littered with old bills and advertisements. He selected several items and carried them to the dirty table in the corner of the room used as the kitchen. The first item he placed down was a letter with a small cross in the upper right hand corner. The letterhead stated it was from a Reverend J. Thomas, Church of Our Savior.

"This is addressed to 'Deacon' Albert Burbakowski. Listen. 'Thank you for all your support in our church's latest renovation project, Albert'," he read.

"This one is a note appointing him as the church's representative to oversee the new Sunday school program. These others are various awards Burbakowski's received from the church during the past year."

"Maybe he's a *religious* serial killer?" Drake suggested.

"Let's pay a call on Reverend J. Thomas," Murphy said.

————

The Church of Our Savior was located four blocks away, in the same neighborhood as the suspect's apartment. Drake and Murphy were both surprised to discover a small, neat two-story structure surrounded by well-tended flower gardens and bubbly water fountains. Unlike most of the other buildings in the surrounding area, the Church of Our Savior's walls remained unmarred by gang graffiti. A smiley face sign on the front door invited them, *COME IN AND PRAISE THE LORD.*

Inside the church, it was just as neat and tidy as the exterior had been. Long rows of freshly painted pews and vases of fresh flowers filled the elongated room. An impressive altar, highlighted by the splashy spring colors of lilies and azaleas, beckoned at the far end. Everything was immaculate. An old man gazed up from his work as they entered.

"May I help you gentlemen?" he said, smiling warmly.

"We're looking for Reverend Thomas," Frank stated.

"Look no further gentlemen. You've found him."

"I'm Sergeant Murphy and this is my partner, Detective Drake — Homicide, Seattle P.D. We'd like to ask you some questions about Albert Burbakowski. He was arrested this morning on suspicion of murder."

The old man's warm smile turned to puzzlement. "Surely there's been some mistake, Sergeant Murphy. I've known Brother Burbakowski for more than two years. He wouldn't hurt a fly."

Frank and Drake shifted uncomfortably, then Frank cleared his throat. "Reverend Thomas, are you aware Albert's a registered sex offender? That he spent six months in jail for attempting to rape a sixteen-year-old girl in Portland?"

The pastor hobbled toward them, his hand supporting his hip, and gingerly lowered himself into a pew. "Albert told me all about that when he first came here, Sergeant." The old man's sad eyes hung on them as he said, "You must understand, gentlemen. Albert has the body of a man but for most things, the IQ of a twelve-year-old. It's easy to see how people like Albert lose their way in this world."

"You say 'for most things'. What things did he understand?" Drake said.

The old man frowned slightly. "Albert's a genius with his hands. Since his arrival, he's practically rebuilt the entire church, single-handedly."

The minister's frail hands floated from the top of his head to his hips, indicating his torso. "As you can see, I'm of little help, but he and I finally finished the altar Saturday night. We worked feverishly so we'd complete it before midnight. That would've been the Sabbath, you know, and we don't work on the Sabbath."

His sad smile held a tinge of pride in their accomplishment. "He did all the landscaping you saw outside, too." The frail old man paused, and then continued. "And while Albert has the cognitive ability of a twelve-year-old, he knows the Bible as well as any man I've ever met. He can practically recite it verse-by-verse; anything you request. Does that sound like a murderer to you?"

"Well, some people seem to think they've got a pretty good case against him, Reverend," Murphy said. "What time did he leave here Saturday?"

Reverend Thomas thoughtfully rubbed his whiskered chin. "I'd say it was just before midnight. Maybe five minutes before. I remember us joking about his running the four blocks to his apartment before the goblins came out. He has to pass the cemetery on his way home, you see." Remembering brought a hint of a smile to the old pastor's eyes. "Can I prepare you gentlemen some refreshment? Some tea, perhaps?"

"Sorry, Reverend, maybe another time. We'll need to be going." They shook hands again, and turned toward the entry.

On the way out Reverend Thomas cautioned, "Gentlemen, you have no idea what this'll do to Albert. Even if he's found not guilty, everything about his previous offense will undoubtedly come out."

The old man's head drooped and he looked tremendously sad. "You see… the church is all he has, and this congregation is all the family he knows. I fear this may damage Albert seriously."

"Thank you for your cooperation, Pastor Thomas. It's been most helpful."

As they walked to the car, an evil gleam radiated from Drake's eyes. "This is sure gonna piss old Butthead, royally."

Chapter 13

Mrs. Sommers smiled warmly as the young man carried her groceries to her white 500 series Mercedes. She'd been shopping at Best Groceries for the past fifteen years, ever since her husband had passed away and she'd moved into the plush retirement community two blocks away. David had been just a bagger then. Now that he was store manager, he still helped the elderly ladies with their bags.

What a handsome young man, she thought, *and he keeps the cleanest store.* Her mind shifted to her own worthless son — she wished desperately that he'd turned out like David Turner.

Mrs. Sommers tried to tip the young man but, as always, he declined, saying it just wouldn't be right to accept money for doing something he enjoyed so much. He suggested she consider donating it to the small church on the corner that supported all the special children's programs.

Such a nice young man.

David smiled and waved as she drove out of the parking lot, gathered up the carts in the area and pushed them to their designated spot near the door. He'd been the manager at Best Groceries for the past three years, and to the owner's delight, had increased the store's profit margin while substantially improving their customer base. He'd received several raises during his tenure, although money was of little interest to him — above what it took to live on. David had other interests. He smiled as he turned toward a frizzy-haired brunette in jeans and her daughter of about ten.

"Here, let me help with those," he said, hoisting the heavy

sack from her hands as he smiled warmly at the daughter. "You folks live nearby?" he said politely.

"Yes. We just moved into the Soundview Heights Condos, just down the street," she answered. "This is our first day there."

David smiled. "Oh, you must be in the older section, then. Right?"

"No, we're in the stone finished condos facing toward the water. A-21, one of the newer ones, with a balcony."

"I know it well," David told her. "I deliver there sometimes. Those are very nice units."

The young woman climbed into a blue Volvo station wagon and started the engine. David watched intently as her daughter slid into the passenger's side, swinging her polka-dot dress over her tan legs with the unconscious ease young girls often show.

"Well, you folks have a good day, and welcome to the neighborhood." David yelled, waiving at them as they headed toward the exit. He watched as they pulled onto the tree-lined street and headed home. His eyes followed until they were out of sight. Then David Turner scanned the lot for empty shopping carts.

On their way back to the station, Murphy and Drake stopped at the 7-Eleven to buy a newspaper.

"Shit," Drake said when he saw the headlines of the Seattle Post. "Looks like the Barracuda strikes again."

He held the paper up for Murphy to see the headlines.

HEADHUNTER SERIAL KILLER CAUGHT!

Murphy somberly listened as Drake read the article aloud, feeling sick inside. He could sense it had the same affect on his partner. Molly Atwood was a good writer, if nothing else. She'd reported about the suspect's previous conviction for rape, and of the smut and porno tapes found in his littered apartment. She made it sound as if a trial wouldn't even be necessary. Every word she'd written screamed, *guilty, guilty, guilty!*

"That poor bastard," Drake said bitterly. "She's just cut off his nuts."

Murphy knew he was referring to Albert Burbakowski. They drove the rest of the way to the station silently, each thinking about that slow-witted man in a lonely jail cell, not fully understanding why he was there.

A message from Borden awaited them when they entered their office. They were both in a surly mood, and the message didn't help it improve any. Murphy read it aloud. "Be at the Mayor's office at ten sharp for a news conference. Don't be late!"

Glancing at his watch, he noted they had only fifteen minutes to make it. "Screw it. Let's skip this one," he off-handedly remarked, just as the phone rang.

Lieutenant Borden screamed in his ear, "*Murphy*? You and Drake get your asses over here, and I mean *now*!"

Murphy grimaced as the phone slammed down on the other end.

"Guess not, huh?" Drake said.

The meeting was well under way in the conference room when they arrived. Borden was relishing the spotlight, already pacing in front of the assembled group. Drake and Murphy tried slipping unnoticed into chairs in the rear, but that was not to be the case.

"Frank, John Henry, glad you could make it," Borden stated as he greeted them in a friendly voice.

Drake rolled his eyeballs at Murphy and sighed, *Feets don't let me...*

The Mayor, Councilwoman Helen Walcott, Chief Williams, Captain Brooks, even Robert James were all present. *All the heavy hitters*, Murphy thought, trying to sink into his chair. He felt like a whore in church.

"I was just turning it over to Councilman James to say a few words, Frank. Then, perhaps you'd like to tell our friends in the press corps just how you were able to nab this monster." He grinned warmly at them.

Beside him, Murphy heard Drake snort softly under his breath. "*Shit.*"

A seasoned politician, Robert James basked in the limelight for as long as possible, frequently referring to his own self-importance and his imagined role in the capture of the killer. He was careful to avoid Murphy's eyes, finally summarizing his points by re-emphasizing that he'd been kept fully informed throughout the investigation. He closed by restating his commitment to a law and order platform, and if elected, promised even more quick arrests in the future.

Borden motioned to Murphy to speak next, and he quickly looked around for a fast way to escape. Finding none, he reluctantly rose. "I'm afraid I don't have a comment at this time. Maybe later."

He began to sit back down, but Borden quickly stopped him. "Nonsense Frank. Say anything you want about the investigation. You're among friends."

All eyes turned toward him as murmurs, laughing, and good-natured clapping erupted. He scanned the crowd and saw Molly Atwood suggestively lick her lips. He recognized several other reporters he'd brushed up against during his tenure with the department, as well. Trying to hide his disgust for a group who'd burned him more than once, and for whom he clearly felt were the lowest form of life in the food chain, he chose his words carefully.

"There're a lot of different aspects to an investigation like this one. Some have developed only within the past hour or two. I don't feel comfortable discussing them until I've had a chance to brief my superiors. Then, I'd be happy to also disclose those facts to you."

Borden slammed his hand on the table in front of him. "Murphy, just cut the crap and tell these people what we're doing to wrap up this case. There'll be no secrets here! We've nothing to hide from the Press, and you have my okay to disclose anything you have about the case!"

From the corner of his eye, he saw Drake softly smiling.

"Yes sir," he said amicably. He surveyed the faces of the reporters once more. "What are your questions?"

Several shouted questions simultaneously, and Murphy pointed at one of them. "When did you know you had the killer and ordered his arrest, Sergeant Murphy?"

"I didn't. Lt. Borden made the decision to arrest him. I believe after conferring with Councilman James. Isn't that correct?" Murphy said, glancing at the head of the table. James and Borden nodded eagerly, relieved that Murphy was going to give them front stage.

"But you're the one in charge of the task force. You must've been involved in establishing probable cause and turning over the evidence to them to support his arrest," Molly Atwood shouted above all the others.

"Nope," Murphy said. "His arrest was as much of a surprise to me as to the rest of you."

A stunned silence filled the room, as those at the head table glanced with uncertainty at one another. Robert James frowned at both Borden and the Mayor.

"Then how do you know he's the one who killed the three girls?" It was Atwood again.

"I don't," he stated. "In fact, I don't think he is."

His statement landed like an atomic bomb, paralyzing the room into silence. He inhaled deeply and went on. "I wish to God I could say it was him. The truth is, the killer's still out there, maybe getting ready to strike again, and I'm wasting time standing here answering stupid questions."

Everyone in the room swallowed hard, as if an awful taste didn't agree with them — especially those at the front table. The room was deadly quiet once more.

Borden suddenly stood and broke the silence. "Ladies and gentlemen of the press, this is all the time we have for today. I promise we'll have more later." With that, he and the others at the head table beat a hasty retreat toward the exit. As Borden and his retreating group made their way out, he glared at Murphy and Drake, and jerked his thumb toward the Mayor's office for them to follow.

"Well, the shit's about to hit the fan now, Pard," Drake stated. "And I got a feeling it's not gonna be evenly distributed. You want me to wait in the car?"

"You plaster your big ass to me like it's glued there, Bear! You're in this as deep as I am."

Drake followed him out, grinning easily.

All eyes turned toward them as they entered the Mayor's office. *If looks could kill, Robert James would be a murderer,* Murphy thought absently. Somehow, just that thought brought him a small measure of joy. All the chairs had been taken, so Murphy and Drake were left standing in the middle of the floor.

"Just what the hell was that all about, Murphy?" James demanded. Gone now, was the amicable *Frank* he'd used earlier.

"I don't understand," Murphy answered innocently. "I did what you *told* me to do. After all, we were all among friends."

"God dammit, quit the *bullshit*, Murphy!" Borden shouted. "We've got the killer in jail and you know it! What's the deal with you, anyway? You're just pissed off because you weren't the one to make the collar?"

Murphy glared coldly at Borden before he answered. "I've made collars before, Borden, remember? All of *my* assignments with the department have been on the streets."

Borden's face colored a dark red as he sputtered, nearly choking.

Brooks took that opportunity to ask, "What have you got, Frank?"

"An air-tight alibi, Boss. Albert Burbakowski couldn't possibly have killed the girl in Magnolia Bluffs. He was with someone else during the time she was murdered." Murphy focused directly on Robert James and felt the same cold hatred reflected back at him.

Borden snorted. Murphy wanted to reach across the table and squeeze his scrawny neck. "Anybody could give him an alibi," Borden sneered. "All Deputy Prosecutor McDonald has to do is discredit their testimony," Borden said, unaware he might be digging himself a bigger hole.

"Well, this 'someone' is the Reverend J. Thomas. The same J. Thomas who hosts the Thanksgiving 'Free Meal Deal', provides shelter for abused wives, and is on the Governor's committee to feed the homeless." He took some delight in their shocked faces.

"Whoever leaked this to the press has probably ruined that boy's life. Not that anyone in this room gives a shit."

"If I find you're pulling a slick one, Murph..." Robert James started.

The explosion was instantaneous and focused. "You want to talk about slick, James?" Murphy yelled, his face glowing crimson as his blood pressure soared. "As slick as fucking someone's wife, right under his nose? Let's talk about slick, you *motherfucker!*"

Livid, Murphy shouted and balled his fists, edging closer to the large table separating them. On the verge of swinging at the councilman, Drake suddenly grasped his arm in a vice-like grip, pulling him toward to the door. The others gasped, stunned at the ferocity of Murphy's near attack on James. The City Councilman's face was as white as a sheet, and his hands noticeably shook!

Once outside of the Mayor's office, Murphy attempted to pull away from Drake, stating calmly, "That went pretty well, don't you think?"

Drake didn't answer, nor did he relax his grip on Frank's arm, which was beginning to grow numb. Making it halfway down the hall, Murphy heard his name being called out behind them. Pivoting, he saw the matronly Helen Walcott waddle toward them.

"Sergeant Murphy, I need a word with you, if you gentlemen can spare a minute," she said, puffing her way toward them.

"Yes ma'am?" both men said in unison. She placed a hand to her ample bosom and breathed deeply until regaining her breath. "You really think that young man they've locked in the King County Jail is innocent, Detective Murphy?"

"Yes ma'am, I do," he answered respectfully. "I think the real killer will strike again, and do it soon. That should answer the question of guilt. The only problem is the irreparable harm it's causing Albert Burbakowski, though that doesn't seem to be a high priority right now."

"It is with me, Sergeant Murphy." The old woman's steel-gray eyes were clear and steady as she stared back at Frank. He had the impression she could be very tough. "One of the victim's mothers — Congresswoman Ethel Holcomb — is a personal friend of mine. I want the person responsible, the real killer, found as quickly as possible. The emphasis here is on *real killer*."

She began to walk away then wheeled and said directly, "I think Robert James is an *asshole*, too, Murphy."

They watched her retreat, and then hearing a noisy crowd clamoring down the hallway toward them, turned and sprinted for the back door. They exited quickly, primarily to avoid more dogged reporters, and had made it all the way to their parked patrol car before Drake finally let loose of his arm.

"You didn't have any future plans concerning promotions... running for office... staying on with the department... anything like that, did you?"

"Why? You think I loused it up back there?" Murphy said.

"If we don't find this guy soon, you'll be lucky if they let you direct traffic in Rainier Valley," Drake said. "Don't worry. I got a bad feeling you're gonna have company."

Drake settled into the driver's seat and Murphy slumped down on the passenger's side. He actually felt surprisingly good since blowing off steam back there.

"Well, until they relieve me of my duties, we've got a killer to stop. Let's get on it."

Lisa was waiting when they arrived back at the task force. Her eyes were bloodshot, and it was clear she'd been crying.

"What's wrong?" Drake said.

"Lieutenant Borden called. He talked awful — cussing and yelling at me. He said to tell you he wasn't through with you yet. That he was going to... to... fry your *nuts*. Tears swelled over her long lashes and she looked as if she might cry again at any moment.

Murphy fought to maintain a straight face. "Oh, don't worry about Butthead. He'll be lucky if he doesn't get fired himself after the press gets through roasting him. Just think...the Barracuda and the other...all those nice stories they printed yesterday. Now they've got to go back and say... oops, sorry."

"Yeah," Drake said. "That ought to keep them off our backs for a while."

"BJ call in?" Frank said.

"No messages."

"Lisa, give her a ring at home and see if everything's all right," Murphy directed.

Charley Booth and BJ chose that moment to enter.

When BJ came in, she informed them she'd taken Amanda to her grandmother's house in Everett, adamant her daughter would remain there until the guy responsible for Kathy's death was caught. She looked pale and shaken. Murphy could see fear in her eyes.

"Drake, you come with me to interview Burbakowski. The rest of you settle in for the afternoon with this computer list of domestic white van owners."

"This is nothing but a goddamned wild goose chase," Booth muttered as they departed.

Murphy smiled. "That's what I like. Unbridled enthusiasm."

———————

Murphy had been checking the booking log for Burbakowski's cell number when a frumpish woman about forty approached, carrying a vinyl briefcase that had seen better days.

"Sergeant Murphy? I'm Peggy Hunter — Public Defender's Office. I've been assigned to represent Albert Burbakowski. You got a minute?"

"Sure. This is Detective Drake. He's working with me on this. What can I do for you Ms. Hunter?"

"I understand you don't think my client's guilty. Do you have any other suspects?"

"It may not be important what I think," Murphy retorted. "If the prosecutor's office wants to push it, they might cause it to stick. If I were you, I'd start preparing a Murder One defense."

"I've already been contacted by the King County Prosecutor's Office. They're going to prosecute it, all right. Murder, First Degree, with premeditation and no plea-bargain.

They're going to seek the death penalty. Probably because of the high profile of the Holcomb name." She smirked disgustedly. "At least, that's what Deputy Prosecutor McDonald said. She's handling the case for King County."

It took a minute to sink in whom she was talking about. Elnore! So, she was using her maiden name these days. *Oh that's just great, Sport. Maybe we can go head-to-head in the courtroom over this one. What a can of worms!*

"Bear and I were just on our way back to talk to your client, Ms. Hunter. Want to tag along?" Murphy said.

"Since you two are about as friendly as it's going to get around here, I probably wouldn't really need to. But, I'd be remiss if I didn't. So...?" She smiled, and its brilliance made one instantly forget that she was overweight and frumpy.

He and Drake hung their badges on their jacket pockets, waiting while she fumbled with the catch on her visitor's pass. He pushed a button next to a heavy door, and when it buzzed, yanked it wide.

On the way down the long hallway, she asked, "How do you feel about the death penalty, Sergeant Murphy?" Her question caught him by surprise.

"Keeps 'em off the streets."

"It certainly does that." She laughed shortly, and then said, "Have you ever seen anyone executed?"

He didn't much care for the direction this discussion was headed. "I've seen people die in the war, Ms. Hunter. So has Bear. Death is never pretty."

"But executed... have you seen a man executed?" she persisted. When he didn't answer right away, she went on, quietly. "I have. The last person to die in Walla Walla was one of my clients. I *made* myself sit through it. Some sort of penitence, I suppose, for not getting him off. It was the most horrible thing you could ever imagine one human being doing to another. They hanged him — his head was severed. Would you like for me to describe it to you, Frank?"

"Not particularly, but if you're enjoying this..."

"I won't. But I do wish every person who advocates the death penalty would be required to sit through it, just once — let them see what it is they're endorsing."

They stopped outside a large metal door with a thick plastic slot for a window, and Drake pushed a button on the wall. From the other side, they could hear hard-soled shoes click, approaching on the tile floor.

"I don't believe it'd change the mind of the families of those three little girls who were butchered," Murphy said as they waited.

"Perhaps. Revenge *is* a strong emotion. Maybe I'd feel differently, too, if one of them had been my daughter."

A burly Corrections Officer opened the door and silently stood back to let them enter. When they were inside, the big guard made sure the door was securely closed, then led off without a word.

Drake spoke for the first time since entering the secure area, whispering, "They must hire these guys by the inch."

Murphy had noticed a long time ago how people tended to whisper whenever they were in these halls, almost as if in a church. Peggy Hunter also whispered. "I felt compelled to let Albert know about it. The execution, I mean. After all, it's not the best recommendation to a new client, you know. I don't suppose he had much choice though, being poor as a church mouse — not to mention this being less than a desirable case to build an attorney's reputation on."

Two wide, steel-bar gates parted and after they'd walked through, clanged shut behind them with a sound of finality. From his previous visits, Murphy knew they'd arrived. The guard unlocked the door to a small interview room containing four stark chairs and a metal table. Murphy seated himself, while Peggy paced back and forth. Drake remained beside the door, peeking through the small slit of a window. Footsteps could be heard approaching; Drake let them know the footsteps belonged to Albert and his guard.

"Why did you take this case then? Do you need the money that badly?"

Peggy said, "I think I took it because I might get him off. I have to."

One of the custodians entered with Burbakowski, who remained standing in the center of the small interview room, as if uncertain what he should do. He looked terrified.

"Albert, these men are detectives," Peggy told him. "They're going to ask you some questions. Just answer them as truthfully as you can, unless I stop you. Okay?"

Peggy Hunter chose a chair and opened her briefcase. Albert nodded and sat in the chair his attorney pushed toward him. He looked stiff and uncomfortable, repeatedly clearing his throat.

Murphy studied the man as the interview progressed. Albert Burbakowski was about twenty-five years old, five-eight, at least twenty pounds overweight, and badly in need of a bath. His neck-length, long unkempt hair, oily from neglect, hung in strands, and his nails were gnawed to the quick. Murphy also perceived he was inarticulate, uneducated, and most likely, mentally deficient. His eyes were dull and listless. He appeared lethargic and seemed to need to concentrate deeply to answer the simplest questions.

The prosecution is gonna have a field day with you on the stand, Albert, Murphy thought, as he scribbled on his pad.

The detectives questioned him for almost an hour, during which Peggy only disallowed two questions — one, when Drake asked if he did it — the other, when he'd asked if Albert would take a polygraph test.

Hunter had countered, "Perhaps I'll consent to the test later."

Murphy looked at the prisoner's bowed head, trying to pick out his features through the stringy hair. "Any questions of us before we go, Albert?"

For the first time he seemed to display some interest in what was going on around him. "Do the people in my church know about any of this?" he said softly.

Murphy hesitated, considering lying, then took a deep breath. "It's in all the papers, Albert. I'm sorry." Burbakowski dropped his head again and never looked up as they departed.

————

Comparing notes later, he and Drake determined that Albert had left the church at five minutes before midnight, just as the Reverend had remarked earlier. They'd also discovered that Albert Burbakowski had never held a driver's license, and if he was to be believed, had never learned how to drive.

"The Coroner's report said the time of death was between 11:30 p.m. and 12:30 a.m., probably closer to midnight, but he was unwilling to swear to it," Murphy said.

Drake nodded his agreement. "That means Albert would've had only thirty-five minutes to get from the church to wherever the girl was kept... maybe his place... then from his address in Queen Anne, go to the apartment and kill the girl."

"Unless he killed her someplace else before he took her there," Murphy reasoned. "That's what the Prosecutor's Office is undoubtedly going to argue."

"Well, if he did, he would've had to carry her all the way to the crime scene on his shoulders, because he doesn't own an automobile, and probably couldn't drive one anyway. Also, he didn't keep her at his place, Frank," Drake stated. "The forensics team didn't turn up any evidence of her and it would've been nearly impossible for anyone to have cleaned up all the traces. Especially in that squalor!"

"I agree," Murphy replied. "So, what if he'd kept her somewhere else, nearby? An old warehouse — storage shed — vacant house, something like that?"

"He'd still have needed a vehicle to transport her, alive or dead," Drake said. "And as far as we can determine, Albert Burbakowski doesn't drive and never has."

"True, true. It just doesn't fit, Bear. They've got the wrong man."

"Yeah, the poor bastard. They're gonna crucify him."

Chapter 14

As Elnore started down the long flight of concrete steps leading from the Public Safety Building to the street below, she saw Frank and Drake coming toward her. Deeply involved in their discussion, neither noticed her until she was almost directly in front of them. Startled, both men stopped and gawked.

"Hello, Frank," she said softly.

He didn't answer, just calmly looked through her.

"Why, hello Elnore," Drake intervened. "You're sure looking *good!*"

Elnore knew she looked *good* these days. After all, she worked out two hours a day at the "Y", had a schedule that would keep anyone trim, and had recently replaced her whole wardrobe.

Still, she wished it'd been Frank who'd said it. She gave Drake one of her smiles that made most men squirm and replied in a silky voice. "Thank you, Bear. You always were such a gentleman." She continued, gazing pointedly at Frank. "I hear you're the ones who nabbed the Headhunter."

Murphy cringed at the name. He still didn't acknowledge her remarks, but nodded noncommittally.

"Congratulations on a good job, Frank. I've been chosen to prosecute him," she said, outwardly pleased at having been entrusted with such a high profile case. "Looks like we'll be working together on it."

That proved too much for him to swallow silently.

"Fat chance! He's the *wrong guy*—just some poor smuck who happened to be in the wrong place at the wrong time." He maintained his dour expression, purposely short with his remark.

Elnore wasn't sure she'd heard him right. Capitalizing on her disbelief, he went on harshly. "Sorry to interrupt your chance at career progression, Elnore. But the simple fact is, this guy just didn't do it."

Elnore quickly regained her composure and drew herself up to her full height. The act had a way of making her generous, firm breasts poke against the front of her silk blouse; a fact she was fully aware of — and the effect it had on most men.

"Lieutenant Borden says you've got an air-tight case against him."

"Borden's an asshole," Murphy answered without malice. Drake was trying to maintain his interest in the decorative trim around the courthouse roof half a block away, hoping he wouldn't be drawn into this.

"Councilman James also claims he's guilty," she said, narrowing her gray eyes. At last, this remark finally evoked some emotion from her estranged husband. It wasn't exactly what she'd bargained for.

"Well now *Ms. McDonald*, just because you're bumping uglies with someone, you can't always believe their *pillow talk* —now can you?"

He shouldered past her up the steps, stating sullenly as he passed, "By the way, Robert James is an asshole, too. Please pass that on to him."

Drake flashed her a warm smile and followed his buddy through the revolving doors, gawking over his shoulder at remarkably long tapered legs below the short skirt.

"*Shit,* Murph! What a dish! I still can't believe you used to bang that!"

He didn't answer, so Drake persisted. "Ya know what?"

"Please don't tell me."

"A railroad spike, my man. An honest to god, diamond cutter."

"Figures."

Drake lost sight of the million dollar legs as he rounded a corner in the hallway, and nearly took out two gray-haired secretaries in tennis shoes leaving for their daily walk around the block. The fat one sneered disgustedly at him, as though she'd read his mind.

"Ya know, Murph. I think something's going on with my *dick* these days," Drake whispered loudly, hurrying to catch up as Murphy lengthened his stride, trying to out-distance his loud-mouthed partner.

By the reactions of several other ladies headed the opposite direction, they'd also heard his raspy whispers. Murphy felt their eyes boring holes into his back.

"For *Christ's sake*, Bear, get it off your mind. And keep it down to a low roar, will you? Where the hell did you learn to whisper anyway? A sawmill?"

Elnore watched the two men disappear into the stone building, then quickly crossed the street, dodging heavy traffic. A cabbie laid on his horn and she flipped him off. He rolled down his window shouting, "Anytime, sweet buns, anytime!"

Shit, she thought. That's not the way she'd wanted her first meeting with Frank to turn out. *Shit! Shit! Shit!*

She hurried toward the Lexus coupe she'd recently leased and eased inside. Gripping the wheel, she stared into space, her thoughts fragmented and confused. *Why does he have to be so hard on me?* She asked herself, tears burning her eyes. *All right, so I screwed up — really bad — but if he'd only give me a chance to talk — discuss it — but no, not Frank Murphy. He'll never forgive me!*

Tears flooded her eyes again, and she quickly blinked them back. No! She wouldn't cry. Not now, not ever again!

Damn you, Frank Murphy! She placed the car in gear and merged into the heavy downtown traffic.

———————

Wiping his hands on a paper towel, Captain Brooks stepped from the men's room, just as the object of Elnore's anger rounded the corner, nearly colliding with him. Brooks halted abruptly, silently gazing at Murphy. "You sure stepped on your foreskin at *that* little meeting today, didn't you?"

"Tromped all over it with baseball cleats," Murphy admitted, honestly.

"When *are* you gonna learn, Frank? You got to go along. You can't fight every battle that comes your way, or eventually, they're gonna get you." Brooks waited for an answer.

"If that means getting into bed with the likes of Butthead Borden and Beavis James, forget it, Tom. I'll just wear a flak jacket and stand with my back against the wall," Murphy said.

"Uh huh, well..." Brooks jerked his head, indicating he expected Murphy and Drake to follow him, and headed for his office.

Captain Brooks retrieved a paper from the stack on his desk, pushing it toward him. "Here's a search warrant for the address where the leader of that Korean shotgun gang has been known to frequent. Kisop Shinn, it says here. Probably spelled wrong, but who's to say? It may be a wild goose chase, but you might as well try to tie up the last loose end of that case."

Within moments, they'd returned to the task force office to see who might be available to assist them. Lisa, sorting through a stack of printouts, looked up and smiled as they entered.

"Grab your gear, Officer Kinard. You get to go on a real bust this time," he told her, then grimaced at her eagerness.

The address in West Seattle was near White Center, a small apartment complex Murphy recalled from his days as a uniformed officer responding to domestic incidents and drug raids. It'd once been shabby, but had recently been painted a pastel pink. It hadn't helped. It still looked shabby. It was a type structure he'd hated going into; three elongated units constructed in a semi-circle, every apartment facing the center, with long deck balconies across the rear of each building.

Because of the way they were built, they were extremely difficult to approach without everybody in the entire complex knowing the cops had arrived. Plus, they were equally easy to exit by the rear, with most suspects beat-feeting it through the back lots into the adjoining woods. Several years before in a similar setup, a few officers had been ambushed as they attempted to enter one of the buildings, caught in crossfire. That's one reason he'd decided to go in with just the three of them.

"Lisa, see the long balcony with the staircases at each end?" Murphy pointed and Lisa nodded.

"You stay on this end. Cover the stairs that lead from that corner apartment that have the throw rugs hung over the rail. See it?"

She nervously nodded again, and picked up her radio.

Murphy was impressed as he watched her prepare. She unsnapped her sidearm, turned down the volume on the radio and checked to see that there was a spare magazine she could get at quickly, if needed. He'd given her the back door assignment because he'd wanted to protect her as much as possible. After all, she *was* the Judge's niece."

That's all I'd need to completely wreck my life — get the Judge's niece shot to pieces by sending her through the front door after a cold-blooded killer. That is, if he's even here.

He and Drake waited until they heard her press the talk button twice. It was the prearranged signal Lisa was to use to let them know when she was in place. He and Drake edged quietly up the soggy, water-rotted steps and stopped outside the apartment door—Drake on the right and Murphy on the left, both hugging the walls.

Standing to one side, Drake knocked loudly. "Police! Open up! Search warrant! Search warrant!"

A faint scraping sound was heard from inside, then silence.

"Police! I said open up and I mean *right now*! Don't make me have to say it again!"

They readied themselves to kick down the door, and were both unprepared for the loud blast that rang out. A large hole magically appeared in the apartment door.

"*Motherfucker!*" Drake screamed.

Murphy kicked the lock and the rotten wood gave up on the first try. He went low and Drake went high, entering with pistols shoved before them. They heard the crash of broken glass in the rear of the apartment. *Lisa!*

Bounding across the room, Frank cautiously peered around the corner of the open bedroom door, seeing a broken window. Sweat streamed between his shoulders, sticking the shirt to his back. Despite that, he felt cold. *Shit, what a way to make a living!*

Grasping his pistol with sweaty palms, he edged around the door, quickly scanning the room. It was empty except for a discarded shotgun lying on the floor. He rushed to the window, flattening himself against the wall. Carefully leaning out, he caught a glimpse of a fleeing man as he disappeared around the corner. Lisa was on his heels; then, she too was out of sight.

Pivoting quickly, he collided hard with his partner. It was like hitting a tree.

"Out the front! *Quick*!"

They retraced their steps through the living room and onto the front stairway, just in time to see the running man stumble down the last few steps at the far end of the complex. Before he could regain his feet, Lisa Kinard landed squarely between his shoulders, driving his face into the pavement.

Murphy charged down the moss-slick stairs three at a time, never taking his eyes off Lisa and the man. The suspect tried to throw her off, and he watched in amazement when she clubbed him in the head with her radio. As she wrenched his arm up behind his back, he screamed in pain. By the time he and Drake arrived gasping for breath, Lisa had the suspect cuffed, staring up the barrel of her 9mm automatic.

"Jeez, *Rambo*, back off. We've got him now," he panted, skidding to a halt.

When Drake, puffing, reached them, he fell to his knees and lifted the man's head. Murphy could see it was, indeed, Kisop Shinn — the leader of the so-called *Shotgun Gang*. Gasping air into his tortured lungs, he sagged to the grimy steps and noticed Drake was bent over, his hands on his knees, also having trouble in that department. *Those damned cigarettes are going to kill you, Sport.* Glancing up, he noticed Lisa barely breathing heavy, busily taking inventory of her gear. *Jeez!*

Drake coughed and spit a lumpy wad on the ground. "I think I'm gonna puke."

After booking the fugitive, Murphy and Drake had both been subjected to some shrill catcalls and friendly ribbing about Lisa having to "pull their nuts out of the fire". Lisa, of course, instantly became everybody's sweetheart and awarded the time-honored, *Super Cop Award*, nothing more than a picture of a pig in a cop's hat. As they trooped together into Brooks' office, he even managed to smile at them for a change. *Never saw him do that before*, thought Murphy. *In fact, I never even knew he could smile. Wonder what he's going to shove to us this time?*

"Great job!" Brooks half shouted. "That should get City Hall off our backs." He pushed back in his chair and smiled at Lisa. "I wouldn't be surprised if someone got a citation out of this."

Lisa blushed and dropped her head. "We all got this guy, sir. None of us could've done it alone. No one could."

"Yeah, yeah, I know. Team effort, and all that," Brooks growled. "But what this department needs right now, more than anything else, is a hero. Like it or not, looks like you're it, Officer Kinard."

Murphy could see that didn't set all that well with her, but the young officer didn't comment. *Wish I could learn to do more of that,* he thought. *She's got a great future in the department if she can keep her mouth shut.*

Drake dropped Lisa off at her car and Murphy reminded her, "Have your report on my desk first thing in the morning, Lisa. I know you have psychology classes in the evenings so I'm giving you a break by not requiring it today."

"Thanks Boss," she said pertly. "It's been a full day. I think I'll head home and get in an hour of studying."

They watched as she climbed into her white Honda Civic and drove away. "That's one hell of a little girl," Murphy said. "I wish I had just half her energy."

"One hell of a cop, too," Drake followed up. "Did you see how she tossed that dirt-bag around? She's in great shape, but I just can't believe she's that strong!"

"The Judge told me she'd trained to be an Olympic gymnast. I understand they have to be pretty strong to do that stuff. Besides, the Judge also said she's pretty heavy into martial arts."

"Man, I hear that! Don't get *Super Cop* pissed off at you!" he exclaimed. They laughed about that for a moment, and then prepared to head home.

"Want to come by for KFC? It's the only thing Mable knows how to make." Drake joked.

"Sure, why not?"

"Why don't you bring your lady... what's her name, Julie? Bring Julie with you."

Murphy snorted. "I'm not letting you get within pissing distance of her, you horny bastard."

Drake laughed and slapped Murphy on the shoulder, which immediately went numb. "I get the impression you're kinda hung up on her."

"Well, she is *one* remarkable woman, but we'll give it time and see what develops. My track record with women isn't all that great." He suddenly thought about BJ.

On the way to Drake's, he called BJ's home number from his cellular, but with no response. He vowed to drive by her house on his way home, just to see if she was all right.

———————

The little black bitch hadn't been there! *Cunt! Stupid little cunt!* He pounded on the steering wheel with the heel of his hand. *She'd better not piss me off,* he thought, as spittle ran unnoticed down his chin. *She don't know what I'm capable of when I get pissed off!* Angrily, he pounded his temples, then froze and stared out the smoked glass windshield. *OK. OK! Calm down. There's still plenty of time.*

The *voice* wasn't real happy about his doing the other girl, but advised him to be sure to get the right one next time. He had time. The *voice* wasn't going to be unreasonable, but he sure couldn't afford any more fuck-ups.

Tomorrow he'd be informed of the little black girl's whereabouts and given more specific instructions. Just thinking about it, his breathing quickened and he felt a familiar stirring. Yes, he had time.

Chapter 15

Abie McNeill was almost seventy-years-old. Born in Birmingham, Alabama, she'd left the Deep South at eighteen and moved to Puget Sound when she married Charles McNeill II, the son of a wealthy land developer. Backed by family money, her new husband had made a fortune in the timber business. In fact, her husband had made no fewer than three fortunes during his lifetime, but had lost two and a half of them. Abie figured he'd have lost the other half too, if he hadn't keeled over from a massive heart attack thirty-three years ago.

Although she was pregnant with their son at the time, she'd never told him. He would've been *furious,* she often mused. It was one of the few things he couldn't control, and Abie felt time running out if she was ever going to have a child. She'd been nearly forty when little Charles was born. It was the happiest day of her life.

During the last twenty years she'd lived pretty much alone except for her three cats named after Charles II's three pompous brothers; Darnel, Pollard, and Alfred. His brothers had shown up right after Charles' death, convinced they were entitled to a part of their brother's *vast* wealth — vast wealth? She'd laughed right in their faces at the absurdity.

Oh, she was comfortable, and had spent little of what remained through the years, except to pay for gardeners, maid services, and her taxes. She'd watched as her investments increased over the years, once again accumulating a considerable fortune from the money Charles had left her. Some time ago, she'd made up her mind to call that slick old lawyer who'd run Charles' legal affairs, Wilford "Happy" Billingsly, and told him to leave it all to one of her favorite charities.

That was before she'd found out she had a granddaughter. It bothered her none that Amanda was "*half-colored*." In fact, it amused her that part of Charles' money would be left to such a child. She could almost hear the old racist spinning in his grave. It'd given her occasion to smile more than once in the past few days.

As Lisa and BJ pulled to the curb in front of BJ's house, they heard the phone ring. Rushing to get it, she was too late, but saw that Frank had left a message. He seemed genuinely concerned about her welfare and she smiled. *Sweet,* she thought. *Now don't go reading anything into it,* she chided herself. He'd probably do the same for any of them. Still, it had been *very* sweet.

She and Lisa had gone out for coffee and a sandwich after work again tonight, the second time in a week. She was beginning to like Lisa — finally glad to have another female presence in the squad room. A little longer of working only around men and BJ felt as if she might begin to grow a penis and sprout hair on her chest.

She was also glad Lisa had offered to stop in Everett and check on Amanda on her way to Bellingham. BJ called her daughter every day, but it wasn't the same as seeing her, and she knew she wouldn't be able to go to Everett until the following weekend. Amanda would remain with her grandmother until they caught the man who had butchered her best friend, Kathy.

Although BJ didn't really think there was any danger, she was glad her daughter was out of harm's way for a while.

She had finally gotten a chance to meet Abie McNeill, too; Amanda's other grandmother. BJ had met Abie's son, Charles, during a fraud investigation of a company he'd once represented. She'd never considered dating a white man until he asked her out, and soon found him to be most charming. Soon, she had no doubt her growing love for him was mutual.

Charlie's problem was that he'd become a recreational cocaine user and had gotten his hands on an ounce far more potent than anything he'd ever encountered. His mother had found him slumped over the wheel of his BMW one morning and called 911, but it was too late. Charles McNeill III, brilliant Bellevue attorney and soon-to-be father of BJ's unborn daughter, was dead—just as was BJ's dream of their life together.

She'd never met Abie nor told her about the child, believing the old southern woman would be adamantly against their mixed union. But when this latest trouble came up, BJ had impulsively called her and was delighted by the warmth she'd heard in the voice on the other end. She'd also been surprised to learn that Charles had mentioned their relationship with his mother. Not all of it, only her first name. That was why Abie hadn't contacted her all these years.

With bittersweet feelings, she'd packed Amanda's clothes and driven her north on I-5 to Everett to see her grandmother for the first time. If things had worked out differently, BJ felt she might've been meeting her mother-in-law.

Julie pulled her sleek green Jaguar into the circular drive of Robert James' house. Carefully glancing around, she strode quickly to the front door, opened it with her key, and slipped inside. She knew her way, and that the help would be off today. Dropping her jacket on the floor in route, she automatically headed for the curved stairs and climbed them briskly, her heart racing. She opened the first door in the long hallway into the master bedroom. James was seated upright in a straight-backed upholstered chair near the bed, fully dressed, a stiff leather riding crop in one hand—intermittently slapping it against his other palm. Julie shivered deliciously.

Without prompting, she moved to the Hollywood king-sized bed, picked up a thick leather collar and snapped it around her neck. Reaching beneath her long red hair, she unhooked a single button and her long cotton dress dropped in a crumpled heap at her feet. She was naked. Breathing rapidly, she descended to her knees and knelt before him, slowly unzipping his pants. She reached inside.

"Did you get the information I asked for?"

"Yes," she mumbled. "Everything you asked for, and..."

He let her talk until she finished and looked up expectantly.

"Go ahead," he ordered, and she obediently lowered her head.

Abie, contently rocking in her favorite chair, observed her granddaughter as she devoured milk and cookies. *Such a beautiful child!* Abie could see her son's likeness in her grandchild's mocha features. The old woman had never been as happy as she watched Darnel's tail switch in the young girl's face, trying to gain her attention. Amanda gently picked him up and let him nibble a small amount of her cookie; quickly the other two cats joined them, seeking their share. Amanda giggled, hugging and feeding them all, one-by-one.

Abie thought Amanda seemed comfortable with her. *After all, she's a child of a new era, and race is less of an issue than it used to be when I was that age — at least among youngsters.*

Abie recalled BJ mentioning Amanda's young freckled-face *boyfriend* from one of her classes, and that her best friend Kathy had been a tow-headed blond.

BJ had cautioned that Amanda had taken the loss of her best friend extremely hard, and to watch for sudden tears or other signs of depression she'd exhibited lately. Noticing a subtle mood swing Abie suddenly stood, and announced, "Come with me, Sugar. I've got something to show you."

Abie led her to a closed room on the second floor of her Victorian home. Pushing the heavy door open, she stood aside and watched as the little girl's eyes lit up. It was the *most magnificent* collection of dolls Amanda had ever seen! Rag dolls, porcelain dolls, wooden dolls, big ones, little ones, even black ones!

"There must be over a hundred dolls!" Amanda stared in awe, her mouth agape, and the old woman chuckled.

"I brought these all the way from Alabama over sixty years ago. I've had 'em ever since I was a little girl — just about your age, Sugar."

Amanda's eyes danced from first one, then to another.

"Go ahead, you can pick them up," Abie prompted softly, enjoying the girl's bewilderment.

Amanda moved toward one with a white-laced dress, but quickly changed her mind, instead selecting a worn antique rag doll with big cloth shoes. Abie smiled.

"That one was my favorite, too. Old Charles 'bout had a duck-fit when I told him I wasn't coming if I had to leave my dolls behind." She crackled, leaning on her cane for support.

"After we were married, I used to sneak up here and pretend they were my children. Then I had my own baby to care for... your father. After he was born, I didn't have as much time as before, but I'd still get up here now and then."

Abie moved to a closet and opened the door. "Come. There's something else I want you to see. A secret just between us girls."

Amanda joined her and peered cautiously inside as the old woman slid a panel aside, revealing a long passageway with narrow stairs, leading downward.

"This leads to the back storage room. It was included when the house was originally built, in the mid-eighteen hundreds. Some say this place used to belong to a smuggler and this was his escape plan. No one knows for sure, but that's how I used to get up here without being detected by 'Sir' Charles." She laughed again. "The old fool thought I was in the kitchen working all the time."

"Did my father ever come up here and play with them?" Amanda said, her eyes large.

Abie crackled her dry laugh. "Oh yes. At least until he started to get older and realized they were for little girls. Then he still used the secret tunnel to play pirates. Hid his little treasures all through it, I would imagine."

The old woman looked a little sad, as though remembering things from days long past, then she brightened. "Now, they're *your* dolls, Sugar. Love 'em and take care of 'em. Someday you may have a little girl and she can enjoy them as much as we did."

Amanda gently laid the doll back into its vacant spot and hugged Abie. "Thank you, Grandma," she whispered. "I love you." She giggled giddily, heading for the dolls again.

A loud knocking at the front door suddenly interrupted them.

Murphy had downed several beers at Bear's. Mable was out with the girls and the kids were studying, so they'd had the kitchen and the TV all to themselves. The Lakers had beaten the Sonic's again and the game had run into overtime. He'd declined the invitation to crash on the couch, opting to head for the boat.

As he wound his way back toward the marina, he suddenly realized how close he was to BJ's place. Turning quickly, he was there within a matter of minutes, surprised to see her lights still on. He drove past slowly, turned around at the cul-de-sac and backtracked.

Without making a conscious decision to do so, he wheeled sharply into her driveway — letting the car idle for several minutes. Eventually the front porch light flooded the lawn, and he switched off his engine.

As he approached the front door, it opened, revealing BJ in her robe — her hair disheveled. She thrust an opened beer toward him. Murphy thought she was the sexiest looking thing he'd ever seen, but quickly shoved the intrusive thought deep into his subconscious, grabbed the beer, and downed half of it.

"God, BJ," he said with satisfaction. "Why aren't you married? Any woman who can read a man's mind... well, you certainly know how to treat a man."

"Don't get your hopes up, Stud. I opened that one for me, but you looked like you needed it worse," she said. "What brings you out this time of night? Don't you know the streets aren't safe?" She moved aside for him to enter.

"Well, uh... I was just checking on you. I didn't know you'd be up and I'd get caught." He looked a little sheepish as he said it.

"You usually do this?"

He blushed again, this time a bright red, avoiding her eyes. "Once in a while. I know it can be kind of rough for a woman living alone, with all the punks running around, so... sometimes I just drive past."

"All those other times, why didn't you just knock on the door and come in for a drink? Sneaking around like that... I might've shot your nose off before I realized it was my boss." BJ smiled, thinking she'd been right; he was a sweet man — though she'd never say it to his face. *Not when he tries so hard to hide it.*

He drained the can in two long swallows. "Well, I better take off and let you get some sleep."

"Why? You tired?"

She walked into the kitchen and returned with two more frosty cans. Murphy reluctantly took one, sat at one end of the couch and drank deeply.

"Amanda still out of town?" He said, more to initiate conversation than for any real desire to know.

BJ nodded and swallowed some beer. "Yes. I expect she *will* be too, until this thing is over." Darkness suddenly clouded her face. "Killing is too good for him."

"You're a cop, BJ. You're supposed to be unaffected."

"Right! Like you wouldn't blow the mother away if you got the chance."

"Well, I'd feel *bad* about it later."

BJ struggled with herself, trying to find the right words to say. "We used to be kind of close, Frank. Remember?"

"You want to start going out for beer and pizza again?"

"That's *not* what I meant and you know it, asshole!" Fire shot from her eyes and frost tinted her words. "What happened, Frank? You were a nice guy. Everybody liked you. Oh, I know all about your daughter… and Elnore. But it's more than that. For the last six months you've gone out of your way to piss people off and keep them at arm's length. It's as though you *want* to self-destruct."

"Oh come on, BJ, don't try to sugar-coat it! Just tell me how you really feel," he retorted sarcastically.

BJ silently stared at him until he began to feel uncomfortable. Softly, she said, "That's what I mean, Frank — a smart-ass answer for everything. You've shut everyone out except for Bear. I thought *we* were friends, too." She quickly turned her face away, but not before he saw the moisture in her eyes.

"I'm sorry, BJ. We *are* friends. We always will be."

When she wouldn't face him, he knew she was really angry—or hurt. "I *said* I was sorry. Look, see all the little sorry marks on my face? See?" He craned his neck to look into her eyes. At last, she rewarded him with a tight smile.

Something about that smile made Murphy recall the evening that he and BJ had first discovered their mutual attraction and how dangerously close they'd come to letting it ruin their friendship. He'd been happily married then, and while he'd liked to admire a well-turned ankle as well as the next guy, he was still devoted to his marriage — especially to his daughter, Tina. He'd never cheated on Elnore, even through the worst of it after Tina's death. Not until he'd caught her in bed with James.

He wondered if BJ ever thought about the nightly struggles they'd gone through, resisting the sweet temptation to head for the nearest motel and give into what they'd both wanted so desperately.

"What happened with Elnore? Oh, I know all about James. I mean, couldn't you somehow forgive her?"

Murphy mulled over the remark before answering. "Despair is like a black bottomless pit, BJ. When two people love and trust each other, they build a rock. Every year their love gets stronger and the rock grows larger. If you fall into the pit you can climb back onto the rock and pull yourself out. But when that trust is damaged, a chunk of the rock falls off, and it never grows back. The bigger the hurt, the larger the chunk. Over time, it erodes completely, and you have nothing left with which to pull yourself out of despair."

Murphy swallowed hard, his face reflecting his pain. "First losing Tina that way, then Elnore... I was near the edge anyway. In the early going, I almost ended it. Just two pounds of pressure on the trigger of a service revolver, and it's over. I carried a 'special bullet' around for months. Once I had made up my mind to do it, life somehow became a bit easier, because I knew I had the solution if things got any worse."

He smiled sadly at her. "The 'special bullet' was Doc Larsen's idea. She helped me get through the worst of it."

BJ stared horrified, contemplating for the first time, the true depth of Murphy's despair. Once started, he let it all pour out. "It got bad, BJ. Nightmares, cold sweats, drinking binges."

He drained his can and held it aimlessly, then went on in a raspy whisper. "Everyday I woke up, I had to find a reason to go on living one more day. Twice, I put the muzzle in my mouth and tried to pull the trigger. Close, but no cigar. Guess I just wasn't ready to concede yet. I saw Doc Larsen almost everyday — and called her even more often. Couldn't have made it without her help. Then this case came up. I had to get involved — things became a little easier after that. Or I've just grown numb. Either way, it gave me purpose, a way to seek closure. I'm better now."

He smiled weakly. "Hell, I don't think about killing myself but about once a week anymore."

She didn't return his smile, so he sobered and went on, "Some days it would get so bad I didn't want to get out of bed in the morning. I started hitting the sauce... built up a wall against anyone who might hurt me."

He stood and walked to the large picture window facing the street. He turned back, looking at her steadily. "It used to kill me to see you and Amanda together. I loved my little girl so much that I just couldn't handle it. I was eaten up with jealousy over the two of you together. So I stayed away. Pretty stupid, huh?"

BJ went to him, placed her hands on his shoulders, hugging him. Murphy felt the urge to pull her closer and kiss her. He felt his face redden, and suddenly stepped back. "I really have to be going, BJ."

She smiled and inched toward him again, touching his cheek. "I know what lonely is too, Frank. Remember?"

He covered her hand with his and put his lips to it. "I know. But this is just not a good idea. Too many complications."

Suddenly, their mouths crushed together. Murphy's hands slipped inside the robe, finding soft, warm breasts, feeling her nipples harden against his palms. Her tongue darted into his mouth and her hands tugged wildly at his belt. He had a railroad spike! Abruptly, he shoved her, retreating several steps. She followed, and he fended her off.

"No! Dammit, *no*, BJ!"

She'd never looked so good to him, her robe parted — the plump, bee-stung lips — her half-closed eyes, gasping for breath. She heard the desire in his voice as he spoke softer. "I want to, BJ. Lord knows I do. But it's not fair to you. I roam the bars at night and pump the local police-groupies. You know why? Because there's no pay back, no obligations, no regrets."

"Maybe that's what I want, too," she finally whispered.

"Bull-shit! That's not you. I've never known you to even go out on a date! Hell, you don't have the time."

"It could be that I don't want just anybody, Frank. Maybe it's you I want. Did you ever think of that?"

"I'd be a fool to say I haven't thought about you and me together, BJ. A lot of times, in fact, and I'm not the only one. Just about every man on the force would give a month's pay to jump between your sheets, including me. But I... well, hell, BJ, I think too much of you." BJ smiled seductively and Murphy felt himself move below the belt again.

"Do you, Frank? In what way?"

"Well... as a friend. A fellow officer... a..." he stopped. "I've got feelings for you BJ. You know that. But we can't let it happen. If we did, we couldn't work together anymore. Don't you see?"

She moved to him and placed her head against his chest. "Frank. Sweet Frank," she murmured. "You try so hard to make everybody believe you're a hard-ass." She looked up. "I have feelings for you, too, Frank. Don't wait too long, okay?"

BJ felt miserable as she stood in the doorway and watched Murphy drive away. She suddenly shivered, pulling her robe tightly around her as she glanced toward the wooded area across the cul-de-sac, as though expecting to catch sight of someone there. She saw nothing, but had an unsettling feeling she was being watched. She hurriedly closed the door and slammed the heavy dead-bolt lock into place.

Just jumpy, I guess.

Still, she made a resolution to keep her 9mm automatic nearby, just in case.

Amanda hurried down the stairs well ahead of her grandmother and reached the front door first. Standing on her tiptoes, she peered through the peephole, just as her mother had instructed her to do. There was a lady outside — a *pretty* one, too. Amanda attached the chain and cracked the door open a few inches.

"Yes? Can I help you, ma'am?"

The lady smiled, confirming Amanda's first impression. She *was* pretty! "I'm Lisa Kinard. I work with your mother, and I'm a police officer, too. She asked me to stop and check on you. I have friends who live further north, so I thought I'd just drop by."

"Oh, yes," Amanda cried, opening the door wider. "She said you'd be by to visit. Won't you please come in, Miss Kinard?"

As Lisa stepped in, she glanced briefly at the dirty white van parked just up the street, surprised she hadn't noticed it before when she'd parked. Something tugged at her subconscious, and then was just as quickly forgotten.

Amanda delighted the two women by playing the consummate hostess, serving tea and cookies to their guest, telling funny antidotes about the cats, and describing the dolls in remarkable detail. The secret tunnel, she kept to herself. After all, she'd promised her grandmother it would be *their* secret. Abie and Lisa conversed lightheartedly, secretly stealing smiling glances at one another, amused by Amanda's attempts to act grown-up.

"Your mother will be up to see you on Sunday," Lisa said. "Hopefully, we'll catch the bad guy soon and everyone can feel safe again."

Amanda smiled at Lisa, struck by the young officer's beauty then rose and hugged her, smelling the rich fragrance of her perfume as she often did with her mother.

"When all this is over, would you like to go skiing with me when the season opens, Amanda? Your mother tells me you are a fine skier," Lisa said.

"Yes! Oh, yes. I *love* to ski! I can hardly wait!"

"Okay, consider that a promise. We have a date."

Lisa's visit was brief, but as she left, she did notice the white van that'd been parked across the street was gone.

Driving home after leaving BJ, Frank Murphy did a lot of thinking. He'd always known she'd liked him, and he knew *damned well* he liked her. For the second time that night, his mind drifted back to when she'd first come to work with him and Bear, and the three of them had spent a lot of time together. He'd never tried to touch her, even after that night they'd danced and the fiery attraction had developed. She'd hinted through small subtleties that she wouldn't have minded too much if it happened again, a fact that had often played on his mind. Having a beautiful, classy woman covet him was good for his ego, but being married was a full-time job and he'd had a daughter he thought the world of.

He still got goose bumps every time he recalled that night after pizza and beer, and both of their heated reactions to a perfectly innocent slow dance. Deep down he wondered if his reluctance to get involved with her was all that noble. Was he just being selfish?

Was it because she was black and he was white? He was aware of his own human prejudices. Everyone had them, but they hadn't influenced him since he'd been a youth in high school. Why now?

He didn't see Bear as a black man, only a man; someone he loved like a brother. BJ was slender, mocha-colored, with fine classic features. Her hair, brunette rather than black and large dark eyes made her appearance more Hispanic than anything. But, she *was* black. Could that fact be the reason he was subconsciously pushing her away? He thought of other interracial couples who'd overcome such obstacles. Was it the obstacles that scared him? If so he were indeed being selfish, for little Amanda, being half of each race would have more than her share to endure, and without a father.

The image of BJ when he'd left her crossed his mind, and he felt another ping. No, he decided, it wasn't prejudices. He wanted her — a lot — but that still wasn't it. Then, it dawned on him. He was scared. He'd been burned before and that was enough. He'd *liked* Molly Atwood, and while they'd been lovers, it'd been more like a great friendship than a connecting of souls. Still, it'd taken a long time for him to get over the loss of that friendship and her betrayal.

Elnore? She'd been different. He'd been head-over-heels in love with her. He'd always taken it for granted that Elnore loved him as much as he did her. Perhaps she did in the beginning, but separate careers have a way of pulling people apart. That's why when Tina came along, he'd been so happy — convinced the baby would be the glue that would hold them together, made them a real family.

He'd been wrong and now knew that he should've realized her resistance to having a baby went deeper than simply a concern for her career. He didn't try to fool himself about his part in the breakup. He knew what had happened between them had been partly his fault, too. Still, to forgive her sleeping with Robert James… no, that was too much to forgive.

Things were different now, though. He no longer had a family, but couldn't imagine getting seriously involved — ever again. Oh, there was wealthy, glamorous, Julie, but he suspected he was just a passing fad until she found another interest. That's the way he wanted it, too!

Shit, BJ! Why do you have to complicate my life?

He picked up his cellular and poked a single programmed number. It rang.

"Hello," said a sleepy voice.

"Julie. It's me, Frank. Can I come over?"

"Oh, yes, baby. I've been missing you."

At work the following morning, BJ acted as though nothing had happened. Murphy came in late, feeling ill at ease, but determined to put it behind him. Still, he found his eyes following her as she went about her duties, and once, when he discovered Bear gazing at him, his face suddenly turned warm. Drake suddenly brought the subject up in the unit as they headed toward Capital Hill.

"You and BJ carrying on?"

The question caught him by surprise. "No, BJ and I are not *carrying on*," he retorted sarcastically.

"Well, it looks that way," Drake persisted.

"I don't give a damn how it looks! We're not screwing around, so just drop it. Okay?"

"Good," the big man said. Then after a lengthy pause, he said, "Because if you were, I'd hope it wasn't like all the others."

"What the hell does that mean? All *what* others? You talk like I'm into triple digits, for Christ sake. Who the hell do you think I am, *Wilt-fuck'n-Chamberlain*?" Murphy indignantly puffed up, then said more quietly, "There hasn't been that many, anyway."

"Frank, the three of us have been friends for a long time and I just wouldn't want to have anything happen that'd change that for us. That's all," Drake concluded.

"Don't worry. It won't."

"Okay."

"Okay, okay, *already!*"

They rode in silence about a mile.

"I just got one more thing to say, then I'll shut up about it, okay?" Drake said looking straight ahead.

Fuming, Murphy puffed up again, hesitated, then exhaled loudly and reluctantly grunted.

Drake breathed deeply, also exhaled loudly then stated, "Do you think if Payton had taken that three-pointer instead of passing off to Kemp, the Sonics would've still lost last night?"

The two men burst out laughing. They were still laughing when Hooter's husky voice broke in on the radio.

Charley Booth came on next. "Ya better get over to the jail right away, Frank. Albert Burbakowski hung himself in his cell about an hour ago. Step on it, if you want to beat the news-hounds."

As it was, the reporters were already arriving and two uniformed jail personnel were trying to detain them outside. Booth was waiting on the steps as Drake whirled into a no-parking zone and Murphy placed the police plates on the dash. A news van had illegally parked, and traffic was already beginning to jam behind it.

Taking the steps two at a time, Murphy said, "How'd it happen, Charley?"

"We better get inside, Frank. You ain't going to like this."

As the three men rushed by the group of reporters, one shouted, "Hey, Murphy. Why don't you let us do our jobs?"

That comment brought him up short. "When you get a chance, go take a look at what's laid out on the floor of cell block W-4. That's what your '*job*' did, pal."

Hurrying to catch up with him, Drake grinned. "You sure do go out of your way to win friends and influence people, partner. You thinking about running for office?"

When Murphy didn't answer, Drake grabbed a young uniformed officer's arm as he rushed by. "Officer, get out front and ticket that illegally parked news van."

The young man grinned and nodded. Pulling away Drake yelled after him. "Ticket every fucking car on the block! You got that?"

Searching for a quiet place to talk, they finally selected a narrow spot in a stairway alcove. Murphy stated without preliminaries, "Talk to me, Charley."

Booth took a breath and started. "One of the deacons from Albert's church dropped by, just before the noon meal. Apparently he told Albert the congregation didn't want him to come back when he was released."

Murphy swore softly.

"They brought his noon meal by earlier, but he'd just sat on the edge of his bunk stoically staring at the wall. When they returned to pick up the tray thirty minutes later, they found him hanging. He'd taken off his shirt, looped one sleeve around the top of a door crossbar, placed the other sleeve around his neck and just sat down. He must've lost consciousness pretty fast, and gravity did the rest."

"Poor bastard didn't even have a family. The only thing he had was his church, and when they took that away he couldn't handle it," Drake said.

"Pastor Thomas claimed the body. Said he'd see to it that Albert got buried properly. He seemed real saddened about it," Booth said.

"Check with him and see if he needs a few bucks to help out," Murphy said, avoiding their eyes.

It was an uncomfortable silence, as each tried to think of a reason to change the subject. "I talked to Captain Brooks last night and he gave me permission to visit John Lee West," he said abruptly. "I'm driving to Walla Walla tonight."

Booth stopped in his tracks, mouth gaping.

"Holy *shit*!" Drake said under his breath.

"I know, I know," Murphy continued, acknowledging their perplexed faces. "But he's offered to help and it sounds sincere. We're at a dead end as it is — we've got to do something! Right Charley? *Right*, Bear?"

Charley whistled softly and rolled his eyes, without replying. Drake grunted, then said, "You couldn't pay me enough to face that bastard. I'd reach through the bars and throttle him if I got that close."

"Well, I'm not exactly looking forward to it myself, old buddy. I saw him once before and he scared the crap out of me. If either of you can come up with something better, let me know," Murphy said sarcastically.

Drake shrugged and walked away. Murphy stared after him, not feeling one bit better about the prospects.

166

John Lee West was awaiting execution for the rape and murder of fourteen eastern Washington housewives over a six-year period. Everyone agreed there were probably a lot more, too, if the truth were ever known. After dismembering them, he scattered their remains over the countryside for unsuspecting hikers to find. He'd finally made a fatal mistake when one of his victims survived, despite him cutting her throat and pushing her from his moving car.

He'd hurriedly left her on the side of the road to die when his police scanner alerted him about a State Patrol roadblock set up ahead. They were searching for a pair who'd just robbed the First Interstate Bank and believed to be headed in his same direction. It was John Lee West's bad luck, and the poor woman's good luck that a miracle had saved her. When she was finally able to talk, she'd identified her assailant as someone she'd seen on a local TV program, remembering him as the son of a respected family.

His prominent father had spent much of his fortune trying to get his son acquitted, but in the end, he was found guilty and sentenced to die at Walla Walla State Prison. After five years of appeals, it looked as though his capital punishment would finally be carried out the following month.

Murphy had attended the trial and recalled how unremarkable West had seemed, not at all like the monster everyone knew him to be. A son of one of the Tri-Cities original families, he'd sung with his church choir, attended WSU, excelled in their acclaimed sports program and graduated, if not with honors, at least respectfully.

But as those who followed the trial soon discovered, John Lee West was indeed, a monster. He'd taken most of his victims to an isolated family cabin in the Cascades, tortured and repeatedly assaulted them, then growing tired of them, murdered each. West was easy to label during his lengthy and costly trial; psychopath, deranged, madman. The one that stuck most in Murphy's mind was *monster*.

He'd followed the investigation and trial with interest, attempting to learn from it. As the evidence unfolded, he'd watched West change like a chameleon, from an articulate, charming young man, to a sinister and pernicious individual, who left most of the witnesses and jury shaken and fearful.

At the end, when he stood during the reading of the sentence, he'd smiled individually at each juror, seemingly disinterested. When asked by the judge if he had anything to say to the Court, he'd remarked in a quiet, friendly tone, "I'll be seeing all of you soon." Murphy recalled it'd been a singularly disquieting experience for the entire courtroom.

He hadn't seen West since his incarceration, but had heard from several security personnel that he'd become even more despicable, though many begrudgingly admitted he'd been a model prisoner. When Warden Cummings had first housed West within the general prison population he'd nearly been killed by the other inmates, so he'd soon been isolated pending his execution. Murphy had heard little of him until receipt of the letter offering to assist in his investigation of the recent Seattle murders.

Although it was clear that West was insane, several 'do-gooder' groups were working frantically to get his death sentence commuted to life and have him committed to an institution for the criminally insane. However, the common man-on-the-street opinion was that he'd be executed right on time, if Washington citizens had anything to say about it.

Later that day, Murphy drove alone to Walla Walla to see the *monster*, John Lee West.

Returning home after visiting Amanda and her grandmother, BJ was calmer than she'd been since she'd first learned of little Kathy's violent death. Similarly, the house seemed almost friendly again, particularly since Amanda was now out of the reach of any potential danger. She caught herself humming as she washed her clothes, and put away others belonging to Amanda. Finally, her chores out of the way, she stretched tiredly and went upstairs to take a hot bath.

BJ opened the dresser drawer where she kept her underwear and noticed one of her panties — a blue floral pair trimmed in white lace — was missing! She knew they'd been there earlier because she'd considered taking them with her in case she decided to remain overnight in Everett. She was certain she'd laid them out, but changing her mind returned them to the drawer. Now, they were clearly gone.

Someone has been in the house!

Unnerved, she knew it immediately. A chill crept up her spine, making her hair tingle. She felt nauseated by the idea of someone creeping around inside her home, handling her under-garments. She felt — *violated!* Frightened, she trembled, listening for sounds outside — or in the house.

She was deeply aware her violated feelings came from a sense of helplessness. She needed to regain control of the situation. Pulling herself together, she removed her pistol from a drawer and stuck it into her waistband.

Anger replaced fear as she searched the house, checking every door and window. Relieved and finally feeling more secure, she went to the kitchen and made tea, trying to sort it out in her mind. *Kathy had been with Amanda the day she'd been murdered. Now, someone's broken into my home and stolen my panties. Coincidence? Maybe — maybe not.*

From the corner of her eye, she detected the living room curtain move just slightly. Quickly, she got up and turned off the lights. She stood quietly for a long time, listening intently, scarcely daring to breathe. Her heart hammering violently against her ribcage, she tried to swallow, but her mouth felt like cotton. It took all her force of will just to edge closer to the window.

Her mind raced as she tried to think back. Perhaps she'd overlooked the window while checking the house. It was open several inches and the curtains softly billowed against her face. She remained very still, unaware of the tears running down her cheeks.

Holding the pistol in her right hand, curling her left forefinger around the edge of the curtain, she drew it aside just a crack. Outside, the cul-de-sac was vacant. Most of the streetlights were on and a slight breeze rustled through the willows in her front yard. Nothing seemed out of the ordinary. About to turn away, she thought she saw the flare of a match just inside the tree line across from her house.

BJ recoiled from the window, a tiny involuntary cry leaving her lips. Clutching the pistol, she watched where she'd seen the light but saw no further movement. She was greatly relieved when the next-door neighbor's car drove up, their headlights illuminating an empty tree line.

Still shaken, she locked the window and wearily climbed the stairs, realizing that for the first time the safety she'd so enjoyed in her own home had only been an illusion. She would never feel completely safe there, again. BJ thought about calling Frank, or Drake, then, feeling silly, poured a hot bath and climbed in — but not before she placed the pistol on a stool, well within reach.

Later, ready for bed, she turned back the covers and there were her blue panties. They were lying on her pillow. Someone had apparently ejaculated on them.

———————

Amanda had a feeling her grandmother had sent her on an errand to the small 7-Eleven so she could talk business with that creepy old lawyer. She was about four blocks from the house when she'd noticed the Darth Vader van for the first time. She probably never would have if she hadn't decided to cross in the middle of the block. It'd nearly knocked her down, but she'd been able to jump backward between two parked cars as the van continued down the block.

After buying the milk for her grandmother's hot chocolate, she headed back using the same route and then, there it was again. Only this time, it had been parked on *her* side of the street.

Sensing something drastically out of whack, she paused, gawking at the black ominous windows more closely. She just *knew* she'd seen it somewhere before. Suddenly goose bumps rose on her arms and her hair prickled her scalp.

In front of the school! That's where!

It'd been just a few days before Kathy had been killed. And, she had a distinct feeling that's not the only time. Quickly deciding not to pass too close, she took the alley instead; it was starting to get dark so she hurried, casting furtive glances over her shoulder. When she exited on the other end, the van was there again — facing her this time, its dark windows peering toward her, like large bottomless eyes. Inexplicable terror shot through her!

Go away! Leave me alone!

Amanda had run track in school but she'd *never* run any faster as she dodged cars, jumped hedges and cut across lawns. Finally she reached her grandmother's front yard. Out of breath and unexplainably frightened, she paused and searched carefully up and down the street. The Darth Vader van was gone.

Amanda didn't know exactly why she should be so scared of a dirty van, but something unerringly reminded her of another one, about the time Kathy had been abducted. *Might not be even the same one, but I'll probably go through the rest of my life just hating the sight of them!*

At the thought of her little dead friend, tears sprang to her dark eyes. Sensing a movement beside her on the porch steps, she turned. Pollard crawled into her lap and purred against her face. Hugging him, she placed her head on her knees and held him close, remaining that way for a long time.

She never noticed the Darth Vader van as it passed again, crossing at a street one block away.

Chapter 16

Washington's Walla Walla State Penitentiary had opened in 1887 to house the state's worst and most chronic offenders. At one time, its name was synonymous with the state's meanest prison, and though recent efforts had been attempted to rehabilitate the facility, Murphy had heard it was still no summer camp. Perched on a small hill in a quiet farming community, its imposing brick facade looked much like the old brick factory it'd originally been. Still, there was no disguising what it really was; a cage for hundreds of the country's most dangerous human beings.

If you could bottle evil, I suppose this is what it would look like, Murphy thought, suppressing a shudder as he pulled into the lower parking lot. Stepping from his sedan, he stared at the building's imposing entrance a moment longer, as though hesitant to enter, and then walked toward his encounter with John Lee West.

A uniformed toothy young man closely scrutinized his badge and said, "The Warden is expecting you, Sergeant Murphy. Please follow me."

Warden Cummings was equally friendly and Murphy soon found himself seated in a large comfortable office, drinking coffee. "Here to see my famous resident, huh?"

"I hope he can give me some ideas about the kind of person we're looking for."

"Well, don't place too much credibility in what he tells you. Johnnie's a polished manipulator—intelligent, to be sure—but he *always* has a hidden agenda."

"Thanks for the warning, Warden."

Cummings leaned forward. "Frank, have you ever met West?"

"I went to a couple of his trial sessions. Why?"

"Just be careful what you disclose, that's all. When it meets his interests, he can come across as your wholesome next-door neighbor, eager to please — so pure that butter wouldn't melt in his mouth. I think I know him as well as anyone can know a creep like him, and even I have to be careful not to be taken in by his act — and an act is *all* it is.

Make no mistake about what you see, Frank. He's world-class when it comes to exploitation. Everybody has an Achilles heel. He has a way of using what you tell him — reading your body language to find your most vulnerable point — then gets *inside* your head. Done it to me a couple a times, until I wised up and quit going near him.

Once he identifies what gets under your skin, he undergoes a… well… a metamorphosis. I don't know how else to describe it. His eyes change first, then his entire face and demeanor, until he seems almost a stranger. It's like he needs to feed off the pain of others."

Cummings laughed, embarrassed, breaking the tension. "I can assure you, it's quite… intensive."

The Warden poured more coffee, then continued, choosing his words carefully. "Since I last saw him a couple of weeks ago, I understand he's shaved his head and barely eats — just enough to stay alive. The transformation has been awesome, or so I'm told. I suspect it's just another ploy to get me back to see him. Fuck 'em. He can starve himself to death, for all I care. The only time I'll go back will be when they fry his skinny ass."

The warden's eagerness at the thought was unmistakable.

"I've been warden here for eight years, and I've seen some real bad ones come and go. We've executed three during that time."

Cummings killed time spooning powdered cream into his coffee and stirring, then sighed heavily. "I've *never* seen another like Johnny West. He scares me shitless, and frankly he hasn't done a thing for me to feel like this. He's accommodating, friendly, appears almost eager to be liked. But he seems almost supernatural."

Cummings offered Murphy a long cigar, but he declined, reaching for a cigarette instead. The warden went on.

"You know how hard it is to keep a thousand inmates straight, Frank? We find a ton of weapons each year—made from anything you can imagine — drugs are rampant, prostitution and murder for hire flourishes. And all this from people who have IQ's lower than a rock. But you take a near genius like John Lee West and you've got a whole new set of problems. Problems you can't even fathom—affecting even the personnel who work to make this place function on a daily basis. Add the bleeding heart civil liberties groups who've taken up his cause, and you can see why I'm getting nervous."

"How do you secure West?"

"IMU...sorry...that's the Intensive Management Unit. We keep him isolated from other inmates. If I didn't, they'd kill the little slime-ball in a heartbeat. Just like the others in IMU, he hardly ever leaves his cell. If he absolutely has to go somewhere, he backs up to the wicket, sticks his hands through, and we cuff him. Then we do the same with his feet.

Everybody in IMU gets the same treatment. I've got a guy in 'B' Pod who shot three people through the head for a measly twenty-six dollars in change. Another stomped his pregnant wife to death, and a third shot-gunned his own grandparents, for Christ sake! I never hear a word from the staff about interacting with those people. But you know what? I can't find anyone who wants to go in there with West."

"I had an idea it'd be important for you to get close enough to him to observe his body language — see his expression — hear the inflection in his voice. That would've been hard from outside, talking through the cell door. I've had him placed into a cell next door. It's completely empty, except for two chairs bolted to the floor. He'll be wearing body shackles and anchored so he has to remain in the chair. We've installed a panic button for when you wish to terminate your visit — or have a problem. It wouldn't make any difference, any of my IMU prisoners would get the same treatment. But in his case, it's warranted."

Murphy stood and they gripped hands. The warden still seemed troubled.

"If there's anything else you need, tell one of my officers. Officer Kendall will give you instructions for when you get inside. Good luck, Frank. I hope you get what you've come for."

Within five minutes, a burly male guard and a sturdy female officer replaced the toothy young man who'd originally shown him in. They escorted him toward the maximum-security section of the prison.

Murphy was led half a mile down a fluorescent-lighted cold gray corridor, past an aging prisoner carrying a mop and bucket. The old prisoner never glanced up as they passed, as though his only existence in his dark and lonely world was the hallway, the mop, and his task.

God, what a depressing place! Frank thought, watching the old man swipe half-heartedly at the gleaming floor.

They'd already passed through two high security doors, and he could see a third one ahead. It opened into the sunlight where a van waited. The burly male guard remained behind while Murphy climbed in the front passenger seat beside the female officer. He was immediately whisked through two more security gates; their IDs checked each time. Finally, they were dropped off in front of a round concrete structure with a large door. The female officer pushed the buzzer; a guard peered through a small opening, then let them in manually.

The female custodian assigned to escort him hadn't spoken during their long march through the cavernous halls, and Murphy had wondered fleetingly if she *could* speak. His question was soon answered. She addressed the huge guard outside the 'D' pod.

"Officer Kendall, please advise Detective Sergeant Murphy of the procedures."

With that, she wheeled and marched back the way they'd come. He felt certain that if he were to see her later in the day, she wouldn't remember him.

The new guy was at least six-foot-four, two hundred forty pounds, his muscle mass sizeable. His bulk sprawled in a straight-backed wooden chair. He mechanically outlined the procedures without looking at Murphy.

"Mr. West is in the next to last cell on the right. He's sitting, shackled to a ring in the floor and is cuffed—both hands and feet. Go directly to the other chair and sit down. Don't leave it for any reason — not even if he dies right in front of you. There's a button installed under the seat of the chair.

If there's trouble or if you want to leave — push it. You're not to give Mr. West anything. Reveal only the information you must in order to accomplish whatever you've come to do. You are not to get within an arm's reach of Mr. West, for any reason. Do you understand the instructions?"

The officer finally looked up. The guard's eyes were cold and lifeless, like cops Murphy had known who'd seen too much and lost a piece of their soul by living too near evil. A thought about the around the world sailboat trip with Olaf suddenly entered his mind.

"This isn't on my list, Murphy. It's free. I work here, but I don't go in unless I'm specifically ordered to. When it's absolutely *necessary*, three of us go together and we carry a long curved-end pole, just in case we have to back him against the wall. There's no dialog with the inmate.

I'm the *smallest* of the three. He may or may not be crazy, but he's one smart dude. He's never done anything to make me believe he's dangerous, but he's the creepiest asshole I've ever known. The truth is, he's said things to me that make me wake up at night in a sweat and think about. I don't know what you need that's so important you have to see him, and I don't want to — but it damned well better be critical to you. Once you meet him he knows who you are; from then...he never forgets."

Murphy nodded with uncertainty, then walked to the metal door and waited. When the buzzer sounded, he hesitated briefly, then pushed against the heavy door and entered.

David Turner had put in a hard day, harder than usual, even by his standards. He lived in a large three-story home his parents had left to him when they died several years earlier. An only child and never married, it only seemed logical he'd continue to stay. Last year, to help offset the high maintenance fees and ever-increasing taxes, David had finally converted the house into three separate and distinct living areas and began renting out the other two. His first two tenants had both been college students, a boy and a girl. But they'd discovered each other one day in the laundry room, and soon ran off to get married. While he was glad to play the role of cupid in the drama, he'd had to start over and find two more tenants. Although the upper level remained vacant, he'd eventually rented out the lower apartment by telephone.

Now he was sorry. The next time, he'd meet potential renters first and thoroughly check them out. Then he wouldn't have gotten stuck with twenty-year-old Arty Hicks, a weird pimple-faced skinhead with a glass stud in his nose and wild eyes. The guy was *sick*, he was sure of that. Or maybe, a 'druggie,' which was even worse. To top it off, he suspected Hicks was mixed up in some of that occult crap, because he'd found the hide of a small animal and a chicken foot buried in a shallow grave in the backyard flowerbed. Then there was the mystery about all those rattraps in the crawl space. *What could he ever be doing with all those rats?*

About a week ago, David thought he'd heard a child crying. He couldn't be certain because Arty always kept that boom box of his blaring all hours of the night and day. The one time David had complained, he'd stared into those lifeless eyes and beat a hasty retreat.

God, and I've signed him to a lease for a whole year, too!

David had considered calling the police, but what could he tell them? He was only guessing, and they'd probably just laugh at him. He shivered. *One weird dude, that's for sure!*

John Lee West sat in his chair bolted to the concrete cell floor. As Officer Kendall had assured him, he was secured with both belt cuffs and ankle restraints. Despite Warden Cumming's grim descriptions of West, he was still shocked. This wasn't the clean-cut young man he remembered from the trial. This horrifying creature stared at him through black sunken holes — his translucent skin tightly stretched over his bony skull. He was thin to the point of being gaunt, his chin long and pointy, teeth yellowed. His head, shaved recently, sprouted short uneven bristles, causing his facial bones to appear even more prominent. Looking closer, Murphy could see the eyes were clear — no, *sharp*! Focused, intelligent, piercing eyes, capable of reading the soul. Murphy understood fully what the guard had been trying to tell him.

"Well, well, Frank. Do come into my humble abode and take a seat. My, you are looking fit these days. Not as fit as you were during my trial, but fit, nonetheless. Like me, you've cut your hair shorter, too."

His remark jolted Murphy for a second time! Was it possible? *No!* He'd never seen John Lee West before the trial. He'd always remained near the rear of the courtroom, and dozens of others were present the entire time; his was just another face watching the proceedings. There'd never been any reason to even say his name. *How could he possibly remember me?*

"How's your lovely wife... Elnore, was it not?" A chill shot down Murphy's spine. "I'd love to meet her some time. Perhaps when all this is over?" The remark could've been from a close family friend instead of an insane killer. "Tell me Frank, to what do I owe this unexpected pleasure?"

Murphy repressed the urge to run from the room, but instead, steeled himself and answered. "I got your letter, John Lee. You seem to think you might be of some help to my finding out who's been stalking, then murdering young schoolgirls. I came hoping you'd give me your opinion on the matter."

West still smiled slightly. "I suspected that was it."

There was a long silence until Murphy began to feel uncomfortable. He realized it was exactly what West had intended. Still he couldn't seem to help himself, and rushed on. "I really don't expect you'll be able to help us find him, but you might help me understand how he might think, what makes him tick, so we can catch... him." He'd started to say 'the sick bastard' but had an idea West already knew that.

"What's in it for me?" John Lee West said casually.

It was Murphy's turn to attempt a smile. It felt strained. "Some company — a chance again to let everyone know how intelligent you are. Besides, it was your idea." He placed a small recorder on the floor near his foot and turned it on.

"I see," the prisoner said again, waiting.

This time Murphy didn't bite. West continued after a few minutes. "I was going to ask if you were intelligent, too, Frank. I can see now that you are." West smiled again. "I like intelligent people. There's only a bunch of Neanderthals working in here." He suddenly shifted subjects without warning. "I can help you catch him. I'll need a telephone."

"Not a chance."

West observed him closely, as Murphy fought to maintain a blank expression, feeling as though he was a specimen under a magnifying glass. Finally, West broke the silence. "I would have to see some of the material, naturally. Pictures, police reports, that sort of thing." He said this as though disinterested, convincingly hiding his aching desire to see pictures of the crime scenes.

Murphy sensed that, and this time fought back a real smile. *Just love to see some wet shots, huh, Sport?*

"I'll give you all you need to know about the case — if you're really serious about helping. If not, tell me now and I'll leave." He was quickly tiring of the cat and mouse game and decided to get off dead center. "That's all I can offer."

Again, another long silence.

"Tell me about the murders, Frank. I get the newspapers, but they don't tell you everything. I need more of the details. The things the public doesn't get."

Murphy felt those dark holes boring right through him, as he fought down another wave of panic and urge to shudder.

Over the next hour he told the prisoner only the facts he wanted him to have, without names or places. Finished, he waited.

"You'll have to leave the recorder with me, of course — to study."

Murphy knew that wouldn't be acceptable to Warden Cummings, but stated, "I'll check with the warden."

West nodded, as though satisfied with his answer. Then he softly murmured, "Ah, such beauty I envision, for all alike, you are as sisters."

Murphy listened to the deep rich tone more than the words and could suddenly see how such a man could easily lure women into a stranger's car, only to be knocked unconscious and hauled away. The smooth inflection had a lulling quality.

"...and for all seeming impossible things? We complete with ease — for we do not toil alone."

Murphy listened until he was finished. *Mad as a hatter*, he thought. "I didn't come to listen to poetry, John Lee."

Those deep penetrating eyes locked on his, and again he felt the chill in his bones. "No, I am aware of why you came, Frank. You came because you're being eaten up inside." His lips curled cruelly at Murphy, then he abruptly said, "Tell me about all the guilt, Frank. The guilt you carry around. The horrible nightmares … and about how you hear your little girl crying after you go to bed at night."

Murphy sat dumbstruck. He couldn't seem to look away from those hypnotic eyes.

"Do you still see her, Frank?"

He was having difficulty breathing, yet, as if being mesmerized by a large snake, he was locked on those deep, clear eyes.

"Every one of the little dead girls look exactly like her, don't they Frank? When you dream at night, do they all become her?"

Murphy felt anchored to the chair, struck mute, unable to move. A ringing in his ears grew increasingly louder — what they'd referred to, as kids, as death bells.

"Tell me about the guilt, Frank. Why so guilty? You weren't the one responsible."

Murphy felt nauseated. West wasn't just talking to him he was *absorbing* him! He suddenly remembered the warden's comments about West feeding off the pain and discomfort of his victims. The newspapers, of course! That's how he knew. West got all the news here, and he had a computer. Someone as brilliant as West could get virtually anything he wanted from a computer; court transcripts, personnel records, archives — the works.

John Lee West rejoiced at his latest victim, hesitated slightly, then suddenly beamed and droned on in his soft hypnotic voice. "Or, *were* you responsible? Were you supposed to pick her up from school that day, Frank? Maybe you were just a little late — trouble at the office or something? You really had no way of knowing something bad would happen, besides, you'd been late several times before, right? But on that day…on that *particular* day…" West's voice dropped to barely a whisper. "…someone *else* met her and gave her a ride, didn't they? Is that it, Frank?"

Murphy jumped to his feet! "You *son-of-a-bitch!* I'll ask the questions. If that isn't good enough for you, I'm out of here!"

The fucker's mad, he thought again, his mind racing. *Insane! Just as I am, to have come here hoping he could help me!* "If you think of anything you want me to have, let the warden know! He'll get it to me!"

Murphy turned to leave.

"The killer is demonstrating his control of the situation by leaving the bodies right under your noses, Frank. He feels superior to you, and may very well be. I was, you know — superior, I mean.

"Another thing. It's just beginning. Remember John Wayne Gacy? Ted Bundy, Wayne Williams, and now, this Headhunter? They don't stop. They never stop — unless they're caught. Now that he's had the taste of blood, he'll know it's the greatest aphrodisiac ever discovered. The pleasures of sex, food and blood are the essence of primitive man's hunter spirit, Frank. Did you know that?"

He looked intent, as though sharing something important with an old friend, but Murphy vowed not to be caught off guard again. As he spoke, Murphy slowly cooled off and studied the convicted rapist and murderer. He found himself briefly wondering about the crossroads that he'd encountered that made him one of the nation's worst serial killers.

John Lee West had come from a good family, had all the benefits of a good education, and apparently hadn't been abused as a child. Once, he'd been an extremely handsome young man, personality plus, charm, manners — so what was it? A genetic flaw? Something left out when growing up? Murphy was convinced the man he was after was a psychological double of this man sitting before him. If he could just understand what made this monster tick, he might be able to catch the other one.

West spoke with cultured tones and phrases of the intellectually elite, as though he were a college professor from a prestigious East Coast university. "The reason your killer is invisible to you is perhaps because you are looking for a stereotype murderer, as in the movies; salivating lips, lewd manner, dirty, black broken teeth... someone like young Albert. You know the type."

Uh huh, Murphy thought. *Like you.*

West curled his lip again as though he knew exactly what the police officer was thinking, and went on. "Tax your brain, Frank. You're intelligent. Break away from conventional thinking and let your mind run wild. The beautiful person you see on the outside is not necessarily the person living on the inside. '*Within*. There's where the monsters lurk,'" he quoted some obscure source again.

"We need to find him so he won't kill again," Murphy said softly. West didn't answer, and his mannerisms suddenly made Murphy's skin crawl. "Are you finished?" he blurted at last.

West grinned and reclined against the hard back of his chair, staring up at the ceiling. Despite his restraints, he looked almost comfortable. "He comes back, too, Frank. He always comes back to see every site.

He kills them all at the same place — but dumps them where they'll make the most impact. He returns to each place to relive it, while others are around. Maybe even cops. That way he can share his enjoyment. Find the murder scene and you'll find your killer. Watch the dump sites and he'll eventually come back — he won't be able to help himself." The smile was gone and a vacant gaze replaced it.

"I'm tired now. Maybe you could come back later? In a few days I might have something else for you." He closed his eyes as though dismissing an unwanted guest, then continued, "Don't wait too long. I have a date with my own killer in a couple of weeks."

Murphy pushed the buzzer under his seat and rose to stand near the door. It seemed to take forever, but after only a few seconds he heard an audible click, then lunged against the cell door — it swung lazily open. He went through the same procedures at the outer door. This time the big guard didn't look up at him as he left.

The van was waiting — and the same female driver. She deposited him in silence at the door of the main facility. Murphy hurried into the endless gray corridors from which he'd entered — it seemed a century before. He finally busted through the last door, finally rewarded with sunlight and fresh air. Bracing his hands on the long sidewalk railing, he paused for several minutes, his head bowed. Shuddering, he inhaled deep satisfying gulps of fresh air, the cool breeze drying the sweat beads on his face. His hands trembled.

Goddammit to hell! What a God-forsaken, fucking place!

Rushing toward the parking area on rubbery legs, he felt as if he'd been wallowing in slime for hours—that he was leaving the presence of something unbelievably evil. Still nauseated, he desperately craved a bath. He slammed the car into gear and sped from the parking lot, like the devil had been behind him. As far as Frank Murphy was concerned, he was.

———————

Dinner was over and Amanda had begged Abie to let her clean up the kitchen and feed the cats. That had been thirty minutes ago. Abie hadn't heard so much as a whisper coming from the kitchen for quite a while. In her cotton house-slippers, she slipped noiselessly to the doorway and peeked in. Amanda was peering apprehensively out the kitchen window as she scrubbed absentmindedly around a plate. Abie came up behind her and spoke said quietly.

"Something bothering you child?"

Amanda startled, then smiled up at her and said, "No, Grandma Abie. I guess I'm just a little nervous tonight. Do you think we could call Mom later?"

Abie wasn't fooled. She saw the worry in the little girl's dark eyes. *Something is troubling this child*, she thought. "You can call your mother anytime you want to, Sugar. I'd even like to talk to her myself."

Amanda wrapped her arms around Abie and hugged her tightly. The old woman patted the girl's thin shoulder, smiled warmly and trudged back toward the large living room, leaving Amanda alone to finish the dishes.

Poor child, Abie thought. *She must be missing her little playmate. I'll get out the Scrabble. That'll take her mind off things for a while.*

After several failed attempts at contacting her mother, Amanda finally left a voice message, and they got carried away playing Scrabble until almost nine o'clock. Even the cats tried to get into it. Towards the end, Amanda was rolling on the floor with them, laughing and scolding Darnell, who seemed to be the instigator of the bunch.

"Why, it's way past my bedtime... and you've won three straight. We'll have to have a rematch tomorrow night," Abie said, as she stood and stretched. Leaving Amanda to place the pieces back into the box, she said over her shoulder, "I'm going to fix you a big glass of warm milk and draw you a bath to help you sleep."

The thought of warm milk just about made Amanda barf, but out of politeness she kept it to herself. Just as she'd finished toweling off and slipped into her PJs, the old woman carried the warm milk up to her room and gently tucked her in. Sitting on the edge of Amanda's bed, Abie took her small hand in her own wrinkled ones and said gently, "I love you, Sugar. I'm so proud that you're my granddaughter."

"I love you, too, Grandma Abie. Tomorrow can I take the cats for a walk around the park?"

The old woman chuckled. "We'll see, child. We'll see." She bent, kissed her on the forehead, pulled up her covers, and was gone.

———————

Yates was on his eleventh address, checking up on the list of white van owners, when he pulled in front of the old Victorian home. Once stately, the dilapidated four-story peered at it's visitors through two tall gabled windows. The windows, turreted corners and sweeping wrap around front porch had once been in vogue. The grand old house had initially been painted white, but neglect and the damp Seattle weather made it a dingy gray, peppered with greenish blotches where the sun never seemed to shine enough to quite dry it out.

He advanced up the cracks in the sidewalk to the askew porch and searched for a doorbell. Unsuccessful in locating it, he finally just knocked loudly. After several tries he finally heard someone moving about inside and within seconds the door swung open. A disheveled unshaven young man with short trim hair scratched his sides and yawned widely.

"Yes?" the young man said, sleepily.

"Detective Yates, Seattle P.D. You own a white van?"

"No," *sleepy eyes* said. "Oh, that one. It belonged to my tenant. I wouldn't be caught dead driving something like that. I haven't seen it around for a while now, though."

"What's your name and who is the tenant?" Yates said.

"Please come in Detective Yates. You'll have to excuse me for the way I look, but I worked late last night and slept in. I'm David Turner. I manage Best Groceries, ten blocks north of here."

In sharp contrast to the exterior, the interior of the old house was immaculate! It'd most likely been renovated during the past five years and many modern conveniences were evident, such as a built-in large screen TV. Still, the additions hadn't disturbed its original romantic character and charm. The ten-foot high ceiling held its original antique lighting fixtures, the windows were crafted of stained glass, and the woodwork had been recently restored to a rich sheen. A large iron grated gas fireplace, framed with a walnut mantle, was a visual focal piece. It wasn't burning.

The young man motioned to a chair and asked, "Can I get you something, Officer? Coffee, tea…?"

"No, thanks. The tenant….?"

"Oh yes, that would be Arty. Arty Hicks. He's lived here for almost a year now. Well, actually, about eight months."

"Do you know anyone by the name of Cecil Patterson?" Yates said.

"No sir. Should I?"

"That's the name registered on the van. It was registered six months ago… at this address."

David looked puzzled. "Never been anyone here by that name. Could there be a mistake?"

Yates nodded without answering, then said, "What does this Hicks guy look like?"

"Six-foot, skinny, one of those skin-head types. Wears a stud in his ear and jackboots most of the time."

Yates digested that bit of information. "You ever see him driving the white van?"

"He drove up and unloaded it the day he moved in. I don't remember ever seeing him drive it since though," David answered. "It just sat there for months, getting moldy and rusting away, then about a week ago — it was gone. Don't know where it's at now."

"Anything else strange about him — other than being a skin-head? Hear anything odd? Stuff like that?"

David contemplated the question. "Well… two nights ago, I thought I heard a child's voice coming from his room. Though it's hard to tell, the way he keeps his stereo volume up all the time. He's got one of those big boom-boxes and listens to some pretty raunchy stuff."

"Can I use your phone, Mr. Turner?"

"In the hallway. Help yourself."

Frank Murphy answered on the third ring. "Murphy here."

"It's Yates. I may have a lead on the van. The twenty-three hundred block of Rainbow Avenue. I need a search warrant, Frank. This could be a serious lead."

Something in his voice told Murphy this was indeed, serious. "I'll be there in fifteen minutes, Joe. Sit tight until I arrive."

Murphy hung up and shouted at Booth, "Charley, get me a warrant for twenty three hundred, Rainbow Avenue, and meet me there with the crew. We don't have time to fool around with it, so see Judge Stoner if you can. I'll give you an hour then we're going in, with or without it. Let's go, people."

Within forty-five minutes, they were assembled outside the old house. They'd parked their vehicles three blocks away, and Murphy had sent Booth and Drake to cover the back while he joined Yates in front. Joe Yates smiled broadly as he approached.

"This is your bust, Joe. How do you want to go in?"

"Me first, then you. Okay?"

"You're the boss, let's go!" Murphy said. They moved in as David Turner watched from behind one of the police cars.

The lower apartment was actually on the basement level. Murphy used the key Turner had given Yates earlier, unlocking the heavy wood door as quietly as possible. Yates went in first with Murphy right behind, then they branched off; Yates veered right, toward the bedroom and Murphy entered the small kitchen. It was empty.

"Jeez, would ya look at this?" Yates called from down the short hallway.

Murphy had seen a lot of porno films during his time with the department, but the observation shocked the hardened veteran. Two walls were completely lined with shelves, chock full of every type porno film imaginable. There were snuff films, pedophile films, lesbians, men with men, bestiality; everything possible for a living being to do to another was depicted on those films. Occult and supernatural posters plastered the remaining wall space. A small altar had been placed in one corner, positioned with several burnt candles and a stained stone chalice.

Drake and Charley Booth joined them. "*Holy shit!*" Drake said, wide-eyed. "This is one sick puppy!"

"Charley, get this guy's description on the wire," Murphy instructed. "Joe, call the CSU. I want them to go over this place with a fine-tooth comb. Check the area for tire tracks. If any are found, have them checked against the plaster mold we took earlier."

Within three hours, the Crime Scene Unit had finished and left, the last of the videos had been loaded up. Murphy turned the lock in the door while Yates strung yellow crime scene tape across the doorway. Instructing Turner to call them immediately if Hicks returned, they finally departed.

————————

Stupid cops! Stupid shit for brains cops! How dare they try and take my van! I'll kill them all for doing that! The whole thing had gone all wrong. Tits up, right from the get-go.

First, he'd gotten the wrong girl by mistake — then the little black girl had disappeared and it had taken forever to find her again. Now, they knew about the van, too! He'd have to be more careful, maybe hide it for a while. *Goddammit,* he loved that van!

Cocksucker, motherfucker, eat a bag of shit! I will not let them fuck up my plans. I'll kill them all first! Starting with the black cop-bitch — right after I do her daughter. Then, I'll get that fat-assed nigger —maybe his whole family. Last, but best, I'll nail that motherfucker, Murphy! Watch his eyes as he realizes he's going to die—and why! Ah, sweet!

Beating his hands against his head, the spittle drooled as he imagined the awful things he'd do to those who'd wronged him. But first, there was tonight. How he looked forward to that.

————————

Amanda lay awake for a long time as sleep evaded her. At last, she slipped into a fitful sleep, only to be stirred awake by faint scratching sounds. *Maybe one of the cats was left outside?* Silently crawling from beneath the covers, Amanda moved to the window and peeked outside. Her heart suddenly jumped into her mouth! *Darth Vader!* The white van with the black windows was parked under a streetlight, halfway down the block! She was sure it was the same one.

Quickly, her mind flashed back; but she couldn't remember if her grandmother had set the burglar alarm. She quickly made her way to the bedroom door, silently opening it, listening. There was no moon and the hallway was pitch black. She reached to the right of her door and flicked the light switch. Nothing happened. She instinctively knew that somehow, she must get to the kitchen hallway and trip the burglar alarm.

Earlier, she'd been shown how to enter the four-digit security code, and Abie had cautioned her it screeched horribly — ringing also in the security company headquarters across town. It would work even if the electricity were cut off.

More importantly, it had a panic button. Just push it, her grandmother had said, and the noise would raise the dead.

Slowly feeling her way along the wall, Amanda headed in the direction of the stairs, until at last she felt the familiar coolness of the oak railing. She inched her foot downward carefully until she felt the first step, and *froze*. Someone was moving downstairs! She was certain of it! Grandma Abie would *never* be moving around the house in the dark!

The old woman had renovated the den on the first floor ten years ago, converting it into her bedroom after she'd fallen on the steps and broken her leg. Her room was at the bottom of the stairs, just around the corner. Amanda knew she had to somehow warn her grandmother and set off the burglar alarm.

Terrified but steeling herself, Amanda started down the long stairwell once again. She tried to breathe quietly, but to no avail. Her heart beat so loudly she was certain that what ever was downstairs would surely hear it. It was *so dark* —like looking into a bottle of ink.

She heard nothing more and wondered briefly if it'd been her imagination. No! That *was* the Darth Vader van out there! She was certain of *that*.

One last step and she'd finally reached the first floor — *at last*. Her hands, anchored against the wall, inched their way along its coolness toward her grandmother's room. She tried to recall the furniture placement between her and the old lady's bedroom door. All she remembered was a small table with a bunch of photos about two-thirds of the way down. Her legs trembling, she made her way around the stand by touch, then her foot bumped against something soft. Bending in the total darkness, she felt something furry. She could tell by the size that it was Alfred. He was dead. Amanda fought down sudden hysteria, forcing herself to breathe deeply. After a few seconds, she stiffly resumed her tedious journey toward the doorway of her grandmother's room.

She felt the edge of the door. *It's open!* Scarcely breathing, she dropped to her knees, crawling silently toward the bed. Carefully reaching out, she felt her grandmother's leg beneath the thick comforter. *How to do it?* She didn't want to startle the old lady, but she had to wake her up *somehow*.

Placing her mouth close to Abie's ear, she whispered, "Grandma. Grandma, it's me, Amanda. You have to wake up and be real quiet. There's somebody in the house. *Please*, Grandma?"

Getting no response, she gently shook the old woman and felt stickiness on her hands. There was an odd smell she hadn't noticed earlier. Frantically she ran her hands up to her grandmother's face, and felt more of the same sticky stuff all over it. She gasped. *Blood!* It had to be blood! Amanda recoiled and huddled on the floor in despair. She shook violently as a sob stuck in her throat and hot tears sprang to her eyes. She ached to scream out for her mother and curl up on the floor until she came for her.

Stop acting like a baby! It sounded like Abie's voice prompting her. Amanda swallowed hard, forcing herself to fight down the panic. If she made a noise, any noise, she was dead. *Like Alfred!* She'd end up just like Kathy… dead, cold, in the ground… *forever*. She'd never see her mother again. So, okay, she'd stop acting like a baby. Suddenly, she knew what she had to do.

Crawling silently, she backtracked through the bedroom door, inching her way back along the wall. She carefully stepped over the dead cat, finally feeling the cool oak handrail of the stairs. Bracing herself for a swift move toward the kitchen and the alarm box, she caught the sound of a soft footstep, just around the corner. *He's between the kitchen and me!* Amanda fought down a scream, and backed toward the steps. *Jesus, oh please, Jesus help me.*

She felt the first step press against her heel and grabbed for the railing. Not bothering to maintain her silence to the degree she did when coming down, she climbed the stairs much faster this time.

Reaching the top, she paused briefly to listen. *Oh, no...* a slight creak emanated from the hardwood landing at the bottom of the steps. Amanda quickly made her way back toward her room, then, at the last minute continued down the hall to the doll's room.

She could plainly hear the heavy breathing behind her as someone — *or something* — moved up the stairs behind her. Amanda opened the doll's room door as silently as she could manage, slipped in and closed it softly. As in her bedroom, the distant streetlight cast a slight glow in the darkness. She moved quickly toward the closet, opened the secret passageway, and peered inside. *It's like midnight in here!* She looked back, wondering if she could somehow slip past her stalker.

Stop being a baby! Abie's voice again? *No. Just my imagination.*

Breathing deeply and praying there were no spiders lurking, Amanda slid through the small opening, closing the passageway panel behind. The air was stuffy and stale. She crawled forward a short distance, then stopped to listen — and heard the doll-room door quietly creak open!

Forcing a sob back down, she scrambled as fast as she could for what seemed to be an awfully long time. She finally bumped into the panel at the far end, removed it and crawled outside.

The distant streetlight cast faint hues over the kitchen, helping her to find the alarm box just outside in the hallway. She heard heavy steps hit the bottom of the stairs just as she struck the panic button on the alarm and sprinted to the back door, all in one swift motion. Rough grabbing hands tore at the collar of her robe, forcing her to hesitate in mid-stride, but then the collar ripped away. She never looked back as she flew out the door, across the wet lawn and into the street!

Sobbing and still running at top speed, the headlamps of Sergeant O'Brady's cruiser spotted her, her snow white nightgown covered with her grandmother's blood. Recognizing the familiar uniform, she flew sobbing into his arms.

Chapter 17

Murphy hadn't seen BJ since his return from his Walla Walla meeting with John Lee West. Although he'd promised he would call the minute he got back, he still hesitated. For a reason he couldn't explain, thoughts of her made him feel uncomfortable, confused. When she'd answered her phone earlier tonight, he was still feeling guilty about not calling, and hadn't explained why he was picking her up — only to be ready to go. He knew how much she loved Amanda and decided what he had to tell her was best said face to face.

He'd received his own call about twenty minutes before from Sergeant Liam O'Brady in Everett. O'Brady knew he'd been heading up the new task force and immediately figured the two situations were in some way connected. He'd told Murphy he had BJ's little girl with him, then went on to explain how he'd answered a silent alarm and found her running down the middle of the street covered with blood A subsequent check of the residence had revealed the old woman's body.

Now, as they traveled at a high rate of speed toward the coastal city just north of Seattle, Murphy shared with her all the details he'd been provided earlier. He could see her frightened eyes in the dash-lights of the patrol unit, and silently cursed a faceless, nameless monster that thrilled in harming little girls. Beside him, BJ moaned quietly.

"Now... she's all right, BJ," he said softly. "Sergeant O'Brady is a good man and he's staying with her until we arrive."

"What about her Grandma Abie?"

He didn't answer right away on purpose. BJ had seen him use the technique before to pass on unpleasant news. It was all her trained ear needed as an answer.

"BJ, I'm really sorry. Sergeant O'Brady said it was over quickly for her, if that's any consolation. She was killed in her sleep. We just have to be grateful now that Mandy is all right." He kept his eyes glued to the street, hearing her sniff softly and blow into his handkerchief.

They were almost there. As he turned onto the familiar street, they could see the red and blue lights of several police cars, flashing off the trees and houses along the wooded lane. About a dozen neighbors stood in their robes clutching at umbrellas, huddled silently under two of the largest trees. They looked cold— scared. A large ruddy-faced policeman with his sergeant stripes waved and walked toward them. Murphy pulled in behind a police car.

"Where is she?" BJ shouted frantically.

"She's in my unit, ma'am—that one—curled up asleep in the backseat. She wanted the two cats with her. Hope you don't mind. I covered her and the cats with a blanket and they all dropped right off."

O'Brady was as large as Bear and just as soft-spoken.

"Because she belongs to one of our own, I called ahead and Doctor Larsen will meet us at the station-house to check her over— if you agree." BJ nodded her agreement. She knew Amanda would be in good hands. Dr. Larsen was the departmental choice because she was both a psychologist and medical doctor rolled into one.

BJ hurried to the cruiser, peering through rain-streaked windows into the rear seat. Amanda and the two cats were huddled under a blanket, apparently sleeping. As BJ opened the door, Amanda peeked open her sleepy eyes and with a small cry, flung herself into her mother's arms, sobbing. The two men watched briefly as BJ soothed her daughter tenderly. Then they moved toward the large house where all the activity seemed to be.

"I'll get someone to drive them back to Seattle, Murph. Then I'll walk you through it and tell you what I know up to this point," the big man said.

Startled, they looked up as car brakes screeched to a stop. It was Lieutenant Borden, one of his flunkys, and his usual entourage of reporters.

O'Brady motioned to the three officers standing drinking coffee under a large tree. They immediately dropped their paper cups, then moved to block access. He could hear Borden arguing with the officers as he and O'Brady went inside. "I am Lieutenant Borden, Seattle P.D., Homicide. I need to..."

"...really sorry, Sir..."

"I've known that son-of-a-bitch for ten years," O'Brady muttered. "He couldn't even write up a halfway decent traffic ticket back then. Heard he hasn't learned much since, either."

"Liam, could you see that my people get in when they arrive?" Murphy gave him all their names and O'Brady sent a female officer to assist the three others outside with instructions to bring the task force members in without delay.

"The little girl told me most of what happened and we were able to piece together the rest," O'Brady said. "She's one brave little girl. Anyway, he came in through the kitchen window after first shutting off the electricity. Broke a pane and unlocked it from the inside. If the burglar alarm had been set, it would've gone off right then. The sound of the glass breaking probably woke up the little girl and she..."

Murphy listened while the story unfolded, his rage simmering just below the surface.

"...I saw her in my headlights, covered with blood, running like all demons of hell were after her. I guess in a way, they were." O'Brady paused, then said, "You don't know it, but I have a daughter about that age. I'd give a year's pay to get that sick son-of-a-bitch all to myself for ten minutes."

Murphy could tell he meant it.

Someone approached. Murphy glanced up as the female officer led Booth, Yates, and Lisa toward them. He could still hear Borden shouting profanities outside in the rain.

"The LT ain't very happy with you right now, Murph," Charley stated. "Kind of feels like he's the ranking man present, or something."

O'Brady growled, "Fuck 'em. He's out of his jurisdiction. I'm paying the bills tonight. The Chief can take it out of my hide later, if he wants. Doubt it though. He don't much care for Butthead, either. You fellows go ahead and work the area. I'll keep those assholes in the rain 'til you're done."

He lumbered off in the direction of Borden's commotion.

"Hemphill coming?" Murphy slipped on latex gloves.

"Should be here any minute," Booth answered, also pulling on his gloves.

"Good! As soon as it gets daylight, scour the outside area. Then start knocking on doors. See if anyone saw or heard anything during the night—or the past few days, for that matter. We don't know, but there might've been someone with insomnia out walking the dog... you know the drill. Specifically ask about a white van. I'll have an artist standing by if you get anything."

He turned to Lisa. "You go with BJ and Amanda. Don't let them out of your sight, and don't let anyone you don't know come near them, particularly anyone from the Press. If someone you don't know grabs her, shoot 'em — several times. If Amanda goes to the bathroom, you go with her. The next time I see her, I expect to see you, too."

"Yes, sir." Lisa headed into the misting rain.

Borden screamed again and they turned to see Bear, lumbering toward them, grinning. "It's almost worth it—getting out of a warm bed with my Mable—just to hear such displeasure coming from our leader."

Murphy hurriedly briefed him and they split up to complete their missions. By the time they'd finished, Lieutenant Borden and all the reporters had enough of the cold drizzle and were gone, except for Molly Atwood. Murphy tried to avoid her as he and Bear sprinted to the car, but she cut them off, halfway.

"Frank, is this the Headhunter again?"

Murphy didn't answer, increasing his pace. Sometimes if you ignore a menace, it'll go away. Not always, though.

"How well do you get along with your boss for this investigation, Frank? Is it true your wife has left you, and you're drinking?" Atwood pummeled him with questions.

He stopped with one foot outside the car door. "That isn't any of your fucking business, Molly. Stay out of my private life or I'll slap a lawsuit on you so big you'll be working the rest of your life to pay it off."

Drake gunned it and the big car sped away, leaving the reporter alone in the street.

They'd decided to temporarily let Amanda go home with BJ, and Captain Brooks had provided two officers for around-the-clock security on the house. Murphy escorted BJ and her daughter home, and told her he'd be back in the evening to check on them.

As he returned to the station, he received a message that Brooks wanted to see him immediately. He figured it was about Borden, and ignored it. Pulling into a vacant parking spot, he slumped in his car for a moment, tiredly rubbing his eyes. They felt as if someone poured half a cup of gravel into each of them. Too much coffee and no breakfast had left him with a sour stomach, and an even sourer disposition. At the moment, the *last* thing his stomach needed was more *leadership*.

Drake was just pouring the last of the coffee when Murphy joined him in the task force room. "You want the rest of this? I've had all I need," Drake offered.

"What do you have against me?"

"I guess I could make some fresh," Drake said.

"Don't strain yourself. Why start anything new?"

Drake gazed at his partner, amused. "You're in a cheerful mood. What's the matter? Someone leave the lid off the tooth paste this morning?"

"Cute." Murphy stared aimlessly at the desktop then stated quietly, "Something's wrong with this picture, Bear. How'd that sick bastard know where to find Mandy? How'd he know about the alarm system—how to get around inside the house—where her grandmother slept, any of it?"

Drake hesitated. He knew what Frank was suggesting, but was unwilling to put it into words.

Murphy went on. "I've been in this business too long to believe in coincidences, old buddy. I've never trusted them. So, what's happening here?"

"We've got someone on the inside." It was not a question.

They stared at each other; both reluctant to voice what they knew had to be said. Finally, Drake stood and paced. "I can't buy that Frank. We *know* these people. Some of them might be assholes, but they're not sicko's or freaks and they don't give out information to sicko's and freaks.

Everybody here knows it's us against them, that we have to keep their kind on the outside." He shook his big head sadly. "No, I don't buy it."

"Well, you've got to admit, there's sure as hell something funny going on." Murphy was unwilling to concede coincidence as the answer. "Just give it some thought, okay?"

His big partner nodded half-convincingly as Murphy started thumbing through the long list of white van owners again. His mind wasn't on it. It was on coincidence.

———

It was late afternoon when Murphy and Drake pulled into BJ's drive and one of the two security men came out to ID them. Murphy had to give Brooks some credit; he'd put two of the best on it; Clancy Gates and Paulie Haskill. He wouldn't want to be the smuck who tried to get to the kid with those two guarding her! BJ walked silently into his arms as Drake looked on disapprovingly. She raised her liquid brown eyes to stare into his bloodshot ones.

"You getting any rest, Frank?"

"Been real peaceful without you around," he answered, smiling.

He could feel her hard breasts pushing against his chest and gently pulled away. She curled her upper lip where Drake couldn't see, and led them into the living room. The blinds had been closed. Clancy sat with his back against the far wall, watching Amanda do her homework. Two pistol butts protruded from shoulder holsters beneath his jacket. *His clone is probably out lurking in the woods just looking for someone to kill,* Murphy speculated about Haskill.

Under Murphy's watchful eye, BJ gave Bear a hug and a kiss on each cheek. "Hey, no fair," Murphy growled. "All I got was a hug."

Drake smiled at him with droopy eyelids. "That's 'cause you ain't a brother and don't have what it takes, white bread. Haven't you heard? Chicks dig me. Besides, black men have the secret of what it takes to make a woman happy?"

Murphy scowled disgustedly and waved his hand. "Yeah, yeah. You take her then, I'm too tired to argue about it. Besides, it's all bullshit about black men anyway. Mable told me so."

BJ left the room and returned with three beers. She jerked her head toward Gates. "I offered him one, too, but he won't touch the stuff. Says he's on duty."

"Lisa coming back tonight?" Murphy asked. "If she does, tell her to call in tomorrow. I have a few things for her to do—it looks like everything's under control here, with Rambo and Conan the Swarts-sen-hammer over there, on the job."

They dallied for a while longer, BJ hugging both men as they prepared to leave, intentionally poking Frank with her breasts again and taking satisfaction in his sudden discomfort. After he drew back, she got serious.

"I'll be in tomorrow, Frank. I want to get this creep off the streets as quickly as possible, too" she assured him. "I think Amanda is as safe as we can make her with these two commandos around."

As BJ smiled and waved to Murphy and Drake from her doorway, *Corky* dropped another candy wrapper, thoughtfully chewing the last of the chocolate in it, and watched from the tree line as the police cruiser pulled away.

The presence of the new bodyguards clearly called for a change in direction.

Murphy dropped Drake at the station and hurried to keep his appointment with Doctor Linda Larsen. Although she worked exclusively for the police department these days, she still maintained her office in the Professional Building in nearby North Gate, a robust area several miles north. If you had to live in the city, it was a nice part of town. That was where he was headed now.

Murphy stopped at the nearby Starbucks and grabbed a couple of muffins and two cups of coffee.

The interior of the North Gate brick building was tasteful and serene, as nice as the exterior. Marble floors and wide carpeted stairways made the lobby eloquent, as did large oil paintings along the pastel walls. He'd always liked its ambiance, even when he'd had to come during his worst days for *specialized* treatment. Since Linda's secretary was not at her desk, Murphy peeked through the half-opened door, spotting the pretty doctor laboring over an opened file folder.

"Frank, come in. So good to see you." Doctor Linda Larsen rose as he entered and came around her desk to hug him.

After Tina had been found he'd started coming to see Linda, and he'd be the first to say it'd helped. During that short time, he and Linda had developed more than simply a doctor patient relationship. They'd become friends.

Still, after only two months he'd abruptly ceased making his appointments. He'd reached a point where he felt he either had to make it on his own, or not at all. He always felt that she resented his sudden dropping from the treatment program, and their developing friendship had substantially cooled. If so, she hid it well now.

"Hi, Doc," he said, setting one of the paper cups of coffee and muffins on her desk. He seated himself in the chair he'd used many times, placing his own coffee on a nearby stand. "You get a chance to go over that material?"

Linda reached into a top drawer and retrieved a thick folder marked *Confidential*. Laying it on the desk, she studied its contents for several moments. Murphy settled back, bit into his muffin and sipped his coffee as he studied her. Linda was a beautiful woman with long blond hair she always tied up in a knot. Her professional wire-rimmed glasses couldn't disguise her deep blue eyes. She appeared to be a youthful thirtyish, but he figured her true age closer to forty. The years had been good to her. She looked up.

"What specifically do you want to know?"

"A profile, Linda. I need to know what I'm looking for here."

"Well, I've put together a tentative profile using the limited information you've provided." She handed him a single sheet of paper and he scanned through it.

"Why do you think he's "Joe Average", Linda?" he said.

"Makes sense. He comes and goes pretty much as he wants, and nobody ever seems to see him. If he was a freak or dressed weirdly, someone would've spotted him by now."

"Yeah, that's what I thought, too," Murphy said, remembering that John Lee West had essentially said the same thing, but in a more round-a-bout manner. "Just wanted to hear you say it, I guess. Anything else?"

She thought about it for a minute. "It's all in the report. I'd place him in his mid-to-upper twenties, maybe early thirties. He'll be average-looking, neat—maybe even a *neat freak* type.

Probably lives in a big house—I'd guess alone—perhaps isolated from others nearby. He'd need the privacy it would afford him to carry out his enterprises. Also, I'd say he's the type who'd want to work at home."

Murphy marveled at her detachment from the terms she used for the mutilations.

She continued on in a clinical fashion. "More likely, he works in a public job close to his own neighborhood. That way, he can target victims without being obvious about it."

She waited until he'd absorbed the information, still studying the folder, her hair hiding her features. "I'd surmise he thinks he hears voices telling him what to do and how to go about the mutilations. Like a voice of God. Some do. It could be deeply psychological based upon a disturbing childhood experience, or, even a religious experience for him. The sex is secondary. It's the violence that gets him off."

She hesitated then met his eyes.

"It's likely to escalate until he's completely out of control, like a runaway train. He'll be a virtual killing machine, like a shark, which kills even when not hungry—simply because of its nature. That doesn't mean he'll be any easier to catch. He's probably quite good at manipulating and deceiving those around him. His IQ may be near genius."

Murphy recalled John Lee West's similar comments. "Why do you suppose he positions the heads as he does, Doc?" he broke in.

"Why do you think he does?" she countered.

Murphy hesitated, so she pressed him. "You must have *some* idea, Frank."

"I'll admit I've given it some thought. It's just that all my ideas are so sick, I hate to give them any credibility by talking about them."

"Remember, Frank, this guy is so far out, the worst thing you could possibly imagine is mainstream for him. So, take a shot at it." She smiled encouragement.

He took a deep breath, and began. "I figure it's his way of saying, 'if you won't let me do what I want to do with you while you're alive, I'll make you do them to yourself after I kill you." His face colored slightly as he ended.

"Bravo!" She smiled, quickly reverting to a more professional somber look. "I've had some experience with cases like this, Frank. Not a lot, but enough. Remember, I assisted the Green River Task Force, and to some extent, on Ted Bundy's case. Then, I was new at it, but I've learned enough to know that no case two cases are exactly alike. There's no common denominator. Whatever makes one of them tick wouldn't get another's motor turned over.

What I'm trying to say is this, Frank. This isn't an exact science. Your ideas are as good as the next guy's is, or, in this case, as mine are. I'd encourage you to brainstorm and the wackier the ideas the better. Nothing's too far out to be considered."

"I guess my job's cut out for me, huh Doc?" Murphy rose to his feet and turned to go. "Thanks for taking the time to see me."

"Frank?"

He turned back to face her.

"You look tired. How are *you* handling this?"

"Linda, I'm going to nail this madman. I have to, for myself as well as everyone else. See you around."

Linda Larsen stared stoically at the closed door long after he'd departed.

———————

Murphy had planned to have a late lunch at Julie's apartment, hopefully a *nooner*, too. It'd been some time since they'd been able to connect, and when he'd called her earlier, she'd seemed eager to see him. Since she hadn't yet arrived he used her hidden key to let himself in and poured a beer into a frosted mug he knew she kept iced in the freezer. As he took his first sip, the telephone rang; Julie's voice message responded briefly.

Probably Julie, calling to tell me she's running late, he thought absentmindedly.

Setting his glass down, he moved slowly forward to pick it up—only then her recorded message ended. He hesitated a second longer, then a familiar voice broke in.

"Julie—call me as soon as you get home. There've been some major developments and I want you to arrange another of your little cuddling sessions with Murphy. Find out what he knows about this latest suspect, ASAP. When you do, call me. Maybe I'll let you do your little trick for me again."

As the connection was broken, the click was deafening as Robert James hung up.

Julie had seen the unmarked police unit by the sidewalk as she pulled into her garage. Despite her relationship with Robert, and her self-despised spying for him, she still felt her breath quicken each time she met with Frank. Maybe she'd just break it off with Robert James—stay with Frank. *No.* She knew in her heart it would never happen. What she had with Frank was *nice,* but what Robert gave her she desperately *needed.* There was no reason a girl couldn't have it *both* ways.

She smiled as she entered the apartment and saw his back as he stared out the window at the spectacular view. He must've heard her enter, but never turned.

"Oh darling. It's been *so* long! I've missed you!"

He slowly pivoted. His expression stopped her cold. Instantly, she knew it was over. She stepped toward him, her hand reaching in a weak gesture. "Frank, oh darling, I'm so sorry. I...."

He slapped her face hard and she staggered backward, grabbing at the counter to keep from falling. He towered over her, his fists balled, tears of rage flooding his eyes.

She blurted out over the ringing in her ears, "You don't understand! He's got a hold over me. I need help to get away..."

Without a word, he spun and left, the door open wide. Sobbing softly, Julie slumped to the floor.

On the drive back, his mind washed over his entire relationship with Julie while fighting to keep his rage under control. He felt alone, forlorn, as though he'd lost something he'd never really quite had. He felt betrayed, disoriented, and a little sick. Not only because he'd been deceived by yet another woman, but because he now realized why she'd been using him.

Shit, I can't believe I blamed Joe Yates for our leaks. All the time it was that double-crossing bitch and Robert James—and my own big mouth.

In a way, it seemed almost amusing. He'd always thought of himself as a worldly, street-wise, cosmopolitan kind of guy who understood women as well as the next guy. *All right, dammit, a cock-*

hound. Yeah, old-Frank-dumber-than-a-rock-Murphy. Ladies man and mushroom. Keep him in the dark and feed him shit and he'll tell you anything. He realized what a fool he really was, a walking jerk with a big target on his back, *Sucker.*

Molly Atwood, Elnore, and now Julie—Christ, will I never learn?

Somehow he had to make it up to the others for all the times he'd chewed *their* asses for the task force's leaks.

Pulling into the parking lot, he turned off the ignition yet hesitated to enter the office immediately. Frank Murphy felt totally rotten.

Finally getting up his nerve, he entered. He'd seen a message from Drake, indicating he'd gone upstairs to run some prints through the system. Joe Yates had photocopies of several drivers licenses spread out, trying to match signatures against the one on the white van's registration.

Glancing up, he could tell the rage in Murphy's face, and a confused, uncomfortableness crossed his face. Silently he continued his work, then deeply sighing laid his project aside.

"Boss, I have to clear the air. I didn't tell Borden about Albert Burbakowski, or anything else we do. To tell you the truth, I like being here and I don't want to leave the task force. This is the best bunch I've ever worked with and I'd never betray them. *Never*, Frank!"

Murphy listened, his head down, then gazed at Yates. "I know, Joe. I shouldn't have accused you. I know who's responsible now, and I apologize for acting like a horse's ass. If anyone should leave, it's me. I was the one at fault. I told someone I thought I could trust, and she broke it off in me. You're doing a great job and I'm glad you're working with us. Keep it up."

The relief washed across Yates' face, then he nodded appreciatively and returned to his signatures.

Glad to have gotten it off his chest, Murphy dug into the mess on his desk. A second message from Captain Brooks was among the scraps of paper he uncovered. This one meant business! On the way up, he picked up Drake for moral support—and to help him keep his ass out of trouble. Knocking respectfully, he waited until Brooks told them to enter.

"What's the hell's the matter with you? Didn't you get my message yesterday that I wanted to see you?"

"Sorry, Captain, it must've gotten misplaced. What's up?"

"Sit. Borden met with Chief Williams and Councilman James

earlier today," Brooks started off. "He told them he's ready to make a press release that Burbakowski was the serial killer. He wants Williams to disband the task force."

"That's just so much crapola and you know it, Captain," Murphy said, leaning forward in his chair. "That murdering slime ball is still out there, ready to grab another young girl off the street and slaughter her. You've got to intervene in this. I need more time."

"He's right, Tom. This ain't over yet," Drake agreed.

"I'll do what I can, but when Borden came back from Everett, he was pretty pissed about how he was treated up there. He seems to think you two had a hand in it. Anyway, they'll want to see you this afternoon at three, Frank. You won't do your cause any good if you don't show up."

"I'll be there."

It'd been three days since the Everett incident and under BJ's watchful eye, Amanda had settled down in the safe company of her two bodyguards. Bored to tears and believing Amanda to be in good hands, BJ decided her mind might be better if she could keep busy. She used this day to return to the office to pick up any tasks she might bring home to work on.

It felt good to get some fresh air. She was in a happy mood when she arrived at the task force office. Joe Yates still poured over his stack of printouts, and she offered to relieve him so he could grab a sandwich and stretch his legs.

The time quickly flew by. Finishing a second cup of coffee while immersing herself in Joe's stack of printouts, her cellular phone rang, jolting her.

"Officer Burgess here."

The whisper came so quietly she almost didn't hear it.

"Mommy?"

Her heart lumped in her throat, she blurted, "Mandy? Darling, is that you?"

Pulse pounding, she waited anxiously, then another whispered response. "Mommy, they're gone. The guards are *gone.*"

Cold terror gripped her and she fought to sound calm. "Where did they go, baby?"

Again, a faint whisper. "I don't *know*, Mommy. They got a telephone call and just up and took off."

"Are all the doors locked and shades down, Amanda?"

"I don't know. I think so."

BJ tried to calm her ragged breathing. "Now listen to me, darling. Do exactly as I say. Okay?"

"Okay," came the ragged whisper from the other end.

"Get the portable phone and keep it with you. I'm going to talk to you until I get there." Already retrieving her purse and car keys, she gripped the phone, her hand trembling slightly and waited until Amanda confirmed she had the portable phone. "Now, I want you to go check all the doors and windows. Make sure they're all locked and the shades closed. I'm leaving *right* now. Don't hang up. I want you to stay on the line until I get there, okay?"

BJ sped out the door, running as fast as she could and still listen to her daughter. Sticking the portable emergency light to the top of her car, she activated the siren and squealed from the parking lot, startling some off-duty police officers arriving for their shift.

Suddenly, a more urgent whisper, "*Mommy!*"

"I'm right here, sweetheart."

"There's someone outside!"

Oh God, BJ thought! *Be calm. Be calm!* She couldn't let the fear show in her voice. "Go back to your room, *now!* Hurry, darling." She could hear her daughter panting hard as she ran up the stairs.

"I'm there." She sounded out of breath.

"Now, lock the bedroom door and shove your dresser chair under the door knob, real hard. *Go!*"

BJ glanced at her speedometer and saw she was traveling nearly eighty miles an hour on straight stretches through the city. Thank god she'd taken the smaller house two years ago because it'd been closer to work.

BJ cringed as she thought of the pretty framed one she'd nearly leased in Bellevue. She'd finally decided against it because it'd been at least forty minutes from the station, the commute was a killer, and she'd wanted more time to spend with her daughter. Now, she prayed her choice had been close enough. BJ's car slid sideways around a corner with a sickening lurch, and fighting for control, she finally regained it. Cold sweat beaded on her brow.

"Okay Mommy, I did it."

BJ heard a sob catch in her daughter's voice. Fighting to sound calm, she said, "I'm real proud of you, honey, and I love you so much. Now go into the bathroom and bolt the door. Take the phone with you so we can talk. I'm just a few blocks away now. I'll be there in another minute or two."

Ahead, a King County Transit bus slowly entered traffic, it's left-hand turn signal blinking, blocking two lanes and her ability to pass.

"Goddammit, move!" she screamed, her hand slamming the steering wheel.

Unaware that she had screamed at the driver, she yanked the wheel hard to the right, scraping the fender of the motorist to her rear, jumping the curb, careening across Washington Mutual Bank's manicured lawn, coming to rest on the adjoining street.

She floor-boarded the big Chevy again, jerked the wheel sharply and squealed around the right hand corner through a red light—in front of the angry driver's car she'd just damaged. She caught a glimpse of his up-your-ass finger as she flew over a hill out of sight.

BJ was still ten blocks from home when Amanda screamed!

"Amanda? Amanda, can you hear me? Answer me, Goddamn it! BJ shouted, her heart sinking.

"He busted down the front door, Mommy!" Amanda was openly sobbing now. "He's in the house! Oh god, oh god, he's going to get me like he did Grandma Abie and Alfred..." her voice trailed off to a small incoherent whimper.

BJ could tell she was near hysteria and that somehow, she had to keep her daughter rational. "Amanda? *Amanda*! Listen to me! No he's *not*! I'm almost home now! Just keep talking to me. Can you hear the siren?"

BJ slid into her cul-de-sac sideways, just as a loud crash and a scream ripped from the phone, then—silence.

She fishtailed across the lawn, slamming on the brakes, skidding to a halt in front of the porch. Jumping out, she left the car door dangling open and sprinted to the shattered front door. It had been splintered and the lock ripped out. Holding her 9mm in a two-handed stance, she rounded the door, quickly scanning the room, then raced across it, flattening herself against the wall as she inched her way up the stairs. Reaching the top, she could see the splintered door-jam to her daughter's room.

Come on you bastard! Just show yourself and I'll blow your fucking ass to kingdom come!

She covered the distance in only three steps and immediately saw the bathroom door ajar. Her heart pounding, she quickly moved to one side, braced herself, and cautiously peered inside. It was empty!

A scream of rage rose in her throat and she struggled for control. She wheeled and raced back toward the hallway. Just as she exited the bedroom, a faint sound caught her attention — she turned back.

"Mommy?"

It'd come from inside the bedroom. Instantly she returned and saw Amanda crawling from beneath her bed, her face streaked with tears. BJ ran to her, knelt and held on as if she'd never let go.

"Darling, darling, my darling," BJ crooned, stroking her daughter's tear-streaked face.

"Mommy, oh, Mommy, I was so scared," the girl sobbed against her chest.

Enraged, BJ was on guard again. *I'm going to kill that bastard!* She jumped to her feet, moved toward the door, gripping the automatic.

"Do you know where he went, sweetheart?" she asked through her teeth, her eyes never leaving the doorway.

"I think he left when he heard the police car coming. I heard him run down the steps, then the kitchen door slammed and... I didn't know if it was him coming back when I heard you come in, so I stayed hid."

"You did real good, sweetheart. I'm proud of you. Now, grab your blue suitcase and get some clothes; jeans, sweatshirts, a nightgown, things like that. We're going away for a while. Okay?"

Keeping her automatic within easy reach, she quickly packed her own clothes into a battered brown bag and carried the two suitcases down to her car. She never acknowledged the perplexed old man next door shaking his head as she left, leaving more deep ruts in the lawn.

Murphy and Drake were kept waiting thirty minutes before being called in. Chief Williams motioned Murphy toward a chair in the middle of the room, while the huge Drake melted into the wallpaper toward the rear. Only Borden, James, and Brooks were present this time. Councilwoman Helen Walcott, his ally from the last meeting was conveniently missing. Murphy had a bad feeling about this. *Looks like an inquisition,* he thought.

Chief Williams started the ball rolling. "Frank, we'd like to commend you for the fine job you did in tracking down this serial killer. Your record will reflect it."

Borden smirked, but no one else seemed to notice. Williams went on. "We all think the time has come to disband the task force and get back to the routine of running this department. Lord knows we need the manpower."

Murphy watched Borden whisper to James, who ignored him. *Shit draws flies, but sometime even shit don't care for them,* he thought, cursing the events in his life that had brought him together with such a group.

The Chief was still speaking, "...any loose ends, Frank?"

Murphy sighed wearily. "If you mean like the little thing of catching the real killer before we close up shop, yeah, there is."

Drake snickered quietly behind him, and Borden's face reddened. He hurriedly went on. "Look Chief, I know there're hard feelings in this room, but this goes way beyond that. There's a killer out there who makes Ted Bundy look like Mother Teresa. Linda Larsen says he's becoming totally out of control, and that means more dead children to answer for."

James leaned forward and stated, "It's quite interesting you should mention Doctor Larsen, Detective Murphy. I too, spoke with her recently and she seems to think *you* might be the one out of control — the strain of losing your daughter... other family crisis's... may be causing you a great deal of stress."

Murphy steeled himself, struggling to maintain control. He knew James was trying to provoke him so he'd lose his temper and hasten things along. He was certain he couldn't bring up Julie without making himself appear unstable, and this was too important an issue to let him be drawn into a pissing contest with his archenemy. He ignored James and directed his remarks toward Captain Brooks.

"Is this how you see it, too, Tom? The DNA samples — teeth marks — nothing matched with the Burbakowski boy. This creep is going to strike again, very soon. We're getting close, Tom. Give me a month, even another week. If there're no more killings, or we haven't made any more headway, I'll gladly step aside."

Brooks cleared his throat, clearly under stress himself. Just as he was about to answer, the Chief broke back in. "Well, Frank, there hasn't been any activity since the little Farmer girl was killed," Chief Williams said.

"Three days ago one of your officer's daughters was stalked and her grandmother brutally murdered by this guy. Borden *must've* told you that, Chief."

"A burglary, pure and simple," Borden blurted. "All the facts support that. Someone tried to rob the place, the old lady surprised him, and he killed her. End of story. It'd have to be a pretty big coincidence in a city this large, if this Headhunter guy just happened to randomly select a police officer's daughter. And an even bigger one considering she's on the task force charged with catching him.

Come on, don't be so paranoid Frank! Or, maybe you think there's more to it? You're seeing conspiracies in too many things lately, Frank."

He thought of Julie again, but kept his gaze leveled at Williams, ignoring Borden completely. "I don't understand it all myself, sir. I'll admit it sounds strange, but it happened. If Borden wasn't so full of hatred for me, he'd confirm it."

"We're not here to bargain with you, Murphy!" Borden retorted. "The task force is dissolved — as of today! Get your desk cleared out and report back to Captain Brooks!"

"I'll do it when I hear it from Chief Williams! I can't believe he'd let personal feelings and politics influence a decision this important." He stared straight at Williams and waited.

"I'm afraid it's over Frank. I wish there were some..." Murphy's cell phone rang loudly, interrupting him. Borden smirked, clearly enjoying Frank's embarrassment of having his phone ring in the middle of a meeting.

Shit, not now, thought Murphy, as he reached into his pocket and flipped it open.

"Yeah?"

He tensed, listening intently as the color rose in his face rose, then said, "Take her to the Cozy Cove Marina. It's on the north end, near the locks. See Mama Elsa, tell her who you are, and that I asked her to help you. Ask to see a big Swede — name's Olaf. Tell him I asked him to look after you until I arrive. I'm leaving now, it should take about twenty minutes." He quietly listened intently. "Okay, bye."

Murphy returned the small phone to his jacket pocket then removed the small black case containing his badge and credentials from his inside jacket pocket. He gazed at it briefly then unceremoniously flipped it onto the table in front of Chief Williams.

"You fools," he said softly. "You dangerous, arrogant fools. This city is approaching a bloodbath and you're playing politics with children's lives. I'll give you my letter on Monday morning."

As he strode to the door, he paused and faced the group once more. "Oh, by the way, that was Officer Burgess. After you geniuses pulled her daughter's security, the *burglar* returned a few minutes ago and tried to kill the little girl again. Some persistent burglar, wouldn't you say?" He slammed out, leaving them in stunned silence.

Brooks was next and moved toward the door, too.

Chief Williams cleared his throat and said, "Tom, we'll need you to stay and discuss this a little longer...if you don't mind."

"It just so happens I do mind, Chief. I just lost the best cop in my division. I agree with Frank and I'm going to write a memo to that effect as soon as I get back to the office." He turned to leave again, then paused. "Or do you want my resignation, too?" He exited without waiting for a reply.

Drake followed Brooks out. Exiting the building he heard a shout from behind.

"Detective Drake!"

He halted, and waited for Borden and James to catch up. Panting hard, Borden drew close and began to talk rapidly. James stood to the side and remained silent.

"With Murphy gone, we'll have an opening for a promotion. I'd say you deserve it. This could be a great opportunity for you,

Drake. Interested?"

Drake drew himself up to his full height, his stance exactly like the large hairy beast for which he was named. His deep rumbling voice reached several uniformed officers standing nearby.

"Frank Murphy is my partner, but more than that, he's my *friend*, and has been ever since Desert Storm. Now, being someone's friend might seem like a foreign concept to you 'cause I doubt if either of you assholes have a single one. So let me say this just one time — clearly, so you both understand it," he snarled through clinched teeth.

"Stay the fuck away from me. Don't talk to me, don't look at me, don't *think* about me. If you see me in the hallway, turn around and go the other way. Don't *ever* speak to me in public, and *never* — *ever* — say anything bad about my friend, Frank Murphy that I might hear about."

His jaw clenched, he edged closer to the white-faced Borden, flicked an imaginary piece of lint from his lapel and whispered low and dangerous. "Now go crawl back into your hole, slime ball, and remember what I said, 'cause I will."

With that, he turned his cold hostile eyes on Robert James for just an instant before he lumbered down the steps toward his parked police unit, leaving Borden, white and shaken.

Chapter 18

The Cozy Cove Marina was situated on an inlet nestled between two of Seattle's largest marinas. Mama had once confided in Murphy that the owners of the other two had been trying unsuccessfully for the past six years to buy her out. He could see why. Though small, she had the prime property, a small, secluded cove, not one jutting out into the elements like her neighbors. The other two marinas were positioned on her flanks, giving them an oblique view, while Cozy Cove faced directly into Elliott Bay. He'd fallen in love with its charm the first time he'd seen it. Approaching it now, the waves slapped against the hulls of moored boats, their gentle rocking motion and saltwater spray calming his frayed nerves.

His eyes caught Olaf and his ugly bulldog first. Then he spotted Amanda and BJ inside the Swede's tug. The big white-haired Swede was six-foot six, weighing nearly three hundred pounds. His neck size resembled a small tree trunk and knotted arm muscles bulged beneath his shirt. Murphy had seen him lift incredible weights while working with the boats. Despite his bulk, he moved with grace, as effortlessly as an athlete.

Murphy had once visited his cabin and noticed his framed award, a fourth place in the Olympic Iron Man event as a young Marine. He'd left the service after his enlistment and immediately gone to work for Mama Elsa, helping her run the marina. He'd said more than once those boats were his first love.

When Murphy had first applied for a slip, Olaf had noted from his application that he'd also been a Marine, in Force Recon. Like flypaper, the usually quiet, standoffish Swede bonded to the policeman, helped him refurbish his old boat and provided free security when Murphy was not around. Over time, their friendship grew stronger as they renovated Mama's ancient sailboat together. Olaf observed the love Murphy had for fine teak and classic boats and was quick to remark that he was his friend. It was a term he didn't use lightly.

The bulldog raised his big, ugly head, a hungry growl deep in his throat. "I see him, Apeshit. He's a friend."

BJ saw him approach down the floating dock and ran into his arms, holding him as tightly as she could. He could tell she was crying softly and held her until she was ready to pull away.

"Bear called to see if you were here yet. He told me what happened. I'm so sorry Frank."

"Don't be. I never did fit in with that bunch anyway. How's Mandy holding up?"

BJ grasped his arm and walked back toward Olaf's tug. "She's a tough kid, Frank. After everything she's been through, she can still smile—and that ugly bulldog loves her." They were able to laugh at that and it felt good.

"Thanks, Olaf. I knew I could count on you." He shook the big man's weathered hand.

"I'll keep watch as long as it's necessary, Frank. No one's going to hurt that little girl while I'm around. Don't worry about that," Olaf assured him.

Murphy had the vague sense he'd relish the opportunity to pull the arms off anyone who threatened Amanda.

He'd stopped by the market and loaded up on galley supplies. After grilling steaks and corn ears, they discussed the arrangements while they ate, followed by Amanda washing up the dirty dishes while the grownups relaxed. He and BJ enjoyed a glass of wine on the deck, quietly planning their next move.

"I'm leaving the department too, Frank. I won't let them put my daughter at risk any more," she told him after Amanda had gone to bed.

The air was chilly. She'd changed into jeans and an oversized sweatshirt that made her look even younger and more vulnerable. "Those bastards pulled off her security and didn't even tell me about it. Why did they do it, Frank?"

He could see she was nearly in tears again. "I'm afraid you just got caught up in something between Borden and me, BJ." He felt badly and just a little guilty. "The innocent always get hurt when people play politics."

"It's not your fault, Frank! Don't you think for an instant that it was."

Watching her hug her knees for warmth, she stared at him with large dark eyes. He suddenly ached to take her in his arms, but forced his mind away from that track and instead, said, "Thanks, BJ, I just feel badly for the two of you, that's all."

He left momentarily and brought back the half bottle of wine. Pouring her glass, his hand gently brushed against her arm. He jerked his hand away quickly as though touching it to a flame, and BJ turned her head as she smiled secretly to herself.

"What are you going to do now, Frank?"

"You mean with my life?"

She nodded, and he shrugged, thinking about. "Maybe I'll take a little vacation. I haven't had one in over three years. They'll have to pay me for the vacation time I've got saved, so I might take the loot and cruise the San Juan Islands a few months. It's real cheap to get by on a boat up there."

They watched as a long graceful sailboat cut through the water at the end of the cove, barely leaving a ripple in its wake.

"You and Mandy could come with me." It just came out naturally as he gazed after the sleek sailboat. Glancing back at her, she stared into his eyes. The wind had swept her hair loose from the one lone hairpin and strands swirled around her face.

God, is she ever lovely.

"What are you asking, Frank?"

He swallowed hard, clearing his throat twice before answering. As he said it, it sounded very noncommittal. "Well, you said you wanted to get Mandy away for a while, so I just thought it'd be a good way. Besides, I know the situation and could keep an eye on the two of you. How about it?"

It was clear she wanted to, but she hesitated. Finally, she said, "No... I don't think so, Frank. I appreciate the offer, but it wouldn't be a good idea."

He nodded then poured the remainder of his wine into the water. Placing his glass down carefully on the wood trim, he pulled her into his arms, kissing her deeply. BJ responded, sliding her tongue past his lips, moaning softly into his mouth. Her arms circled his neck and she pulled him tighter. Murphy dropped his hands to her buttocks as he pressed her to his hardness. She moaned softly again.

As the kiss ended, she pulled back slightly. "The answer's still the same, Frank. There's no future in it for me."

"You want it all, don't you?"

"Yes."

He pulled her close again, this time placing his lips close to her ear. "I love you, BJ. When this is legally over between Elnore and me... I'd like you and Mandy to be with me, forever. Will you?"

She pulled back and smiled, her face brightening. "Of course." Taking his hand, she led him inside to the king-sized berth at the aft of the boat.

Elnore awoke suddenly, remembering she had to present a brief in court at nine. Swinging her shapely legs over the edge of the king-sized bed, she groaned in discomfort, stiff and sore from the previous evening's activities. *Robert's a damned animal*, she thought, grimacing again. Hell, so was she.

Like a bitch in heat. What's happening to me?

All James had to do was to say it, and she did it. No, she *wanted* to do it! It was always the same the morning after. Guilt... despair... a deep down dirty feeling, like swimming in the sewer. *Where in the hell did Robert get that ugly giant?*

Through it all, he'd just silently sat nearby and watched as that huge *animal* had used her in any manner he wanted—hour upon hour. A shiver shot through her at the thought.

God, what is happening to me? What have I become?

It was Robert James' fault. He's the one who'd changed her. He was the sickest, most depraved person she'd ever known, and she realized she was becoming just as bad. Remembering the stack of magazines she'd discovered in his closet, she was certain that he'd meant for her to find them—suggesting she select some pictures of acts they could try later. She knew if she didn't get away from him soon, he'd destroy her sanity. She wondered how many other women Robert had debauched. She had no illusions about him. He was extremely handsome, wealthy, powerful and persuasive. He could do whatever he wanted to do—and she knew she'd let him.

That phone call she'd overheard, though, disturbed her. What had it been all about? Elnore was sure she'd heard Frank's name mentioned. Robert was extremely upset, as he'd discussed her *ex* on the phone with someone late last night. She'd clearly understood him to say that Murphy "wouldn't be a problem much longer".

Despite her and her estranged husband's difficulties—mostly her fault to be sure— she didn't want anything *bad* to happen to Frank. She knew she wouldn't be fit for him anymore, not after Robert got through with her, but she'd never intentionally want to have bad things happen to him. Not while she was alive. Elnore closed the door, locked it, and hurried toward her parked car.

———————

Eyes closed, Corky reclined and daydreamed about a lost love. Jennifer had been the love of Corky's life. Corky had been young when both parents *tragically* perished in that accident. Corky had lived with several relatives and a godfather until age ten before attending a private school. It had been the one Jennifer went to, and they soon became great friends. Jennifer was the daughter of a prominent black family, the most beautiful girl Corky had ever seen. Even more special, their families lived only a few blocks apart and were friends, which made it easier to see each other during the summer.

After Jennifer's murder, Corky had been intrigued with other girls, but none as special as Jenny. That is, until Amanda Burgess came along. She resembled Jennifer, so much that Corky could almost believe Jennifer had been reincarnated.

Yes, I've got to have Amanda. I will have her—and soon! Until then, there're always others to amuse myself. Like the sweet little thing in the basement.

Corky smiled and headed down the long dark steps.

———————

With some trepidation, Murphy and BJ informed Amanda of their plans the following morning. They were pleasantly surprised as she excitedly discussed the possibilities of being away from school for such a long period. BJ explained that school would be out within the next couple of weeks anyway, and she already had sufficient credits to continue to the next grade. It'll be easy to enroll somewhere different, long before the next school year began.

Amanda's spirits dropped briefly, but soon excitedly asked if they were going to live on fish the whole time. Still laughing about that, Murphy noticed two people advancing, instantly recognizing them. He shuddered with an ominous foreboding.

The two matronly women made their way cautiously down the sloping ramp and floating walkway leading to his slip. *High heels.* He cringed, thinking about his glossy teak finish. *Nice practical footwear for walking on decks, docks and fiberglass.* Helen Walcott flipped a half-smoked cigarette into the water just before they arrived. Both women looked as if they meant business.

"Detective Murphy," she shouted as she neared. "My, but you do live in a difficult place to reach."

He opened the small door off the transom, and allowed them to enter the salon.

"Sergeant Murphy, this is Congresswoman Ethel Holcomb. You recall that she's the mother of one of the killer's earlier victims."

"Ms. Holcomb," Murphy acknowledged, as she shook his hand. "I'm sorry about your daughter, Ma'am. Maybe they'll catch the guy before he can harm any one else."

BJ joined them standing near the door, silently watching. Then both ladies greeted her warmly, as they all settled safely on board.

"But it's not *Sergeant* Murphy, anymore," he went on, correcting her. "I'm just a regular citizen now, ma'am."

"You haven't turned in your letter of resignation, have you?" she said.

"Not yet. But that's just a formality anyway. I'm taking it by the administration office this afternoon. Then I've got a little vacation time coming and I plan to spend it in the San Juan Islands with this nice lady and her wonderful daughter. Please ladies, have a seat. Can I get you something to drink? Tea, coffee, soft drinks?"

"Iced tea would be great," she said, and her companion eagerly nodded.

Ethel Holcomb stuffed her broad butt into one of the empty lounge chairs Murphy kept on board for company, while the much slimmer Helen Walcott eased into the other. Amanda relished her usual role of a grown-up hostess, placing glasses of iced tea down on a small table before quickly vanishing inside.

Holcomb squeezed a wedge of lemon into her glass and sipped, eyeing him. "Well, that sounds like loads of fun, Detective Murphy," she said, ignoring the correction of his title. "Does it bother you at all that someone is still out there killing our daughters?"

He'd known it was coming, but sighed heavily and looked off into space. "Ma'am, I'm sorry about your daughter, believe me when I say that. I know what you're going through right now because I've been there, too. But I took my best shot at it and didn't get the job done. Now, it's someone else's turn. Besides, the party-line is Albert Burbakowski was the killer and he's dead."

"Have you read the morning paper yet, Detective?" she said expressionless.

"No ma'am."

Murphy saw her age dramatically as her shoulders slumped and her facial muscles sagged. Composing herself, she said, "Two more girls were taken last night. One hasn't been found and most of the experts are assuming it's the same guy."

The news stunned him. *Two! Jesus, Doc Larsen was right. He's out of control.* Murphy quickly detached himself by tidying a boat line while blinking rapidly. "Who are they?"

"Nobodies. One is the daughter of a poor hard-working black family, and the other is that of a single mother on welfare. No one the press will get excited about," the old woman said.

She laid out two large color photos on the table in front of him. The first, a smiling little blond girl, her dark freckles sprinkled across the bridge of her nose... playfully sticking her tongue out at the camera. The other, a young black girl about Amanda's age, her wide infectious grin reminded him of her. He felt BJ stiffen and she'd placed her hand on his arm. Swallowing hard, he struggled to keep his voice from breaking. He was only partially successful.

"What are their names?"

Congresswoman Holcomb pointed at the photo of the little white girl. "That was Peggy Sue Anton last year in the fifth grade. The other is Sherry Underwood." She rummaged inside her folder again, retrieving what she was seeking, and said, "This is Peggy Sue today."

Out came another picture, this time a glossy black-and-white official photo. Murphy had to look twice to comprehend the image. It was only a torso. No arms — no legs — just the torso. The head had been positioned as all the others. It was as if someone hit him with a hammer! He lost his bearing, the boat began to spin, gorge rose in his throat and he suddenly stood, knocking over his glass of tea.

Amanda hovered instantly, trying to wipe up the spill, but BJ wasn't quite fast enough to hide the photos. A sob caught in the girl's throat and she ran back inside, crying. BJ glared, incensed at the older woman then followed her daughter below.

"I'm very sorry she saw those," Ethel told Murphy, busily stuffing the photos back into the folder.

"No you're not," he said coldly. "You knew exactly what you were doing, Ms. Holcomb. Why did you really come here?"

She closed her attaché. "We need you to get this guy, Frank. I need you to do whatever it takes to get him off the streets."

"There're lots of cops in Seattle P.D., Ms. Holcomb. Any one of them would do as well, or better. What makes you think I have the silver bullet?"

"Well, for starters, you were the only one who wasn't satisfied with the arrest of Mr. Burbakowski. Secondly, you're not intimidated by the so called *party-line*." She hesitated, shifting her body closer to focus on his eyes. "And lastly, you too have lost a daughter in this manner. I frankly don't believe you'll be able to stop until you catch him, Sergeant Murphy."

Murphy felt immensely weary, his shoulders sagging under an invisible weight. "I'm not a *cop* anymore, ma'am. I've quit."

She reached deep inside her large handbag and retrieved a small black case. She laid it on the table. It was his badge. "Frank, I heard from your supervisor, Captain Brooks, about what happened yesterday. I saw Chief Williams early this morning and explained the awkward position he'd placed me in.

I told him that I might be forced to hold a press conference to discuss the lack of progress in my daughter's murder. I also related that I intended to bring up these two latest disappearances, and the fact that you've resigned, rather than agree to a cover up. He blustered and squirmed a bit, but finally ended up asking what I wanted. I told him I wanted you back on the case. Now, I'm asking you. What do you want Frank Murphy? What will it take to get you back on the case?"

"You said *two* girls are missing. What about the other one?"

"We don't know about her, yet. We're praying we can find her before it's too late."

BJ had quietly returned and stood beside him. He couldn't read her expression. "I can't do this again, Ms. Holcomb. I feel sorry for those little girls and their families. I really do. But I can't help them any more than I could've helped my own daughter. I have a family that depends on me, too."

He dropped his eyes, and more softly said, "At some point people have to get on with their lives, or they start to die, too." A soft hand rested on his shoulder. He reached up, covering it with his own.

BJ knelt beside him, placing a hand along each side of his face. "Frank Murphy, I know you too well. You could no more walk away from this than you could stop breathing—not if there's one chance in a million of finding that little girl. Amanda and I'll be safe if you ask for the right things now. Tell her what you want, quit feeling sorry for yourself, and go back to work. We'll never be free of this until he's caught, or dead." She kissed him softly on the lips. "Go on back. We'll be fine, darling."

Murphy focused his eyes on Ethel Holcomb. She hadn't budged.

"I want free rein to go after this guy any way I want. I'll answer only to Brooks—if I have to answer to anyone. I want security of *my* choice for Amanda, and I—and *only* I—say when that security is removed. The task force stays in operation until either we catch him, or *I* say it's over—*period*. I also want the same men who asked me to leave, to ask me to come back and take the task force again. That way I'll know there'll be no misunderstandings as to who's running the show. I may have other conditions before it's over. Can I count on you to intervene if necessary?"

She smiled and nodded, then stood. "I'll set up a meeting with that group right away. You ask for whatever you need, Detective Murphy. I'll kick ass if I have to. Agreed?"

Solemnly shaking hands, she and Helen Walcott precariously waddled off the boat, tettering back up the floating dock in their high-heeled shoes.

———————

Sherry Underwood couldn't move. She could only sense what was above her or directly to either side. But she felt she was going to be safe, *now*. The person walking down the steps toward her was smiling, and she could tell by the bright buttons and stripes that this was a *safe* person who'd finally found her.

Like the familiar clothing, the heavenly smile was so wonderful to see—she instinctively knew her safety was at hand. She'd always been told she could rely on *them* if she were ever lost or in trouble—and boy, was she ever in trouble… *they always came to help*! Sherry tried to smile, her lips held back by an *awful* rubber taste. She watched as the kind face came closer to the rescue, then averted her eyes to her savior's hands.

Her eyes widened in terror as she struggled to cry out, but only muffled screams leaked through the rubber gag. In a latex-gloved hand, her smiling rescuer grasped a large flesh colored rubber object that filled her with stark terror. As she turned her focus to the other hand, her bladder released, soaking through her thin panties onto the table beneath her. Terrified, she arched and struggled against her bonds, a bare light bulb reflecting from the knife's shiny serrated silver teeth.

———————

Frank Murphy received his first call back from Drake less than an hour later. "Hey, old buddy. Want a job chasing bad guys?"

"I kind of thought I might take a crack at it again. Want to give me a hand, or has Borden offered you a better deal?" he deadpanned.

"Well, I ain't sure I want to work for anyone stupid enough to come back to this viper's den once they're free of it, but if you're offering job security I guess I'm still in. I got two tickets for the Sonics game tonight, but now I suppose I won't be going."

Murphy told him about the meeting Congresswoman Holcomb was setting up with the Chief, James, and Borden. "Since you're not going to the game, want to come along and watch the fireworks? I know you wouldn't want to miss it for the world."

Drake snorted loudly into his receiver. "I'd enjoy that about as much as a dirt sandwich."

"Well then, how 'bout contacting Clancy Gates and Paulie Haskill, ASAP. Tell them to set up security on Amanda at Cozy Cove not later than noon today!" Drake was silent, but Murphy knew him well enough to know he was scribbling furiously in his little black notebook.

"And another thing, I want the task force team to schedule stakeout shifts on the marina during the hours of darkness, until we find a more secure place for Amanda."

"I'll get it set up, Murph," Drake agreed. They talked a few minutes longer and hung up. Less than ten minutes later the phone rang again. It was Borden.

"Murphy? We need to talk to you. Be at the Chief's office at three."

"Fuck you."

There was a long silence on the other end. "*What?*"

"I said, '*fuck* you.' I don't work for the department any more, so take your shitty meeting and shove it where the sun don't shine."

On the other end of the line, he could hear Borden having breathing problems. He made sure his next words were ultra-pleasant. "*Bye now.*"

As he hung up, he glanced at BJ. She flashed him an amused smile. *Boys will be boys*, it clearly said. Less than thirty seconds later, the phone rang loudly. Borden again.

"Now Frank, don't hang up on me. *Please!* The Chief said he'd have my ass if I didn't get you in here today," the voice whined.

"So what do you want to ask me, Borden?" BJ's smile had returned, but her arched eyebrow indicated she was becoming a little annoyed with his antics. A thought crossed his mind, *cute expression*.

"Frank, will you come to the Chief's office at three o'clock?" Borden finally asked.

"Please."

"What? Oh, yeah. *Please* Frank." He sounded pathetic.

"Well, I'll *try* to be there. I was going to scrape the bottom of my boat this afternoon. If I can't make it, just start without me. Okay?"

"Please try hard, Frank! *Really*, Frank! Williams will fry my nuts if you don't show up," Borden pleaded.

Murphy struggled to keep from laughing, recalling how much Borden had enjoyed using that particular phrase when threatening others. "We certainly wouldn't want anything like that to happen to *you*, would we Borden? I'll be there. In fact, I think I'll rather enjoy it this time." He hung up.

"You still trying to win friends and influence people?" BJ asked, as though amused by his childish display.

"You've got to take your pleasure whenever you find it," he insisted as he stretched. "Mandy napping?"

BJ nodded slowly, but with sudden suspiciousness. Springing to his feet, he pulled her up, slipping a hand under her sweatshirt. "You sleepy? Want to take a nap?" he said, feeling her nipple harden.

"Sure."

———

Elnore hadn't stayed at Robert James's house last night. He'd been in an awful mood and she'd suspected it was because of Frank's reappointment to the task force. He'd been so pleased when he'd first told her of Murphy's resignation a few days ago. At the time, the news had hit her like a bomb. Elnore couldn't see Frank doing anything but being a cop, and she'd had a sinking feeling it'd be the straw to break the camel's back — *Frank's* back.

The truth was, she'd almost resented James's enthusiasm concerning Frank's demise as he'd droned on about it. Finally, she'd just gone home—early—without even going to bed with him. James hadn't called her all day, and then last night he'd become so surly and mean to her that she'd left early again. Elnore had a feeling he was still smarting from her early departure.

Take a cold shower, darling, and get used to it.

She might've cheated on her husband — have a few twisted hang-ups — a little too much ambition — but she wasn't a *bad* person. No one could make her believe that she was. While she'd accepted the fact that she'd never get Frank back, she still wanted him to think well of her — to be friends.

I'll tell him what I heard James talking about on the phone when he thought I was in the bathroom and couldn't hear.

Yes, she'd tell Frank today.

———————

Vacant eyes bored into the little black girl who'd slightly resembled the lovely Jennifer, once upon a time. *Then, she lost her head.* Corky giggled, then laughed insanely at the joke.

Eyes lovingly stroking the dismembered corpse, it all became clear! *Why, of course! The perfect place to dispose of the body. It was absolutely genius! Just wait until those assholes get a load of this! This'll teach them to try and hide little Jennifer... uh, Amanda. This'll show them all!*

This would let them know there wasn't *any place* they could hide her where she couldn't be found.

Chapter 19

The meeting with Chief Williams, Lt. Borden and Captain Brooks had not gone well for them. Brooks had just stared silently at the table, leaving it totally up to Borden and Williams to say what had to be said in order to make Murphy happy. It hadn't gone well because Frank Murphy hadn't been the least bit magnanimous about the situation, making them say aloud all the things he could've just let them gloss over. It was a pound of flesh, pure and simple, or as his partner Bear always said, "Forget and forgive — but first get even."

He could tell every word out of Williams mouth was flat-out insincere and wouldn't have been spoken at all, had he not been coerced by Congresswoman Holcomb. Still, Murphy knew that once the words were out, it would be extremely difficult for him to take them back. So, he'd sat silently until he was satisfied they had run out of concessions, thinking, *Wonder what she said to Williams that scared the crap out of him like this?* He'd grinned, with just a hint of maliciousness, not bothering to conceal it.

At the end, he'd risen and simply told them what he expected if he agreed to come back. He began with Borden's removal from the task force chain-of-command, and ended with the lieutenant's exclusion from being remotely connected with it.

He knew he was on firm ground because Congresswoman Holcomb had told him she'd laid the law down to Chief Williams. Aware of her power with the press, he had no doubt she was capable of it, too. He suspected Helen Walcott had informed the congresswoman about his own daughter's similar death, and that he hadn't bought the story of Albert Burbakowski being the killer.

Well, if she wanted Frank Murphy on the job, she'd get Frank Murphy on the job.

Then he'd laid a list of demands in front of Chief Williams, abruptly turned and left, followed by the lumbering Drake.

———————

A grinning Joe Yates was still at the office when he arrived. Joe looked up, grinning hello. "Welcome back, boss. What do you want me to do?"

He heard subtle voices through the door. An instant later, Charley Booth and Lisa Kinard entered. Relief flooded her face as she spontaneously hugged Frank, placing her head against his chest for a moment; her pretty blue eyes brimmed with tears. When she looked up, she was smiling.

"Glad to have you back, Frank. This is a rotten place to work without you around." Lisa hugged him again, then stepped back, blushing, embarrassed.

Murphy spent the next several hours bringing them all up to date and assigned areas of concentration.

Yates said, "I've got a list of about fifty names to check out. Hopefully I'll be able to identify the real owner of that white van. The tests came back on the tire molds and they matched perfectly with the tire tread we found in the lawn at David Turner's house. That means our man may be Arty Hicks... or whatever his real name is."

"Good job, Joe."

It was well after 6:00 p.m. when they broke up for the evening. Halfway to the marina, Murphy called BJ. The security team was back on the job, as were Olaf and his ugly mutt. She sounded relaxed and confident that she and Amanda were safe. He'd barely hung up when another call came through. It was Drake.

"Frank? Meet me at the sheriff's office in Auburn. They just called. Our friend, Arty Hicks? They found him floating in the Green River, his throat slit from ear to ear."

Murphy opened up the gas hungry V-8 cruiser and arrived in twenty minutes. He found Drake pacing outside. Drake hustled to meet him, filling him in on the details. "They think he's been dead for about a week... that means prior to the death of the little Anton girl. That also means we got nothing, Murph. Not a fucking thing!"

Murphy could see the weariness and growing frustration on his partner's usually calm face. He was also smoking a cigarette.

"Don't let it get to you, Bear. We'll get this sicko. We're getting closer every day — don't go losing it on me now. I need you too much."

Drake wrinkled his nose at the butt, tossed it on the ground and crushed it under his big foot. "Now I know why I quit these fucking things," he said. "They taste like shit." He jerked his head toward the station and lumbered away, Murphy following him inside.

Drake introduced him to a youthful officer sitting behind an old metal desk. "This is my partner, Frank Murphy. Frank... Detective Tim Parker, Auburn P.D.'s lead investigator in the case." They extended hands, shook, and Parker indicated chairs for them to sit.

"Still some coffee left in that pot. Anybody takers?" Parker ceremoniously reached for his pipe, filled it, and struck a match to its bowl. It was easy to see why. The pipe added ten years to his youthful appearance.

Murphy and Drake edged nearer to the stained coffeepot, cautiously peering inside at the thick mixture. They looked at each other, horrified, and hastily declined.

"Don't blame you," Parker said, as he poured himself some. "This shit'll kill ya." He took his seat and pushed the preliminary forensic report across the desk to them. Murphy quickly perused it, noting the crime had been committed with the same serrated type knife as all the other murders. He pulled out his cellular and pushed several buttons.

"Charley? Sorry to bother you at home. We've got Arty Hicks stretched out on a slab in the Auburn morgue. I'll fax the information we have on him. I want to know everything about this guy by ten o'clock tomorrow morning... where he was born, went to school, lived, criminal record, family life, friends, the works. If you can't get it all by then, just bring what you can."

He hung up and looked at the report again. "You I.D.'d him by his drivers license. Can I see it?"

Parker tossed a small plastic baggy and Murphy up-ended it on the desktop. He sifted through nail clippers, folding knife, condom, a crushed pack of smokes, four crumpled one-dollar bills and a damp wallet. In the wallet was a California driver's license, issued the previous month. The photo was that of a tall skinny youth with a shaved head, a stud in his right nostril and one earring. Above his left eye was a tattoo of a bird.

"Nice clean cut kid," Drake said sarcastically.

"That doesn't make him a killer," Murphy retorted.

"No, it just makes it easier to believe that he is," Drake insisted reading through the preliminary forensic report. "Now, why can't we get these things this quick? Look! Less than a day and it's already done."

They both knew the large number of crimes committed in the metro area precluded them from getting the reports quickly, but Murphy sensed it was more frustration talking and didn't address the real issue.

Drake pushed the report across the table to him and pointed toward a particular passage. The dead man had been stabbed twenty-six times. It described the weapon as most probably a long thin kitchen type knife.

"Guess we can rule out suicide, huh?" Drake muttered.

"Sounds like the kind of weapon our guy uses," Murphy agreed. "This estimates he was killed about five days ago. That would be right after we searched his apartment."

It also placed the time of his death *before* the latest killing — which meant the killer was still out there. Murphy fought a strong urge to call and check up on BJ and Amanda.

On the drive back to the city, Murphy called BJ twice, but the line was always busy. Each time, he unconsciously increased his speed by another ten miles per hour. Fretting, he arrived at dusk as the sun set, just as he saw Lisa Kinard carrying a large stuffed purple dinosaur down the ramp. He paused, inhaling the fresh salt air, realizing how foolish he'd been. They were both safe and the kid was sure to get her share of attention from everyone as long as she was under wraps, he mused.

Olaf sanded the seat of a small dingy, while ugly old Apeshit panted, sprawled contentedly in the shade of the boathouse. *Makes me wonder why the hell I keep doing what I do for a living.* Suddenly, he felt very weary.

He spoke with the big Swede briefly, then spying Mama nearby, strode over to pay his respects. She nimbly jumped three feet to the ground and smiled as he approached. Barely five-foot four but weighing nearly two hundred pounds, he'd seen her leap from boat to boat many times despite her bulk.

"You be sure to drop by the office before dinner. I made you one of my special Scandinavian dishes," she with a big hug before she continued her project.

Lisa was just departing as he began walking down the ramp toward the *Crime Pays*. Meeting him halfway, she'd informed him she was scheduled for the midnight-to-three shift guarding Amanda, and was on her way home to get some rest. Murphy watched as she jogged to her little white car, her ponytail bouncing pertly. She sped away with a short wave visible through her rear window. He shook his head at her youthful exuberance, as well as the prospect of spending a peaceful evening with the other two women in his life.

Just like clockwork for the past four years, every morning on her way to the marina, Mama Elsa had stopped by her favorite bakery to buy jellyroll donuts. This morning was no exception, and she'd already stuffed three of the sweet sticky rolls into her mouth during the drive.

Carefully pulling her new Ford SUV into the marina's small parking lot, Mama first waved to Olaf, then smiled at the tall good-looking policeman who'd been assigned to guard Amanda. He was just the kind of Italian hunk Mama could fantasize about during slack periods today.

Using her master key, she unlocked the double dead bolt and pushed the office door open, wrinkling her nose at the heavy metallic odor that rushed to meet her. *Jeez, gotta air this place out today*, she thought. *Smells like they've been gutting fish.* Setting the jellyrolls aside, she unlocked the supply room to retrieve the key box. As she flipped the light switch, the small, windowless supply room flooded with light. She began a moan, a low deep rumbling, hurriedly backing away, trying to put some distance between her and the awful sight. Horrified beyond words, she wheeled, knocked over a small table and tipped the fresh rolls onto the tile floor. That's when Mama Elsa finally started to scream. It was only then, as she hit the outside railing, that she lost her jellyroll breakfast.

———————

Frank had almost reached the office when Hooter's deep breathless voice alerted units to finding a body at the Cozy Cove Marina. His heart in his mouth, he flipped on his emergency lights and siren and made a swift U-turn against a red light. Traffic was always heavy at this time of the morning, but he weaved the heavy cruiser between crawling cars and buses, as they too, fought against each other, inching closer to their morning destinations.

Squealing into the parking lot that he'd left only a short time earlier, he found two police units had already arrived, their flashing lights spoiling the usual tranquility. His heart raced out of control. As he exited his car, he spied Charley Booth laboring up the steep ramp to meet him.

"Amanda? Is it Mandy?" he screamed. "What the hell is going on, Charley?" he shouted before they were close enough to talk.

"Amanda and BJ are fine, Frank." Booth yelled breathlessly when he was close enough to dispel his fears. "It's the little Underwood girl that's been missing. The sick son of a bitch planted her right here in the marina. The old lady who owns the place found her when she opened up this morning. They think she's had a heart attack. She's on her way to the hospital."

Mama Elsa...the Underwood girl. Murphy's head spun. *How could this happen? Something's so wrong about this whole damned thing!*

His hands trembling, he took out a cigarette and stuck his lighter to the tip, inhaling deeply to get a hold on his nerves. Trying to stay calm, he said, "Anybody call Hemphill?"

"On the way, Frank. We've done all we can for the moment."

Murphy inhaled deeply, blew out smoke, studied the ash of his cigarette for a few seconds, and then flipped it into the water below. Dreading his next move, he said, "Let's go take a look."

It was low tide and Booth led him down the steeply sloping ramp, then up toward the narrow stairs leading into the small dingy office space. Booth waited near the door as Murphy went to the storage room and peered in.

During all his years as a cop, and even during the war, the hardest thing to do by far was seeing the death of a child, particularly a needless, gruesome death such as this one. A little black girl, about the age of Amanda, had been placed in the same taunting position as all the others had. That made it seem even more obscene.

He heard Hemphill and his crew coming, giving him a reason to wheel around and rush for the door, gulping in fresh air as he exited. Seeing his ashen face, Hemphill had the good sense not to say anything as he entered.

"Does BJ know yet?" he asked Booth, still shaky.

"I told her just before you got here, Murph. She took it as well as you might expect. Gates and Haskill are fit to be tied. Nothing like this has ever happened on their watch before."

Murphy gazed out over the marina, seeing nothing. "Let Hemphill wrap this up. Get everybody on the team together in the office, ASAP. I want some ideas, and… I want to know who was on watch last night. I don't know how it's possible for something like this to happen, but I'm damn sure going to find out!"

Charley made eye contact with him through his sad deputy dog eyes, then said softly, "I had the last shift, Frank." As he turned and trudged away, his shoulders were slumped like those of an old man.

Murphy made his way down the long ramp, much steeper now from low tide, and BJ met him halfway to the boat. She just walked into his arms and stood until she stopped shivering. He smoothed her hair back and held her tightly.

"*How?*"

Her one word was enough; he heard her anguish. Unable to answer, he held her in silence, each drawing their strength from the other.

The office was quiet and subdued—none of the happy give-and-take banter that usually went on when the whole squad was together. Murphy had just poured a cup of the thick coffee when Booth joined them.

"Sorry I'm late, Boss. I waited around until Hemphill could give me a preliminary report. It's handwritten and he's only guessing for the most part, but he said maybe it'd help."

Murphy nodded his thanks. "We need to discuss everyone's activities last night. No finger pointing, but that sicko got into and out of a highly secured area without ever being seen. It falls on our shoulders to figure out how he did it. Who was on watch first?"

"That would be me, Murph," Yates said. "It gets dark later now, so I didn't come on until around nine thirty, relieving Paulie Haskill. That's when all those big floodlights around the marina flick on. I never saw or heard a thing during my entire watch. Lisa relieved me at midnight." Yates looked at Lisa expectantly.

On the verge of tears, Lisa took a deep breath and began. "I was parked out in the front lot with the rear of my car backed against the left side wall. From my position, I could see the entire marina, both piers, the repair shop, and the office where the body was found. Those big halogen lights lit up everything bright as day, Frank. Nobody — and I mean *nobody* — moved while I was there."

"Did you doze? Go to the bathroom? Eat a sandwich? Do *anything* else?"

"*No!*" Lisa's face flushed bright red and she still looked as if she'd break into tears at the least provocation.

Frank's voice softened as he said, "No one is accusing anybody of neglect. We're just trying to get to the bottom of this. Everyone all right with that?"

They nodded their consent.

Charley began next, without being asked. "I spelled Lisa around two-fifty. I was running a little late." He smiled apologetically at Lisa and she favored him with one of her own brilliant smiles in return.

"I stayed until Mama Elsa showed up to unlock. I was off-site about ten or twelve minutes, sometime around four-thirty, Frank. I had to take a dump. I swear it was no more than that. I defy Houdini to drive up, unload a body, carry it two hundred feet, pick a lock, position the body, lock up the place, return to a vehicle and drive off—all in twelve lousy minutes—all without being seen!" His face glared beet-red.

"I agree," Murphy said. It seemed to calm Booth down. "Okay, what about by water?" he said to no one in particular.

"Not a chance, Murph." Drake spoke for the first time. "You got two of the craziest bastards who ever baby-sat a client either perched on your boat or roaming the docks, just itching to blast away with one of those big magnums they're so proud of. They love their job and they don't sleep. *Period*! Shit, I'd trust all the gold in Fort Knox in that marina!"

Murphy nodded his agreement. "To top it off, there's Olaf and that man-eating dog of his, blocking the entrance to the marina with his tug all night. Not to mention all those bright lights again. Anybody got any other ideas?"

From the expressions, he could tell that nobody did. Murphy reached for Hemphill's report, scanned through it briefly, and tossed it aside. "Same as the others. Raped, sodomized, and butchered. No semen present however. He estimates she's been dead about thirty-six hours. Have her parents been notified?"

Drake straightened up and leaned forward. "Brooks and BJ went to their house right after you left, Frank. Brooks said they took it hard."

"I can imagine." He suddenly changed the subject. "Charley, what were you able to get on Arty Hicks?"

"DNA record and teeth plaster both negative. The California driver's license is legit. Issued just recently, and ya know why? Because he's been in the Vacaville prison the past two years for Grand Theft Auto. Seems he's got a taste for BMWs — the big ones. They let him out about eight months ago, but after just two weeks, he violated his parole by stealing another 750 and went right back in. That's the only sunshine he's seen in two years."

Puzzled, Murphy stared at Booth, then at Drake. "Then David Turner lied to us about the period he'd rented the room, and about owning the van. It was registered in Washington several months ago...while Hicks was still in Vacaville."

Drake nodded and followed up. "If he lied about that, he's probably lying about other things."

"Right. The question is, why?" Murphy said. "I think we need to take a run by Mr. Turner's place and have another talk with him. Joe, he was your find. Who do you want to go with you?"

Yates appeared pleased by his boss's public show of confidence in him. "Lisa and I can handle it, Frank. We'll do it right after lunch, if that's okay."

Murphy nodded. "Charley, while you're working on Hicks, get all you can on David Turner, too. He seems just a little too good to be true. We already know he's a liar. See if he's ever been arrested, especially for any sex-related offenses. Do a complete background — friends, neighbors, family, clergy — the works. Also, get that registration on the white van from Joe before he leaves. See if you can match the bogus signature with David Turner's handwriting."

The phone rang loudly, interrupting their discussion. Murphy picked it up — it was Julie.

"Frank? Please, give me one minute. I'm so *sorry* for everything. Just let me explain, don't hang up…"

He hung up. Glaring around the room, it was evident the others had suddenly become obsessed with other things; the room's paint job, a speck of lint on a trouser leg, their notebooks. Except for Drake, who just raised one eyebrow.

"Wrong number?"

Murphy didn't answer — it rang again. He grabbed it and shouted into the mouthpiece. "God dammit, leave me alone, *you bitch*!"

After a noticeable silence on the other end, BJ said softly, "That's *not* what you said last night."

"Oh *Jeez*. I'm sorry baby. I didn't know it was *you*," he whispered, quickly deflating. He swiveled in his chair until his back was to the group, several snickers erupting from his rear.

Assholes!

Yeah, Darl'n. We all knows you ain't a bitch!" It was the unmistakable deep voice of Drake, mimicking him quietly. His remark was followed by more stifled snickers.

Murphy stiffened. "When?"

The room fell instantly silent, all eyes on him.

"How's Olaf taking it?"

He listened intently for a short time then said, "I'll be there as soon as I can. Take Amanda to see him. If she can't cheer him up, no one can." His head nodded at the invisible speaker as he finished. "Right. Bye."

He slowly faced the group; his face pained and drawn. "Mama Elsa passed away about an hour ago. She never came to. Her heart just gave out."

The others finally began to drift away to their assigned tasks, leaving Murphy and Drake alone. He raised his sorrowful eyes to Drake's. "I'm going to kill that bastard, Bear. I'm going to save the state a lot of money and trouble by putting a hole right between his sick eyes!"

————————

The Turner house looked deserted when Joe and Lisa pulled up in front. All the curtains had been drawn and it was dark inside.

"Take the back, Lisa," Yates instructed. "If I have to, I'll kick the door down and just hope the warrant we used before still covers us. If not, we'll cross that bridge when we get there." He allowed Lisa a few minutes to reach the back, while he called in and reported to Murphy.

"Don't wait. Go in," Murphy said. "I'll back you up on this."

Yates rang the doorbell and waited. No sounds came from within. He rang it again... nothing. Removing his pistol, he smashed in one of the front door's small windowpanes and reached inside, unlocking it. Holding his gun high in both hands, he slid around the door, pressing his back against the inside wall.

Empty.

Joe slowly moved through the house, checking each room, then arrived at the rear door, flipped the lock, and let Lisa in.

"The downstairs is clear. Let's go upstairs."

They conducted a thorough search, but it was clear from the first. David Turner was gone.

Yates called in again. "He's gone, Frank. Looks as if he left in a hurry, too. TV's still on and there's food on the table. Looks like he was eating his lunch when he decided to go. It was as if he got a phone call, and booked."

"Stay put, Joe. I'll get the CSU out to go over the house from top to bottom. Don't let anyone in until we get there."

Just as Joe broke the connection, several cars pulled up in front. From the window, he could see Molly Atwood, four other reporters from local newspapers—and Robert James.

"Get the back door, Lisa. No one — including Councilman James — gets in until I say so. I'll take the heat on this one."

He sped toward the front door, just as James and the reporters reached the porch.

"That's far enough, Councilman." Yates stated firmly. "This is a crime scene and it's off limits to all but police personnel. If you'd be kind enough to withdraw to the sidewalk, I'd appreciate it."

How the hell do these damned reporters find out everything so fast, Joe asked himself. Then looking at James, he was pretty sure he knew the answer. The question was though, how did James find out?

"Oh, come on, Joe," Molly said with her sexiest voice. "Surely if I promise not to touch anything, you'd let *me* in, wouldn't you?"

He replied just as sweetly. "Honey, if you try to get past me or refuse to back up to the sidewalk as I've instructed, I'll slap handcuffs on your pretty little butt so fast your head will spin. Then, I'll have you arrested as soon as the backup comes. When I say now, I mean *now*! *Move* it!"

The reporters, exhibiting a measured hostility, slowly made their way toward the street. James tried to shoulder past Yates, but Joe swiftly stepped in front and reached for his handcuffs. James immediately retreated, his face burning a bright crimson. "Your days are numbered, too, Yates!" he snarled. "You can join Murphy in the bread line when I'm through with *you*!"

Yates smiled back thinly, dangling his cuffs on one finger. Having lost his staring down contest, James stomped backward toward the street, entered a waiting vehicle and was quickly driven away.

Another car immediately took the space vacated by James' vehicle. Exiting on the passenger's side, Murphy smiled as he saw the reporters milling in the street. Two more marked police units followed and parked across the street. A young uniformed officer exited the rear one and started to string yellow crime scene tape around the house.

Murphy and Drake stood near the porch and watched as Molly Atwood approached the young officer and smiled sweetly. She said a few words to him as she stood with her legs wide apart and a hip thrust slightly forward. The pose had a nice affect. The young cop momentarily paused to appreciate the view, then pointed toward Murphy and went back to his task of marking the crime scene.

Molly looked their way as Murphy raised his eyebrow. She chuckled and raised her hands shoulder high, as if to ask, "Why not?" He ignored her and went inside.

"The Crime Scene Unit's on the way, Frank," Yates said with exuberance as they approached. He looked as if he were having a good time.

"Good. Looks like you have things under control here, Joe. I want to know as soon as they get a positive DNA match. Where's Lisa?"

Joe tilted his head toward the back of the house and grinned. "Out back, scaring off reporters."

"Tell one of the uniformed guys to spell her so she can observe and participate with the investigation inside."

Joe moved off to comply.

"Oh, Joe?"

Yates turned back toward him.

"You done good here today," Murphy said sincerely, and it seemed Yates stepped a little lighter toward his task.

David Turner had indeed left hurriedly, leaving most of his clothing, food, and shaving gear. There was still money on the upstairs bedroom dresser.

"Something spooked him, all right." Drake confirmed, searching through a closet.

Murphy removed a plastic bag of change and a stack of neatly folded jockey shorts from one of the dresser drawers. "Could be," he answered, half listening. Then he straightened suddenly, the movement catching his partner's eye.

"What?" Drake asked over his shoulder. When he didn't answer right away, Drake repeated, "Well, *what* spooked him?"

"We got a leak, Bear. I don't know who, or how, but this guy's got someone on the inside."

"I was afraid you were going to say that." Drake abruptly stopped poking through the closet and fidgeted, unwilling to put into words what they both suspected. "Do you know what you're suggesting, Murph? There are a few bad cops around, nobody is going deny that... and, there are a few that'd probably knock someone off, if the price were right. But, a cop that'd help a serial killer get away? Like this sicko? Sorry Murph, I just can't buy it!"

Murphy began to think out loud. "How about someone on the periphery then? Someone close enough to know what's going on, but not *directly* involved? A politician, or upper level manager?"

Drake gulped, stupefied. "*Shit*, Murph," he whispered. "You can't mean *Robert James!*" He glanced around nervously to see if anyone had overheard him, and then edged closer, lowering his voice more. "I know you hate the no-good fuck for what he's done, Murph, but you've got to be careful with that kind of talk! Lord knows you've got reason to hate the son-of-a-bitch, but to accuse him of murder? Boy, that's a stretch!" He rolled his eyes while whistling softly.

"Yeah?" Murphy walked to the door and paused. "Then you tell me for Christ's sake, just how this maniac is able to stay one jump ahead of us all the freaking time!"

Robert James, seated comfortably in the back seat of his chauffeured car, pointed toward a small blue Toyota with its dark tinted windows parked near the sea wall. His driver, catching a movement in the rearview mirror, nodded, and nosed the long sedan in the indicated direction. A steady rain cascaded down the Toyota's windshield, obscuring the driver. The rain was a lucky break, for no one else parked nearby, or walked along the pier.

His driver pulled along side the Toyota, stopping just inches from the other car. James pressed down the automatic window button and reached out, placing a small package into the outstretched, gloved hand of the Toyota's occupant. There was no need for words. As his man immediately drove away, James pressed the window button up to close. A slight smile played at the corners of his mouth.

Amanda tightly held Olaf's big hand. Clancy Gates walked ten paces to their front while Paulie Haskill trailed about the same distance to the rear, as BJ and Lisa followed. Forced to leave everything behind when they'd fled their home, BJ and Amanda had been able to take little clothing. BJ felt the need for warmer clothes and asked to go shopping at a small mall nearby.

Before returning, Gates and Haskill had given in to Amanda's pleas and declared it safe to walk along the sea-walk before returning to the Cozy Cove marina. The weatherman's forecast of "scattered showers" had chased everyone else inside; still her two bodyguards didn't relax. BJ and Lisa both carried their packages, leaving the two men's hands free for an instant response, should it be required. The marina remained under surveillance by two uniformed officers who'd leave upon their return.

What a way to live, BJ thought! *I'll give Frank one more week then Amanda and I are out of here!*

BJ had a lot on her mind. She knew she loved Frank, but still didn't feel as if she really knew how he felt about her. Anyway, that would have to wait. Amanda was all that was important now, and it was up to her to see that nothing happened to her daughter. Then…she also had to respect Frank's opinion that their leaving might not keep them safe anyway. The killer seemed to know everything they did, so wouldn't it stand to reason if she took Amanda to another city, this creep would know…and follow them? Why Amanda? Of all the people in the world, why was this guy so determined to kill her daughter? There had to be an explanation.

Just the thought gave BJ a headache, but the weight of her heavy automatic in the middle of her back was reassuring. *As long as I'm with her, he won't get close enough to see her, let alone harm her. Just one shot, that's all I'm asking, Lord, just one…shot!*

Corky exuberantly danced in a tight little circle. *Oh Corky, don't bust a gut! Keystone Cops! Every fucking one of them!*

Corky reflected back to earlier in the day for the tenth time, reliving just how close the little black girl had been. Close enough to touch! In fact, *did* touch! Those big stupid goons guarding her hadn't suspected a thing. Not a thing!

I can do her any time I want and there ain't a thing they can do about it. But first, there's a little loose end to take care of. A very important loose end! Then, fun and games, Jennifer!

Fun and games.

Chapter 20

CHIEF DETECTIVE OF HEADHUNTER SERIAL KILLER TASK FORCE—TROUBLED!

Is he the one for this job? Inside sources' revelation of past mental problems say it may affect his job. People are beginning to ask—who's hunting whom? Informed sources within the department....

By Molly Atwood

The damning headlines of the Seattle Post had gone on to say that Frank Murphy had recently been under the care of a prominent local psychiatrist for an undisclosed condition. The Post claimed it'd obtained documents and a *confidential source* had confirmed that within the department the task force leader's mental instability was well known. The article concluded several conditions as significant factors in the police department's inability to apprehend the serial killer terrorizing the city.

Murphy calmly read the screaming headlines for the third time before he went to Brooks's office. Captain Brooks glanced up from the morning paper as the door opened, but wasn't surprised to see Murphy enter. He *was* surprised to find his subordinate didn't have his usual case of "red-ass," he'd always displayed whenever he was under conflict. This was an entirely different Frank Murphy. Brooks nodded toward a chair and Murphy sat, crossing his knees.

"Guess you've seen that, huh?"

Tom Brooks studied Murphy's face before he answered. The anger, stress and uncertainty he'd seen as recently as two weeks before were gone, replaced by dogged determination.

"Any of it true, Frank?"

"It's all true, Tom. At least it was six months ago. Right after Tina's death," Murphy admitted.

"Who do you suppose leaked it?"

"That's a good question. The only person who knew is Linda Larsen. She's the one I went to for help."

Brooks reeled, stunned. "You think the department's shrink passed that out? Shit, Frank! There's a lot of stuff in her files! Things about *me*, from several years ago! I don't believe she'd have anything to do with this. She'd lose her license!"

"You want to go see her with me? I was on my way." Murphy stood and looked expectantly at his boss, until Captain Brooks reached for his hat.

Within twenty minutes, they'd both been seated in Linda Larsen's reception area, waiting for a patient to leave. Hearing her inner office door open, they stood to greet her.

"Please come in gentlemen," she said, as if she dreaded this conversation. "I've been expecting you."

Pointing them toward two chairs, she took her place behind her large executive desk and folded her hands. "The file is gone."

"The file is *gone*. The file is *gone*," Murphy mimicked. "Well, *no shit*, Doc. Is that your professional opinion?"

Larsen calmly gazed at him as if he were a child, and indeed, he felt like one, but something controlled the tip of his tongue and wouldn't let it go. "Well, Doctor, what happened to the *file*? The *file*, I might point out, that you kept in *your* safe? The *file* that *you* assured me would never be divulged to anyone. *Ever*! The fucking *file* the Seattle Post reporter has in her greasy mitts!"

Linda's face reddened and deep inside, she secretly felt very alarmed. The file *had* been her responsibility and it'd gotten out. Not withstanding any legal implications, there was an ethical question, as well. She decided to take the logical approach.

"Who might be out to cause you harm, Frank?"

Both men snorted simultaneously, Murphy answering first, calmer this time. "Got a couple of hours? You are aware, I presume,

241

of the inquisition just two weeks ago in Chief William's office? It resulted in my offering my resignation. Anyone in that room has good reason to want my nuts on a skewer, my dear…and the hotter the fire, the better."

Linda almost smiled. She'd always liked the gruff detective, figuring him to be so honest that he wouldn't know how to lie to her. People like Frank made her job as a psychiatrist easier. During their sessions she'd seen his anguish over the loss of his daughter, the despair of how his faithless wife had forsaken him, and his gradual isolation from those who cared about him most.

More than once, she recalled, she'd talked him away from the edge, away from a permanent suicidal solution to his pain. She'd also been witness to his rapid recovery when given a task that would ultimately help him find himself once again.

It was plain to both of them that she felt badly and would do anything she could to get to the bottom of it.

"Give me two days, Frank. I'll find out how your file ended up in Molly Atwood's dirty little hands. I give you my word. If anyone in my office had anything to do with passing that file to her, I'll have… *their nuts on a skewer* before this is over." This time, she did smile.

Murphy struggled momentarily, then gave in and returned her smile as he rose to leave.

"Linda, does Robert James frequent this office, or know anyone who works here? By the startled look in her face, he instantly knew he'd struck the target — *dead center*.

She immediately regained her composure. "I'll ask around, Frank, but I seriously doubt he had anything to do with this."

"Well, it's a long shot, Linda. Call me if you find out anything," he said, as he and Brooks exited her office.

Almost to the car, Murphy surfaced the subject both of them were mulling over. "Did you see it, too, or was it just my imagination?"

Brooks crawled into the passenger's side, settled back and sighed. "No, I saw it. She just about came unglued when you asked about James."

Neither spoke for a while, each silently contemplating the implications. Brooks observed the brick buildings as they drove by, while Murphy pretended to be totally involved with driving.

Breaking the silence at last, Brooks said, "Frank, I've known Linda Larsen for twelve years. In every aspect of her work, she's a professional. I refuse to believe she had any involvement in handing over your file to James, or the press. Have a little faith in her, boy. If there's any collusion in her office, I think she'll figure it out and do the right thing."

"Yeah, but will I still be around here to see it?"

"You've still got Congresswoman Holcomb in your corner, Frank. As far as she's concerned, you're the only one who cares enough to get this guy."

"I called her office first thing this morning after reading the headlines. They told me she had to go to Washington for a few weeks. Guess I'm on my own this time. If they make this thing stick, I doubt if even she will want to publicly back me."

————————

During the next two weeks there were no more bodies and David Turner's trail just seemed to dry up and disappear. What didn't disappear was Molly Atwood's continued vicious attacks on Murphy's stability and his credibility. At one point, sorely frustrated, he'd marched into Captain Brooks's office and offered to resign. Brooks had quickly told him to *get out*!

Emotionally bruised and battered by events, Murphy wearily made his way toward his marina mailbox. Lodged among the junk mail and bills was a plain brown manila envelope, addressed only "Frank Murphy." Puzzled, he sandwiched the other items under his armpit so he could tear off the end. Inside, he found a typed unsigned note. It didn't matter that it'd been disguised to some extent; he still recognized Elnore's style.

F.M.;
If you want to know who is behind the Press's attack, talk to the Doc. R.J. took the file and gave it to M.A. He wants to ruin you! The file was purged before giving it to M.A. The later records that pronounced you fit for duty were destroyed. Concerned.

His heart pounded as he read it twice. *Doc* was obviously Linda Larsen; R.J., Robert James; and M.A., Molly Atwood. *It doesn't make sense!* He could understand James and Atwood going after him—both had axes to grind. But Brooks had seemed so convinced Linda Larsen wasn't involved. So, why was Elnore his benefactor now? Or, was it someone else—someone in the department?

He slowly made his way down the ramp along the walkway toward his slip. Amanda laughed and waved through the side window. Waving back, he felt a sharp pang. Her gesture reminded him of how Tina had waited by the window until he came home at night. In that moment, Frank Murphy vowed he'd always take care of her. Smiling, BJ joined Amanda. He suddenly winced, remembered their earlier telephone call.

As he unlatched the transom gate, both of them ran toward him, hugging him tightly, refusing to let go.

"All right you guys, that's enough mushy stuff! What's for dinner?" He caught Lisa's smile over their shoulders. *You're one lucky man, Sport.* Amanda grasped his hand and led him inside, the table all decked out in a red and white-gingham checkered tablecloth and candles. They waited expectantly for his reaction.

"Spaghetti with meat sauce! That's-a-my favorite!" he shouted in his best Italian accent. A bottle of Chianti chilled in a frosty ice bucket. "What's this? The condemned man eats his final hearty meal?"

Laughing and taking his jacket, BJ said, "You can thank Lisa for the food. It was catered."

"Thank you, Lisa. I deeply appreciate it." Lisa beamed at his praise.

"Besides, we all saw the morning papers and figured you'd need cheering up," Amanda squealed happily.

As they laughed, Murphy thought about how great it felt. He hadn't had much to laugh about lately, but here, with BJ, Amanda, and his friends, there seemed to be plenty of good reasons for it—even when things got really bad, like they were. With gusto, he gratefully dug into his spaghetti as Lisa poured the wine.

Yes sir! I'm one lucky guy!

After Lisa had left and Amanda had been tucked in for the night, he and BJ made slow deliberate love on the upper bridge deck, their sounds masked by the waves slapping against the hull. Afterward, relaxed and wrapped together in a blanket, he felt her weeping softly against his shoulder.

"Things will get better, babe. It just looks bleak right now," he told her gently.

She raised her wet eyes to his. "You fool (sniff). That's not why I'm sniveling. Things couldn't be any better, and (sniff) I'm so happy."

"So, the tears. They're a *good* thing?"

She smiled, blinking rapidly. "They're a *very* good thing."

He tenderly kissed her eyes and within minutes her deep peaceful breathing joined the gentle slapping at the boat's hull. He let her sleep for a long time.

––––––––

At first, David Turner had tried to resist the *voice*, but ultimately knew he would comply. Once he'd given the plan some thought, it was brilliant! He could kill that meddling cop—maybe lots of cops—then, just disappear. He'd be rewarded with any girl he wanted—and as many as he wanted! It *was* brilliant!

Once his mind was made up, he was eager to get started. But, the *voice* had cautioned '*wait*,'…the timing had to be just right. David waited.

––––––––

On Monday morning, Murphy paid another call on Doctor Linda Larsen. This time he went alone and didn't call ahead first. Hessy Furman, Linda's secretary, had arrived and had been hanging up her jacket as he suddenly strode past her into the doctor's office.

"Don't bother, Hessy. I'll just be a few minutes," he said over his shoulder.

She stammered, "But…"

She followed him in anyway, wringing her hands with uncertainty, until Linda Larsen nodded. "It's okay, Hessy. I've been expecting him."

As Hessy left, Linda stared calmly at him, then broke the ice first. "Sit down, Frank."

He stoically stood his ground, glaring at her.

"*Please.*"

He begrudgingly sat, maintaining his silence and cold expression.

Linda smoothed her skirt and cleared her throat softly. "Robert James and I have been lovers for more than a year. I always thought he loved me and we'd eventually get married after his divorce. But his divorce came and went, and nothing happened. There were persistent rumors about him and a woman named Elnore at the Prosecutor's Office—and others. Until your last visit, I just never pieced it all together... that... *that* Elnore was your wife.

She called me last night and told me she'd overheard Robert speaking on the phone about your file. She'd finally gotten enough out of him to understand what it meant."

She laughed shortly, a cold cutting laugh. "At first, he was charming... attentive... tender... everything a woman could ask for. But, you have no idea what he's really like, Frank. Over time he changed — wanted me to... do things... awful things. I did to a certain extent, at first. He can be so damned persuasive... and I wanted to keep him.

After I'd been away from him for a while, I could look back and see his depravity. I don't know how I could've mistaken what we had... for love." Her eyes traced the patterns on the carpet.

Murphy could tell she was embarrassed and ashamed, but she bravely plunged ahead. "It's been over between us quite a while, but the bastard must've waited until he had an opportunity and stole your file from my safe. I asked Hessy, and she told me Robert had been in my office while I was out."

Linda lit a cigarette and inhaled deeply, tossing the pack to Murphy. He shook one from its opening and stuck it between his lips, his eyes never leaving her.

"It wasn't Hessy's fault. He'd often wait for me here while we were seeing each other. He always argued we had to be careful about going out in public until his divorce was final." She laughed bitterly.

"They're going to hold a no confidence meeting at the Mayor's office tomorrow at ten a.m. I've been asked to testify concerning your competence. I think it was Robert's idea to have me do that. He must've figured I'd back him up because of our relationship... or what he held over my head."

"Will you?"

"Do you have to ask, Frank?"

"Can they do that? I mean, aren't there laws about privileged information between doctor and patient... confidentiality issues?"

She nodded thoughtfully. "The law used to be more defined, Frank. But in the last few years some judges have sent doctors to jail for failing to honor a court order regarding their client's medical records. I'd certainly resist, but that's not the problem. The issue is, these files have already been leaked. Once that happens—especially if the information happens to be true—the media believes it's on firm footing to print it.

Only, in your case, Frank, it *used* to be true, but not anymore. I think they're treading in dangerous water—but it's still muddy water."

"It doesn't seem quite fair."

Linda snorted. "Life's *not* fair, Frank. Remember the pro-tennis player who died of AIDS he caught by receiving a blood transfusion? He wanted it to remain a secret to protect his family, too. But the media found out and splashed it all over the country. Don't expect fairness from this liberal press."

He mentioned the note he'd found in his mailbox. As he spoke, his shoulders slumped and he sagged forward, his elbows resting on his knees.

"What can be done, Linda?"

"I've reconstructed your file as best I can from memory, and always kept a back up on floppy disk. The latest notes I'd made after you were doing better and my recommendations for your return to duty are on that disk. You'd already quit coming to appointments before I could finalize the evaluation, and since you swore me to secrecy about our meetings, I felt I had to hold on to them. Now, I'm glad I did."

"So am I Linda. So am I," Murphy sighed heavily. "Brooks

told me about the no confidence meeting last night. He said I'd scared the shit out of Chief Williams when I threatened to resign the last time, and to sue his ass if he ever tried to come after me again. He's afraid this action will look like harassment... retribution. He's already stepped in it, as far as Congresswoman Holcomb is concerned. Anyway, according to Brooks, the Chief asked for — now get this — an Administrative Law Judge to serve as final decision maker about whether there's 'reasonable cause' to boot me out. *Medical retirement,* I believe he called it. The little chickenshit doesn't have the balls to take me on! Any respect I ever had for him just went out the window! A fucking ALJ! For pete's sake, Linda, this is unprecedented."

Linda nodded, agreeing with him. "Elnore will be there, too. Robert wants her to tell about your behavior after Tina's death; any violence toward her, mood swings, nightmares, that sort of thing. I don't think she'll do it, Frank, but I can't be sure. I believe she sent you the note. If you ask me, she's still in love with you."

He ignored her last statement. "Brooks wants me to hire a lawyer and show up to fight the good fight." He sadly shook his head. "I won't be there, Linda. Not this time. Hell, I feel I've been in a dogfight ever since I took this case. I almost resigned once over this kind of crap. When Congresswoman Holcomb asked me to reconsider I thought things might be different. Now I can see they're never going to let me do my job."

"Why does Robert want to destroy you, Frank? I've heard him say despicable things against you, but he'd never tell me exactly *why* he hates you."

"I caught him with his hand in the cookie jar during one of my early cases. It should be water under the bridge by now, but James's ego is so huge he has to demean others to maintain control and the upper hand. I think he wants to get rid of anyone who could possibly endanger his political aspirations—namely, me."

He stood, his shoulders slumping. "Either I go down, or he does. It makes no difference. At this point, I don't much care, except for the fact that it would seriously hamper my capability to protect Amanda. The killer's still after her and I've got to hide out for a few days until this is over and I can evaluate my options.

I spoke with Brooks this morning and asked for some time off until it's settled. He knows I haven't been happy with the department for a while, so he okay'd it. James is such a sick bastard he'll probably just keep coming after me until he's finally able to make something stick. I'm not sure I'm up to the fight anymore."

"I'm sorry, Frank. I'll do everything I can to get you out of this. Then I'll resign."

"You'll do no such thing, *Doctor*! Even if I come out of this okay, I'll still need your help! If you think I'm going to suffer alone trying to catch this sicko, you're crazier than he is!"

Linda rose and moved toward him, warmly hugging him. "Good luck, Frank. I'll be with you, whatever it takes."

———————

The cold rainy days of a late spring were gradually turning into real summer — the kind of mild climate most people moved to Seattle for and kept secret by the locals. The deep blue waters of Puget Sound sparkled in morning sun, sea gulls picked at the scraps left by Pikes Place Market tourists, and the gentle kiss of a slight breeze felt warm and clean — a taste of days to come. The natives knew there'd be more rain before the three or four months of fabulous weather, but until then, the boaters, hikers, and bicyclists made it clear they'd take advantage of any day like this one.

Murphy slowly guided the *Crime Pays* through the marina entrance, tooting two blasts on the horn, as tradition required. Sitting beside him, Amanda squealed as the horn broke the silence. They were underway!

"Hey, you guys! Do you mind?" BJ had come out of the cabin, glared at them for a moment, then disappeared inside, slowly shaking her head.

"Landlubber!" he shouted, and Amanda laughed. "First Mate, Mandy, give me a depth reading," he instructed. She flung herself into her task exuberantly, reading off the illuminated numbers from the antiquated depth-gauge. Her joy was contagious and it radiated to embrace him. He covertly watched her, not having felt this carefree since… well, he couldn't remember when he'd felt this good. Even at their present slow rate of speed, a slight chill still hung in the air.

The wind whipped against their unprotected faces. Murphy

had intentionally folded the canvas back from the command-bridge to take advantage of the scenery; the summer sun warmed their shoulders more than compensating for any discomfort. He slipped on his sunglasses as protection against the sun's dazzling reflections off the clear blue water. Small crafts jockeyed for position in the crowded channel, or sped past.

Amanda mimicked his actions by reaching for her own gaudy sunglasses. He heard BJ approaching behind and glanced around as she joined them with cool drinks and snacks.

"Did you check the head?" Murphy growled in his best gruff, seafarer voice.

"Don't push your luck, *Peaceman*. I don't totally trust these floating contraptions," she answered curtly.

"Oh, *Mom!* Really!"

"Well, I *don't!*"

He remarked seriously, "If we start to sink, I have a dingy."

"I don't think I trust your little *dingy* either," BJ's tone gave a slightly off-color meaning to her play on words.

Murphy's ears flushed a bright red. Making eye contact, the adults hoped Amanda didn't get it. The heavy traffic of the harbor behind, he relaxed completely and pulled Amanda to his chair, instructing her to take the wheel. As she grabbed hold, she expectantly watched for other crafts. Carefully, Murphy slid away from her and moved closer to BJ. Sipping on a chilled beer, BJ watched her daughter easily handle the craft, then covering his hand with her own, she squeezed it. Murphy closed his eyes against the warm sun, contented and relaxed with his two special girls.

At the conclusion of a smooth two-hour trip, they reached Poulsbo, a quaint Norwegian village and Liberty Bay, highly sought after by boaters and tourists. It's off the beaten path of the heavy ships servicing Seattle's commercial harbors. He carefully backed *Crime Pays* into a transient moorage slip at the small public marina. After tying off and adjusting the lines, the three of them hurried toward the pier and the ramp leading to the small, tidy waterfront park. Regardless of the day of the week, families always lolled about on the grass, ate ice cream and picnicked while their children energetically climbed on a large rock near the edge of the seawall. A young boy flipped a yellow Frisbee toward Amanda.

250

Startled, she caught it, then questioningly looked at her mother. BJ nodded and she ran off to join the other children. Murphy and BJ, reclining on a bench, watched as the children laughed and yelled between tosses.

"God, Frank. This is what life's all about. How'd it get away from us? I just can't believe she's finally safe." She stiffened, her eyes widening. "She *is* safe here, isn't she, Frank?"

"She's safe, babe. I didn't tell anyone where we were going. Not even Bear, though I'd trust him with my life." He gazed deeply into BJ's eyes. "Of all the places we might've gone, it'd be impossible for that sicko to accidentally stumble on this destination. Relax and enjoy, because eventually we'll have to go back."

She rested her head in the cusp of his shoulder and watched as the taupe colored clouds merged into the sunset.

Later in their berth that evening as he reclined against his pillow, he gazed at her smooth mocha skin. He realized more than ever just how beautiful she truly was.

"Why did you decide against being a model?"

She squinted through sleepy, just been loved eyes and groaned softly. "Oh god, let me rest! I beg of you! I need sleep! *Sleep!*"

Sensing he wasn't going to let it drop, she braced herself on an elbow and sighed. "Okay. I quit because I was getting too old and fat."

"Bull pucky! I see older women who are models and even fatter ones who are still working."

She punched him playfully. "Cute. I hope you like sleeping in the bilge for the rest of the trip, Bucko."

"Seriously, was it Amanda?"

BJ groaned softly as she pulled two pillows behind her and leaned back. "When I was modeling there was always an agent, or someone with more money than sense trying to get his hands into my pants. It went with the territory. It meant I had to travel almost continuously, and had to leave Amanda with others. The reward would've been great if I could've handled it. But it just wasn't worth it to me."

He pulled her toward him and brushed away a strand of hair. "I'm glad you decided against it, too, because I'd probably never have met you."

He kissed her lips gently, heard her soft moan, then accepted her darting tongue and frantic hands for the second time of the evening.

———————

The blue Volvo parked under covered carport slot 2G of the masonry-faced condo. *Idiots!* He chuckled. *Don't they know there's dishonest people out here?* It was well after midnight. The last light had just been flicked off in this part of the complex. Still, he waited another half-hour before moving toward the stairway leading to the second level, careful to stay in the shadows.

His dark clothing, black sneakers, and wool ski mask blended together like a Ninja as he moved through the darkness. Silently, he crept upward, pausing briefly once as an interior light was turned on, then flicked off. A small penlight aided his search for apartment door numbers.

2-G. *Excellent! It's a corner apartment.*

Gliding, he moved to the end of the outside hallway, slowly peered around the corner and smiled. A balcony was reachable within a few feet of the rail and the sliding glass door left partially ajar. He'd counted on it being open, choosing a cool night when most folks wouldn't feel a need to run an air conditioner. *I'll bet there are many more doors and windows open tonight. They'd all shit if they knew what was out here.*

Pulling on latex gloves, he effortlessly climbed over the railing and then jumped onto the small balcony, catching his breath as a loose board slightly squeaked beneath his feet. He listened intently before silently sliding through the half-open door.

To the right side of the living room, adjacent to the breakfast counter, a hallway led toward the bedrooms, the kitchen illuminated by a small night-light. Within seconds, he'd silently moved down the hall and peeked into the first bedroom. The mother, wearing only her panties, sprawled on top of the sheets. She breathed deeply and evenly, sleeping soundly.

Moving quickly to the next room, he found the daughter asleep in her pink nightgown, also on top of the covers.

Thank god for hot weather.

He retrieved a small bottle and white cloth from his pocket. Turning his head aside and holding his breath, he poured some liquid onto the cloth. Holding it well away from his face, he took the final three steps to the girl's bed. His attention focused on the saturated cloth, his leg loudly bumped against the side of the bed! The girl's eyelids suddenly fluttered open... her abrupt scream cut short by the dampened rag covering her face.

He wasn't aware of the *bitch mother* until she'd landed on his back, pounding at his head, gouging through his ski mask with her lethal nails. He hurled her to the floor violently then kicked at her, but she sprang to her feet and charged back at him.

She fought a good battle for her daughter, but in the end she was no match for his superior strength. His hand masked her mouth and nose with the damp white cloth until her limp body sagged against him. Helpless from the drug, but still conscious, she finally ceased to struggle as he dragged her into the bathroom. In one smooth movement he slit her throat, pausing only to watch her life ebb across the cold tile.

Keenly aware of a severe burning sensation, he raised his hand and removed the ski mask. Gingerly touching his face, he discovered the blood and deep gouges left by her nails. Sobbing at her with an insane rage, he attacked her still form, stabbing repeatedly until he was exhausted. Sucking several deep ragged breaths into his tortured lungs, he returned to the girl's bedroom, hoisted her small frame onto his shoulders and retreated into the night.

Chapter 21

"**W**here the hell are you, Murph? No, don't tell me, I don't want to know. Just get your ass back here. Have you read the paper lately? The shit hit the fan, *royally*!" Bear's gleeful voice exploded through the phone line.

"Good. Let someone else handle it," Murphy told him. "I just discovered that *living* beats the hell out of what I've been doing for the past ten years! Tell Brooks to extend my vacation for another year or two."

"*No*! Murph, you don't *understand*! James has resigned — he could be facing indictment due to the alteration and disclosure of confidential files — and Molly Atwood has been reprimanded and printed an apology to the department, and to you!"

Fuck em all," Murphy retorted. "I might even resign for real this time. That'll make *twice* I've tried to do it. Most employers allow people to quit when they want to."

"You've *got* to come back right now, Frank. Linda Larsen went to bat for you. Elnore too. She told the world about overhearing James plotting to discredit you and generally what a total rat's ass he is. Why even the Chief has come on line and said you are — now *get this*, Murph — the best officer on the *entire* force! Why, shit, you could run for *governor*!"

"What about you, Bear? Did *you* go to bat for me, too?"

Drake snorted. "Are you crazy? I wasn't about to walk into that viper pit and draw attention to myself!"

"Can't thank you enough for your support," Murphy said dryly.

Drake's laugh boomed through the receiver, deafening him. "Think nothing of it. Joking aside, Frank. This time, I really do believe you'll have carte blanche to run it the way you want. Crap, at this point, we could stage a *coup* and take over the whole damned department. But call anyway if you decide to head for the San Juan's. Ya hear?"

He sighed for Drake's benefit, and said, "I'll be back in a couple of hours. Anything else happen on the case since I've been gone?"

"Well, we're still looking for David Turner. Oh yeah... Frank, we found the white van. Turner's prints are all over it—along with several blood types. We're having it worked over now. Well, got to run, old buddy."

Murphy held the dead phone, contemplating how he was going to break the news of going back to BJ and Amanda.

———————

It was hot. Sweat exuded from his bare muscled arms and the small of his back. Though slender, he had a stomach like a washboard, a fact he was proud of. Wearing his drab clothes and tattered cardigan, he appeared rather ordinary, but underneath he was all muscle. He'd been working on his *project* for weeks and at last, it was nearing completion. His tunnel was ready, he'd obtained the guns and ammo, and the last of the equipment he'd ordered by catalog had arrived. An orgasmic-like excitement pulsated through his veins.

I can pull this off —I know I can!

The *voice* had told him exactly how. Well, he'd resisted at first, but suddenly it all made absolute sense. He'd earn his place on the mountain! No rules to follow — the freedom to select any girl he wanted — to take to *his* mountain. The *voice* would always guide him!

He paused and straightened from his task, wiping sweat beads from his eyes. That should do it — now, get back to the girl. She was probably already awake. His face still smarted from the attack, and his hand instinctively touched his right cheek. It was just starting to scab over, tender to his touch.

The bitch! I should've taken her alive and fucked her over — made her watch what I've got in store for her daughter.

He furtively glanced over his shoulder as he'd been doing all day. He was frightened. Not of the cops, but of the *voice*. This was the first time he'd ever acted on his own without instructions. He'd never done this before — but those damn tanned legs and short skirt had played on his mind ever since she'd stepped into her mother's Volvo at the grocery store that day. Thoughts of her had just about burned a hole in his mind for the past month! He couldn't *help* himself. Surely the *voice* would understand! *Well, I'll just keep it a secret.*

Grabbing a half-filled sandbag, he trudged to the green pick-up and tossed it on the truck bed beside a dozen others. *That should be enough. It ain't like I'm building a fucking bomb shelter!* The instructions had been precise, though, so he counted the bags again.

Murphy was troubled. The short stay in the little seaside village had been like a tonic to them all. When he'd reluctantly informed BJ about Bear's call, it'd been like throwing cold water on their good mood. The trip back from Poulsbo had been much different than the one before. They'd both been quiet and withdrawn, as each contemplated what waited.

After he'd docked, BJ had remained below and hadn't come up as he'd hosed off the saltwater spray. He'd tried to talk through the cabin door but she'd remained silent. At last, he'd simply departed. Reaching the ramp, he recalled how he'd looked over his shoulder and thought he saw her face peering through the side window. Amanda had been on deck. He'd waved, and she'd waved back.

He was troubled about what he might find once he got back to the office. While Bear's message had been filled with hope and excitement, he wondered just how much of it was fact, and how much Drake had adlibbed in order to coax him back.

He soon discovered the hearing *had* been ugly, just as Drake described on the phone. It'd been all the Administrative Law Judge could do to maintain any semblance of order. The press had been on hand as Lieutenant Borden presented the painful and often embarrassing facts outlined in Linda Larsen's *sanitized* psychiatric evaluation. He'd practically made Murphy out to be a slobbering lunatic! All the while, corridor phones had been ringing off their hooks, while inside, cameras were capturing the nonstop action.

Next, it'd been Linda Larsen's turn, and she'd stunned the crowd of participants! She testified that Murphy's file had been stolen from her office and that Robert James had been the last person present before it was missed.

As Drake related the story to him later, when James heard her comments, he was aghast and bellowed right out of his seat. The ALJ had to threaten him with removal to quiet him down.

Then Linda had told about how the file had been purged and altered to reflect only the most detrimental and incriminating information against Murphy, none of which was currently correct. Then, she'd presented her backup notes concerning Frank's total recovery, and her recommendation that he be allowed to return to full duty.

Congresswoman Holcomb, Councilwoman Walcott and lastly, Elnore had followed. It'd been Elnore who'd really hammered the final nail into James' coffin. When it was all over, the scene had resembled the Hindenburg wreckage. According to Drake, some very important people were in "deep shit!"

Murphy arrived back to a rush of high-fives and congratulations, not to mention the usual comments about Lazarus and the Phoenix. The noise and commotion continued to buzz at such a decibel that Brooks had to finally stick his head out, and yell, "This is a police station, ya know! If ya can't find enough to keep you busy, come and see me...oh, and by the way, Frank, welcome back."

Brooks had even *smiled*.

Laughing and joking aside, the task force personnel adjourned to their own area to bring Murphy further up to date. Their routine meeting was just finishing up when Murphy's desk phone jingled loudly, interrupting them. It was the unlisted line, used only for interdepartmental conferences and task force emergencies.

"Hello, *Frankie boy*. Welcome back."

The voice was soft, non-threatening—absolutely unremarkable in every respect, yet it made the hair stand on the back of Frank's neck.

"Who is this?" he asked calmly, snapping his fingers to get everyone's attention and motioning to trace the call. Drake hurriedly picked up another line and began working on it. Murphy pushed a conference call button and the voice oozed through for others to hear—a second mode was quickly activated to record it.

"It's who you *think* it is, asshole," the voice snarled, turning savage. "Don't even think about tracing it. I'll be gone long before you can get a fix on me."

"What do you want, sicko?" The others sat motionless, hardly breathing.

"Sicko? *Sicko, is it?*" A nasty laugh jarred the other end of the line. "All the big bad cops in this shit city and you haven't gotten a smell of me yet!" It was a sticky snicker.

"David Turner," Murphy said softly, as if to prove him wrong. "A loser at everything he ever attempted in his life. Mother and father died when he was a child. Washed out of college and joined the Peace Corps—then quit because it was too tough. *Never* had a relationship with a woman. At age twelve, you raped a two-year old girl in Spokane — sentenced to reform school until you were eighteen. Now you're a registered sex offender. Our profile says you're probably a homosexual, David. At least, that's what I'm going to tell the press for tomorrow's papers."

"No! *No!* I'm *not* a Fag! You can't put that in the papers! I have my *rights!*"

"Well, that's the story for the media. That is, unless you want to come in and discuss it with me," Murphy urged.

The line fell silent for almost fifteen seconds, then in a tone as soft and gentle as it'd been when he'd first spoken, Turner began speaking. "I don't think so, Frank. Not just yet. First I've got some young pussy that needs breaking in. Her name's Lottie. A *sweet* tender little thing, Frank."

"Let her go, David. It doesn't make any difference. We know who you are, and it's only a matter of time before we get you. Let the girl go, and come in. There are a lot of hard feelings about you in the department. I wouldn't want to see you get hurt. I'll protect you, if you turn yourself in to me. How about it?"

"Well, *shit, Frank!* Sure, I'll just come right on down and turn myself in. You *asshole!* Who do you think you're fucking with? One of your brain dead druggies?"

"You harm that little girl, Turner, and I swear…"

"Ah, *threats*. That's more like you, Frankie. But don't worry. I'll be calling to let you know where to come pick me up — real soon. Expect my call in a few days. And, oh, by the way, how's the little black cunt on your boat? You tapping that yet? Be seeing you around, Frankie boy. Bye."

Click.

Murphy glanced up at Drake questioningly. He shook his head regretfully and slammed the other phone into its cradle. The rest sat silently, frozen in place. Turning his eyes from one to the other, Murphy could feel a mixture of rage, fear and revulsion. He finally broke the silence.

"Now you know the face of the enemy. I want someone on this phone constantly in case that sick son-of-a-bitch calls back, and I want equipment set up that can get a trace on him as soon as the goddamned phone rings. Keep your vests and head gear here, ready to roll the next time he calls!"

Murphy's voice was a harsh whisper. "I want this guy so bad it hurts. You better feel the same damned way!"

They found the next victim the following morning.

———————

The call had came in at 8:00 a.m. from a hysterical Walter Brown. He'd gone by his ex-wife's condo in Southern Heights to give his daughter a lift to school. When no one answered, he'd used his passkey to enter thinking they'd overslept again. He'd found the place splattered with blood, his ex-wife with her throat slit, stabbed repeatedly on the bathroom floor. His young daughter was missing. Police had responded within minutes, and the Special Task Force had been notified within the hour.

Murphy solemnly watched as the CSU finished processing the scene, while Drake spoke with one of the uniformed officers who'd been the first to arrive. He had an empty feeling that he was missing something obvious but just couldn't put his finger on it. Earlier, he'd told Booth and Yates to review everything known about David Turner, no matter how trivial.

Lisa remained at the boat with BJ and Amanda and had called in a few minutes previously to report that Clancy Gates and Paulie

Haskill were on site, "armed to the teeth." At least, he could feel good about that.

BJ hadn't been all that keen about bringing Amanda back to Seattle anyway, but he'd persuaded her because there was simply no way to protect them anywhere else. They hadn't spoken much since their return.

A short portly figure rambled toward him. It was Hemphill, and as usual, he was frowning. Hemphill quickly briefed him on what was known.

"Her name was Judy Brown, killed sometime early Sunday morning but undiscovered until this morning, when Walter Brown, her ex-husband, came to pick up his daughter, Lottie, and take her to school. Lottie is fourteen. She's missing and presumed abducted. Mister Brown is taking it real hard, so go easy on him.

The mother put up one hell of a fight; blood's all over the freaking place — early blood typing says its more than just one person — skin and blood were under her fingernails, defensive bruises and cuts on both hands and arms. I'd say cause of death was her throat wound. But as if that that wasn't enough — he continued to stab her about forty more times. Probably after she was already dead. Sick bastard."

Murphy fought down an urge to spit out a stream of profanities. Instead, he said, "Nobody saw or heard anything, as usual. We found blood on the steps over there, and marked it. Maybe she hurt him."

"I hope she tore his nuts off," Hemphill growled. "Well, good hunting." He waddled off to a waiting car and was driven away.

Drake approached, catching him deep in thought. "Just for shits and grins, I asked the neighbors if they knew David Turner, and guess what? He worked at the Best Buy Groceries store two blocks away. One of the neighbors said she saw him loading groceries for Mrs. Brown and her daughter a couple of weeks ago. She remarked she always thought he was the spitting image of Mr. Rogers."

Murphy blankly looked at him, puzzled.

"You know, *Mr. Rogers*, on TV. Only younger, of course."

Drake continued to explain. "It's a *kiddies* show, Frank! For god's sake, get a life!"

Murphy slowly shook his head. "Bet you watch all the cartoons, huh?"

Drake turned away. "My favorite is Porky Pig... T-t-t-th-that's all folks!"

Murphy laughed softly and followed his partner to their vehicle. It was stuffy and hot, even with the windows rolled down. Drake quickly started it up and drove more for the breeze than for being in a hurry.

"Murph, if Turner isn't at his house, where can he be? He can't be moving much, because every frigging cop in the state is watching out for him. He has to eat, and those photos we found have been shown on TV for the past week. I've got an idea. Let's do a real estate check and see if his parents owned any other property around here. What d'ya think?"

Murphy gawked at him in complete amazement. "You're not just another pretty face, are you? You really *are* a cop. That is a pregnant idea, Hoss. Let's get back."

Anita had been stacking new computer printouts on top of the others when they arrived. The stack appeared ready to topple over. No one else was present. After pleasantries, she departed, leaving the officers to their work. Drake got on the phone and called the tax assessor's office while Murphy studied the wall, now filing up with the photos of smiling little girls. Lately, they'd all began to look the same. He averted his eyes quickly as Drake yelled.

"Hot damn! *Bingo!*"

Drake finished jotting notes and hung up, smiling widely. "Turner's parents owned a house near Magnolia bluffs in West Seattle. It's been condemned, but David Turner continues to pay taxes on it. What'd'ya think?"

"I think we'll keep it just among us chickens for now. Put someone on the house day and night, and when we know for sure he's there, we'll go in."

"Who?" Drake said.

"Yates."

Drake's eyebrow shot up.

"I owe him one, Bear. Include Lisa. They work well together."

The phone interrupted loudly and Drake picked it up. He immediately began to write, the one-sided conversation punctuated only by Drake's head nodding. Hanging up, he said solemnly, "That was the Snohomish County Sheriff. They found the body of a young girl in the river and they think it might be Lottie Brown. He asked if we wanted to come up and look over the site before it was disturbed."

More than a million tourists take the leisurely drive east along SR522 to enjoy the natural unspoiled beauty of Snohomish. Murphy had been a dozen times — fishing, camping, or just sightseeing. Few homes could be seen from the highway, just mile after mile of pristine green freshness. Fleetingly, he realized he'd never be able to make the drive again without remembering it for this purpose.

The cruiser's red, white and blue emergency lights carved a path through the heavy city traffic, shortening a normal two hour drive to just over an hour. Following the sheriff's directions, they'd proceeded northbound on I-5 to the SR522 cut-off, then east toward Monroe. Winding along mostly secondary roads, they'd finally turned left onto a marked dirt road leading to the Snohomish River. A green four-wheel drive Sheriff's Department vehicle waited to guide them into the difficult terrain. Drake followed slowly with the cruiser, down the deeply rutted road for about a mile and a half, across a small creek, then yet another quarter mile through thick brush. The ill-defined trail ended at a small turn-around where three more county cars were parked.

Murphy spotted Sheriff Walker speaking into the hand-held mike of his unit's radio. Although friends for more than ten years, Walker was all business when he got out and approached.

"Howdy, Bill. This is my partner, John Henry Drake. Everybody calls him Bear. What ya got?"

Walker was a big beefy man, prone to bluntness. He wasn't unfriendly, just direct. Murphy understood that about him and it'd formed the basis for their friendship through the years.

"A fisherman found her early this morning, Frank. On his second cast, he got hung up and figured he'd probably break his line if he continued tugging, so he waded out and tried to unhook it. That's when he found the body, weighted down with rocks."

"Weighted down with rocks?" The Sheriff's information surprised him.

"That's right. Just a quirk of fate she was found this quickly. Otherwise, she might not have been found for years — if ever. If you want to see it, you'll have a hike."

"Let's go."

The sheriff was right. It was quite a hike, especially for two men in suits and shoes more suitable for sidewalk work.

Disheveled, panting, splattered by mud, they approached the riverbank. The meandering muddy river with its lazy whirlpools understated its treacherousness. In a low marshy clearing, a tarp-covered body lay near several deputies standing slightly off to one side. Among them, an elderly man, seventy-five to eighty years of age, was dressed in calf length rubber boots, flannel shirt and a denim jacket. His white knuckles clutched a small fishing rod.

"He's the one who found the body," Walker stated, jerking his head toward the group. "He said he likes to come here because hardly anyone else does. Guess we were lucky, huh?"

Murphy nodded and advanced toward the tarp. He knelt and lifted the corner. The head was in its proper place! Nude, she'd been stabbed repeatedly. He gently lowered the cover, rose and returned to Drake and Walker.

"Who did you have process the scene, Bill?"

"Jessie Hagan. He heads up the CSU."

Murphy nodded. "He's a good man. Could he tell if she'd been sexually assaulted?"

"In his opinion…"his voice trailed off. "She'd been used every way possible, Frank. Of course, the ME's report will have to confirm that, but I'd say he's correct."

Murphy nodded again, puzzled. "Anything else?"

Walker shook his head. "Nothing that we've found so far. Sorry, Frank. We'll keep working it and I'll call you if more comes up." This time he smiled warmly and shook Murphy and Drake's hands before trudging back into the marsh.

On the return trip, Murphy was unusually quiet. Drake concentrated on his driving in heavy rush-hour traffic, respecting his partner's solitude. At last, Frank sighed deeply as he stirred.

"It just doesn't make sense, Bear. After flaunting the others by placing them right under our noses, Turner takes this one to an isolated place a hundred miles away and hides her in the middle of a swamp. She wasn't even killed in the same manner as all the rest. What do you make of it?"

"Maybe he thinks we're getting too close."

"No, he already knows we know who he is, and that it's just a matter of time before we nail his ass. So why try to cover up this particular one?"

Murphy scanned several notes in the log left by his staff, and leaned back heavily in his seat. "I'm gonna see Brooks first thing tomorrow and get permission to see John Lee West again."

Drake whirled to stare at him.

"If he okays it, I plan to drive out in the morning."

"Why don't you just fly over? Thirty minutes and you're there." Drake was acutely aware of his partner's fear of flying.

"Yuk, yuk."

The last sandbag heaved snuggly into place, David lay behind the burlap-covered berm, sweating and trying to catch his breath. Peering through each of the small apertures he'd built into the bagged wall, he checked each one's field of fire to the large room below. An M-16 automatic rifle leaned against a wall, while loose ammo was scattered beside each aperture. He carefully reviewed his checklist one final time, checking his entrees. Black-out curtains covered each window, electrical throw-switch within easy reach, escape route ready—down the laundry chute into the basement— through the wall hole he'd cut into the old factory sewer—to the stowed car—and away! Genius! The *voice* was a pure genius!

Fucking cops!

A surge of adrenaline pulsed through his muscles. His perspiration dampened his T-shirt causing it to stick against his back. He felt like Rambo! They'd remember him long after he was gone!

He'd been forgiven for the last one, although he hadn't been given permission to *do* her! Thinking about it, he laughed aloud, smug about how worried he'd been. He'd sensed not a *trace* of anger in the voice, only — *pride*. He was leaving this place for good. *To the mountains,* the voice had said. A small modern cabin with it's own built-in hide-a-way. That's where he'd be provided

anything he ever wanted from now on. All he had to do was ask—
all the girls—anything at all!

David closed his eyes as he leaned against the sandbags,
daydreamed, and pondered what the mountains would be like.

———————

Murphy's second visit with John Lee West had left him
shaken, sticky with sour sweat. West's hair had grown back and
neatly trimmed. Murphy was surprised to discover he'd
transformed himself, more to the clean-cut youth he resembled
during his long trial. He'd filled out, too, as Murphy had
remembered him from before. *The eyes haven't changed a bit, though.*
Murphy shuddered as he scrubbed in the shower, trying to wash
West's image away along with the sour sweat.

Checking out of the hotel early, he called his office before
driving back. Drake answered on the second ring.

"It's me. What's happening, Bear?"

"Our man's using the old homestead, Frank. I spelled Yates
and Lisa for a few hours, and right after I took over the shift, he
carried a bag of groceries inside. That was around ten this morning,
and he hasn't stirred since. When'll you be back?"

"I'm heading back now. Will you be at the office when I
arrive?"

"Yeah. I'll meet you there this afternoon."

"How's BJ and Amanda holding up?"

"Both are doing great, Murph. Lisa is with them and BJ said if
you called, to tell you that they send their love and miss you.
Mable and Jo Jo said to hurry back."

Murphy perked up and smiled for the first time since leaving
for Walla Walla the day before. Once on the road, he switched on
his recorder and listened twice through the entire tape of West's
interview. It made his skin crawl. But resolved, he continued
combing over it. He now he had the advantage of not being able to
see West's face when he spoke, and could finally concentrate more
on the inflection and emotion associated with key words.

He listened intently as the cultured voice caressed certain
words, sliding over them like an evil touch. It was evident
whenever he mentioned blood, death, or spoke of killing, his
words hung in the air, sticky with desire, poignant with longing.

The oozing voice emitted a raw hunger that Murphy had somehow missed during their first face-to-face conversation. He forced his attention back to the tape, and the beguiling voice.

"…when I think about your killer, I can see what's running through his head. There's a strong, almost religious connection between sex and violence — no — that's *too* strong. The killer believes that by the victims giving up their lives, they are demonstrating an ultimate level of love for him. To the killer it's not a violent act, or a sexual one for that matter. It's far more. Who knows the variables… all the intangibles that come together to motivate him to the point where he acts out like he does? For me, it was… ah, but let's not talk about me, Frank."

Murphy could almost see him smile on the tape.

"He fantasizes a lot, masturbates, too. Probably as much as fifteen — twenty times a day, though, logically, not all the way to climax. Most likely, he can do it in front of the people around him and feels smugly superior that he can get away with it.

He fantasizes because it provides a way to vicariously experience the only thing that gets him off — killing young girls—and, it's safer. He's obviously seeking a certain quality in his victims that can only be found in a very few. Otherwise, you'd have bodies stacking up at the rate of ten or twenty per day. Now, wouldn't *that* be fun, Frank?"

West's lecturing revealed him to be an experienced sexual, thrill killer, one who believed he understood the dark motivations lying behind the recently butchered victims. His words exposed his beliefs that he found little abnormality in sexually manipulating bodies, or dismembering victims after they were dead. His words were chilling, demonstrating a complete void of conscience—and just how much he was able to accept without remorse.

"My guess is that your killer is selecting his victims because of some kind of love-hate grudge… a hang-up that goes far beyond viewing them *only* as young females. That's why he doesn't shop prostitutes, such as the Green River Killer did. By selecting within this particular group — young school-aged girls I mean — he's fulfilling a need to defile something as yet unsoiled, something pure. He looks for the most *tender* of *prey*, Frank. That's what makes his act so *exquisite* —*intense*! I can't see him stopping — he doesn't consider himself to be bad, or a monster the papers make him out to be. His actions are all justified in his mind. Maybe he thinks he's being guided by divine 'voices'..." West's voice trailed off on the tape at this point.

"Or... possibly... *pictures* he sees in his mind. Yes. I tend to think that's it."

"I don't see him collecting souvenirs from his victims, at least not like clothes and jewelry... but he may photograph them either before or after killing them. That's so he'll have *wet* pictures for his masturbation sessions."

"Certainly, he toys with them for a prolonged period — maybe a couple of days. For that reason alone, I believe his house has a basement — located well away from others. Possibly an indoor garage so he can transport them with ease. He'd need a large vehicle, too, for the same reason."

Murphy heard his own voice break in with a question. "What race is he? How old would you guess he is?"

West's pace picked up, not hesitating this time, delving deeper into his analysis of the killer's profile. "The killer is white, but definitely an equal opportunity killer, because the victims he selects are both black and white — about fifty-fifty. My guess is he's educated and twenty to twenty-five years of age because he'd have to have a lot of energy to recon his targets and select dumpsites. He probably works for a living, too. Remember Frank, as people get older, their energy levels drop."

West's tone had been admonishing and condescending with this last remark.

"Athletic?"

"Certainly! How would he be able to overpower them so quickly and carry them around so easily? Ever carry a dead person any distance, Frank? It's *dead* weight."

Murphy remembered how John Lee West had smiled sheepishly at that point.

Murphy's voice continued. "Do you think he's keeping them for any length of time?"

"Since the victims turn up missing throughout the week, I'd say the killer lives alone, with no family to speak of. So in that regard he's your typical garden-variety serial killer. With such flexibility, he probably keeps them for varying periods. It's the

267

thought of having someone so vulnerable, tender and helpless… completely at his mercy that compels him. It's *exquisite*, Frank!

Murphy swallowed hard as the sick emotion in West's voice lightly caressed the final words, as though reliving some wonderful experience of his own. He forced himself to listen closely as West's excitement caused him to breathe into the microphone more intensely.

"I'd say his state of excitement dictates when he kills them, more than any fixed time requirement. He controls the timing. In other words, he plays with them until he reaches a state of exultation, he has to experience the ultimate high… that's when he can slowly cut off their head, look into their horrified eyes… and climax… *exquisite*, Frank!"

Murphy felt West had toyed with him by his choice of words, watching his eyes for reaction, and secretly *getting off* on it.

The sick bastard!

At that point, he'd quietly told West, "What would you say if I told you we already know who the killer is, John Lee? That we have him under surveillance at this very moment?" He was determined not to leave West with his smug superior expression.

Whatever reaction he'd been hoping for, he was disappointed. John Lee West's expression never changed. "*Do* you now, Frank?" The dark eyes were open, but Frank recalled fathoming that he couldn't see into them anymore.

"Are you absolutely *certain* about that?"

At last, Murphy clicked it off and just drove, deep in troubled thought.

Chapter 22

Drake lurked in the parking lot, waiting while Frank maneuvered the big sedan into his stall. Without preliminaries, his huge partner blurted, "I have Booth and Joe on surveillance. Turner's still inside. When do you want to take him down, Murph?"

"We'll watch the place today and if he doesn't try to make a move tonight, we'll do it tomorrow at first light. If he steps out before then—we take him! I want a sniper across the street and one in the rear. He will not get away from here."

Drake nodded and led him to the illegally parked police unit outside on the street. "You get anything from that psycho at Walla Walla?"

"Mostly perceptions. The guy's a real sick puppy, but slick and smart. I'm going to study the recording more closely later to see if there's anything we can use. Now that David Turner's bottled up, it's probably a moot point."

Drake nodded in agreement, but in the back of Murphy's mind he felt a sensation, as if a spider had crossed through it quickly.

Drake dropped him off in the marina parking lot and drove away just as Lisa was leaving. With a bright smile she animatedly brought him up to date on how his *women* had been while he was away. For the most part, it was hard contending with her bubbly personality this late in the day.

"...and I promised to take Amanda skiing as soon as this is all over," she finished.

Absentmindedly he smiled, nodded, and craned his neck toward the walkway leading to his slip, and those who waited for him. Sensing his impatience, Lisa wisely said, "Glad to have you back, Boss. Catch you later at the office." She was still smiling to herself as she merged into the busy street traffic.

They were in his arms before he could get halfway down the ramp; Amanda squealing and laughing and BJ smiling through her teary eyes. Both held him, as though they were afraid he'd slip away again. He felt as though he'd truly come home. Silently he vowed he'd provide them a home where they could feel completely safe as soon as this was all over. Arm in arm, he and BJ slowly meandered together down the long ramp, Amanda ahead of them. Relieved to be home, he could see Clancy Gates lean against a sailboat mast, cradling a telescoped rifle in the crook of his arm. Although he didn't see Haskill, but had no doubt the man was skulking close by.

On a dock box, Olaf crossed his legs while enjoying a pipe. As he and BJ walked up Apeshit lay with his big ugly head between his front paws, only his mean eyes shifting. Amanda started to rough up his ears. The ugly hound seemed to love it, groaning and stretching in anticipation of a sublime belly rub.

He'd probably tear my arm off if I did that, Murphy thought.

Olaf unexpectedly stood, towering over them and without a greeting, rumbled, "Glad you're back, Murph. Got a minute to spare? There's a little business I need to discuss with you."

At the moment, discussing business was about as unpopular as the idea of being circumcised, but he sighed and nodded as an invitation for Olaf to come aboard. The big man nimbly climbed on board. BJ rounded up cold beers and a soda for Amanda. Herding Amanda to her cabin, they became comfortable on the bow deck. Olaf removed a document from inside his jacket.

"This is Mama's Last Will and Testament, Frank. She didn't have any family that she knew about. She left the marina to you and me."

Murphy recoiled in disbelief. "W… what? You have got to be kidding!"

"It's true. Mama's attorney called me yesterday and wanted you and me to meet with him. I explained your circumstances. He wasn't real happy about your not being available for the reading, but he provided me a copy to give to you." Olaf handed the document to him.

Dumbfounded, Murphy stared at it, the words swimming before his eyes. He pushed the paper toward BJ, and she quickly scanned it.

"It's all here, Frank. You and me get it all—fifty-fifty, down the middle. Except for her old sailboat, she left it to me. She wanted me to take that trip around the world I always spoke of."

Olaf smiled slightly; his eyes brimmed with tears. "The lawyer said she'd known for some time about her heart problem, and had been told to take it easy. She knew she had only about six months left and was on borrowed time. I guess she just wanted to leave the marina to someone who loved it as much as she did."

Murphy slowly shook his head, trying to think clearly. "It just doesn't seem right, Olaf. You should get it *all*. I mean, you've known her a lot longer than I have."

"Nope! Mama knew what she was doing. If I had it alone, I'd just ignore the business end of it and spend all my time sanding and repairing boats. Pretty soon there'd be no customers, and there'd be dog shit — excuse me BJ — knee deep all over the docks."

He shook his head strenuously, as though horrified at the image he'd just conjured up, and the thought of desecrating Mama's marina. "Nope, Mama knew what she was doing, all right. This place needs a level head at the helm. It needs kids, too. Mama knew that. Besides Murph, I got no family either. You guys are all the family I've known in years…except for old Apeshit and he's getting up in years… I need you, too."

Murphy held BJ, as they lay propped against several pillows. "How do you feel about running a marina?"

"Why, Frank! Are you asking what I think you're asking?" BJ stared at him in wide-eyed wonder.

"I suppose so… yes… I am."

A heavy silence hung in the air as he studied the boat traffic in the bay. "Well? Are you going to answer?"

He turned back to her. She was softly crying. Cradling her face in his hands, he kissed away her tears and looked deeply into her eyes. "Why so sad?"

"I'm not sad, you big dummy!" she said, sniffing quietly. "You know I always cry when I'm happy. I just never thought you'd really ask me to marry you. You know a lot of people would say we're nuts to even consider it."

"There are a lot of mixed marriages these days, Hon. Have you ever seen Mandy happier? Mama was right. This place *does* need kids, perhaps a little sister for Amanda. What do you say? Want to help run a smelly old marina?"

She nuzzled against his neck and raised her lips, touching his for an instant. "I love you, Frank Murphy. I'd spend the rest of my life with you, on this smelly old marina, or anyplace else you want to be."

He mashed his mouth against her lips and tasted her sweet tongue as he felt himself beginning to grow hard. They were awake a long time.

He knew they were out there. He'd seen them through his night vision goggles, stumbling all over each other. He'd been fully aware of them for two days now, and they hadn't a clue. *Fools! They think they have me trapped. Will I ever love to see the morning papers when they print what I've got in mind for those imbeciles sneaking around in the dark.*

But, of course, that would be impossible. By then he'd be far away, breathing the cool mountain air. Just thinking about his new adventure excited him immensely. Besides, he was getting a little tired of all the rain.

He'd given some thought to a nice little place he'd heard of outside Denver — secluded, where no one could hear the screams, yet close enough to a major city — a new hunting ground to feed his appetites. He'd even picked up some ski magazines — those with pretty young girls poured into their tight spandex outfits. It'd be paradise for a person of his tastes.

How about that jackass Murphy? Going to see John Lee West about me? I'll send John Lee a letter after I get there—or better yet, something wet from one of his adventures! What a blast!

He reclined, wide-awake, stroking the M-16, daydreaming of the possibilities, savoring what was yet to come.

Joe Yates and Bear moved silently through the mist toward the front door. Once a neighborhood where society's upper crust held decadent parties when most of America was starving, the grand old houses starkly remained as moldy reminders of extravagant lifestyles and flamboyant ways, as though in restitution for those embarrassing lifestyles. The one they focused on had become overgrown with tall grass, weeds, and blackberry vines. Its right front porch pillar had collapsed years earlier, leaving the roof slanted at an odd angle. Several windows visible from the street were broken out.

Abandoned, it was dark, and the chimney emitted no vapors. During its heyday, it'd been an architectural wonder. But that had been years ago. The lack of care had quickly turned the once proud structure into a decaying mass of rotten timbers, lopsided foundation, and overgrown vegetation.

Charley Booth, BJ and Lisa had all been in their positions at the rear of the old house for more than thirty minutes, awaiting Murphy's signal to move in. Murphy had argued with BJ unsuccessfully that she remain behind to ensure Amanda's safety, but with Olaf and the big dog nearby, she was adamant she wanted to be in the final takedown of this "monster" who'd caused her so much grief.

In the shadows, the hands on his watch glowed five a.m. Murphy reached for the *talk* button on his radio. Certain that Turner had a police scanner, he'd decided to use two breaks in the steady stream of normal radio static as the signal to go. He hesitated, then saw Joe and Bear sprint toward the front door. He was only a few steps behind. When he reached them they were already in position on each side of the battering ram.

"Police! Open up! Search warrant. Police, search warrant, open the door!" boomed Drake's deep voice.

He nodded, and the two men swung the heavy metal tubular object, the rotting wood splintering on the first attempt. Drawing their firearms, Drake and Yates rushed into the black void, their flashlights cutting through the darkness. Murphy moved in behind them, instinctively aware that Drake would be to the right and

Yates left. As he quickly scanned the dark big room, his eyes raised toward the high railing across the second floor and vaguely made out a familiar outline running the entire length — sandbags with firing ports.

Ambush! His brain screamed the word, but he couldn't get his mouth to work.

Trying to shout a warning and react at the same time, Drake beat him to it, firing off half a clip.

"Get out! Ambush!" he was finally able to scream, just as automatic weapon fire spewed from the balcony. The unseen assailant raked their exposed positions as the three of them huddled in the darkness; then in what seemed like a lifetime, a deafening pause in the rain of death as the shooter reloaded.

Joe Yates bolted to an adjoining room, pulling an automatic shotgun from beneath his coat. Pausing only briefly, he pushed it around the doorway corner and opened fire at the sandbagged wall overhead, firing until the weapon was empty. Silence permeated the darkness as he reloaded—then an unmistakable sound of feet running across the old floor above.

Joe fired twice more at the footsteps that faded toward the rear of the house — followed by a sliding, bumping noise.

Booth and BJ were near the rear of the house when they heard the first burst of automatic fire. They hit the back door simultaneously, unaware that Lisa had dropped back. BJ slid around the corner of the kitchen to the right, her weapon held in a high, two-handed stance. Booth went the other way, into what appeared to be the dining room. BJ heard a muffled sliding sound through thin walls, and hesitated briefly, straining to listen. Sudden realization flooded her face as she frantically groped for a door leading to the basement. As she reached for the knob, loud reports of more gunfire came from below. BJ flattened herself against the wall and waited, scarcely breathing.

Only minutes earlier, Lisa moved into formation behind the two veteran officers. Pausing, she stared down at a manhole covering. Slightly ajar, it appeared as if it'd been moved recently. Without hesitating, she knelt and tugged, wrenching the heavy lid to one side until she could shine her flashlight inside. The abandoned, unserviceable sewer ran directly toward the old house.

Her flashlight thrust before her, she climbed down the rusty ladder and moved swiftly along the damp passage. As she approached the approximate distance she figured the house to be, she spied a different texture in the sewer wall. It was a *recent* hole disguised by a brownish blanket.

Lisa slowly pushed the blanket aside, peered through, and then crawled inside. Instinct told her she'd reached the basement of their suspect's house. Her ears detected a muffled metallic sliding and suddenly a man popped from a chute, landing hard on the concrete floor, his black metallic rifle skidding across the floor at her feet.

The black-clad figure regained his balance with his back toward her, then suddenly stiffened as he realized he wasn't alone. As he turned, Lisa shot him, and continued to fire until the gun was empty.

BJ and Booth found her rigidly pointing her empty weapon at a riddled David Turner. Booth gently took the pistol, wrapped his arm around her shoulders, and turned her away from the grisly scene. Fear gripped BJ's face and she glanced upward, then wheeled and bolted for the narrow steps.

"It's me, don't shoot!" she shouted. Reaching the landing, she sprinted for the living room.

Just inside the double doors, she suddenly stopped. On the floor, a flashlight provided just enough illumination for her to see Murphy, sitting, his back against the far wall. Bear's head was in his lap. Tears ran freely down his face as he spoke to his partner, too softly for her to make out his words.

The blackout curtains had been pulled aside, and daybreak was just beginning to lighten the room. Even from her position in the shadows, BJ could see Murphy trying to stem the flow of blood. She rapidly moved to help him.

"Hold on, old buddy. The ambulance is on the way. They'll be here in a few minutes. You're going to be fine. Just hang in there."

There were no signs of life from Drake. Joe Yates leaned against the doorframe, cradling a bleeding arm against his body. He cried quietly as he watched the two men, but his pain was not for him. BJ waited, uncertain as to what she should do, then the faint sound of a siren galvanized her to action and she ran to the door. The sirens become louder and closer. Murphy gently rocked his body back and forth as he continued to speak quietly to his injured friend. A crew of white-clad paramedics suddenly busted through and pushed their way in, a stretcher in hand. BJ knelt beside them.

"They've got him now, darling," she said softly. "Let him go, they'll take him the rest of the way."

Murphy looked blank, as if confused about what she was saying. "They're here to take care of Bear, now. Let him go."

Dazed, he slowly released the grip on his friend. The medics hoisted Bear onto the stretcher and rushed for the door. BJ reached to touch Murphy's face, to comfort him in this moment of need. Without a sound, his eyes rolled back into his head and he collapsed sideways. BJ screamed.

"*Frank!* Oh God, help me! Somebody help me!"

Chapter 23

Two major surgeries and as many days later, Frank Murphy finally opened his eyes. His vision blurred, he could make out BJ and Amanda sitting quietly nearby, unaware he was awake. He watched them silently whisper to each other while flipping through a fashion magazine. Suddenly his eyes locked onto BJ's. She was instantly in his arms, crying and kissing his stubbled face.

"Darling, darling! Oh, thank, *God!*"

His throat felt scratchy and raw, and he had trouble focusing. BJ saw his struggles and placed her cool fingers over his lips. "Don't worry, darling, don't try to talk if it hurts. It's from the tubes in your throat."

He drifted in and out of sleep for the next six hours. When finally lucid again, he found BJ was still there, alone, and sleeping uncomfortably in a chair. Murphy swallowed a lump in his throat and hot tears sprang to his eyes as he realized just how much he cared for this woman waiting by his side. Hallway voices interrupted her sleep. BJ opened her eyes and stretched, spying him gazing at her.

"I think I hear Joe," he whispered hoarsely.

Yates burst through the door with two nurses in hot pursuit. One, a pretty slim girl with a shorter than usual uniform—the other, a sturdy brunette with wire-rimmed eyeglasses who could've played linebacker for the Green Bay Packers. Murphy was sure Joe was running from the latter.

"Now... now... I'm an injured man, nurse. A hero, actually. I've been shot recently in the line of duty. Please, don't get physical with me," Yates pleaded as he skittishly flitted around the room—the big nurse trying to corner him, the younger one giggling wildly.

"First of all, *mister* policeman, you don't come in here after visiting hours! Secondly, you certainly don't come in drunk, carrying a bottle of *booze!*"

The pretty young one giggled again, her hand covering her mouth.

"All right. All *right!* I'm out of here, okay? Hell, I was just bringing my friend a little something to ease the pain. Murph? I'll be back when *Lawrence Taylor* gets off duty," Yates shouted over his shoulder. At the door, he returned the pint bottle to his jacket pocket and marched out indignantly, "Lawrence Taylor" and the cute giggly nurse trailing closely behind.

BJ and Murphy enjoyed the moment, then Murphy sobered. "How's Bear?" he said, trying to disguise the dread in his voice.

BJ held his hand and looked at him sadly. "I'm so sorry, Frank. He never made it to the hospital."

Murphy turned his head away to hide his wet eyes. Wrestling with his emotions, he wiped his eyes with the sleeve of his hospital gown then turned toward her, in control again.

"Anyone else?" he said.

"Lisa killed David Turner as he escaped down the laundry chute. He planned to ambush whoever came after him, then leave through a tunnel he'd cut into the sewer. He'd parked the van in the alley and loaded it with enough supplies to last a month. Lisa spotted a partially dislodged manhole cover and went in. If she hadn't had the foresight to check it out, Turner probably would've escaped."

Murphy's eyes were closed, but BJ knew he was listening. "You and Drake never had a chance, Frank. He was sandbagged— fully automatic weapons — the works. Like sitting ducks. He would've gotten you all if he'd been any kind of shot, but probably never held an automatic weapon before. A novice, he thought all he had to do was point in the general direction and pull the trigger, and he'd mow everyone down, just like in the movies. It could've been much worse." She sat on the edge of the bed and reached for his hand.

"Joe was nicked but was able to get to an adjacent room and blast away with his twelve-gauge. Turner probably hadn't planned on anyone shooting back and lost his nerve, real quick. When he jumped down the laundry chute and tumbled out into the basement, Lisa emptied her 9mm into his sorry ass."

BJ poured orange juice from a clear pitcher, hoping it'd help him regain his strength. He nodded.

"Frank, we found a heavy table in the basement with metal hooks screwed in. It's stained with the blood of at least three people. The ME is running tests to determine which victims match. During the search we also discovered a bloodstained knife, latex gloves, shackles, and pictures of Amanda's little friend, Kathy." She took a moment to steel herself before continuing. "*You* got him, Frank. This time, you finally nailed the bastard."

Murphy closed his eyes without acknowledging her remarks. "Mable?"

"She's taking it hard, to be expected. So are the daughters. She and Jo Jo came by while you were sleeping and said they'd be back. They love you, Frank." Her tears flowed freely.

"I know. They're family." He blinked rapidly, turning his head away again. "Oh shit, BJ" he moaned into the wall—then realized he'd just spoken Bear's favorite word.

BJ wrapped her arms around him, gently rocking him, as shuddering sobs wracked his body.

———

The killer wasn't *dead*. Frank could observe the act as the demon raised the long blade, prepared to bring it down on... someone he knew. He couldn't exactly see the victim, it was all hazy, but knew it was someone he cared for. So weary and tired, he moved as if in slow motion, trying to scream out a warning, but no sounds would come. It was all so familiar. He'd been there before. Then the faceless killer raised a grizzly trophy and turned. It was Amanda's head! In his sub-conscience, John Lee West's syrupy voice seeped through, and Murphy screamed.

Around two a.m., a nurse had come in and administered a shot... everything went black. The following morning, his head ached and his mouth parched, as though stuffed with dry cotton balls. *The whole Russian Army marched through your mouth last night,*

Sport. The dream suddenly washed back over him again, filling his senses, shaking him.

"Heard you had a rough night," BJ was saying. "The shift nurse said you scared the crap out of her in the middle of the night."

Apparently BJ had worked out a visiting arrangement with *Lawrence Taylor*, for she'd showed up at six to have breakfast and no one seemed to mind.

"Yeah? Well, I don't remember," he muttered.

BJ could sense it wasn't true, but decided to drop it. She pointed toward a cardboard box. "Here are the things you asked for, but I still think you're rushing it a bit."

He scowled, but she went on. "They tell me you might be able to go home in a couple of days. Amanda's really getting excited. She claims you'd promised to take her to the San Juan Islands or something ridiculous like that. She has a little homecoming all planned for you."

He remained quiet as she babbled on. "She and Lisa are going to Mount Bachelor to ski in the morning. They're opening the season early due to that freak storm. It's the only resort that has enough snow for late summer skiing. Which reminds me, I've got to get going if I'm going to get her ready and be there by ten. I'll have to go by our old house first and pick up her ski clothes and gear."

BJ paused, her expression distant as though she remembered something, but just as suddenly the thought was gone. "It will seem a little weird going back. We haven't been there since that day we left in such a hurry." She moved closer to the side of the bed, hugged him and gazed into his eyes. "You all right, Frank?"

"Sure, just tired. The nurse is right. I didn't sleep well last night."

"I'll get Amanda off and be back by noon tomorrow. You get some rest and leave that box of documents alone for now. You'll be home soon, darling, then, I promise, you won't get a lick of sleep."

She smiled wickedly and for the first time, he felt a tiny surge. *Good to see everything works okay, Sport,* he thought as he reached his hand toward her breast.

"Uh uh," she said, pulling away. "No samples. First you get well so you can come home, then we'll see. You're still a sick man, you know." She kissed him lightly on the lips, waved, and provocatively walked out the door, exaggerating her swaying hips.

———————

Amanda was her usual talkative self as she and her mother loaded her ski boots, bag and outfit into the hatchback, and locked the skis into the ski rack. BJ couldn't help but smile with pride. Observing her, it was hard to imagine the healthy transformation the last few days had made. She'd reverted from a guarded and jittery little girl who'd witnessed her grandmother's murder, into a bright, laughing youngster. It seemed nothing short of miraculous.

"Okay, Moms! Ready to roll!"

They squeezed into the small Toyota, BJ easing it into the street under the watchful eye of her elderly neighbor, as though he expected to witness more squealing tires and deep ruts in the lawn. As BJ drove very slowly past him, with an exaggerated cautiousness she carefully turned out of the cul-de-sac and out of his sight. They broke into a fit of laughter.

"I don't think he's going to miss us, Moms," Amanda laughed. "Hey, I've got an idea! Why don't you drive me to Lisa's, instead of her coming all the way here to pick me up? That way, we can have a chance to talk and plan our trip to the islands. Deal?"

BJ was starved for quality time with her daughter, away from everyone else. It was something she'd really missed while sequestered away on Frank's boat. Caught up in Amanda's exuberance, she agreed, "Deal!"

BJ picked up the cellular, put it on speaker and pushed Lisa's number.

"Hello."

"Lisa? This is BJ. We've just picked up Amanda's skis. It's such a nice day, so instead of you driving down, I thought I'd just bring her up. If that's all right with you."

"It's really no trouble, BJ. I could be there in forty minutes."

"I know — but I want to. This gives us a chance to share some time alone — something we haven't had in months. Okay?"

"Sure. That'll be fine."

"Thanks! See you in about two hours. Bye!"

She smiled at her daughter. "Now, how 'bout a burger?"

———————

BJ saw Lisa waiting for them outside on the porch of her stucco two-story home. Leaving her mother to unload, Amanda bounded up the sidewalk, wanting to be the first to give their friend a hug. Lisa met her halfway, held her and smiled.

BJ witnessed the exchange, experiencing just a fleeting pinch of jealousy. "Okay, you guys, lend a hand here," BJ mocked in a threatening tone.

Unloaded at last, BJ hugged her daughter, heaped on some last minute instructions, never really expecting her to comply with any of them. Driving off, Amanda and Lisa leaned together in her rear view mirror, waving frantically. BJ felt happy as she began her return trip.

It was only when she'd stopped for gas that she noticed the ski poles poking out beneath the powder jacket that Amanda decided not to take at the last minute.

Oh crap! She forgot her poles. Well, it's only a few miles back. Maybe they haven't left yet.

BJ hurriedly paid the attendant, turned around, and sped back in the same direction she'd just traveled. Again pulling in the driveway, she carried the poles to the front porch and knocked. After several minutes with no response, she knocked again, this time, harder. BJ finally detected footsteps approaching. Lisa finally appeared at the door. She seemed out of breath, her face flushed, as though she'd been exercising.

"Is everything all right, Lisa?"

"Oh, sure. We're in the basement, going through some of my old ski stuff. Here, I'll give those to Mandy," Lisa said brightly, reaching for the poles.

Intuitively, BJ felt an overpowering urge to see Amanda. Impulsively, she retracted the poles and brushed by the startled Lisa.

"I have something to tell her, anyway. Which way?"

"Straight ahead, and down the stairs, BJ." Lisa smiled, pointing the way. "You'll probably hear her before you see her. She's going through that old ski stuff like it's Christmas," Lisa called from behind.

BJ hurried down the narrow steps. Reaching the bottom, she turned toward a dim light from an adjacent room. As she pushed on the partially open door, the light flickered, and BJ dropped into a black bottomless hole.

Chapter 24

Murphy had vaguely overheard the duty nurse speak to someone down the hallway, but drifted between sleep and wakefulness, never quite reaching consciousness. Whomever it was spoke in a measured low tone, but the sudden footsteps near his door brought him to full wakefulness. Straining through sleep-caked eyes and forcing himself alert, he focused just as Judge Thurman Q. Woods strode in, his gnarled hands pushing his walking cane ahead of him.

"Well, by God, boy! Looks like you got the bastard, once and for all!"

"We got him, Judge. But at what price?" he agreed groggily.

"You're always too hard on yourself, Frank T. Of all the nieces and nephews I claimed through the years, you and Lisa are the ones I favored most. I don't suppose I ever told you that, did I?"

Surprised, Murphy weakly offered his hand to his mentor. It wasn't like the Judge to show softness or caring. Sensing Murphy's confusion, the old man laughed, his perfect white teeth contrasting against his ebony face. "You're right, boy. I guess I'm just getting emotional in my old age."

He abruptly changed subjects. "Hear you're courting a black lady — pretty one too. I've recently met her and her daughter."

Murphy nodded but didn't answer, unclear about where he was heading with this topic.

"It's serious business, Frank T. This interracial marrying, I mean. It's hard enough to make marriage work these days with all the outside interference, without the added pressure of race issues. You've given it a lot of thought, I suppose?"

"I love her… and Amanda… if that's what you mean."

"Good. *Good!* Glad to hear it, because as soon as I saw them, I knew it was providence. That pretty Amanda is the spitting image of my late daughter, Jennifer. I don't mean she just *resembles* her — I mean, she could be her *twin*. It's uncanny, really. Almost like my Jennifer has suddenly come back to life."

The judge reached into his breast pocket, pulled out a small photo and shoved it toward him. Murphy thought it really was Amanda with a young white girl, about the same age, standing in front of a rambling Victorian home. Only, it *wasn't* Amanda. The clothes and hair were all wrong. It had to be Jennifer, the judge's dead daughter. The resemblance between her and Amanda was simply… uncanny!

"That's my daughter, Jennifer, just before her death, and that's Corky with her. They were the best of friends. The picture was taken at Lisa's parent's home. See the resemblance?"

Despite his weakness, Murphy smiled. *Corky? The Judge calls Lisa Corky? There's a human side to the old man after all. That might be why Lisa has been so fond of Amanda, inviting her skiing and all —she reminds her of her little friend, Jennifer Woods.* Suddenly, Murphy felt more at ease.

"Corky was with Jennifer when she died, and almost drowned trying to save her little friend." The old man suddenly looked older than usual, as if speaking about those memories still caused him considerable pain. "She was a real little hero, but she didn't want any glory. She missed her playmate too much for that. After that, she left and didn't come back until she got this job offer. Now, here at last, I have my favorite niece and nephew, both at home where they belong."

Murphy listened as the old man relived when his daughter Jennifer was still alive, and she and Corky had played together in the park near the river. Quite abruptly, he rose and turned toward the door. His eyes averted Frank's as though he'd exposed too much of himself. He said stiffly, "Well, you take care, Frank T. Come by and see me when you're able to get around. Bring those two young ladies when you do."

Without waiting for a reply, he gingerly exited the room, the tapping of his cane and the shuffling of his feet fading into the silence of the corridor.

285

Murphy smiled after him for a time, reflecting upon their conversation. Then he pulled the brown cardboard box toward him. Reaching in, he removed the recorder, placing it on his tray table, then spread out several files on his bedcovers so he could read the labels.

Those dreams the previous night *had* shaken him. It'd been so real! He'd awakened with a feeling that David Turner was still out there. What was bugging him? It was *over*! Still, something gnawed at him.

Reaching for a note pad, he began to jot down his thoughts, pausing after several entries to study what he'd written. Inexplicably, he realized what had been bothering him. It was the ambush! It'd been meticulously planned and executed, and except for David Turner being a shitty shot, they'd all be dead, and Turner would be planning his next murder.

Murphy concentrated on his notations. First he'd listed all the things that'd seemed so out of place during the investigation. Like… how did the killer know they'd be coming for him at a time when most people would've been sound asleep? How did he find Amanda at her grandmother's, then later, at her home? How did he know when to make a try for her, within minutes of the security being pulled off? How did he know she would be on the boat? And finally, how was he able to leave the body at the marina without being seen?

He scribbled more notations, intently trying to think of any common thread that might link any of these "*hows's*" together. Next, beside each event, he listed the names of those who might have known the details of it, comparing that list with the first for any commonality. As Murphy studied them together he grew increasingly uneasy. Suddenly, he reached for the phone.

"Charley? I'm getting started writing my report and need some information. Yeah, I want to get a head start so I can lay around for a few days." He passed onto Charley the information he was seeking, hung up and quickly punched in another number.

"Officer White, please. Thanks."

He waited impatiently until the officer came on. "Tim? This is Frank Murphy, homicide." Brief and to the point, his conversations and requests for information were hasty, with little time spent on pleasantries. He asked for specific information and then hung up.

Charley swiftly called back. Murphy jotted down the information he'd been able to dig up. Placing the receiver down, he studied the list repeatedly, periodically leafing through various files to confirm a point. The hair suddenly stood on the back of his neck!

There *was* a pattern! All along, it'd been right before his eyes. At first he refused to believe it.

No! It can't be. There has to be another explanation!

His heart hammering, he frantically searched for additional information — and found it! It was *true!* Hastily, he drew a matrix and seeing the information unfold, he knew, beyond a doubt, that he was right.

The phone rang again and he picked it up, made more notes while listening intently, then hung up. He abruptly swung his feet over the side of the bed and slid out onto the cold tile floor. Finding his clothing in a small closet, he struggled to get a leg into his pants. The phone rang again. He hopped toward the bed, plopping down hard. He was already breathing heavily from the exertion.

"Yes?"

It was Officer White, confirming what he already knew. His mind raced. He thought of something else and dialed 'Information' for a new number, then punched it into the receiver and waited.

"Department of Corrections, Officer Jones here. May I help you?"

"Yes, at least, I hope so. I'm trying to contact a George Hurst. He used to be a supervisor there." He was put on hold until Hurst came on the line.

"George? Frank Murphy here. Remember me?"

"Frank! How the hell are you? I thought you'd moved away. To what do I owe this pleasure?"

"I understand that Lisa Kinard worked for you last summer. I head up the task force for those recent murders. Lisa now works for me. Could I ask a few questions about her, for reference?"

"Yes, I remember Lisa quite well. Smart gal. What is it you'd like to know?"

"Just what did she do for you, George?"

"She handled our sex offender case load, Frank. Did a pretty good job of it, too."

"Was David Turner ever one of your clients?"

"Well, I'm not really supposed to give out that kind of information over the phone, but seeing as how I read that he's dead... yes. He was one of Lisa's cases. Funny you should ask about him, though. We did have a small problem during that period. He'd show up, maybe five or six times a month, meeting with her for very lengthy sessions. I was beginning to worry she was becoming too involved with one of her clients, so I mentioned it to her, and that was the end of it. Still, I never felt exactly right about it."

"Do you remember what David's problem was?" He held his breath, afraid to breathe.

"He'd gotten into trouble as a juvenile — raped a family member — a little girl of two. Her family didn't press it, but we were able to make an assault charge stick. It's all in the folder we sent over with Lisa earlier. Didn't you get it?"

"Uh... oh yeah... but I'm away from the office now, so could you fill me in? Who did you say you gave the file to?"

"Lisa. She said you'd asked for it some time back. Three years ago, he manhandled a young girl and tried to rape her, but some neighbors intervened before he sexually assaulted her. He claimed voices told him to do some pretty weird stuff—a lot of bad things. Because the attack was averted, he was only charged with Assault, Third Degree, with sexual motivation. He was put into the SOSSA program. That means he received treatment in the community and didn't have to go to prison. After he was released he was required to register as a sex offender."

"Swell!"

"Is Lisa in any kind of trouble over this Turner guy?"

"No, no... nothing like that. You've been a big help, George. Thanks a heap."

Murphy abruptly ended the conversation and hastily punched on the recorder. He shivered involuntarily as the chilling voice of John Lee West came on. He pushed fast forward and listened, finally reaching the part he was seeking. West's smooth voice cut through the quiet air.

"...the reason your killer is invisible to you, is that perhaps you're looking for a stereotype murderer... like in the movies — salivating lips, lewd manners, dirty, black broken teeth — you know the type..."

Fast forward, again.

"…within. That's where monsters lurk."

Murphy hit the fast forward button. "…ah, such beauty I envision, for all alike, you are as sisters."

Sisters! John Lee West had known! The son of a bitch had known all along! How? Had the killer been in contact with West? He'd probably never know. What was clear, however, was that West had been toying with him.

Murphy quieted his shaking hands and hit the fast forward button again, "…and for all seemingly impossible things, we complete with ease, for we do not toil alone."

He felt certain West had known David Turner had help in committing those hideous murders. That help had been *Lisa Kinard*!

He intently scanned his matrix once again to confirm his suspicions. The thread became even clearer. First the murder in New York close by the hotel, during the same time four department officers had been at the conference, Bear, Captain Brooks, a guy from Bunco and *Lisa Kinard*. Then the time she'd been in Portland during the U.S. Olympic tryouts when another rape — and murder — had been committed.

She'd also been privy to every piece of information regarding the case. The killer had known! Lisa! Pretty, friendly, young, capable Lisa — strong, athletic, fearless — could move freely, *in uniform*, without drawing attention to her. She'd manipulated everyone, getting just what she wanted.

Lisa, with her little black girlfriend, Jenny, suspiciously dead at fifteen — a child the spitting image of Amanda. *Had Lisa also murdered her?* Another problem popped into his head. She was the Judge's niece. *God, what a mess!*

Piecing it all together, his mind raced. She'd probably assaulted the Judge's daughter, Jenny, then killed her so she couldn't tell — while still only a child herself. Then through the years, she'd carefully left other victims in her wake. Like in New York City, Portland, and… how many others? Murphy knew she'd traveled extensively to prepare for the Olympics, so there might well have been more victims, in both Europe and the U.S.!

His mind leaped to his conversation with George Hurst. As a probation officer, she'd apparently met David Turner while handling a sex offender caseload before attending the Academy.

She'd used the knowledge about Turner's instability to her own advantage. It wouldn't have been hard. He'd seen her test scores from the evening psychology classes. She was *smart*—intuitive, and could've easily manipulated a disturbed person like Turner to accomplish her own aims.

Murphy was immensely shaken by this new knowledge, and by its implications. Turner had been only a diversion, someone to help grab the girls and move the bodies. Maybe she'd let him have some of them, too. Then when he'd become a liability and of no further use, she'd killed him.

That's what John Lee West had meant, he thought.

He searched absently for a cigarette, before remembering he was in a hospital. His mind snapped back to Lisa, realizing that she'd finagled her way into the Special Task Force by using the Judge's influence, and had known every move they'd made from day one. She'd cleverly manipulated every last one of them, including him. Now Bear was dead and Amanda was still at risk. He felt sick.

My God, a female serial killer!

The realization brought him to his feet. In all his years with the department, he could recall only two female serial killers, somewhere in Florida, and it was questionable whether they should've legitimately been classified as such, anyway. In any event, it was extremely rare that a female would do this—and the fact that the victims had been young girls, with the primary motive being *sex*.

Suddenly, he stiffened, and groaned aloud. *My God! Lisa's taking Amanda skiing!*

BJ had mentioned they were meeting up with her today. He quickly dialed BJ's cell phone number, waiting until it became clear she wasn't going to answer, then frantically searched for his shirt. He struggled to get dressed and heard someone enter — *Lawrence Taylor*.

"Just where do you think you're going, Sergeant Murphy?" she boomed. "You get your firm little tush right back into that bed before I have to rough you up!"

"I've got a gun, nurse. Don't give me any reason to shoot you," he said sourly, as he buttoned his shirt. He reached for the phone again.

"Charley? I need a car. Right *now*! Okay, get it here fast. One more thing—do you know where Lisa lives?"

He listened and nodded.

"Yeah, I know where she lives. Where are you? Good, you're closer than I am. Swing by, use your emergency equipment. And Charley…just get there *fast* and be careful. You'll be walking into a potentially dangerous situation! If Lisa is there, take her into custody…."

"Yes, that's what I said, I'll explain later. I'll be on the cellular. I'm leaving as soon as you can get me a car."

He slowly hung up and impatiently paced, waiting as the tough nurse periodically brushed past his door, trying to stare him down. The phone rang again, this time the ring came from the phone on his nightstand. A voice informed him that his car was waiting.

He'd only been on the road ten minutes, when his cellular interrupted the heavy cruiser's steady humming, jarring his thoughts.

"It's Charley. No one is home, Frank. Strange though, BJ's car is parked out front and it's got an empty ski rack on it."

"Charley, kick the fucking door down and see if the ski equipment is in the house. If it is, put out an APB on Lisa's car, then stand by the phone and wait for my call!"

He dialed the Judge's home number and the houseman answered on the fourth ring.

"Good afternoon. Woods residence."

As Murphy identified himself and requested to speak to the Judge, the tart British voice rebuffed him sharply. The Judge was out and wouldn't be expected until around five. Murphy asked where he'd gone.

"I'm sorry, sir, but it is the Judge's day out — golf I believe he said — and he rather hates to be disturbed."

"This is an emergency, you *asshole*! A matter of life and death!" Murphy screamed into the receiver. "If anything happens as a result of your asinine interference, it may well be your death, too! Now, give me the fucking *number*!"

He was given the number.

Moments later, Judge Wood's voice came on the line.

"Judge? I've got sort of an emergency here. Lisa was supposed to go skiing today, but there's been a bad situation at the office and we desperately need to contact her."

"Well, how can I possibly be of assistance?" said the gravelly voice on the other end.

"We went by her place, but she wasn't home. Someone overheard her say that she might take Amanda to see her parent's old house," he lied. "The one in the picture. Would you have a telephone number, or know how to get there?" He waited, anxiously holding his breath.

"There hasn't been a phone for years, Frank. It's at the south end of Vashon Island. I can't imagine Lisa taking the Seattle-Vashon ferry and then driving all the way to the south end. It's been vacant for years and the place is in terrible disrepair—but I'll give you the address if that's what you want."

He gave Murphy an address just off Pohl Road, a small, seldom traveled side road skirting a large wooded area. Murphy broke the connection without saying goodbye.

Pushing the *talk* button on the unit's radio, Hooter's breathy voice oozed through. It didn't excite him this time. He had other things on his mind.

"I need to contact our *navy*. I need a boat." The 'navy' he referred to was the Seattle P.D.'s new high-speed chase boat. They'd recently replaced two older ones for a fast, sleek, modern high tech one.

"Sorry, but it's engaged right now, Frank. You should be able to get it in about thirty minutes, though."

"I don't have that much time. How about getting me a schedule for the Vashon Ferry run? I need it *ASAP!* Also, if there are any other units in the vicinity have them call me on my cellular. *Not* the radio... my cellular! Thanks. Call me back because I'm heading out there now."

Hooter was back on in scarcely two minutes. "The ferry to Vashon leaves in ten minutes. It's pretty true to schedule, too. We have a unit close by. Do you want me to call him?"

"Does that unit have a cellular? I don't want to use the radio if I don't have to," he said, thinking Lisa might be monitoring it.

He was in luck. The officer had his own personal cellular phone and Murphy quickly dialed the number. "This is Detective Sergeant Frank Murphy with the Special Task Force. Are you near the ferry?"

"Yes sir. It's arriving now. The cars will begin to disembark in another minute or two."

"Listen to me, officer... I'm sorry, what's your name?"

"Martin. Martin Dewey, Sergeant Murphy."

"Okay, Martin. Do whatever it takes, but don't let that ferry leave without me. Even if you have to put a gun to the captain's head! After the cars have disembarked, block the ramp and don't let anyone else on. We'll be the only passengers this time. Make a lane so you can get up front of cars waiting and block the ramp. I'll leave my car and we'll take your unit. This is life and death mister, so don't blow it."

"You can count on it, Sergeant Murphy. By the way, who's paying the fare?"

He smiled coldly. "I'm paying the fare today, Marty. I'm paying the fare."

True to his word, the young officer first allowed the ferry to unload, blocked off the ramp, and then through the sheer force of only his will and flashing red and blue lights, he'd opened up a lane to drive on. Murphy ignored the waiting drivers' curses and fist shaking. He maneuvered his car into a nearby no parking zone and hurried up the ramp, motioning for the young officer to drive on before latching the safety chain after him.

On board, an equally irritable skipper greeted him. Standing at least six-foot five, he had a head full of wild coal black hair a lumberjack would've been proud of. He bellowed, his hands on his hips and his head thrown back.

"By what *goddamned* authority gives you the *goddamned* right to commandeer my *goddamned* ferry boat, mister policeman?"

Murphy barked, "Shut up and drive this tub, or I'll drive the damned thing myself!"

"Then drive the *goddamned* thing yourself, asshole, and see how *goddamned* far you get!"

The skipper wasn't about to back down. Murphy breathed deeply to try to calm his heart rate and cool off a little. "I'm sorry, Captain. There's an emergency on the island—a matter of life and death. Every minute we waste standing here talking, the more likelihood people are dying."

The big Captain's red face glared down at him as he braced his hands on each hip, unrelenting. The young policeman with Murphy stood slightly in the background with an amused smile. Murphy decided to take a different tack.

"Captain, do you have any children?" The skipper hesitated and his features softened slightly, then nodded.

"Have you been following the papers about the recent killings we've had?"

Another nod.

"Well, a twelve year-old girl is in extreme danger and so is her mother. That little girl must be terrified right now. She's most likely tied up — kept in a dark basement until she can be raped and her throat cut. Her mother is only excess baggage, and if not already dead, she will be any minute."

He waited.

The ferry captain motioned to one of his crew standing nearby and suddenly bellowed, "Don't just stand there, cast off!"

He then wheeled and raced back up the narrow iron steps from which he'd descended. Murphy climbed back into his car and waited, the water quietly lapping against the bow. This was not a day to enjoy it.

During the short crossing, he contacted the Vashon Island Sheriff's Department substation and spoke with Deputy Hawkins. He gave the deputy all the information he had and asked him to respond. "Use your emergency equipment, but turn it off when you're about two miles away," he instructed. "Don't even think about using your radio. This sicko will probably be listening on a police scanner. Now, do you have someone else to go with you?"

"Sergeant, we're just a small outstation of only three deputies. One's sick, the other is on vacation. I'm it."

"Okay, just go in carefully! The person we're looking for is a cold-blooded killer and won't think twice about killing you, too. We think there are hostages — a black female cop and her daughter. The person you might encounter is a twenty-three-year-old female cop, short blond hair, athletic build, a black belt in martial arts and a crack shot. She's killed a lot of people, Deputy, and if she gets the chance she won't hesitate to kill you, too. So if you get the opportunity to take her out, don't let false chivalry get in your way. Shoot to kill. You can bet she will!"

The silence on the other end was so palpable Murphy could almost hear the deputy thinking aloud. At last, the man spoke. "What are you getting me into, Detective?"

"Just be careful," Murphy said, and rang off.

Chapter 25

BJ was awake, but just barely. Groggy, she vaguely remembered she and Amanda had gone to Lisa's house. They'd been going skiing together. BJ's head was foggy, but she faintly remembered going inside, then... nothing.

Where am I?

She tried to move, but couldn't. She realized her hands were bound tightly behind her. The scrape of metal against metal indicated it was a pipe — she was secured with handcuffs, probably her own! BJ tried to make a sound, to swallow, but a sensation of rubber pressed against her lips and tongue. She instinctively knew that it was a rubber ball gag, like those found in porno shops along the strip, Highway 99 — the same kind as those used in the recent killings.

In her hazy mind, she vaguely remembered that those killings had been solved. She fought down panic and as her vision blurred, then became more focused, she tried to make out images around her.

Amanda!

Her daughter lay motionless on a heavy wooden table. BJ fought down another surge of panic. *Where is Lisa? Is she tied up, too?* BJ fought a wave of nausea.

That table! It had a vague familiarity. Her heart pounded as she tried to recall — there'd been an identical table at David Turner's house in the basement where Lisa had killed him — where his victims had been butchered.

Frantically, BJ lunged against her bonds. It was no use. She couldn't budge the pipe. *This is a nightmare! It has to be!* If only she'd wake up in a moment and everything would be fine. She let her head droop, scarcely breathing — listening intently.

Footsteps touched lightly on the stairway to her right. A sense of dread overcame her as she fought to fix her eyes on the floor, as though by doing so, she wouldn't give a face to her terror. Two black shoes stopped directly in front of her. A strong hand gripped her hair, viciously jerking her head back.

Lisa Kinard!

Suddenly, the pieces came together and BJ realized she really wasn't that surprised by the discovery. The answer had been there all along. They'd just been blind to it!

"Well, black bitch, you awake now?" Lisa's bloodshot eyes bulged and the tendons in her once beautiful neck protruded as though she'd recently exerted herself. Spittle clung to her bottom lip. Her profound metamorphosis chilled BJ to the bone.

"What's za' matter, black bitch? Cat got yer tongue?" Lisa slurred, as though heavily intoxicated. In a flash, her hand whipped out, catching BJ on the side of the face, stunning her momentarily. Through the loud ringing in her ears, she could faintly hear Lisa speak again.

"You won't have to worry about it for long. You see, first I'm gonna slit your throat, then missy Jennifer and I are going to have some fun."

Jennifer? Why is she calling Mandy, Jennifer?

Enraged, BJ violently kicked at the shins of this stranger, catching her squarely on her right ankle. Lisa fell against the heavy wooden table edge with a thud and sharply cried out. BJ knew she'd hurt her and struggled to get free, but her bonds held fast. The consequences of her action suddenly dawned on her.

Now, I've done it! Gone and pissed this lunatic off. Helpless as I am, she'll probably just cut my throat!

Lisa rubbed her ankle tenderly, soothing it without looking up, her short blond hair cascading over her eyes. Then she slowly smiled maliciously. "Just for that — you'll get to watch, *black bitch!*"

Grabbing roughly at BJ's arms, she hoisted her to an upright position. Tying a short nylon cord around both her neck and the pipe, she was forced to face straight ahead. If she fell or passed out, she would strangle. Grinning, Lisa moved toward a large cabinet on the far wall, pulled out a drawer and meticulously placed several items on the table in front of the bound woman. BJ watched helplessly as the deranged woman slowly pulled on thin latex gloves, dramatically snapping them. BJ gasped and her heart stopped at the harness and the rubber, flesh-colored dildo Lisa held up for her to see.

Her toying eyes never left BJ's, nor did her demented grin cease. Laying the dildo aside, she picked up a long blade kitchen knife, the curved, serrated notches visible even from her distance.

"Oh, are we all gonna have some fun tonight!" Lisa giggled insanely. Horrified, BJ strained against her bonds, trying to scream through the rubber gag.

Lisa pulled a straight-backed chair toward her and sat, barely out of BJ's kicking range. She straddled it like a man would, facing the back, her arms resting on top. A detached, vacant smile lingered as she silently eyed her captive, clearly wanting to talk, impress BJ.

"I collect them, you know? My first was Jennifer Woods, the Judge's daughter. She was my love for all time." Lisa sounded nearly rational. "We were at a picnic by the river — all of a sudden I just lost it and forced myself on her. It was the most mind-blowing nut I'd ever had — then I killed her."

Lisa glared defiantly at BJ. "Well I couldn't just let her tell everyone, could I?"

Instantly, she smiled sweetly, as though BJ had just agreed with her. "None of the others have given me the out-of-this-stratosphere orgasm I had with Jennifer. But I keep looking, just the same. I kept thinking, maybe someday I'll find another like Jennifer."

She tilted her head toward Amanda.

"Then, I saw Amanda and knew I had to have her, no matter what the consequences. It's like... once you've felt the ultimate high, you have to keep seeking it, BJ."

She spoke inquisitively, as if she were actually seeking her captive's approval.

"I know, you just think I'm another butch lezzy constantly chasing young pussy. I'm not. I have feelings. I actually loved Jennifer. If she'd returned that love, I might've turned out differently."

"I had planned a ski honeymoon, just me and Amanda. If she loved me back, we could've remained together for the rest of our lives. It was all so simple."

Suddenly, Lisa's face turned ugly and drawn, lips pursed, eyes squinted. "Then *you* —you *bitch*. You just had to come back, didn't you? Well, look where it's gotten you— tied up like a hog, waiting to get stuck!"

Like lightening, Lisa stood and slapped BJ across the face. Again, harder! Then she balled up her fist as a man would do and slugged her. BJ tasted blood in her mouth. Moaning, she fought to remain conscious.

"Do you have any idea what I'm going to do now?" Lisa pointed at heavy rings screwed into the tabletop.

"Did you ever question how I was able to get the bodies into the wonderful position they found them in?" She pranced excitedly, as if she were ready to start skipping.

Oh God, she's crazy!

BJ could see Amanda's wrists bound to the heavy rings bolted on each side of her body. Her daughter still hadn't moved, and BJ feared for her. She watched in horror as Lisa guided each of Amanda's ankles to a mid-table ring and fastened them. The girl's knees pointed upward now, her thin relaxed legs spread wide.

"I made this contraption," she said proudly. "When I get through, rigor mortis sets in, and presto, the perfect position!"

Certifiably mad!

BJ lunged violently against her shackles, moaning to plead for her daughter's life, but only succeeding in choking herself as only muffled sounds came. Mesmerized, she watched as Lisa cut through her daughter's thin panties, leaving her genitals bare. Amanda moaned softly and stirred slightly against her bonds.

"She'll be awake in another minute or two." Lisa slipped out of her one-piece dress, completely nude underneath. She attached the stiff rubber device to a belt around her slim waist. It bobbed obscenely as she crawled onto the table beside the girl, waiting for her to regain consciousness.

She gave BJ a smutty lewd wink. "I like to use my mouth first. Some even respond like they like it! Maybe Amanda will, too. You be the judge."

I'll kill you, you fucking bitch! Whatever it takes, I swear I'll kill you!

BJ strained against her bindings until she became disoriented due to a lack of air, and then sagged weakly. *Please let me kill her before I die. Please Lord. Let me see her die!*

The sudden sound of crunching gravel beneath tires jolted both of their attentions to the outside world. Lisa quickly arose, dropped the harness and slipped back into the dress she'd discarded earlier. Darting back to the large cabinet, she removed a .38 revolver and stuck it into an oversized decorative dress pocket. Holding the knife, she cocked her head and crooned pleasantly, "I'll be back in *ex-act-ly ten-n-n-n minutes.*

Chapter 26

Jack Hawkins had been a deputy for sixteen years. For the last five, he'd lived on Vashon Island and considered them to be the best years of his life. Previously a deputy in south King County, he'd become dissatisfied with the type of people he had to deal with and was ready to hang it up. Being exposed daily to druggies, crooks and psychos, he knew he couldn't take it much longer and still treat his family like a father and husband should. Then out of the blue, he was offered this position on the island.

Unable to afford a house in Seattle, he and Helen had immediately purchased a spacious older home with acreage and a greenhouse, remodeling it with most of their savings. The kids had taken to their new social environment like ducks take to water.

Jack even bought an eighteen-foot fishing boat and a four-wheel drive! Life was indeed good for Deputy Hawkins.

That's why the unusual call he'd received from the Seattle detective stunned him. He'd been away from big city crime for so long, that he'd almost forgotten the violence and the dark side of the city. In the past year, the worst thing he'd witnessed was when a carload of teenagers drove off a bridge and crashed into a concrete pillar, leaving them all dead and mangled in the wreckage for hours. He'd had nightmares about it for a week. *But this*? A killer — on his island — holding hostages? He seriously doubted it, but he'd give it a careful look just the same.

He almost missed the old dirt road that led into the dense woods. Tall grass and blackberry brambles easily obscured it from the main road. It looked as if it'd been recently used, but then island teenagers were always looking for a place to drink beer and screw, so he wasn't overly alarmed. Still, he'd planned to be around to draw his pension for at least a *hundred* years after he retired, so he thought he'd be careful just the same.

There, just ahead.

He brought his vehicle to a slow gradual stop and for a moment, just sat, carefully eyeing the old run-down house. Nothing seemed out of the ordinary and he saw no movement. It was one of the older homes built in the late 1880's, most likely for a wealthy timber baron—three levels, balconies and porches jutting from almost every angle. The glass in the windows was long gone, and the rotted front steps had caved in, leaving a large hole where the stone foundation could be seen.

Built to last a hundred years, Hawkins thought cynically. Satisfied nothing was amiss, Deputy Hawkins carefully eased his car into gear, coasting quietly through the matted foliage covering the circular driveway. *Strange. A car is parked in the rear of the house.*

Keeping his eyes glued to the front entrance, Hawkins slid from his seat and got out, careful not to slam the door. Cautiously, he moved toward the front door, now only a gaping hole since the door long ago had fallen into the house. Edging carefully around the sizeable hole in the center on the porch, he eased to the doorway, pulled his service pistol from its holster, and stepped into the musty atmosphere, listening hard for the slightest sound. Nothing.

Wait! Footprints in the dust!

He made his way deeper into the house, grimacing each time he stepped on a squeaky board. Warily scanning the kitchen, he moved on toward the rear of the house. Spying a door ajar and steps leading into an old cellar, he cautiously peered inside.

It happened so quickly that he was caught completely off guard. Someone must've stood on the railing just inside the door, because he hadn't detected anyone on the steps.

A flash of light sliced the air and a white-hot pain shot through his neck. As if fascinated, he watched in slow-motion horror as his blood spurted over the rail onto the cellar floor below. He swayed unsteadily, trying to comprehend, then slowly crumpled into darkness.

Lisa returned a few minutes later, drenched in blood. Returning to the wood cabinet, this time she retrieved a police scanner, activated it, and laid it on the counter. BJ heard her cursing and muttering as she rolled the knob to find the proper setting.

"*Motherfuckers!* They just won't let a person have any peace!"

Amanda had opened her eyes by now, but when BJ urgently shook her head at her, she quickly shut them again, lying very still. BJ felt a surge of pride for her daughter. *So bright! I'll not let her die! She won't!* Helplessly, she watched with dread as Lisa found her channel and listened intently.

"Unit 314, this is dispatch. Are you there, 314?"

Lisa rushed from the room. Within a few moments, BJ heard the muffled sounds of tennis shoes running across the floor above. *She's going to check the vehicle number.* She listened for Lisa's strides on the creaky old floor overhead again, then her steps heading back down until BJ could see her within her limited field of vision.

She huddled over the scanner once again. Every few minutes the same voice repeated the now familiar summons, each time becoming more concerned. BJ knew someone had driven into the driveway not long ago, and suspected it had been a cop. It was probably a deputy sheriff — and most likely, driving car 314.

BJ could only imagine what had happened to the officer. She'd only heard a heavy thud from above, as if someone fell. Then her tormentor had returned alone, covered with blood. She could only assume the worst.

But, maybe there's still hope! If someone had come by, it could mean they'd been sent out! Or, it might be only that they'd just happened to stumble across this old place.

God help me, BJ thought. *I've got to get loose and save my daughter. I can't wait for someone else.* Silently, she struggled with the handcuffs against the metal pipe.

Martin Dewey drove the lone police unit off the ferry ramp as the vehicle drivers lined up to load, or families, obviously waiting for someone to arrive, watched in total disbelief. Dewey hit his siren and emergency lights simultaneously, speeding toward the southern tip of the island. From the corner of his eye, he glanced toward the pale disheveled person in the passenger's seat.

Shit, he looks like he's dying! He focused on a bright patch of blood that appeared larger than when he'd first observed it at the

Seattle ferry dock. Murphy's skin was pallid and his hands trembled noticeably.

"You all right, Sergeant?"

Murphy barely nodded, gazing out the right hand window. Abruptly, he turned to the young cop. "Got an extra gun?"

"I thought you guys were issued weapons in Seattle," he said off-handedly, trying to keep it light.

Murphy was in no mood for humor, nor was he feeling too good right now.

"I was in the fucking *hospital*, okay? They don't let you *have* a gun, because they're afraid you'll get *agitated* at some smart-ass comments and just *shoot* his smart-ass off. Any more questions?"

Martin quickly sobered and became all business. "Just the shotgun in the rack, Sergeant. You want mine?"

Murphy was busy examining his bloody shirt. "No. You keep your pistol. I'll take the shotgun. Remember, when we get there, you take the back and I'll go in the front. Don't shoot me, for Christ's sake!"

Martin laughed. "You got it, Sergeant Murphy."

Murphy really looked at him for the first time. Dewey was a tall good-looking young man with freshly trimmed blond hair.

"You married, Martin?"

"Yes sir. Married for about six months now." He smiled.

"How long have you been with the department?"

"A year. I was working traffic near the pier when your call came in. I'm not going to get into trouble, am I?" He smiled broadly, as if the thought of trouble didn't cause him much concern.

Murphy found himself liking the young officer. "Probably, but don't worry about it. Hell, I've been in trouble ever since I joined the department, and look how successful I am."

The two men grinned at each other.

"Yeah, I've heard about you, Sergeant Murphy. I was on security outside the door on the day you took on that bunch you called the 'viper's pit.' That's why I jumped at the chance to work with you now."

"Call me Frank, if you want. My last partner always called me 'Murph.' You might try that if it suits you better." At the thought of Drake, Murphy withdrew and stared through the side window at the passing fences.

Dewey waited a respectful time before he broke into his thoughts. "What are these people to you, Murph?"

Murphy stiffened, then looked at him steadily.

"My family," he said simply. "A little girl of twelve and her mother—a woman I should've married long ago. If I get them out of this alive, I'm taking them someplace where it's safe to live — where you don't have to worry about sickos and freaks like this one."

"When you find that place, write and let me know where it is. I want to go, too."

Dewey reached to the console and turned off the siren and lights. "We should be getting close to the turn-off now."

They both saw the road at the same time, silently noting the pair of vehicle tracks leading down the dirt trail. Halfway down the lane, Murphy motioned for Martin to stop. Without asking the young cop to follow, he quickly exited the vehicle with the shotgun and walked toward the old house, about three hundred yards in the distance.

Dewey scrambled to catch up, and fell in beside him. They could clearly see the King County Sheriff's car in the front driveway, its door partly ajar. Dewey's face was pale, his lips tightly pursed. He pulled his pistol, swallowed, and glanced nervously at Murphy. He noticed Murphy was struggling hard to keep from faltering, stumbling every few feet, trying to maintain his footing. Dewey wondered just how much help he'd really be if they *did* get into trouble out here.

Giving the injured man another worried glance, Martin Dewey split off to the left and headed toward the rear of the huge old house. As he rounded the corner, his last image of Murphy was of him using the shotgun for a crutch while struggling to climb the few rotten steps up to the front door.

The silence was broken by static, then, "Car 314. Are you up?"

It had come from inside the house.

Although the volume was turned low, the dispatcher's voice came over the radio clear and unbroken. No one answered the call. BJ watched as Lisa straightened and turned back toward them.

"Well I guess we're all right for a while. Let's play some games," she said sweetly, moving to the side of the table. Another voice suddenly broke the silence. "Hey, old buddy, you lose a car?"

Lisa froze, and listened intently.

"Sure did. It isn't like Hawkins to not call in. We're starting to get a little worried."

"This is Seattle P.D. I've got a scanner and couldn't help but eavesdrop. We also seem to have a vehicle that hasn't called in for a while, too. He was headed in your direction to check out some old house near the south end. If you happen to run into him, his name is Dewey. Tell him to call in. Okay?"

"You got it, Seattle. Out."

Lisa shoved her pistol back into her pocket and placed a finger over both lips. "Shush." She winked and edged toward the stairs again, lost from BJ's sight.

Just a quick look, Lisa thought. *Everything's probably okay, but it won't hurt to take a look. Then, I'll get back to the girl and her nosey bitch mother.*

As she reached the top of the landing, she caught a slight movement beyond the small kitchen window and hunkered down, waiting. In one quiet movement, Martin Dewey stepped inside, startled to discover such an extremely pretty young woman before him. A sudden realization flooded his eyes just as Lisa shot him in the chest, her shot reverberating through the corridors. She quickly moved to the door, stood over the fallen man, and glanced outside. Satisfied he'd been alone, she grabbed his foot, tugging him inside. Peering out once more, she headed back down the stairs.

That'll take care of the second cop bastard looking for me. Now, it's time for business, drive to where I hid the boat, and get the fuck out of Dodge.

This time Lisa walked directly to the table, picked up the knife and waved it in front of BJ. "It's party time," she said softly. "Just want you to know there's been a slight change of plans. All of a sudden this place is becoming just a little too popular. So I'm going to speed up the timetable a little. Before I cut your throat, I want you to know what you'll be missing. I won't be able to spend as much time with Jennifer as I had intended — but it'll be enough. When the cops find her they'll know it's not over. Shit, who knows? I might even drop by the hospital and stick a knife in that asshole Murphy on my way out of town."

Lisa's eyes glazed over as she spoke. Her lips half-parted and breathing deeply, she slowly inched toward BJ. BJ could see her madness, her lips salivating, as though about to partake of a fine meal. BJ attempted to scream, lunging violently against her bonds, kicking out. Helplessly, she could only watch in horror as the knife approached her throat. Finally, closing her eyes, she simply waited for it to be over.

Murphy had nearly passed out from weakness after climbing the front porch steps. *If you do Sport, you'll probably fall into that damned hole and not be found until the snow melts next Spring.*

Breathing heavily, he leaned against the rickety old railing until his light-headedness passed. Steeling himself for yet another valiant effort, the loud report of a gun had suddenly punctured the silence. He instinctively crouched, realizing it'd come from within the house. He moved cautiously inside, pushing the shotgun ahead of him.

In the shadows of the room, he reeled, catching sight of the feet and legs lying partially inside the living room. Judging from the dark stripe down the leg of the tan trousers, he could tell it was probably Hawkins, the King County Deputy he'd talked to earlier. Murphy knelt beside the fallen man and touched his wrist to ensure what he already knew. Hawkins was dead. A cold merciless anger rushed through him as he placed the dead man's hat over his face. He pried the pistol from the deputy's limp fingers.

Weakness, more than caution, forced him to continue on slowly, but at last he reached the kitchen. Edging around the door jam, he saw the young officer trying to push himself into a sitting position. Hurriedly, Murphy knelt beside him.

"Where you hit, Martin?"

"Don't worry about me. Just go get that bitch!" he said venomously. Instantly, his tone turned much weaker. "In the cellar, Murph. Be careful."

Murphy saw that the round had just clipped his protective vest and entered his shoulder. He tried to stem the flow of blood, but Martin pushed his hands away. "Go! Get her before she kills someone else."

Murphy nodded, pushed himself to his feet with the aid of the shotgun, and headed quietly down the steep wood stairs. Halfway down, he first saw Amanda fastened to the large table, then BJ, her feet curled under, her body limp, cuffed to a water pipe on the far wall. He could see no signs of life from her. Even though his first instinct was to rush to them, he forced himself to continue to move slowly, making certain no one was hiding under the steps or in darkened corners — waiting to strike.

Satisfied the room posed no immediate danger, Murphy inched toward a partially open door across the room, peered through and detected another set of stairs leading up toward the main floor. His heart in his mouth, Murphy returned to the huddled form near the water pipe.

"BJ," he whispered. "Oh God, Honey, wake up. It's me."

Her wrists raw and bleeding, BJ's eyes filled with tears as he uncuffed her, then removed her rubber gag.

She slumped against him. "Oh Darling. I knew you'd come for us. I *knew* it!" She stiffened as she frantically tried to see onto the tall table. With his help, she climbed stiffly to her feet and stumbled toward it. Amanda was awake, and Murphy kept a tense watch as BJ loosened her bonds and the two of them hugged and sobbed briefly.

"You've got to get Amanda out of here, BJ — *now* — and I've got to find Lisa. Where did she go?"

"She was ready to cut my throat, Frank, and would have if you'd been a minute later. When she heard you coming, I guess she figured there were others too. She left through that door," she said, pointing toward the stairway he'd checked earlier. "She's really freaked out, Frank, and she has a gun. Be careful, she's nutty as a fruitcake."

Murphy handed her Martin Dewey's shotgun. "Go straight to the deputy's car, and whatever you do, stay alert. Use the radio and call for an ambulance and backup. Don't let Mandy out of your sight!"

BJ nodded and looked around fearfully. Murphy touched the side of her face, and smiled. "You were wonderful, sweetheart. Just take care of Mandy, and don't worry. I won't stop until I find her."

He bent and touched his lips to her's. Hurriedly, he slipped out of his jacket, handing it to her for Amanda. Then he squeezed

Amanda's shoulder reassuringly and walked toward the doorway leading to the second set of stairs. Even in the darkness of the shadowed room, he could plainly make out tracks left in the dust leading up the wobbly stairs. He pulled out the deputy's pistol, breathed deeply, and started up.

The door at the top opened into what might've been a sewing room or a study at one time. Another door exposed a wide hallway, almost directly beneath the main stairway that led to the upstairs level.

Holding the pistol ahead of him, he cautiously started up, remembering the day he'd watched Lisa practicing at the pistol range. Almost every one of her shots had been in the black center. He stepped on a loose board, a loud squeak emanating from it. Freezing, his heart lurched into his throat. His eyes furtively scanned the upper landing until he was certain no one was going to blast away before starting to slowly climb once more. Every few steps he paused to listen. Nearing the top he caused another squeak—this one much louder!

Murphy's heart hammered. His sweat-soaked shirt felt cold as it clung to him, his legs quivered, and his breathing labored by the time he finally reached the top. Momentarily catching his breath and leaning against the wall to regain his strength, he surveyed the hallway. There were four doors; the one directly in front of him was partially open, and that's where the footprints in the dust led.

On the top floor of the old house, the frightened child lay curled, sucking a thumb. She'd heard the two loud squeaks those loose boards caused when someone climbed the narrow stairs. Her parents were coming to play their games again. Games that hurt. Games that made her feel dirty. She hated them so much. She wished they both were dead.

Breathing raggedly, Frank forced himself away from the comfort of the wall, edging closer toward the door. Cautiously, he peered around the door jam and in the far corner, curled into a ball, huddled a small figure, facing the wall. Indistinguishable whispers broke the silence. As he edged closer he was finally able to make them out. He shuddered!

"Please daddy, not tonight. Please don't hurt me. I don't want to play the game anymore. Please don't, daddy... please... no games... daddy..."

It was clear; Lisa Kinard had reverted to the child-like presence she'd been before in this very room. As he listened, rage overwhelmed him — rage for all the killings — rage toward her dead parents who'd abused and tormented her, ultimately causing her to be the monster responsible for all those murders.

He slammed his hand hard against the wall and a chunk of plaster fell near his foot. He felt the urge to break — smash things — strike out! And, he wanted to cry.

Such a waste — such a total fucking waste!

Tears of pent-up emotion finally released and he wiped the corners of his eyes with his sleeve. He knelt and slipped a cuff around Lisa's ankle, snapping the other end to the metal radiator pipe near her foot.

She's not going anywhere, but just to be safe.

He picked up her service revolver lying nearby, glanced again at the tormented woman, and retreated out the door. Her muttering pleas to a long dead parent could still be heard as he started back down the wobbly, squeaky old stairs. Corky heard the first step squeak. That one was always the loudest. She knew because it was the fourteenth step and she'd always counted them. *He's going away! Maybe they won't come tonight! Maybe, there won't be any games! Please, Lord, make them stay away tonight. Please!*

Gratefully, the second squeak finally came. She sighed, stuck her thumb in her mouth, closed her eyes, and slept.

Chapter 27

Frank Murphy reclined against a comfortable deck pad, watching Olaf expertly manipulate the large sailboat's colorful spinnaker. BJ was in the cabin, fixing lunch. As Amanda helped the big man with his chore, he could hear Olaf's rumbling voice and Amanda's giggles. Apeshit was out of sight, hopefully, napping where he couldn't be stepped on. Back on shore it was hot enough to melt blacktop, but tacking in the middle of the Puget Sound with the wind whipping past was Heaven. He lay back and closed his eyes, absorbing the fresh salt air.

Murphy hadn't been a cop for more than a year and found he didn't miss it one bit! Managing the marina with Olaf and BJ had kept him more than busy, and now that the sailboat was finished and Olaf's long awaited journey was nearing, he expected it to be even busier.

With the new slips they'd recently added, the expansion of the covered sling-hoist, and the new repair shop, they'd turned a tidy profit at the end of the year—enough to hire another man, anyway. Frank Murphy was happy. He felt a small rustle behind him and glanced at BJ as she placed several cans of beer and two plates of sandwiches at his side.

"Hello, Mrs. Murphy."

"Hello, Mr. Murphy." She smiled back; full of love. He felt his heart skip a beat.

Amanda suddenly jumped between them, grabbed a plate and a beer for Olaf, and rushed back to join him at his task. He marveled at her resiliency. A little love and all were forgotten.

Remarkable! Mrs. Frank Murphy bent and kissed him on the forehead, as though she knew exactly what he was thinking.

He smiled each time he reflected upon the day that he hijacked the Seattle-Vashon Ferry. *Just like Jessie James*. It all seemed so long ago.

Robert James had finally maneuvered himself out of his legal problems and quietly slithered out of town, his tail between his legs. No one had heard of him since. Julie had left around the same time. Despite what she'd done, Murphy sincerely hoped she hadn't gone with him, but the coincidence of their simultaneous departure said otherwise.

He'd left the department with just about everyone having the same feelings toward him. The Chief had been furious over the ferry incident, Brooks had been furious he'd really finally resigned, and the Judge had been furious about Lisa—although he'd seemed to have more or less forgiven him these days. Judge Woods had finally accepted that the real Lisa was someone none of them had ever really known. Locked away in the Special Offender Unit in the Monroe, WA, Maximum Security Institution for the criminally insane, she was never to be free again.

None of the doctors who treated and studied her were ever able to confirm the reason she'd turned out like she had—except all agreed the roots connected with early childhood abuse.

The press had played the story to the hilt for a while, but had finally moved on to more current events. As horrific as she'd become, Murphy never thought about her without feeling some pity for the young woman who'd once been someone's little girl, perhaps not unlike Tina, but one who'd somehow been lost along the way.

The liberal bleeding hearts had finally won out, and in the end persuaded the governor that the interests of justice would be better served if John Lee West were given a stay of execution and also locked away for life as criminally insane. Murphy had seen him on a news channel right after the decision. He had been well dressed, trimmed his hair, seemed alert, and flashed his infectious grin at every camera in view. It was easy to see why some might think he was no longer a threat. Just the same, he could count on spending the rest of his natural life at the SOC at Monroe. It seemed ironic that the only two serial killers he'd ever known would end up a few hundred feet from each other.

Lisa and John Lee. Monsters? Sick? Who knows?

Still, he'd have felt a lot better if West had stretched a rope as scheduled. He'd once looked into those sightless eyes—seen what was lurking behind them. *No. Better to have ended it right then.*

EPILOGUE

There were no squeaking steps in this place, but in her little girl's mind she wasn't aware of it. Every night after she went to bed, she still heard the seventh and fourteenth step, just as if her father were placing his heavy weight on them. And when she slept, she still dreamed of her little friend, Jennifer, whom confusingly, she sometimes thought of as Amanda. But most days, she just huddled against the wall, sucking on her thumb, listening. *Planning.*

She'd overheard some of the staff talking about John Lee West, and how he'd been sent here, too. *Here!* They quietly whispered that they kept him sedated, constrained, and separated from the others. That's why she'd been so surprised when she'd discovered the message in her soup. *A message from John Lee!*

No need to wonder how he'd done it. Everyone knew how smart he was. *He could do anything!* After the first message, there'd been others. Like the last one, just one word, DISPENSARY.

She'd been accompanied to the infirmary on just two occasions. The first was the night she'd arrived and she'd been heavily sedated. The second was after she'd received the message from West. She'd ingested half a bar of soap, waited for it to give her the runs, and then placed the rest under her armpit long enough for it to raise her temperature.

The attendants had responded to her moaning and rushed her to the dispensary. During their examination she'd lain on the cold metal table and eyeballed every minute detail of the room. Only after one of the cramps had doubled her over had she been allowed into the small toilet—had she looked up—and seen it.

There were no overhead bars on one of the windows, and it

was angled open, enough to help ventilate the room's stale air. *Imagine! No bars!*

Oh, the window was small. Probably *too* small for a person of normal size to squeeze through. But she'd always been slightly built and had lost so much weight lately that her anorexic-like frame wasn't much more than skin and bones.

She focused her thoughts on the infirmary supplies. If she were able to get her hands on some Vaseline, KY Jelly—some personal lubricant, she just might be able to slip through the small opening. *It's a thought*! If not that way, then another. She was smart. She'd find a way. Hour after hour she planned—and daydreamed. *One day soon, I'll see Jennifer again.*

Sweet, sweet Jennifer and Corky. Together once more.

THE END

DON'T MAKE THE BLACKBIRDS CRY
R.C.MORRIS
2004

NOW AVAILABLE

ISBN-1-4137-2506-6

From your favorite bookstore or
visit raycmorris.com

TURN THIS PAGE FOR A PREVIEW OF
DON'T MAKE THE BLACKBIRDS CRY...

Chapter 1

Cory Don Sonnet secretly watched them cut the three little girls' throats, all the while trying not to scream his fool head off. Although it was a late humid June evening, he shivered in dread as he crouched behind the stack of discarded boxes and battered trash cans that old man Birdwell had always placed outside his small general store every Saturday evening at closing time. That was the reason for his dilemma now—Birdwell's damned store.

Fourteen-year-old Cory Don had arrived at the store an hour earlier, just past 11:00 p.m., a full hour after closing time. After waiting a few minutes to ensure the place was locked up for the evening, he'd used his prized Buck skinning knife his brother Jack had given him for his last birthday to pry open the rear window, then quietly slipped inside. The knife had been Jack's favorite. He'd found it one day while cutting through the woods to their favorite skinny-dipping hole.

Covered with rust, its point missing, it had obviously either been lost or discarded by an earlier hunter. Jack, who had a knack for fixing things with his hands, cleaned and oiled the old knife until it looked like new, sharpened the blade and filed the point back, even better than before. He liked to wear it anytime they hiked through the woods. Jack always knew how much his younger brother coveted that knife, and for Cory's thirteenth birthday, Jack had presented it to him. Years later, Cory had wondered if Jack had known he was dying even then, and that's why he'd parted with it.

Anyway, it sure come in real handy this night because he would've never have gotten the window open without Jack's knife.

It'd been dark inside the store but Cory knew what he wanted and made directly for it. Where Birdwell kept his weekly cash intake was no secret. Crap, the whole town knew he always put it in that old cigar box under the raw hamburger cases in the meat-locker. But it wasn't the money Cory was after. It was food —and maybe another box of .22 ammo for his single-shot rifle. He was half-starved. As much as he disliked stealing from the old man, it was either become a thief and survive or just lay down in the woods and slowly starve to death.

Not that anyone in this stinking town would care much if he did die. Just another lowly Sonnet getting his just desserts. That's what they'd say. His father had drowned in Carver Creek last summer while on one of his famous drunken binges. He'd jumped into the angry swollen stream while trying to escape from Sheriff Brodie and two of his deputies. That was right after he'd come home drunk and beat Cory and his brother Jack into unconsciousness then choked their pregnant mother to death.

One of the neighbors, probably nosey old Ned Scruggs, had heard screams as he drove past their three-room shanty they called home and finally phoned the law. Used to disturbances at the Sonnet household, the deputies had arrived too late to do any of them much good.

That crazy night had left him and his brother Jack completely alone. Jack was a very mature, two full years older than Cory Don. The two of them were all that remained of the wild and much detested Sonnet family. Oh, their dad had spoken of a sister in California somewhere who he absolutely detested. And he vaguely remembered his mother speaking of an elderly aunt in Maine, or maybe it had been New York—if she was even still alive. Nobody knew either of their married names or how to contact them anyway. What was plain though was that no one in the town of Logan was going to step forward and volunteer to care for the two-orphaned teen's—two orphaned *Sonnet* children.

Although older than his sibling, Jack was even smaller and skinnier than Cory Don. That was due to a unique and rare medical condition that neither he nor his young brother could even pronounce. Always frail and sickly, he'd done his best to act grown up and care for Cory Don, but when the end finally came he was just another scared little boy, crying for his dead mother.

Jack had died only six months earlier of the incurable disease, no more than a skeleton at the time. For years to come Cory Don wondered that if Jack had been the son of one of those well-to-do families of Logan, would the doctors have found some way to save him?

The town did pay to bury him though—right beside his mother and father. Other than Cory Don, only five people attended the funeral, the pastor of the old Negro church, the graveyard caretaker and two laborers waiting impatiently to cover Jack up. Cory didn't cry at the funeral, a fact that was much talked about in the small town of Logan for some time to come. He did later though. Alone and scared in the old shanty, he cried all that day and the rest of the night. That had been the last time he'd cried since Jack's death, and he vowed it'd be the last ever. But it had been hard at times.

During the following months, Cory Don had barely survived on nuts and berries. Sometimes when he got lucky, he had squirrels or rabbits and other small game he could kill with his dad's single-shot .22 caliber rifle. Often, he'd had to get by on what he could steal from people's gardens, and like tonight, from old man Birdwell's store. He didn't like it but it was either that or starve.

The night air had felt heavy with moisture through his thin tee shirt as he slipped back out through the window, leaving the air-conditioned interior of the store. He had just followed his plastic bag of treasures to the pavement when he heard them coming, giggling and hooting as young girls do. He knew who they were even before they came into view. Trapped with his stolen loot and nowhere to go in the narrow alleyway, he'd decided to duck behind the stack of cardboard boxes and trash cans until they passed.

Peeking around one of the trashcans, he immediately confirmed it was Sally and Ella Reid and Betty Lou Parker. Eleven-year-old Sally and thirteen-year-old Ella were sisters, and the daughters of the same black pastor whom had spoken at Jack's funeral—Doctor Samuel Reid. Betty Lou was the daughter of Logan High's eighth-grade teacher, Rita Parker, a tall, striking blond widow with three teenage children.

Betty Lou's older brother, Randy Parker, was two years her senior. Her sister, Kay Sue, was two years younger than Betty Lou's sixteen years. The Parker sisters were the prettiest girls at Logan High, maybe even the whole county. Particularly, Kay Sue, who made his heart race each time he saw her. He'd pretend to ignore her as they passed in the hallway, ashamed of his torn, ragged jeans and long hair. She was royalty—an untouchable princess who resided on a higher level of humanity than Cory Don Sonnet. But secretly, he watched her with fascination every chance he got. If he were ever rich or famous, she would be the kind of girl he'd want for a girlfriend—Kay Sue Parker, the most beautiful girl in the world.

Well…maybe not, if she had a brother like Randy Parker. Her older brother had noticed Cory Don staring at his sister in the schoolyard one day early last year. That was back when Cory Don had still cared enough to even go to school. Randy and his tough crowd of older bullies crowded around him so he couldn't escape, then Randy gave him one hell of a beating. He was so sore he couldn't get up from bed for a week, let alone go to school. Cory Don Sonnet never returned to class at Logan High after that.

Trembling with excitement, he silently watched Kay Sue's older sibling and the little black sisters from his smelly hiding place. Despite his dilemma, he was amused by their naughty young girl talk. He'd always suspected girls talked about the same things boys did when they were alone. He snickered softly at some crass, sexual remark one of the Reid sisters made.

Although it was unusual to see a mixed-race group of kids on Logan's streets, especially this late at night, he was soon able to ascertain that sixteen year-old Betty Lou had tutored Pastor Reid's kids in math earlier in the evening and was now walking them back home. They seemed to be having a good time and enjoying each other's company immensely. That was when things went very bad.

At the identical time the three girls entered one end of the dark alley, a group of five men entered the other. They met less than twenty-feet from where Cory Don sweated in fear. Peering through a slight crack in a discarded Maytag container, he could barely make out the identities of three of the newcomers through the shadows. Joe Bob Turner was easy, due to his huge size and dumb way of talking. Eddie Dean Gash was equally easy because of his filthy whining mouth. And finally, Logan High's heart throb and quarterbacking hero, handsome Kurt Brodie, because…well, one could always identify Kurt anywhere, even in a crowd. He just had that kind of presence.

All of them were at least three or four years his senior. Cory Don knew them well, mainly because of his and Jack's constant bullying through the years. He had seen most of them do things at school that would've gotten almost anybody else kicked out permanently. They were looked up to and feared by the majority of the kids in Logan and if the truth were known, many of the adults, too. The other two men stayed in the shadows and didn't say much, except to occasionally grunt and drink from a bottle each time it was passed to them.

At eighteen, Joe Bob Turner was bigger than most of the fully-grown men around town. More than a few had learned the hard way not to cross him, too. Small, skinny Eddie Dean Gash was the first to reach for the bottle from someone out of Cory Don's view. Gash reminded Cory of a weasel, the way his eyes darted around as though looking for a quick escape route. He was mean, foul-mouthed and shifty, but only when the others were around to protect him. Handsome Kurt Brodie was the son of the only sheriff the town of Logan had elected in over twenty years, and the best quarterback Logan High had ever produced. A year younger than Joe Bob, he was nearly as large, but better dressed and much cleaner. He was also the natural leader of this crowd, but tonight he seemed to be deferring to someone in the shadows. Cory wondered who that could be. He wasn't about to move and try to find out though.

It was clear that Betty Lou knew some of the crowd and felt at ease with the situation. At first, the girls joked and flirted with the young men, giggling and flipping around the way all young girls do. Asking if they could have some of the whisky the men were sharing, they held their noses and backed away giggling when it was offered. When the men's talk shifted suddenly to the subject of sex, Betty Lou finally attempted to lead the other girls past them, but Joe Bob's bulk blocked their way.

"What's the hurry, girls? The boys and me need a little affection. You just wait down by the corner for a few minutes Betty Lou, and we'll send these pretty little Coon sisters to you as soon as we're done with 'em."

Betty Lou didn't back down from the big lout at all, standing firm with her hands on her hips, her cute chin sticking straight out. "Get out of our way, Joe Bob! This isn't funny any more."

She turned her head and spoke into the shadows. "Pistol, you know better than this! Quit screwing around right now and let us pass."

Joe Bob laughed shortly and backhanded her, sending her sprawling against the brick wall with such force that she slumped down and didn't move. To Cory, it looked as though she were either dead or out cold. He was terrified, feeling warmness as his bladder released involuntarily. Screaming sharply, the two Reid sisters broke toward the light at the entrance of the street, but the males were too fast for them. Within seconds, two of the men were between their skinny dark legs, humping vigorously as the others held them down, covering their mouths with big hands. If he hadn't been so scared, it might've looked almost comical to Cory Don.

"Feel good, girl?" Cory heard Joe Bob ask, huffing and grunting between words. "Tell ol' Joe Bob now. Is it good?"

Behind their captor's big hands, Cory could hear the girls trying to beg or scream, as they moaned and whimpered in extreme pain. It went on for a long time, the men exchanging positions periodically with those drinking from the bottle and silently watching. Cory scarcely breathed, holding his own hands over his ears to shut out the brutal sounds, the unnoticed tears streaming down his dirty face. He prayed it would be over soon and that they'd let the girls go home so he could get away.

Movement in the shadows brought him back to the present. One of the men hidden in the darkness had knelt down beside Betty Lou. She had not moved or made a sound during the time the sisters had been repeatedly assaulted.

"She dead, Pistol?" Joe Bob slurred, taking a deep drink. From where Cory Don crouched, it didn't sound as if he cared one way or the other.

"No," the man with the soft voice said. "But from the looks of that hole in the back of her head, she may be soon."

"What do we do with 'em now?" Kurt said as he rose unsteadily to his feet while attempting to zip his trousers. He was the only one who sounded halfway concerned, now that his lust was behind him.

The shadow man Joe Bob had identified only as *Pistol*, stood but Cory could only make out that he wore a hat, the brim covering his face. It was clear the others were willing to take their directions from him. Crouched in the darkness a few feet away, Cory could hear their hard breathing as they silently waited for him to speak. The man in the hat silently stared down at the injured white girl for a full minute before he answered.

"Nothing we can do now. We have to get rid of the *Nigger* girls."

Silence followed, until Joe Bob said, "Okay, *Pistol*. Your call. What about Betty Lou though? She'll shoot her mouth off about this for sure first chance she gets."

"She'll have to go, too," the hat with the soft voice said. "But first, I'm going to sample some of that young meat. I've watched her prance around for years and I've just been dying to do her high and mighty ass. Now's my chance. I'll never get another one."

Joe Bob sounded almost shocked as he half-laughed, then blurted out, "*You*? Well fuck me to tears! This I gotta see! Yes sir, this will be a first! Right boys? Old Pistol's gonna do the old dirt road on Betty Lou!"

It didn't last long. When he was finished, the soft-voiced man rose unsteadily to his feet and moved back into the darkness of the shadows. He sounded out of breath when he finally spoke again. "Give me your knife, Joe Bob."

Cory Don watched in horror as the man in the hat knelt again, his arm rising and falling a dozen times before it stopped. The sounds from the darkness were like those made when sticking a knife in a green watermelon. When it was over, the slender shadow stood and handed the knife to Kurt.

"You first, then Joe Bob. Make sure everyone here takes a crack at it. That way, no one squeals."

The only man who'd been silent up to this point whimpered softly, his voice cracking as he said, "I can't do it, Pistol! I never killed no human before! I can't do…"

"*Shut up*! Just pretend like it's one of those illegal deer you spotlight, Pos. Nothing to it. Just cut her throat and bleed her like an elk. If you don't go along with the rest of us on this, we'll leave you lying here with these bitches. Now take the fucking knife and stick her!"

The man in the hat, *Pistol,* never raised his voice but it was clear that he expected the scared man to do it. Halfsobbing, the whiner did as he was told, his arm seeming to rise and fall almost reluctantly several times. Then he stood and silently stared down at his handiwork, his ragged breathing the only sounds in the dark alley. The meager illumination from the streetlight fifty-feet away fell on his face. Cory almost cried out when he saw it was a man he knew by the name of *Possum* Palmer. He was somewhat older than the others, disheveled, skinny and frail. Cory Don recalled he'd overheard some adults talking one day about Possum Palmer's *drinking problem.* Everyone said he was a moon-shiner and a spot-lighter, which meant he made illegal whisky and shot animals from county roads at night after blinding them with his truck's spotlight. It was obvious to everyone except Possum that the others in this crowd just let him tag along because he owned a new truck that they could use to get around, and he bought them whiskey. Holding his hand over his mouth, Possum suddenly wheeled around and ran toward the deserted street, but he was already spewing his dinner onto the pavement before he reached it.

Joe Bob laughed sharply. "Yellow bastard. We may have to do something about Possum. He's going chicken shit on us."

The man in the hat didn't move. He watched silently until Possum Palmer had staggered around the corner out of their sight. Then he nodded and softly spoke, as though to himself. "Yes. We might have to do something about Possum."

Then the others took their time, seeming to enjoy the task at hand.

———————

Cory Sonnet awoke with a jerk, his clothing drenched with sour sweat. Glancing around quickly to see if any of the other passengers on the old Boeing aircraft had been watching him, he finally allowed himself to breathe a deep sigh of relief. Finally satisfied he hadn't gotten too loud this time, he settled back and looked out of the window as they descended into Atlanta. He hadn't been here for years but as soon as sudden turbulence struck the small craft like a giant fist, he quickly remembered just why he'd avoided coming back all these years. A day earlier, he had been in Kuwait. The world got smaller every day.

Removing a white handkerchief from his inside coat pocket, he wiped the perspiration from his tanned forehead with a trembling hand. Over thirty years had passed since that night in the alley behind Birdwell's store, but it still made him react this way. He thought he'd gotten over it a few years earlier. Lately though, the nightmares had returned, this time with a vengeance.

It'd all started with an article by one of his colleagues at the Baltimore Sun. The article had been about some human bones the Logan County Sheriff had found in a dry well on the old Thomas farm. The short article stated it had been a man who had simply vanished almost thirty years earlier. Nothing but bones now, he none-the-less was easy to identify because he wore a stainless steel watch with his name engraved on the back. The name was that of one, Charles Dale Palmer—old Possum Palmer, himself.

It didn't take a lot of brains to figure out that Possum disappeared about the same time as Cory had witnessed the three girl's deaths behind Birdwell's general store. That was the same day he'd left Logan County for good. Hitchhiking, he'd made it as far as Little Rock before being forced to stop running and earn enough money to live on. First there was a job of setting pins in a bowling alley. Later he'd sacked groceries and worked as a farm hand until he turned seventeen, old enough to join the military. The Marines had shipped him out immediately to Okinawa, then Vietnam.

Of course the war was officially over by then, but it seemed the belligerent Vietcong had the bad sense of timing to capture a small naval vessel and hold it along with the crew on a small island just south of mainland Vietnam. He'd been unlucky enough to be a member of the unit chosen to go on the last raid of the war, a mission to get the boat and crew back from an island that was controlled by about a zillion Vietcong. His wounds had taken months to heal. When they'd finally healed, the government gave him a medal, and better yet, a full medical discharge with a pension. They'd also paid for his high school GED and eventually his entire college tuition. He had studied journalism.

During those first few months back in Little Rock, he'd kept track of what the papers were saying about the brutal murders of the young girls. At first, he was terrified—then furious. There he was, all over the front page of the Logan County Press. They'd used one of his old school pictures, and that was what had probably saved him. It was the one taken while his mother was still alive and she had just given him a fresh haircut, starched and ironed his shirt, and scrubbed behind his ears in anticipation of the event. It looked just like a thousand other uncomfortable kids in any high school picture, but it didn't look a thing like him.

The Logan County Press didn't exactly come right out and say he was the murderer of the three little girls—only that he was a "person if interest" to the investigators on the case. They couldn't have made him sound any less guilty if they'd included pictures of him standing over the girl's bodies with a bloody knife in his hand.

The newspaper was quick to point out that, after all, his fingerprints *had* been found at the scene and *inside* the store. It went on to say, that "local speculation" was that he had probably broken into the store and been seen leaving by the girls who were taking a short cut through the alley. It implied that he *could* have killed them simply to eliminate any witnesses to his crime.

The forensic report from the Highway Patrol lab, however, said it was highly unlikely that a frail, fourteen-year-old boy could subdue three girls nearly his own size, rape them repeatedly, then systematically kill each of them without even tying them up. He was quick to notice that the particular article about the lab report was buried on the fourth page, after the high school sports section. Still, speculation about one of those *terrible Sonnets* being responsible for such a gruesome crime probably made for good conversation during the next few weeks.

Finally though, the story began to grow cold and was gradually dropped by the national media. Eventually, the local papers fazed it out as well. But first the local news hounds drained every last bit of mileage from it they possibly could. After toasting Cory over a low fire for several weeks, they had started putting out half-truthful articles about his deceased family members. His mother and brother were sketchy at best, but their father had been low-hanging fruit—and an easy target.

James (Jim) Odis Sonnet had originally come to Logan from Baton Rouge where he'd eloped with a local schoolmaster's seventeen-year-old daughter, Coleen DeVoe. Jim Sonnet had been twenty-one at the time, handsome, headstrong, with a fire raging in his belly to make his mark in the world. There was an old photo of his dead parents from his mother's photo album. It had been taken about that same time. It was the only one Cory still kept. The album had been lost when he ran, but the wrinkled photo of his parents in better days was safe in his room back in Baltimore. What always struck him was how handsome his father had been, and just how breathtakingly beautiful his mother was, and how happy they'd both appeared.

Something happened through the years to change his father. Maybe it was the constant struggle to provide food and shelter for his growing family. Or maybe it had been the abuse he'd suffered at the hands of the locals, simply because he was married to "one of them *Louisiana Swamp Cajuns*." The Klan had been powerful in Logan around that time, and people were quick to lump *Niggers*, Jews and likely as not, even Cajuns into the same despised group in order to gain favor with the local KKK Grand Dragon.

Although he'd still been very young, Cory could remember his father playing baseball with him and Jack. Sometimes their pretty mother had joined them in the games. Those had been happy days, the kind of stuff memories were made of. Then, around the time Cory had started school, Jim Sonnet had started drinking. Not a lot at first, but gradually it grew worse until he was coming home nearly every night from the fields, staggering, cussing loudly and throwing things.

On good nights, he simply staggered in and passed out on the living room couch, or sometimes the hard wooden floor. But there were some nights when he arrived half-drunk and angry over something that had happened during the work day—being cussed out by his straw-boss, cornered and belittled by some of the local toughs associated with the Klan, who knows? It was on these nights that his father became abusive, violent, cussing them all profanely, striking out at or kicking anyone who got too close.

The last year of Jim Sonnet's shortened life had been a nightmare for all of them—he, Jack and especially their rapidly fading mother. Outcast from her own family, destitute and without skills, their mother had sought ways out of the life she was in.

She'd found an aunt up north who agreed to send money for her and the children to travel to a place she called the Puget Sound to find a job. It was out of the way and no one would ever look for her there. Jim Sonnet had found the letter while in one of his drunken binges and flew into a rage during which he'd killed the frail Coleen. Maybe it'd been an accident, maybe not. Cory never found out for sure, just as he never found out the truth about how his father died.

There had been several stories about the events of that night. Some said that Jim Sonnet had run from Sheriff Brodie and his deputies, jumped into the swollen creek and drowned. One whispered story said the lawmen had caught up with him before he even got to the creek. During his arrest they had beaten him to death and tossed his body into the creek. There were variations of these stories, as well as others, completely different. The truth probably lay somewhere in between.

After a couple of months of milking all that could be had from the torrid affair, the papers dropped the story completely and moved on to the POW talks, national elections and the closure of the local mill. Cory always suspected that had it not been for the death of the white girl, Betty Lou Parker, the whole thing might not have made the front page.

So here he was, doing something he swore he'd never do. Going home again. Home? He wanted to laugh, wondering if the Logan County Sheriff still considered him a "person of interest" in the unsolved case of the three murdered girls. Not that he was too worried about it. He was returning a different person than when he'd left. A decorated war hero, respected correspondent, and a man of property to boot. He supposed the whole town would erupt into a total riot when they learned one of the notorious Sonnet boys had purchased the old defunct Logan County Press.

He hadn't really planned any of it. Nobody ever *plans* on getting the *prize*. The *Pulitzer*. The granddaddy of them all. He'd been as surprised as anyone had by the award. Probably more so, because he'd been so wrapped up in his own work that he'd failed to pay attention to the gossip about it. Anyway, he'd just won the Pulitzer for his story on "Crack Babies." While looking around for a smart investment for the cash award he'd received, he'd discovered the advertisement stating the old Logan County Press was for sale due to back taxes. The McCarthy family, who'd run the paper for over half a century, had all finally died off and either no one else was interested in publishing the news in Logan, or wasn't smart enough to do it. He suspected it was a little bit of both. His boss at the Sun had given him a leave of absence, assuring him his job would always be open should he chose to return. He may.

A plan had been slowly materializing ever since he'd bought the old press. Even now he didn't want to admit the truth, but it was there nevertheless. In his uneasy mind it laid like a lead ball, always with him. He knew the time had finally come. It was time to write an end to the story that only he knew. The true story about the deaths of three little girls.

———————

Printed in the United States
44715LVS00002B/1-87